MAKING MAGIC

"The key to this trick is the transfer of the bullet from your mouth to mine—it must be seamless and natural." Marc stepped closer to Salome, and his breath ruffled the tendrils of hair that fell about her face.

She put her hand on his chest, keeping him from getting any closer. His heart pounded beneath her fingers, and she wondered at the strength and fury of it. If he kept talking and looking at her like this, she feared the magician would mesmerize her.

"Fine, Marc. We'll practice the kiss. But only once. I *have* kissed before, and don't believe it requires much rehearsal."

Trying to still her own heart, which had suddenly started racing, Salome slid the bullet into her mouth. It felt cold on her tongue. Best to get this over with.

Leaning forward, she closed her eyes. Marc gently grasped her by the shoulders and pulled her close. His strong, full lips pressed against hers. This soft kiss was a lovely sensation—even thrilling—but then she remembered she'd have to open her mouth. How else to pass the bullet to him?

She knew she shouldn't, but still, her mouth opened. She felt him push the bullet to the side of her mouth as his tongue danced about hers. She moaned in protest—at least she thought it was protest—but still she didn't break away. Instead, she opened her mouth wide, molding her mouth to fit his; it was soft, tender, exquisite.

Magic & Moonlight

Sharon Pisacreta

LEISURE BOOKS   NEW YORK CITY

For Mom and Dad with love.
May you both have many more years of magic and moon-
light together.

A LEISURE BOOK®

June 1999

Published by

Dorchester Publishing Co., Inc.
276 Fifth Avenue
New York, NY 10001

ISBN 0-8439-4541-9

Magic & MOONLIGHT

Chapter One

May 1893

For the first time in her twenty-six years, Salome Hall felt wicked.

Wickedness felt nearly as strange to her as the new garnet-red slippers she was wearing. She rubbed her hands along her bare arms, shivering. Not even the bathing costume she wore when swimming in the river showed this much flesh. And perhaps her pink gown was a shade too bright and garish. But Lyndon Whittier loved her in pink, and Lyndon was a man worth pleasing.

"How ya doing, Mizz Hall?"

She nodded and returned a greeting to the child waving at her across the lawn. Luckily Jacob Rausch was only seven years old and wouldn't think it strange that his prim and proper schoolteacher was

Sharon Pisacreta

tottering about on French heels and wearing a scandalously revealing dress.

Up ahead, she could see the band park, awash with color and light beneath the strings of Japanese lanterns. It looked as if the entire population of Black Horse, Missouri, was here. Children chased each other around the plank tables, screaming with excitement, while the Fourth Street Glassworkers' Band played beneath the bandstand's lattice roof. The air smelled delectably of bratwurst, fried cucumbers and hickory nut cake—strong enough to overpower the new store-bought scent she was wearing. She was grateful for that; she wanted to turn heads tonight for Lyndon's sake, but she didn't want to look like a hussy. Or a fool.

A young woman came running up to her. "Sally, isn't this the most exciting thing you've ever seen? Half the county is here tonight. And the mayor bought Mrs. Dupree one of Mr. Edison's talking machines for their wedding anniversary!"

"A gramophone?"

"Yes, and everyone will get a chance to speak into it. Although I don't know if I care to hear my voice played back to me. Everyone sounds so different on that little wax cylinder. Except Jane, of course. She sang 'After the Ball' and it came out sounding as smooth as morning cream."

Her cousin stepped back, eyes wide with amazement. "Salome Ruth Hall, are you wearing lip rouge? You are. And where did you find such a dress? Why, if that bodice were cut an inch lower, the Ladies Guild would demand you step down as president." She giggled. "Wait till Lyndon gets a look at you. He'll regret not courting you serious all these years."

Salome tugged self-consciously at the offending bodice. "I just wanted to wear something special tonight. After all, Mayor Dupree and his wife are my godparents, so it's only proper I should dress for their anniversary party." She wouldn't elaborate, not even to her cousin. Ella Bremer was the worst gossip in St. Charles County, and she didn't want her announcement spoiled before it was time.

She rubbed her bare arms again. Perhaps she should have worn gloves, even if the May night was warm and humid. Thank goodness her father wasn't alive to see his youngest daughter traipsing about in public like one of the Dupree sisters.

"Is my dress really too shocking? After all, I'm a schoolteacher, not an actress." Now that she was so close to the crowd and Lyndon, she felt her confidence beginning to wane.

Ella leaned closer. "Compared to the Dupree girls, you look as modest as Granny Mueller. I actually saw Julia smoking a cigarette this afternoon right on the front porch of her parents' house. Tonight she's decked out in some flashy green dress that not even a saloon dancer would be caught dead in." She pointed to the woman standing next to a table groaning with torte cakes and fruit cobbler. "And she's dyed her hair since she left. I think it's supposed to be blond, but when you get up close, it looks just like burnt straw." Ella patted her own pale blond curls.

To Salome's less critical eyes, however, Julia Dupree looked like a woman from an Italian opera, alluring and dangerous. "Oh, you've never forgiven Julia for breaking your hobby horse when you were five. You haven't liked her since."

Ella made a face. "She's never given me any reason *to* like her. Acting all uppity when half the time she sounds as rude as a mountain moonshiner. It must get her back up to have an older sister as fancy and famous as Jane."

9

"Where is Jane, by the way?"

"Surrounded by admirers, meaning the entire male population of the county." Ella linked elbows with Salome, and began strolling toward the crowd clustered about the bandstand. "I have to admit that even if she does make her living on the stage, she seems like a real lady. But then Jane always could put on airs. Of course, one can't imagine what will happen to the Dupree girls in a few years when they lose their looks. No respectable man will have them."

Although Salome murmured in agreement, secretly she envied Jane and Julia. No other females in Black Horse had ever had the courage to run away from home, only to turn up years later as successful performers in the theater. Well, Jane at least was a success. The new Jenny Lind, according to the New York and Boston newspapers. She'd sung for the Vanderbilts only last year, and was said to be considering an offer to tour Europe. If Salome hadn't been so happy at the prospect of being Lyndon Whittier's wife, she might have felt frustrated with her own placid life in comparison.

"Even men who aren't so respectable are rejecting them now." Ella lowered her voice. "Mrs. Dupree told Mama that Julia had a falling out with that magician fellow she was working for."

"Wasn't his name Merlin the Magnificent?"

"Marco the Magnificent." Ella rolled her eyes. "Sounds like some dreadful foreigner. Anyway, she and Marco were quite the twosome until last month. Now she's without a job, which doesn't surprise me. I have no idea how she made a living this long onstage. It isn't as if she had any talent."

"You really should try to overcome your jealousy of Jane and Julia."

"I am not jealous of the Dupree girls," Ella said in

a furious voice. "They're nothing but—but floozies. Just because they're the daughters of the mayor, we have to treat them like they're as good as us. Well, they're not. I'm simply grateful they only come back for a visit every two or three years. They bring trouble wherever they go. No doubt it's that Creole blood they got from the Dupree side of the family. You wouldn't catch German girls being so proud of the fact that they're hussies."

"Well, I always look forward to their visits home." Salome cast another glance at the young woman in green satin. "They add a touch of excitement to our little town. And I wouldn't be surprised if they both marry English lords or Wall Street millionaires. The whole world isn't as small-minded as Black Horse."

Ella gave her a long look. "Lyndon Whittier agrees with you."

"What does that mean?"

Before she could answer, Salome heard her fiancé's voice booming out over the crowd. Lyndon stood on the stage of the bandstand, waving at everyone to be quiet.

A delicious warmth suffused her, as it did every time she saw him. Just listening to his sonorous voice sent shivers down her spine. Not only was Lyndon a successful lawyer, but he was tall, green-eyed, and endowed with the waviest chestnut hair she'd ever seen on a man. She thought it made him appear positively leonine.

Not surprisingly, she had been in love with Lyndon since the moment he came to work for her father's law office a decade earlier. To her joy, they had begun courting four years ago, although at times their courtship was so leisurely and respectful, Salome feared it had turned into simply friendship. But then two weeks ago, Lyndon had made her the happiest

11

woman in Missouri by proving his love and his passion. After so long a wait, they were at last engaged.

"How handsome he looks tonight." Her heart felt near to bursting with pride. Compared to the elegant figure he cut in his linen frock coat and shiny spats, the other men in the band park seemed like country hayseeds.

Ella patted her shoulder as though she were sick with fever.

Salome wondered what the town would say when they announced their engagement. They had been keeping company for so long, she suspected many people thought a marriage would never come to pass—at least not for her. But it would.

Although she had wanted to tell their family and friends immediately, Lyndon convinced her that it would be more proper to announce their coming nuptials at the mayor's anniversary party. The whole town would be gathered to celebrate and Lyndon liked making a show of things: a trait she didn't share, but found endearing. And although she was a private person, tonight she would allow herself to bask in the public's attention. Tonight the people who had grown up with her would learn that she was desired by the most eligible bachelor in the county. Salome felt giddy with anticipation.

"Ladies and gentlemen, we have come together this evening to celebrate thirty years of wedded bliss for our beloved mayor and his wife." Lyndon's magnetic smile seemed to embrace the entire gathering.

The milling crowd erupted into joyous hoots and applause.

Lyndon looked so distinguished and assured. It surprised no one in the community that he planned to run for political office in the near future. Governor perhaps, or senator. She smiled. Given Lyndon's dazzling attributes, she might even find herself living in the White House one day.

Lyndon motioned for everyone to quiet down. "But we have also come to listen to the most angelic voice this side of heaven. After a long absence, Jane Dupree has honored us with her presence tonight. As we all know, she is blessed with a voice so pure it is practically divine. Jane, please come up here and accept your accolades."

Jane Dupree stepped onto the stage amid the roar of more applause and cheers. This time, Lyndon didn't try to hush the crowd. Salome clapped as well, but her anticipation and excitement grew dimmer.

Jane looked exquisite tonight, as regal as a young duchess. Her honey-blond hair was piled atop her head, tendrils of curls falling about her neck and ears. She wore a silver crepe de chine creation that seemed as sophisticated and costly as the woman herself. Jane Dupree made every woman in Black Horse look common, Salome thought with dismay, looking down at her own homemade gown of pink taffeta and ruffles. And Jane had real presence; she knew how to show herself to advantage in front of an audience.

Salome glanced over at Lyndon. He was gazing at Jane as though the sun had just risen before his eyes. The nerves in her stomach tightened.

When the crowd grew quiet, Lyndon spoke again. "Had I her artistic gifts, I would have written a poem in honor of our Jane. But instead, I will bow to the talents of one of the greatest poets of the English language. If you will all pardon my poor delivery, allow me to express my devotion by reciting the poem 'To Jane' by Percy Bysshe Shelley."

"What is he doing?" whispered Salome.

"Making a perfect fool of himself," Ella replied.

No, she thought, he's making a fool of me. How would it look when he announced their engagement later tonight, after he'd done everything but kneel in adoration at Jane Dupree's feet?

Then to her shock and horror, he did just that. Kneeling on the bandstand floor, hand on his heart, he began to recite in a strong voice.

" 'The keen stars were twinkling,
And the fair moon was rising among them,
Dear Jane!
The guitar was tinkling,
But the notes were not sweet till you sung them
Again.' "

The night suddenly felt too humid, the air alive with hungry mosquitoes and moths. She closed her eyes, but couldn't shut out his fawning voice.

" 'As the moon's soft splendor
O'er the faint cold starlight of Heaven
Is thrown,
So your voice most tender
To the strings without soul had then given
Its own.' "

She covered her ears as Ella patted her shoulder once more. How could this happen? Jane had only been in town less than a week. And Lyndon had never shown any interest in Jane, either when she still lived with her parents or when she came back for one of her infrequent visits. What had happened to change all that?

After what seemed an eternity, she uncovered her ears and opened her eyes. He was still on his knees.

" 'Though the sound overpowers,
Sing again, with your dear voice revealing
A tone
Of some world far from ours,
Where music and moonlight and feeling
Are one.' "

As the crowd burst into cheers, Lyndon bowed his head and kissed Jane's outstretched hand. Salome let out a sob, the sound as frightening as the sight of Lyndon on his knees before another woman. She wanted to cry, but felt too stunned to even breathe.

"I told you the Dupree girls bring nothing but trouble," her cousin muttered. "The floozies!"

Salome had to gain control of herself. So Lyndon had fallen victim to Jane's considerable charms—so had every other man in Black Horse. Just because Lyndon took it into his head to recite poetry to a famous singer did not mean he was in love with the woman. After all, he had proposed just two weeks ago to *her*.

And here she was sitting on the steps of the feed store, crying and feeling sorry for herself.

She fumbled for her handkerchief and blew her nose. She hoped neither the full moon nor the Japanese lanterns would reveal her red eyes.

Pity was the last thing she wanted from the town or from Lyndon. Hadn't she endured enough pity when all five of her sisters married and set up households? Then last year her widowed mother remarried, sending the gossips into a positive frenzy. How sad that Salome was the only female in the Hall family who couldn't find a man, they all said. And what a joke that she bore such an exotic name. Salome was a name fit for a temptress, not a quiet school-

15

teacher who lived dutifully with her mother and stepfather, washed her hair every Saturday with rain water, and never ventured out of Black Horse save for quilting bees in the neighboring valley.

But now Lyndon Whittier wanted to marry her. So what was she doing sniveling like a ninny in front of the feed store?

She stood up, dusting off her skirt. In the distance she heard the band playing "Swanee River." At least Lyndon had stopped reciting poetry. She'd go look for him. She would run into his arms and kiss him so hard he'd forget how lovely Jane's voice was or how elegant she looked in that silver gown, blond curls tumbling about her face.

Taking several deep breaths, she grew calm again. What did a brief moment of infatuation over a golden-haired singer matter when weighed against the years Lyndon and she shared? Eager to find her fiancé, Salome took the shortcut to the band park, stepping quickly behind the feed store and around the stables.

Hurrying through the moonlit darkness, she paused a moment under the willow trees. Here was where Lyndon had proposed two weeks ago as they walked home from church. And here was where Lyndon had kissed her for the first time, beneath the largest willow, their bodies hidden behind the swaying greenery. Her body ached with the sweetness of the memory. She closed her eyes, letting her mind drift happily to memories of Lyndon that were even sweeter and more passionate.

Something rustled in the darkness.

With a start, Salome realized that a couple was standing just under that same willow. The moonlight showed a man and woman locked in a tight embrace.

Salome tried to tiptoe past, hoping a cracked twig

16

wouldn't give away her presence. The band stopped playing at that moment and in the sudden silence, she heard a man's familiar deep-throated laugh. She froze.

"Lyndon?" Without thinking, she marched over to the willow, drawing aside the branches as if they were a curtain. "Lyndon, is that you?"

Outlined by the moonlight, Lyndon's handsome figure and profile were unmistakable—as was the woman he held in his arms.

Her hands flew to her open mouth, stifling a gasp.

"Good lord, Sally, I didn't mean for you to find out like this." Lyndon pushed Jane behind him with a protective gesture that made Salome's pain even greater.

"What are you doing?" Her heart began racing. "I don't understand."

Jane stepped out from the shadows. "We should have told you earlier." Even in such an awkward situation, Jane Dupree sounded as lighthearted as a songbird. "I'm sorry, Sally. We're both very sorry. I fear this will come as a great shock to you, but it must be said. Lyndon and I are going to be married."

Salome felt as though she'd been knocked to the ground. "But *I'm* his fiancée!"

Lyndon took a step forward. She cursed the darkness that prevented her from seeing his expression. "I feel terrible about this, Sally. I know I asked you to marry me last month, but that was before Jane came back. Before I realized how strong my feelings are for her."

"You're lying." Salome tried to keep her voice from trembling. "It isn't true. You don't care a fig for Jane."

Lyndon groaned. "I don't know how to say this so as not to hurt you, but I've always loved Jane. I just didn't know how much. Seeing her this past week

17

showed me how wrong it was for me to marry anyone else. Especially a kind, honest woman like you.
You deserve to marry a man who loves you."

Tears welled up, but she wouldn't give Jane the
satisfaction of making her cry. "Two weeks ago, you
claimed to love *me*. Don't deny it now just because
she's hanging all over you."

Jane cleared her throat. "I'd best leave you two
alone to settle this."

Picking up her skirts, Jane gracefully stepped
through the curtain of willow branches. She stopped
a few feet away from Salome. Her face was lost in
the shadows, her silhouette feminine, fragrant and
terrifying. "I hope one day you can forgive me, and
we can be friends again."

Salome clenched her fists, trying to keep from
tearing out all that lovely honey-blond hair. "Obviously, we were never friends, Jane. Friends don't behave like scheming she-cats."

Jane shrugged, then went on her way. The moonlight bathed her retreating figure in a silvery glow.

"Try not to be bitter," Lyndon said quietly.

She let out a harsh laugh. "How do I do that? Forget all the years we've spent together? Forget the
plans we made only a fortnight ago, here under this
very tree! Or did I just imagine that you asked me to
be your wife? Or that we were going to move to Jefferson City so you could run for office one day. I
don't understand how everything can change so
quickly. Please explain it to me. Please!"

He gave a great sigh. One would almost imagine
he were the injured party. "I'm in love with her.
Years ago, before she left, I thought it was just infatuation. Jane was so pretty and vivacious, so talented. It seemed fitting that she had to go out in the
world; Black Horse was too small, too provincial for

18

her. And I thought I was too small and provincial for her, too. But things have changed since then." He paused. "*I've* changed."

"What are you saying? That you've grown worldly and important in her absence? I can't believe you're that arrogant, Lyndon, or that gullible."

"Sally, I've always been fond of you. And maybe I wanted to love you so much that I forced myself to believe it. Because I enjoy your company. I do, Sal. I tried to convince myself that my affection and respect for you would one day turn into love. I was willing to risk both our futures on it. But not anymore. Not after seeing Jane again."

Each word he uttered felt like a physical blow. If he said much more, she feared she would crumple to the ground in pain.

"So you never loved me?" She could barely get the words out.

"I have great affection for you, maybe even a kind of love. But not the sort of love that ties a man and woman together for a lifetime. Would we have courted endlessly for all these years if there were great passion between us?"

An anguished cry escaped her. "How can you say such a thing? Of course, there was passion between us! Do not play me for a fool, Lyndon Whittier. My memory is as sharp as your ambition."

He shook his head. "I—I didn't mean to say there were no strong feelings between us, but not enough. Not enough, Sal. What I feel for Jane is beyond my control. It's wild and urgent and unstoppable. Like the poem I recited tonight. My love for Jane is as glorious as 'music and moonlight.'" He reached out for her. "I'm so sorry. Please forgive me."

She backed away. "You don't know what you're saying. When this madness passes, you'll see how wrong this all is, how wrong Jane is for you. You know you love me. You do."

"I don't expect forgiveness now. Maybe not for a long time. But it may make things easier for you, knowing that Jane and I are leaving tomorrow. Perhaps when we return one day, you'll—"

"You're leaving?"

"Yes, Jane needs someone to manage her career," Lyndon explained, a hint of smugness in his voice. "Who better than a loving husband who also happens to be an attorney?"

If the earth had cracked open at that moment, she wouldn't have been surprised. In twenty-six years, she had never been faced with such upheaval. Maybe it was the full moon. It was said to drive people mad. Certainly none of this felt sane or reasonable.

"You're marrying her right away?" Hot tears spilled down her cheeks, but she was helpless to prevent them.

"No, she has engagements to fulfill, and we both feel it would be more appropriate to wait. We don't want to shock her family and her fans too much. She'll be singing in Chicago at the Columbian Exposition in October. What better way to celebrate the Exposition than with the famed Jane Dupree marrying her trusted manager? Besides, I don't want people to think I'm riding on Jane's coattails. These next few months will let me prove to the world that I'm as necessary to her career as I am to her personal life."

She felt the last of her pride crumbling away. "But you're necessary to *me*, as I am to you."

"Sal, please accept what I'm—"

"Let me finish!" Even she was surprised at the anger—and the strength—in her voice. "You've hurt me terribly tonight. Hurt me worse than if you'd shot me dead. You're a fool—a selfish fool!—to break our engagement and run off with that woman. And I think you'll regret it before the summer is over. Moonlight and music may sound delightful to poets, but they're weak things to build a marriage on. And I guarantee you won't be able to do it."

She wiped the tears from her cheeks. "I've loved you since you came to work for my father ten years ago. And I know what we've shared was tender and comforting and real. Yes, and passionate, too. Jane Dupree will never love you as I do. She'll never make you happy. And I love you too much to let you make such a terrible mistake."

"You don't understand." He shook his head. "Jane is every exciting and beautiful dream a man could wish for. She's glamorous and irresistible—everything pales beside her. Suddenly I'm willing to change my entire life just for the chance to share some of that excitement. Sal, I'm so sorry, but I love her as I could never love you. Please accept that. Don't cling to any false hope. I fully intend to marry Jane this October in Chicago."

"You're wrong." Salome took a deep breath, determined to finish this conversation without collapsing in hysterics. She couldn't let Lyndon's last sight of her be of a crying, pathetic woman. "Take these next few months and try to live this exciting, glamorous dream with Jane. But I promise you, when we talk again in October, you'll have had your fill of all that moonlight and music."

She turned on her heel, marching off into the darkness. Away from the willow tree. Away from the man she loved so desperately.

"Sal, I told you," he called after her. "I'll be in Chicago this October."

"So will I!" she shouted back.

21

* * *

Spinster schoolteachers didn't run away from home every day, but the stir caused by Salome's decision to leave Black Horse was nowhere near as remarkable as that caused by Lyndon and Jane's engagement. The day of their departure, almost the whole town had escorted them to the station as if they were visiting heads of state. Three weeks later, Salome found herself sitting alone on the train platform.

Beneath the brim of her straw hat, she peered down the railroad tracks. Her head pounded and her eyes felt as though they'd been rubbed in salt. No wonder. She had cried nonstop ever since the night Lyndon broke their engagement. For two days, she'd been so distraught, she couldn't even leave her bed. But she was done with crying. Done with allowing life to happen to her. Starting today, she was going to take charge of her own destiny.

She heard footsteps on the wooden train platform, but didn't bother to turn around. None of her family were likely to come say their farewells. Her kinfolk had grown weary of trying to discourage her from leaving. If she was set on chasing after a man who didn't want her, then they wouldn't be party to it. And her female friends wouldn't have the nerve to be seen publicly with a woman who was making such a spectacle of herself.

Despite their disapproval and shock, Salome knew that her family and friends believed she would be back in a week: contrite, shaken by her foray into the world. They were wrong. She wouldn't come back until she was Lyndon Whittier's wife. And to do that, she had to become the sort of daring and exciting woman who could inspire his undying devotion and love.

"So, you're really going to leave?"

Salome looked up in surprise. Julia Dupree stood smiling down at her, her dyed hair looking harsh in the morning sun.

"I wouldn't give up my teaching position and waste good money on a train ticket if I wasn't going to leave."

Julia sat on the bench beside her. "The gossip is that you're set on winning that lawyer fella back."

She nodded.

"I hope you don't have any hard feelings against me, seeing as how it was my sister that run off with him."

"Of course not. You had nothing to do with it." Salome hoped she sounded sincere. In reality, she had no desire to associate with any Dupree right now, not even the blameless mayor and his wife.

"Jane always was a charmer. Could charm a fox from a foxhole or a gent from his blushing bride. And she does it with so much style, you hardly know you been robbed till you look around and find your man has run off."

"It appears that Lyndon likes charmers. So I'm going to have to become one myself, and in short order."

"Your cousin Ella has been saying that you have plans to go onstage."

If only Ella could keep quiet. A town didn't need a telegraph as long as Ella was alive and well.

"I'm going to apply for a job in the theater," Salome said with determination. "Singing, if I can get it. Acting. Dancing. I don't know. Anything at all that will get me to the Chicago World's Fair by October. When Lyndon next sees me, I want him to find me as glamorous and alluring as he does your sister." She frowned. "Obviously schoolteachers don't set his

23

heart racing. So I'll just have to show him that Jane isn't the only woman who can create a stir."

"It's not so simple to get a job in the theater. Even if you can sing or dance, you're going to have to show off more of your legs than you're used to." Julia pointed to the long brown skirt that covered them now. "Are you willing to play the chorus girl, flouncing about half-dressed for the world to see?"

Salome swallowed hard at the image. "If I have to."

Julia laughed. "I'd like to be there to see that. I don't think you know what you're getting into. A nice respectable lady like yourself. I've been on the boards since I left eight years ago, and I've had to do things that would choke Reverend Fletcher dead."

Salome prayed she wouldn't elaborate. "I'll find a way to get by. When you left home, you were just fifteen. And you survived."

"I didn't do so well until I got hooked up with the magician. Now that was a nice job, nearly as easy as teaching children their numbers."

"Maybe I'll look for a magician in need of an assistant," she joked.

"I think I know just the one."

Salome stared at Julia. Julia wasn't as pretty or refined as her sister, but she was a striking young woman nonetheless, buxom and curvaceous with big blue eyes and a mass of curly hair that probably looked fine when left to its natural color. Salome suddenly wondered why Julia Dupree was still in Black Horse a month after she and her sister had come for their visit.

"Do you mean Marco the Magnificent?"

Julia's expression changed slightly. The mention of his name was obviously painful. Salome sympathized with her. She felt a twinge every time she spoke of Lyndon.

"His real name is Marc Cooper. And he's almost as good a magician as he thinks he is. He had himself a few lucky breaks, so now he's working the Orpheum Circuit. With a little more luck, he'll be a headliner soon. A couple months with him could get your name in the papers, make your lawyer fella sit up and take notice."

She leaned over. "And you won't have to show a lot of leg. Marc likes his assistants to distract the audience, but not too much. The man has a strong hankerin' to be center stage."

"Why would you imagine he'd take *me* on as his assistant? If he's as good as you say he is, he must have women begging to join the act."

Julia shook her head, a wide grin on her face. "Friends in the theater have been writing me. Seems Marc has had three different assistants since I left. Three in four weeks! No, Marc is a hard one to please, but I think you're bright enough to hold on to the job for awhile. But not too long." She held up a warning finger. "When the time is right, I want it back."

"Why not rejoin the act now?"

"Marc and I had us a misunderstanding. After all, here we were keeping company for two years, if you know what I mean. And even among show folk, sharing the bed of a man who won't buy the wedding license ain't something to be bragging about."

Salome felt herself blush.

"Well, I finally insisted that he make an honest woman out of me. And Marc plain refused. Refused! I told him that if he didn't marry me, I'd leave him, and the rascal called my bluff. So now I'm sitting here in Black Horse, swatting flies and smoking cigarettes on the front porch. Waiting till Marc comes to his senses and realizes how much he needs me. On and off the stage."

Hearing the whistle of an approaching train, Salome grabbed her drawstring bag. Julia stopped her from getting up.

"Marc can't do without me. I know him well enough. It's just his stubborn pride that keeps him from asking me to come back. One of these days, he'll come to his senses, but until then, some pretty young thing might join the act and make him forget how wonderful I am. Then where will I be?"

"I see." Salome's pride, already battered, sunk a bit further. "You want me to become his assistant because there's no chance he'd ever be attracted to me."

Julia had the good grace to look sheepish. "Well, you're not exactly Marc's type. I can't see you flirting and flouncing about, or worming your way into his bed. Even better, you have your eyes trained on another man. So even if you was a looker, you wouldn't be a threat to me."

How plain and colorless I must seem, Salome thought sadly. Maybe she would never be able to lure Lyndon away from Jane. Suddenly she was weary of both Dupree sisters. "Thank you for thinking of me, but I'll take my chances with the other theaters in St. Louis. I'm sure I'll find something, even if I'm not a looker."

Julia squeezed her arm. "Now don't be getting offended. All I'm saying is that I trust you around my man. You should be flattered."

"I have to go. My train is here."

"You're going to St. Louis anyway. Marc is supposed to be there until the end of the week. It won't hurt none to call on him and ask for a job. He won't be pawing you like some others I could name, and you won't have to do nothing but what the act requires."

"Thank you. I'll think about it." Salome got up, signaling for the porter to get her bags.

"Here, take this." Julia pulled out a crumpled letter from her skirt pocket. "This letter will let him know that you and me are old friends from Black Horse. And that you're sore in need of a job. Then you ask him real nice if you can work with him for just a few months. And don't forget to tell him that I'm thinking about him all the time."

Salome tried to refuse the letter, but Julia pushed it into her hands.

"Now you remember what I said. Theater is a tough life for a woman, tougher than you know. I've just given you a way to make things easier."

The train was ready for boarding. Salome stuffed the letter into her bag.

"I can't tell you how much this means to me. I'll feel so much better knowing you're there looking after Marc." Grateful tears formed in those blue eyes. "Don't let no wild woman get her hooks into him. Keep him safe for me."

Salome was suddenly overcome with sympathy for the younger Dupree sister. After all, they were both in the same predicament. Rejected by the men they loved, they were both willing to do just about anything to get them back. If working for the magician would get her to Chicago *and* help Julia, maybe it wasn't such a bad idea.

On impulse, Salome leaned over and hugged her. "Wish me luck."

"You're goin' to need a lot more than luck, honey," Julia murmured.

"What did you say?"

27

Sharon Pisacreta

But the train whistle blew again, drowning out Julia's reply. Not that it mattered. Salome's course was set. And she wasn't about to let the Dupree sisters or any magician named Marco get in her way.

Chapter Two

The sabers glittered in the spotlight. Amazingly, atop these three large swords, a young boy lay immobile.

"Remember that I perform the impossible, ladies and gentlemen," the man dressed in black announced to a rapt audience. "The impossible *is* possible for Marco the Magnificent."

Salome held her breath as the magician slowly removed one of the swords. The boy remained suspended in midair. A moment later, the magician removed the middle sword. Behind her, a woman let out a scream. Salome's eyes widened as the boy still did not crash to the stage floor. Instead he seemed to be supported by the single sword, its menacing tip resting beneath the nape of his young neck.

As gasps sounded from the audience, Marco the Magnificent held up a shiny silver hoop. Slowly, he passed the hoop along the suspended boy's body. Salome could not understand how the trick was accomplished. She was sitting in the fifth row, watching as closely as possible, yet she still could not fathom how the child remained afloat with only a single sword to bear his weight.

The audience applauded, but in a restrained manner as though fearful of rousing the boy. Then with grace and speed, the magician replaced the other two swords beneath the child. A moment later, the boy awoke as if from a trance and was assisted off the swords by the magician. He looked dazed, yet otherwise unharmed. This time the applause was deafening.

Joining in the applause, Salome felt a bit dazed herself. She had expected the magician to pull playing cards from his sleeve or a bedraggled rabbit from a hat. But she never thought to see children balanced precariously on swords.

This was the second time today she sat through the magic act at the Solti Theater. Both shows had been thrilling, even though the magician hadn't performed the saber trick earlier, perhaps because his assistant at the matinee was a burly fellow in shirt-sleeves, no doubt a stagehand. This evening, he had called upon the services of a boy who looked no older than eleven. Maybe he was no longer interested in hiring a full-time assistant, and was willing to make do with whomever seemed available backstage.

And maybe she wanted to believe that so she wouldn't have to work up the nerve to ask him for a job.

The stagelights dimmed, and the magician clapped his hands. A sparkling gold scarf appeared out of the darkness. After pausing in midair for a heart-stopping moment, it floated toward his outstretched hands.

Salome shifted in her seat. What was she doing

here anyway? She had a decent singing voice—everyone in the Black Horse church choir told her so. And she could sing both soprano and alto. Certainly there were revues in the city that could use a young woman who could sing and read music.

But she couldn't imagine being onstage with Marco the Magnificent.

To be truthful, she couldn't see herself getting too close to any man who looked like he did. No doubt stage performers had to exaggerate their characteristics in order to impress an audience. Clearly this Marco fellow was exaggerating his masculinity. He seemed far too male, like a hero from a Bronte novel.

He wore tight black trousers—as tight as riding breeches—and a black satin shirt with flowing sleeves. But what really riveted her attention, she was embarrassed to admit, was the broad expanse of chest that was bared for view beneath his unbuttoned shirt. It seemed to ripple with muscles and dark curly hair. She couldn't seem to stop her glance from returning to that vulgar display. Even worse, she wasn't certain if she was repulsed by the sight— or excited.

She did know, however, that she was fascinated by the magician's face. He had a pirate's features: rakish and strong. The unnatural shadows cast by the footlights gave him a dramatic, devilish appearance. She wondered if he was wearing makeup, and bit her lip at the thought. In addition, he wore his thick raven black hair unfashionably long so that it nearly touched his shoulders. He looked so unconventional a man that it seemed hardly any wonder he was able to balance children on sword-tips and cause glittering scarves to float above the stage.

"So what would he want with someone like me?" she muttered.

31

The audience was filled with admiring females.
There had to be dozens of ladies waiting for the
chance to meet this dashing man, let alone have the
thrill of working with him.

Salome pulled out her handkerchief and patted
her damp brow. What was the matter with her, for
heaven's sake? Only two days in St. Louis and she
was sitting here dazed by the sight of what was simply a good-looking entertainer. No more, no less.
And if dozens of women were clamoring to be his
assistant, then why was he performing his act with
only stagehands and children to help him?

Onstage, the magician leaned back and waved his
hands. The scarf danced in the air above him, seem-
ingly as mesmerized by the magician's gestures as
the young boy lying atop the swords had been. In
that moment, she spied a flash of gold and realized
with a start that he was wearing a hoop earring in
his right ear. Her mouth dropped open. A pirate indeed! With each passing moment he seemed to grow
more exotic and indecent. Were all men and women
who worked in the theater this strange?

She leaned forward, her eyes trained on his every
movement. The very idea of working with the magician seemed absurd. She was too plain for him and
he was too shocking for her. But Julia was in love
with this man, and feared another woman would
steal him away. Salome understood only too well Julia's pain and humiliation. The least she could do
was attempt to help her out, even if she was Jane
Dupree's sister.

Besides, to walk away now would only prove that
she didn't have the courage to be brash and daring.
And she needed to be brash and daring to land a job
in the theater and win Lyndon back. Even if Marco
the Magnificent laughed in her face, she owed it to

herself to not play the old maid schoolmarm.

She settled back in her seat. Yet what if he did decide to hire her? What would she do then? Salome thought she could grow accustomed to being placed atop razor-sharp sabers.

But she quaked at the idea of having to look at that muscular, hairy chest every night.

Marc Cooper slammed the dressing room door shut behind him. If he didn't find a proper assistant soon, he'd lose his chance of headlining on the Orpheum Circuit. He might even get dropped from the circuit, and that would relegate him to playing dime museums and carnival sideshows again.

Bad enough he had to use Fred at the matinee; the man was too fat to fit into any of his trick cabinets. He had been forced to employ the water boy for tonight's performance. The little scamp had spilled soda all over his twenty-dollar deck of cards, then lost the special needle he required for the balloon trick. Heaven save him from stagehands and curious boys.

He whipped off his damp shirt, flinging it on a chair. No matter how bad things got, however, he refused to send for Julia Dupree. Better he end up playing the strong man in the circus rather than link his fortunes with that troublesome female again.

He bent over the washbasin and washed off the black paint that exaggerated his eyes.

Still, he did need to find some woman who could do the job decently. He'd already had three replacements since Julia stormed off, each one of those ladies worse than the last. The first was too fond of imbibing spirits. The next one kept forgetting how the tricks worked and sprang open trap doors prematurely. Finally there was the assistant who was far more interested in the magic Marco was capable of producing offstage than on. He made sure to send that predatory female on her way quickly. He'd already learned that lesson too well with Julia.

No, the next time he signed on a female assistant, she would have to be so wonderful that he'd make her his wife and thus keep her in his act forever. Or he'd make certain to hire a woman who was competent and intelligent, but one he'd never feel a drop of desire for. Nor she for him. It was the only way to ensure success in the act and serenity in his personal life.

Someone rapped on his door. Grabbing a towel, he wiped his face. "What is it?"

The stage manager stuck his head in. "There's a little lady here who wants to see you about a job."

He smoothed his damp hair back. "If she wants to work with me, Billy, then she's no lady."

Billy laughed, his Adam's apple bobbing up and down above his faded collar. "I don't know. This one looks like a real lady to me, Marc. Dressed drabber than a preacher's wife."

Marc shrugged into his robe. "She give a name?"

"Miss Salome Hall. Sounds like a great stage name, don't it?"

"She goes by the name of Salome but looks like a preacher's wife?" Marc smirked. "This one I gotta see. Show her in."

After every performance, at least one young woman ventured backstage to see him. Most simply wanted a chance to shake the hand of Marco the Magnificent or, even better, peek into his dressing room and catch a glimpse of the magician in a scandalous half-dressed state. He didn't mind. It was good for business.

"Here she is." Billy opened the door wide, gestur-

34

ing for the woman to walk in. "Miss Salome Hall, this here is Marco the Magnificent. A most dangerous man onstage and off."

Marc shot him a warning look. "Thanks, Billy. I'll give a holler if I need you."

The woman threw an anxious glance at the departing stage manager.

"Come in and sit down." He plucked his shirt off the chair.

His cramped dressing room was no more than a glorified closet. If he sat in the dressing table chair across from her, their knees would touch. And looking at this lady, he doubted she would be able to tolerate such close proximity without blushes and swooning.

He remained standing, leaning back against his dressing table, arms crossed in front of him. In all the years he'd been performing, he'd never seen such a prim, demure person come looking for a job in the theater. It must be a joke. Yet as he peered at the woman sitting in front of him, her head bowed, he didn't think she was the sort of lady who indulged in pranks.

She did look like a lady, he'd give her that. She was very petite, barely five foot tall, and slender as a reed. Her gray twill jacket was buttoned up to her neck, even though the theater was hot and airless. Her dark gray skirt was as severe as a nun's habit though its narrowness hinted at slim legs. Since she wouldn't look up at him, he couldn't judge her age, but she did boast lovely dark brown hair. Too bad it was coiled tighter than a fisherman's knot beneath her straw hat.

"So you're looking for a job, Miss Hall?"

She nodded, her face still averted. "Yes, I am seeking employment in the theater and was informed that you were in need of an assistant."

Marc raised his eyebrows. She sounded far too cultured to be working with the likes of him.

"Pardon me, miss, but you don't look like the type who hangs around stage doors. Who told you about me?"

Instead of answering, she fumbled in her drawstring bag. A moment later, she held out a letter. Even when he took it from her, she refused to look at him.

"Is there some reason you're afraid to catch my eye?"

"I'm sorry, it's just that I'm not accustomed to being alone with a man who—who is not properly attired."

He glanced down. What was the problem? He still had his breeches and boots on, and his robe covered most of his bare chest. Damn, but if this wasn't one of those tight-corseted ladies, afraid to glimpse even an inch of naked flesh. With a frown, he wrapped his robe tighter about him.

"I don't mean to dash your hopes, miss, but if you're going to start blushing when I'm just standing here in a robe and trousers, I can't see how you'll bring yourself to wear the costume that the job requires."

"But I was told that the assistant's costume wasn't that revealing." This time she looked straight at him, her eyes wide in alarm. They were lovely eyes, big, brown and dark, nearly the same color as her hair.

"Who told you all this?"

"The letter will explain everything."

He looked at the paper in his hand and felt anger rising up. "Can't you just tell me straight out what this is about?"

Magic & Moonlight

"Forgive me, I'm probably going about this completely wrong. It's just that I'm a bit nervous. I've never had to apply for a job before, except for my teaching position and that was under quite different circumstances."

"Wait a minute. You're a schoolteacher?"

She nodded.

Marc swept his hands over his hair. "Miss, I don't know who sent you or what this is about, but I can assure you that you don't want a job as my assistant."

"But I do want this job. I need this job." She sat there, eyes wide and serious, gloved hands primly folded upon her lap.

"Who told you about my assistant's costume?"

She cleared her throat. She was so obviously nervous, he felt a wave of sympathy for her. "Julia Dupree," she said.

"Julia Dupree?" Whatever sympathy he'd felt went flying out the window. "Julia sent you to me?"

"Yes, she and I grew up together in Black Horse, Missouri. She came home for a visit last month and when Julia learned I wanted to work in the theater, she suggested I come see you." She nodded towards the letter. "That might explain everything more coherently than I am."

With a growl, he tore open the letter. He looked at it for a moment before crumpling it and throwing it aside.

"Julia wanted me to tell you that she thinks of you often."

He tried to curb his anger. "Look, Miss Hall, Julia has no right to be using you as a messenger between us. And she certainly had no business letting you think you could work as my assistant."

Her expression grew even more confused. "So you don't need an assistant?"

37

"Oh, I need one all right, but what I don't need is someone who's spying on me for Julia."

"No, you're quite mistaken. I'm not spying for anyone. I need a job in the—"

"Save your breath, Miss Salome Hall, assuming that really is your name. Or did Julia suggest you tack on the 'Salome' part so as to seem more exotic?"

Miss Hall stood up, clearly flustered. "Of course not. How could you think such a thing? I was christened Salome Ruth Hall and I can get the birth records to prove it."

Marc waved her objections aside. "That doesn't matter. I wouldn't be surprised if you were as ignorant of your friend's character as I once was. All I can tell you is that I refuse to work with anyone who is connected to Miss Dupree. That's final."

She took a deep breath. "Thank you for seeing me, Mr. Cooper. I'm sorry that my visit upset you. It was not intentional, I assure you. I simply need a job in the theater and Julia said you were a decent man to work for."

He felt like a bully, yelling at her like this, but springing a blasted letter from Julia Dupree on him was too much. It had taken him over a year to be rid of Julia, and now a month later, she was sending this little schoolteacher to spy.

"No, I'm the one who should be apologizing to you. It's not your fault that Julia and I have a bad history between us."

She held out her hand. Miss Hall even felt like a lady, he thought as he shook her hand. Delicate, graceful, restrained. Why in the world did she want to work as a magician's assistant?

"If you'll take my advice, Miss Hall, you won't go looking for a job in the theater. You're just not cut out for that sort of thing. The theater is no place for an educated, respectable woman. You'd be much better off going back home, teaching those school-children, and finding a nice gentleman to marry."

She stiffened, drawing her hand out of his grasp. "Thank you, Mr. Cooper, but I've already found the gentleman I plan to marry."

"And your intended doesn't mind his future wife working in the theater?"

She drew herself up, seeming tall for a moment even though she barely reached his chin. "On the contrary, my future husband seems to require it. Good-bye, Mr. Cooper."

A moment after she swept out of his dressing room, Marc still stared after her. When he finally shut the door, he was chuckling to himself. Well, he didn't have betrothed schoolteachers coming to him every day asking for a job. What kind of female did Black Horse, Missouri, produce anyway? Damn contrary ones, apparently.

Throwing off his robe, Marc flung himself into the chair Miss Hall had just vacated. Still, he had to admit she was an intriguing woman to look at. And it might have been worthwhile hiring her if only to see how those slim, petite legs looked in pink silk tights.

He poured himself a glass of whiskey, and swigged it down. Schoolteachers named Salome, he thought with amusement. What next?

Five days later, she was back where she started. Not one booking agent or theater manager had given her a second look, and many of them had refused a first one.

She tried not to get too discouraged. She knew it was going to be difficult. After all, she was past her first youth, had no experience in the theater, and was as plain and unexciting as yesterday's tea. Still it was hard returning to her boarding house every evening, exhausted from the continual rejections, worried about her dwindling savings. And unable to sleep from the ache in her heart.

A real ache, she discovered. The poets were right. A broken heart actually ached with pain. There were nights when she lay for hours in the darkness, unsettled by the sound of strangers snoring in the rooms above and below her, reliving over and over that terrible last conversation with Lyndon. How could he ask her to be his wife, then fourteen days later, run off with another woman? She simply couldn't accept it. And the pain in her heart wouldn't let her forget it.

Despite her heartache, however, there was no turning back. As humiliating as the auditions and begging for jobs were, she would do whatever it took if it gave her a chance to attract Lyndon's attention once more. That's why she'd returned to the Solti Theater. According to the newspapers, last night was the final performance of Marco the Magnificent. This afternoon, he would be interviewing young women interested in hiring on as his assistant.

It didn't matter that he'd already rejected her. Everyone in St. Louis had done that. But of all the people she'd seen about a job, he was the one who'd treated her with the most respect, the most kindness. If only she could somehow convince him that she was willing and able to be his assistant. If only she could convince him that she wasn't spying for Julia and that she needed this opportunity more than any woman in Missouri.

So many "if onlys," she thought with a sinking heart. And the last was the most insurmountable. If only she were beautiful and curvaceous, able to dazzle magicians and country lawyers alike. Of course, if she were, she'd be Mrs. Lyndon Whittier by now.

As she entered the empty theater, she glanced at her watch pin. She was two hours early. She wasn't going to let any other woman get to him first. Two hours was plenty of time to beg, plead and generally make a complete fool of herself.

Walking down the carpeted aisleway, she noted that the bare stage looked different than when she'd seen it last. She ran a gloved hand along the surface of the stage floor. Without the blazing footlights, floating scarves and sabers, it now seemed ordinary and lifeless. And, without the presence of the raven-haired magician, the entire theater seemed devoid of energy and color.

"You looking for someone, miss?"

Turning around, she was surprised to see a man sitting near the back of the theater. He was an older gentleman, bald and round, a walrus moustache decorating his jowled face. The seat beside him was piled with papers.

"I'm here for the interview with Marco the Magnificent."

She tugged at her short fitted jacket. Dressed in her finest "calling" outfit, she hoped the lavender silk gown would give her confidence. Although perhaps the ostrich feathers decorating her satin turban were too ostentatious for early morning. The only time she'd worn this outfit was for her mother's wedding; even then she hadn't had the nerve to wear the turban. But she suspected that she needed to appear as sophisticated as possible to convince the magician to hire her.

"You're early. You girls weren't supposed to be here for a couple of hours." With a grunt, he pulled himself up. His embroidered vest strained against his stomach. "I don't think Cooper's in the theater yet. These magician fellows get up late in the day if there's no performance. I just came in to go over last night's box office receipts."

"Well, I'll wait here then. If that's all right."

He walked down the aisle towards her, his bald head shiny beneath the illumination from the chandelier. "I don't think you have much of a chance, miss."

Frustration and anger stole through her once more. "I'm only trying out for a job as magician's assistant, sir. Hardly a position demanding great skill or talent. And I'm willing to do whatever it requires to get the job."

"I see." He stopped before her, wheezing slightly from the exertion. "But you misunderstand me, Miss—"

"Miss Hall."

"Well, Miss Hall, allow me to introduce myself. I'm Amos Jenson and I own this theater."

Her heart sank. She was going to be turned out by the theater owner without ever getting a second chance with the magician.

"Are you responsible for hiring the acts, sir?"

He nodded. "This is the finest variety and vaudeville house in the city, and I pride myself on knowing how to pick the best talent. That's why I'm telling you that this magician won't take you on." He held up a hand to stop her protest. "And you shouldn't be upset about that, not at all. What's so great about working with a man who makes scarves fly through the air? Not much to be gained by being in a magic act. It's only a step up from the carnival."

"It may not be comparable to acting in a Shakespearean play, but I want the job just the same." She paused. "I need this job and I'm willing to go to great lengths to get it."

42

His already small eyes narrowed further. "Would you be interested in performing in a Shakespearean play, Miss Hall?"

"Me? Shakespeare?" Her voice rose to a shocked squeak.

"Sure. I book all sorts of acts here. Starting in July, I got a company coming in from Washington with a production of *Midsummer Night's Dream*. They always hire extras from the locals. I can't offer you a speaking part, but how you'd like to do a walk-on?"

This man was unbelievably kind and generous. But she couldn't let him think she was more qualified than she was.

"I'd be very interested in working with the company, but I must confess that I have no acting experience. However, I was a schoolteacher so I'm not afraid of public speaking. Not that I'm expecting a speaking role, of course."

He reached for her elbow, gently steering her towards the nearest seat. After she sat down, he squeezed himself into the chair beside her.

"A schoolteacher, eh? I thought so. Moment I laid eyes on you, I thought, 'Now there's an intelligent looking woman.' Perfect for Shakespeare. A couple years of acting under your belt, you'd make an ideal Portia."

"Portia?" Her head was reeling. Suddenly her whole future had changed. What would Lyndon say when he heard that she was a Shakespearean actress? He would be stunned. And exceedingly pleased. Lyndon adored Shakespeare. Every Saturday evening, they read to each other from both the sonnets and the plays. Wait until he learned that she was appearing in a real production of *A Midsummer Night's Dream*. Jane and her pretty songs would pale in comparison.

"Yes, Portia. And Titania, too. Maybe even Juliet."

"Oh, no, I'm too old for Juliet."

"Nonsense." He reached over and covered her hand with his own. "Would you be willing to go into my office and discuss your future, Miss Hall? If you agree to my terms, we could sign the contract right here and now."

Her heart raced with excitement. This was more magical than anything she'd seen in Marc Cooper's act the other night. "Oh yes, I would be more than willing to sign a contract."

"Good, good." He squeezed her hand. She knew it was an impertinent liberty for a stranger to take, but no doubt theater people behaved with less propriety than Missouri farm folk.

He squinted at her for a moment. "Do you mind my asking how old you are, Miss Hall?"

She felt the familiar dread again. "I was twenty-six on March the twelfth. Do you think that's too old to become an actress?"

"Not at all." He took her chin in one hand, then slowly moved her head first this way and then the other. "I would have taken you for younger. I just wanted to make certain I wasn't offering a contract to a woman who's not of legal age."

She could barely keep from laughing. It had been a long time since anyone had mistaken her for a mere girl.

"But I can see now that I have a real woman before me," he continued. "A woman who won't be shocked by the sins and decadence of theater life."

"Sins and decadence?" Salome was so startled by his statement, she barely registered the fact that his hand was now caressing her shoulder.

"I venture to say you might even be excited by it, eh?" He grasped her arm.

"Mr. Jenson, please." She pulled back, her hands pressed hard against his chest to prevent him from getting any closer. "Excuse me, sir, but—but are you attempting to seduce me?"

He chuckled. "Amen, lady. You got that right."

She shook loose from his grasp and stood up. "I'm afraid I can't allow this."

Grabbing her by the waist, Jenson hauled her into his lap. He was so big, however, he barely had a lap left to sit on, and she was left to dangle on his knees.

"I warn you, sir. I shall resort to physical force if you do not refrain from manhandling me."

"Now, my dear. You don't have to pretend with me. No one will show up for at least an hour so we have the theater all to ourselves. More than enough time for negotiating the contract, eh?" He squeezed her waist. "Enough time for you to prove to me that you're willing to do anything for the job."

For a moment, Salome could only sit rigidly in his grasp, baffled at this sudden turn of events, and repelled by his huge stomach pressing against her.

"Please, Mr. Jenson. Let me go or I shall hurt you."

His only response was a sloppy attempt to kiss her neck.

This was really quite appalling. It was as if one of the hogs on Ellis Hoffman's pig farm had tried to wrestle her.

"I fear you leave me no other choice, sir." As he pulled her closer, trying to kiss her again, she slid the hat pin from her satin turban. "You've only yourself to blame for this."

She stuck him full force on the top of his hand, making sure the pin went in at least an inch.

He yowled like a man who'd been properly stabbed. "Great jehosophat! What in the hell do you think you're doing?"

45

While he grabbed his bleeding hand, she leapt off his lap. Scurrying down the aisle away from him, Salome held up the long hat pin. "If you attempt to molest me again, I promise I shall use my hat pin with much greater force." She looked at him with her sternest schoolteacher's expression. "And in a much more vulnerable place, sir."

He stood up, cradling his hand. "Why, you deceitful little chit. How dare you stab me! Did you think I was offering you a job as an actress and expecting nothing in return?"

"I thought you were expecting me to perform on-stage," she said indignantly. "Not on your lap. But I see that we are at total cross-purposes. I could never accept a contract from you now."

He snorted. "As if I'd offer you anything but a swift kick in your bustle. And don't think that you'll find even the meanest stage job in St. Louis after this. I own five theaters in the city and the owners of the rest owe me favors. I'll see to it that you don't find work with any of them." He pulled out his handkerchief and wrapped it around his hand.

"Come now, it's hardly bleeding at all."

"You stabbed me with a pin as long as a knife! Don't tell me it ain't bleeding." His expression grew more forbidding. "In fact, I think you're dangerous. The police should hear about you."

"For pricking you with a hat pin? Don't be absurd."

"Absurd, eh? Well, maybe they wouldn't bother to arrest you for sticking me with that pin, but they might be interested in how you make a living in this here city. A woman as desperate for work as you are can't be earning wages. They might consider vagrancy charges against you."

"That's ridiculous. I've been looking for work all week."

"And ain't found any. I'm not without friends on the police force either. Maybe a few days in jail for vagrancy will take some of the starch out of that petticoat of yours."

"Vagrancy won't work, Jenson," a male voice said loudly from the stage. "You'll have to go with attempted murder."

Salome whirled around. Marc Cooper stood center stage, glaring at Jenson. She wondered how long he'd been there. He looked different with his hair pulled back and an ordinary sack suit covering that disturbing chest. But even without makeup, his dark eyes commanded attention.

"But a little prick on the hand won't move the police," he continued. "How about if I rough you up some? Make it look as if you've really taken a beating." His voice hardened. "We both know you deserve it."

"Stay out of this, Cooper," Jenson warned. "This trollop led me on and then viciously attacked me."

"Trollop?" Salome's mouth fell open. "I am a primary schoolteacher, sir, and once studied with the esteemed Susan Blow of the Des Peres School."

"I don't care who you been studying with. All I know is that you come sashaying in here, telling me you're willing to do anything for a job in the theater." He held up his bandaged hand. "And when I offer you a job, you turn around and stab me!"

Marc jumped down from the stage, as light and surefooted as a panther. He seemed to radiate strength, and Salome instinctively took a step towards him. "Save your yapping for some fool who doesn't know what a polecat you are, Jenson." He walked over to Salome, his eyes taking on a gentle expression. "Are you all right, Miss Hall? I hope this idiot didn't hurt you."

She shook her head. When his voice wasn't booming majestically from the stage, it had a lulling, hypnotic quality.

"I told you, she's the one who hurt me." Jenson pushed himself into the aisle. "And I'm going to make sure she don't hurt any other theater owner in the city either. When I'm done spreading the word about this scheming little schoolteacher, there won't be a soul in greasepaint who will even glance her way."

He huffed his way to the top of the aisle. "And I'll bring vagrancy charges against her, too." With that threat hanging in the air, he stormed out into the lobby.

In the uncomfortable pause that followed, Salome put her hat pin back in the turban. Maybe she had reacted too precipitously, but what was she expected to do? Allow the man to molest her? Perhaps females accustomed to fending off male advances had other, less direct ways of dealing with it. Even so, she suspected Jenson would follow through on his threats. He looked like the sort who enjoyed making trouble.

"Knowing Jenson, I'm afraid he'll do exactly as he says." Marc Cooper echoed her own thoughts. "It's unlikely you'll find work in a St. Louis theater now."

"I suppose I'll have to move on then," she said with a sigh. "I have enough money to get to Joplin. Surely there are theaters in Joplin."

He leaned over and peeked into her eyes. "Yes, I was afraid of that. You look as serious about working in the theater as you did in my dressing room the other day. Is there anything I can say that will convince you to go home, Miss Hall?"

She shook her head. "I can't go home, Mr. Cooper."

He held out his arm. "Allow me to escort you outside then. You look as though you need a little fresh air."

After a moment's hesitation, she curled her hand about his elbow. He felt as solid as a strong tree. They walked up the aisle together. "I actually came here today to see you again."

"Me?" Marc stopped. "What did you want with me?"

"I read in the newspaper that you were going to interview female assistants this morning."

"You are one stubborn woman, Miss Hall. Haven't you learned to take 'no' for an answer?"

"Not when it's something this important."

"I guess I should feel flattered." He laughed. "It's been a long time since a real lady considered either me or my act important."

"I am a very fast learner, Mr. Cooper. And I'm comfortable speaking in public, so I shouldn't have a problem with stage fright." She sensed he was more receptive today and she needed to press her suit. "And I swear on the souls of my schoolchildren that I am not spying for Julia Dupree. I simply need this job very much and you seem like a kind man."

His expression grew serious. "I believe you, Miss Hall."

She held her breath. "Then will you allow me to be your assistant?"

He shut his eyes a moment, as if thinking. "I must be crazy for agreeing to this," he muttered.

Her hand tightened about his elbow. "So I have the job?"

When he looked at her once more, Salome caught her breath. Those impenetrable dark eyes seemed to see into her all-too-desperate soul.

"I always was a sucker for hardheaded women. If you don't come to your senses before morning, meet me at the train station. We leave for Kansas City on the seven o'clock train."

Although he wore a grin, she sensed that his offer was entirely serious. For the first time since Lyndon deserted her, she felt a lightness of spirit, a faint belief that perhaps one day she could know happiness again.

"Thank you so much, Mr. Cooper. I'll work hard, I swear. You won't regret this." Suddenly giddy, she felt like twirling down the middle of the aisle, but feared that would worry the magician. Instead she merely smiled back at him. "There were times this past week when I feared it might not be possible to find a job in the theater."

Marc Cooper held out his hand in a gesture she had seen him perform during his act. "With Marco the Magnificent, the impossible *is* possible," he said in a dramatic voice.

He held out his arm once more. "I just hope that Missouri schoolteachers don't prove too impossible."

Chapter Three

The train had barely pulled out of the station when the magician thoroughly shocked Salome.

Ten minutes after their departure for Kansas City, Marc Cooper stood up and excused himself to go into the smoking car. But before he left, he handed over a small valise containing the costume she would be required to wear as his assistant. Hours later, she was still shaken by what he had given her.

Craning her neck around the upholstered seat, she was relieved that all she could see were the train conductor and several booted feet sprawled in the aisle. Facing forward, she swallowed hard and once again examined the flimsy article of clothing. She could never bring herself to wear this. Not even for Lyndon's sake. Why, it was little more than a glorified camisole. Her upper thighs would be on vulgar display, and the tight fit of the material would emphasize the shape of her buttocks. She frowned at the

51

black lace that edged the shoulder straps. Surely assisting a magician didn't require wearing a revealing midnight blue costume that dripped with cheap rhinestones.

She neatly folded the costume, laying it back in the valise. Before she closed it, she also fingered the pale pink tights that peeked out from beneath. From the back row, she was certain it would look as though her legs were bare. She pursed her lips in disapproval.

Never. Not in a million years. As nice as Mr. Cooper had been to take her on as his assistant, she simply would have to insist that he find a more modest outfit. Something with a skirt that would hang low enough to expose only her calves and ankles. And that would be mortification enough.

"Tickets, miss."

Salome fumbled in her bag and pulled out her train ticket for the conductor.

"Is there a dining car on board, sir?"

"Dining car is right behind this one," he said as he punched her ticket. "The special today is frankfurters and hot potato salad. But mind your step when you're walking between cars. Them newfangled vestibules we got don't cover all the train platform. Wouldn't want you to lose your footing and find yourself dangling in midair."

"Thank you," she murmured, doubting frankfurters and potato salad were worth the risk.

She wasn't that hungry anyway, she told herself. With a sigh, she reached into her satchel and pulled out the second volume of Mr. Henry Adams's *History of the United States*. She'd barely read three paragraphs before her stomach growled. Luckily, no one was sitting close enough to hear. She should have eaten breakfast, but she'd been so nervous this morning. Unaccustomed to traveling, especially with a man, Salome worried that people might think she and Mr. Cooper were married. Or worse.

After all, what did she know about this man, aside from the fact that he wore an earring, worked with saber swords, and drank spirits? The brief time she spent in his dressing room had been long enough to spy the bottle of whiskey on his table. Half-empty too, if she recalled correctly. She wondered if he drank to excess. Maybe he'd gone off not to smoke but to sip whiskey from a silver flask he kept hidden on his person. She shook her head. And maybe she was letting her imagination get the better of her, like a child reading one of Mr. Poe's horror tales.

She couldn't let herself forget that he was the only person in St. Louis who had been kind enough to help her. It was ungrateful to think ill of a man who had come so gallantly to her aid.

Turning her attention to Mr. Adams's description of the Jefferson administration, she found her mind wandering back to the magician. She was surprised to see that when not performing, he tied his shoulder-length hair back in a queue. Just like one of our Founding Fathers, she thought. Although she doubted Thomas Jefferson or Benjamin Franklin routinely exposed their bare chests to respectable ladies.

"Stop referring to yourself as respectable," she said aloud.

An elderly woman was walking past at that moment. "I beg your pardon, miss."

"I'm so sorry," Salome mumbled. "I wasn't speaking to you."

The gray-haired matron scanned the empty seats about her before moving on with a bemused expression.

Salome wished she could stop feeling apologetic and flustered all the time. And she definitely had to stop trying so hard to be respectable. The man she loved apparently didn't give a fig for respectable women. A shameless blond siren had seduced him right out from under her respectable nose.

She threw the book back into her satchel. Jane Dupree wouldn't sit here reading American history while her stomach growled with hunger. Jane was probably unafraid of the most daunting train platform, while here she sat, too timid to even venture off to the dining car on her own.

Flinging herself up from her seat, she turned purposefully into the aisle, only to bump right into a broad male chest.

"Where you off to in such a hurry?"

She looked up into the dark brown eyes of the magician. Even without the makeup he wore onstage, his features were striking and dramatic.

"I thought I'd go to the dining car for lunch."

"Good idea. I'll join you." He stepped back, allowing her just enough room to squeeze past.

Her body brushed against him, his suit jacket catching on the pearl buttons of her glove. As he bent his head to unfasten them, she could smell cigarette tobacco. She wrinkled her nose, although she didn't disapprove of smoking. Her father had smoked pipes incessantly, an aroma she found pleasant. But if she was going to work with Marc Cooper, she would have to become accustomed to the mingled scent of cigarettes and bay rum that permeated the air around him.

"There, I've got us untangled." He had an infectious smile, no doubt all stage performers did. She couldn't help but smile back.

As they moved down the aisle, she was keenly

aware of him right behind her. Sometimes she could feel his feet brushing against her skirt. Surely he could maneuver them safely between cars.

When they got to the door leading out to the train platform, another passenger was coming through. Mr. Cooper grabbed the door before it slammed shut. He pressed against her for a second, both of them swaying with the train's movement. She felt with startling clarity the strength in his arms and chest. Like a young bull, she thought wonderingly. He wasn't a particularly tall man—although everyone seemed tall next to her—but he certainly was a robust one. With one shove, he pushed the door back and then gently nudged Salome through.

The platform was only partially covered, and she spied the ground whistling past. Out here, the sound of the train seemed deafening, although she enjoyed the warm summer air that whipped through the open sections of the vestibule.

Even though the platform rocked wildly, she felt no fear. As they moved along the narrow passageway, he held on to her shoulders, gently moving her along. The train jarred suddenly, and she was thrown back. But the magician was right behind her, as steady and solid as a wall. For a moment, they were pressed together as intimately as lovers, his hands clasped about her shoulders. No man had ever held her this close except for Lyndon. If she weren't so relieved to have Mr. Cooper guiding her between cars, she might have remembered to blush.

"Here, let me open this and then we'll be through." As he held on to her with one arm, he easily pushed open the door in front of them. They stepped into the dining car together, like dancers moving to music.

A waiter approached them. "Will that be two for lunch?"

"Yes, please," she answered in a tremulous voice. If stepping from one train car to the other took her breath away, she couldn't imagine how the first performance in Kansas City would affect her.

And the prospect of working closely with the man now sitting across from her didn't make things easier. He was a most unconventional gentleman, although she was grateful to see that he didn't wear the earring offstage. Even so, his long hair and theatrical looks attracted enough undue attention. Yet he no longer intimidated her. In fact, since leaving St. Louis, he had been surprisingly solicitous of her, as though they were brother and sister.

She frowned as she stared at the small print on the menu. Brother and sister, she thought with dismay. Was she really so plain and unappealing that no man seemed able to regard her with passion? She dismissed the lewd advances of Mr. Jenson back in St. Louis. That scoundrel probably forced himself on every female from nineteen to ninety. But the rest of the male population, it seemed, found her as desirable as a cold rain shower.

"You don't seem too pleased with what the Missouri Pacific is offering today."

"What?" She looked up and met his questioning gaze. "No, I was just thinking of something else."

The waiter came back to their tiny table bearing two glasses of water. She quickly took a sip from hers, and bit back a grimace. The water was warm as soup, and the sunlight trying to break through the clouds outside showed that the glasses were not altogether clean.

"I'll have a frankfurter and potato salad, please." She settled back in the uncomfortable seat.

"Bring me the same." Mr. Cooper pointed to the couple sitting behind them. "What kind of pudding is that lady eating?"

"Peach, sir," the waiter said a bored voice.

"Well, bring me some peach pudding when I'm done with my frankfurter." Once the waiter left, he sat back, crossing his arms. His gaze was much too intense. Salome didn't know whether to be embarrassed or alarmed.

"So what's the problem?" he finally said. "Something is. You're looking just like a woman who ate a bad dish of clams."

"I—I don't know what you're talking about." Now that they were alone together, she didn't know how to tell him about the costume.

His expression softened. "You're not still upset about yesterday, I hope. Jenson may be a slimy rascal, but he's a coward to boot. I wouldn't worry about him ever bothering you again. He knows I'll break both his fat little arms if he does."

"No, no, I'm not worried about Mr. Jenson at all." She fiddled with the pearl buttons on her gloves. "And please allow me to thank you again for taking me on as your assistant."

He waved her thanks aside.

She reached for her water glass and drained its tepid contents. Now was the time to be brash and assertive. Now was the time to tell him that she absolutely refused to wear that disgraceful costume.

"If you're nervous about performing in Kansas City, that's only natural," he said, apparently convinced that was the cause of her sudden jitters. "The first time before an audience is always unpleasant."

She gulped. "It is?"

The magician grinned. He looked quite devilish and exciting when he smiled like that. Despite his

Sharon Pisacreta

long hair and dramatic appearance—a bit too dramatic for a man—Salome was beginning to see why Julia Dupree was so desperate to hang on to him.

"Nah, it's not that bad. After the first ten minutes of being terrified, it starts to get easier. Then you'll just feel as though you're going to be sick. But once you've been doing this about ten or twelve years, you'll only break out in a sweat every other night or so."

"You're joking." She leaned forward on the wooden table between them. The train whistle blew four times, and she waited until the dining car grew quiet once more. "Surely you never feel nervous. I've never seen anyone take control of a stage like you do."

He laughed. "And how much theater do you get a chance to see in little old Black Horse?"

"We're not a backwater, you know. Our population is close to three thousand and we have the biggest glassworks factory in the South. And two years ago, the town council built an auditorium. With electric lights around the entranceway."

Cooper still wore an amused expression. "I might be more impressed if you told me the city fathers had put the lights *inside* the theater."

"Well, it's still a fine auditorium. A theater company from Springfield has visited four times. I doubt if Chicago or New York sees finer productions."

He shrugged. "Maybe."

The waiter brought their food. Salome pulled off her gloves as he set the plates and flatware before them.

"Well, don't worry about the audiences in Kansas City. The theater we're booked in is almost as bad as a dime museum, even if it is on the circuit. They'll

58

be grateful if we just show up sober." He took a big bite of his frankfurter.

"Julia says you have a good chance of headlining on the Orpheum Circuit." As soon as she said that, a look of anger swept over his face.

"Let's try to keep Miss Dupree out of our conversations," he said in a tight voice.

They ate for a moment, the awkward silence between them filled with the rattling of cutlery and the clicking of the train wheels on the tracks below.

"Well, we're going to be onstage in forty-eight hours so I may as well start explaining what I want you to do." He wiped his mouth with a cloth napkin. "I'll try to keep the first couple of performances simple. No 'Bed of Nails' or sawing you in half. You're not ready for that yet."

"You're going to saw me in half?" She was so startled by the thought, she spoke with her mouth full.

"Of course. What kind of magician would I be if I didn't saw someone in half? That's the problem with not having a female assistant. It just doesn't look as terrifying if I cut Fred the stagehand in two. But a pretty girl showing a bit of leg? Why, the audience eats it up."

"Pretty?" she repeated softly, but he didn't hear her.

"Besides, it's hard to find a stagehand who can fit into the cabinet." Excited to be talking about his work, his speech quickened. "But you—you're nice and slim. And small enough to fit into the Zigzag Mystery Box. I haven't been able to do that one in awhile. I need an assistant who's small and flexible. And she also has to be smart enough to know how to get out at the proper time. Seeing as how you're an educated woman, I'm sure you'll have no problem."

She swallowed hard. "You mentioned showing a bit of leg."

He nodded, his mouth full of potato salad.

"Well, I looked the costume over and I have to admit to some trepidation about wearing it."

His dark eyebrows lifted. "I need an assistant, not a schoolmarm. That means you dress like a magician's assistant. With flash and daring. You're supposed to take the audience's attention away from me at the right time, so they don't see how the tricks are put together. And to really grab their attention, I need a pretty woman showing her legs."

She felt herself grow warm, but not with embarrassment. With pleasure. He had referred to her—however obliquely—as pretty. And he had done it twice.

"But Mr. Cooper, if I could just add a few things to the costume so as to make it less—less vulgar."

He shook his head.

"A scarf, perhaps?" She still felt so happy at being referred to as 'pretty' that she didn't want to refuse to wear the costume outright. He had pleased her by the description, so now she was reluctant to displease him. "Just a scarf or two. Flowing scarves to make me appear more exotic."

He looked closely at her, as though trying to figure out why she wore such a wide smile. "Maybe. Let me think about it."

She bit into her frankfurter with renewed appetite.

So a worldly man like Marco the Magnificent found her pretty. Pretty!

A moment later, she startled both of them by bursting into laughter.

He must be going soft in the head. Maybe all those years of working with smoke and mirrors had finally addled his brains. He had no business hiring a modest schoolmarm to be his assistant. She should be back in that little Missouri town of hers, preparing arithmetic lessons. Not getting ready to be sawn in half in front of a crowd of Kansas City cattlemen.

Well, it wasn't as though he hadn't given her a chance to go back home. But apparently things weren't as serene in Black Horse as he would have believed. And he just couldn't let the little fool remain in St. Louis where she would never get a decent job. Not with that fat weasel Amos Jenson talking against her. Marc barely knew Miss Hall, yet he would have felt like he was abandoning her. Damn funny feeling for him to have, especially about a lady so fond of book learning.

He stretched out his legs, careful to avoid the neat pile of bags lying on the floor between them. No doubt Miss Hall had crammed them full with books. He peeked over at her.

He'd never met a woman who read so much—or a man either. It gave him a bellyache just to know she was sitting beside him, her nose buried in a dusty book. Frustrated by her lack of interest in conversing with him, he finally asked her what the book was about. To his dismay, she proceeded to tell him far more than he ever wanted to know about the Jefferson administration. Heaven help him, but he'd hired a woman who not only knew how to read, but one who enjoyed reading about something as useless as a long-dead president.

Marc Cooper had no use for presidents—living or dead—or any politician. In fact, all he'd ever cared about was magic and the men who practiced it. Now if she were reading a book about Jean-Eugene Robert-Houdin or Harry Kellar, he might understand it. But Thomas Jefferson?

How in the world did this demure lady ever get hooked up with a hot number like Julia Dupree? He cast a sideways glance at her. Julia was a real looker; it was the sole reason he'd hired her. Patrons weren't watching his sleight of hand as long as Julia was slinking about the stage. Julia was voluptuous, bold and fiery. She had the sort of looks that struck men immediately, but somehow she grew less lovely the longer one examined those generous curves and brassy hair.

Miss Hall, on the other hand, seemed as refined and delicate as bone china. She was too slender. If he did nothing else while she was with him, he'd do his best to fatten her up. But she had the loveliest neck, just like one of those trumpeter swans he'd seen once in Canada. And from this angle, he could see that her little nose was turned up ever so slightly. He liked how smooth her skin seemed too, and wondered if the rest of her body boasted such soft, pale flesh. He felt briefly excited by the thought.

He shook his head. He'd be in a bad way if this little schoolteacher ever started to give him indecent thoughts. Still, she did have the loveliest eyes, large and velvety brown. And very long lashes. He loved women who had long lashes.

She glanced up at him at that moment, those same eyes now looking bewildered to find him staring at her.

"Is something wrong?" she asked shyly.

He pointed out the window. "Just watching all that nice green grass go by. I don't think I've seen any state as green as Missouri."

She nodded politely, then returned her attention to her book.

He hoped the gentleman she was set on marrying

was a professor. Only a professor would be able to put up with all that reading.

But maybe only a professor would look closely enough to appreciate her quiet beauty. Women like Julia paraded their obvious charms; Miss Hall's restrained manner kept males from giving her much more than even a first look. And dressing as plain as she did didn't help matters. He'd been surprised to see her yesterday in that purple dress, her waist looking tiny and sweet, showing a nice curve to her hips. And that outlandish turban gave the schoolteacher a saucy air. When he saw her dressed like that—and fighting off Jenson's clumsy advances, too—his first thought was that he'd misjudged her. She wasn't a mouse at all, but a very feminine woman.

His mistake. This morning, she was back in her dowdy duds: navy blue jacket and skirt, a dull brooch on her lapel, her hair coiled beneath a little straw hat. It was as though she had briefly performed a magic trick of her own: transforming herself into a mysterious, turbaned lady only to change back into the demure Missouri schoolmarm.

He moved slightly, kicking the valise that held her costume. Chuckling to himself, he tried to imagine Miss Hall wearing that little scrap of blue spangles. Would his mouse be turned into a vixen? Or would she run screaming for a blanket? Not that he blamed her for being reluctant to wear the costume. Only a woman with Julia's nerve—and loose character— would enjoy slipping into it.

Still, that was the costume his assistant was required to wear. And Miss Hall had begged for the opportunity. He'd never admit it to her, but he was quite looking forward to the moment when he could see for himself just how lovely those slender legs of hers were.

63

He glanced down at them now, so chastely covered in navy blue serge. Her legs were crossed, and she was absently moving her right foot back and forth. The late afternoon sun poured in from the window, revealing her ivory hose and the slim ankle it covered. His gaze remained fixed on her ankle, as well as an enticing glimpse of her calf.

Outside, the train tracks clicked endlessly and he felt himself drift off into a daydream, a daydream in which he boldly knelt at her feet and placed his hands on that slender ankle. He'd caress it softly, so softly she might not know for a moment that he was touching her. When she looked down at him in surprise, he'd move his hands beneath her skirt, caressing her knees, burrowing beneath the petticoats until he reached the top of her garters. Then he'd press his hands on her upper thighs, rubbing slowly before venturing further. And when he reached that lovely sweet spot between her legs, his hands would grow more insistent, more daring until—

What in tarnation was he doing? Marc tore his gaze away from Miss Hall's ankle. He was acting like some green boy who had never even brushed up against a female before. Poor Miss Hall. First Jenson slobbers all over her, and now he was sitting beside her, entertaining some very lewd thoughts. Lewd thoughts about a real, genuine lady. He felt like a heel, dreaming about her as if she was as bawdy as Julia Dupree.

He had to get himself under control. "Excuse me, Miss Hall, but I'm going back to the smoking car for awhile."

She looked over and gave him a polite smile.

With a groan, he waited until he could stand up without embarrassment.

Weaving his way down the passageway, he was almost at the door when a heavyset gentleman stepped into the aisle in front of him.

"Excuse me, I'm trying to get by," Marc said.

The man turned around. "I think you're tryin' to get by with too much, Cooper."

Marc cursed under his breath. What the devil was Chauncey Farrell doing on this train? Were they dogging his every step now?

"You got your cut in Independence, Jefferson City *and* St. Louis," he said, his voice low but angry. "So what's your problem?"

The man leaned closer, his ruddy face a mask of dislike. "I gotta answer to the same boss you do, and he don't like being short-changed."

"Yeah?" Marc pushed the man away.

As usual, Chauncey Farrell reeked of orange water. Bad enough he seemed to turn up at every stop Marc had been booked at, but this thug had to smell like a hootchie cootchie girl, to boot.

"And Mr. Baer thinks maybe you're not givin' him his fair share."

"Then let Baer come talk to me himself. I'm tired of dealing with his goons."

"Well, maybe you'll be less tired if we break an arm or two," Chauncey hissed. "Or maybe a leg."

Marc stared back at him. "And if I have a broken arm, how will Baer get his cut of my salary? My act requires a magician with the use of two good arms and two good legs."

"If you keep stiffin' us, you won't be needin' the use of your limbs." He straightened. "Or maybe we'll rough up that little lady who seems to have joined your act. Seein' as how you're such a softhearted gent, you might not want to see the lady hurt."

Marc grabbed Chauncey by his stiff collar. His

movement was so unexpected, the man grunted and his face turned beet red.

"You stay away from her, Chauncey, or I'll be working some bad magic on you. Baer will get his money as always. I don't welch on a contract, no matter how rotten that contract is. So keep out of my sight except when it's time to collect. Until then, I don't want to see you," he sniffed, "or smell you around me. You got that?"

He shoved the bigger fellow away.

Chauncey spluttered for a moment, straightening his collar and jacket. "You don't make enough money to be worth this kind of trouble, Cooper. One of these days I'm going to convince Mr. Baer of that. When I do, you and that little lady up there will have more trouble than you know what to do with. All your magic tricks won't save you then."

Marc glanced back. Miss Hall was still reading, oblivious to the violence only twenty feet away. "Maybe I have a few tricks up my sleeve you haven't seen yet."

Chauncey only snorted, and sat back down in his seat.

Not until Marc exited the car, did he pause and take a breath. Standing on the narrow train platform, he wondered if he had done Salome Hall a great disservice by hiring her. The poor young woman thought her only problem was a skimpy blue costume.

Little did she know they both had a lot more to worry about.

Chapter Four

If Salome came anywhere near him, he feared he'd be tempted to cut her in two with his saber sword. Unfortunately, Marc couldn't find the sword. Somehow she had managed to misplace a three-foot-long steel saber during this morning's rehearsal. And the way he felt right now, it was a lucky thing for her he couldn't find it.

As he spoke to the audience, he kept one eye on his little schoolteacher. She was wisely maintaining a wide berth between them. They were already on the fourth trick of the evening, and she'd ruined three of them. Marc hadn't felt this angry since a circus clown had accidentally set his shirt on fire with a Roman candle.

"Ladies and gentlemen, Salome the Fair will now brave the Zigzag Mystery Box."

He turned to glare at Salome, who was slowly wheeling a tall lacquered cabinet to the center of the stage. She should have been done long ago, only she was preoccupied with keeping her costume covered with what looked like a hundred scarves. Creeping along an inch at a time, she pushed the box with one hand, while the other hand fussed incessantly with the scarves.

"Hurry up," he hissed.

She stepped behind the cabinet. He could see her rearranging the scarves about her legs.

"Come, Salome!" he shouted. "I command you to enter the Mystery Box."

"A moment, please," she whispered back. "One of the scarves fell off."

Laughter erupted from the front row. If only he possessed real magical powers, Salome Hall would be gone in a flash of smoke faster than you could say "old maid schoolteacher." Stifling a curse, Marc pointed towards the three visible sections of the cabinet before swinging wide the three corresponding doors.

"As you can see, the Mystery Box holds nothing but thin air," he intoned in a forbidding voice.

He gritted his teeth. "Now the lovely Salome *will* enter."

Of course, she missed her cue. Reaching behind the cabinet, he grabbed Salome's arm.

"Get out here now," he said between clenched teeth.

"But the scarves are falling off."

He yanked her around to the front, his grip like iron. The pair of them must look ridiculous up here. During the last trick, she'd knocked over the magic fish bowl, splashing the contents into his face. The water had thoroughly smeared his greasepaint; no doubt he looked like a two-legged raccoon by now.

Even so, he couldn't cut a more absurd figure than

68

her. She'd wrapped and fastened so many scarves about her, only her head, feet and hands were visible. To make matters worse, she refused to wear any makeup except for lip rouge. Beneath the blazing limelight, her face looked as pale as cake flour. And without black liner, no one in the back of the theater would be able to see her eyes. It was like working with a headless, moving mass of cloth.

"Enter the box, Salome," he commanded, adding under his breath, "Get in there before I strangle you."

She had the brass to shoot *him* an irritated look. "Just see that you don't get any of the scarves stuck in the doors," she whispered.

He could feel the veins pop on his forehead. Without another word, he grabbed both her arms and shoved her none too gently into the Mystery Box.

"Mind the scarves," she said, right before he slammed the top panel shut over her face. A face hole was cut out of the top section, and he was instantly greeted by a pair of accusing brown eyes.

Even as he was closing the remaining panels, her hands were fidgeting, trying to cover herself even more. Twice the scarves did catch and he had to stand there like a tailor, rearranging and pulling at the masses of silk and cotton. At last the scarves were tucked out of sight, and the box firmly shut.

After briefly considering leaving her there while he left the stage—and possibly the state—Marc instead gestured towards the Mystery Box. Depicted full-length on the outside was a painting of a young woman, with openings cut out in order to show his assistant's face, hands and right foot.

Salome peered at him through the opening provided for her face. Although she obligingly wriggled her boot through the foothole, her hands were still not visible.

Sharon Pisacreta

With a low growl, Marc banged on the side of the box. After an excruciatingly long moment, she finally extended her hands through the holes. Blast the infernal woman! She was fussing with those scarves even when hidden from view.

Quickly, before she pulled her hands back once more, Marc inserted steel blades between each section of the box, sliding them into the front, then dramatically slamming the blades through to the back. As expected, the audience gasped with the insertion of each blade. It appeared as if he had just sliced his assistant into three equal pieces, yet her face smiled at them from the opening, and her foot wriggled through the foothole.

As the applause died down, he pulled up his sleeves. A drumroll sounded from the orchestra pit. Grabbing the middle section of the box, he tried to slide it towards him, completing the illusion of a woman cut in three. The section didn't move. He yanked again. Nothing.

As he tried a third time, he glanced over at Salome who mouthed, "A scarf got stuck." In that moment, he would have given up the secrets to ten illusions if the blades he'd shoved through the box were real.

She wanted to scream with frustration. Nothing was going as planned. Salome withdrew one of her hands from the holes and tugged on the scarf, but it would not come loose from whatever it had snagged on. Actually, she suspected that more than one scarf had gotten entwined in the moving parts of the trick box. Maybe she'd fastened a few too many onto her costume, but she just couldn't bring herself to walk onstage with her legs and buttocks on full display.

Even draped in scarves, her first moments onstage had been an experience of unbridled terror. Staring

70

out into the audience, eyes blinking from the glare of the footlights, she could barely bring herself to take a step. Only Marc's urgent whispers gave her the courage to move. Looking into those furious dark eyes, Salome dreaded his anger far more than the audience's disapproval. And heaven knew, the man did seem nearly at his wit's end with her. At least the audience wasn't booing, although she suspected that Marc's act was eliciting far more laughter tonight than it usually did.

Marc looked as if he were about to explode. He bent over the box one last time and pulled. Mercifully the middle section slid towards him as planned, making it look to the audience as though her head and feet were aligned, while her torso was now standing completely to the left.

What the audience didn't know was that the middle section didn't move as much as it appeared. The edges of the box were painted black, the dark border concealing the fact that the box only moved a few inches. Inside, Salome was actually curled around the two blades and the middle section; an uncomfortable position, especially with boned corsets cutting into her rib cage, but not impossible. A layer of black cloth covered the top and bottom of the movable middle section, and this black material moved with the box and concealed the box's true interior.

She took as deep a breath as she could in her curled position: her head and left arm leaning over as far as possible in the box, one blade resting only two inches beneath her elbow. The picture of the ramrod straight woman on the front of the cabinet enforced the illusion, and Salome knew it mystified the uninitiated. It appeared as if her torso had been removed and placed entirely to the side.

She tried to get Marc's attention. He should have

pushed the middle section back into place by now. Another minute curled into this contorted position, and she would have leg cramps for a week.

She could hear Marc muttering to himself. An occasional curse was audible and she tried to move her neck into a less painful angle. He banged the middle section of the box, causing her to jump.

As the music continued to play, he circled around the box majestically, pausing only to whisper, "It's stuck again."

Her heart sank. She couldn't remain like this much longer, but if she straightened up, the audience would detect the false borders of the box. Salome again removed one hand, searching for the scarves that must be jamming the mechanism.

The audience was getting restless. The gaslit chandelier and wing lights shone down on a crowd of people who seemed not only hot and sweaty, but impatient.

She felt around the small space frantically, her fingers encountering a wad of silk and chiffon. If she could only pull it free, Marc would be able to slide the box back into place. Then she could run offstage—with Marc in enraged hot pursuit.

Salome jammed her fingers into the ball of scarves, searching for a way to unknot the mess. She knew that if she moved too much, the Mystery Box would wobble. And if that happened, Marc might start shoving steel blades in her direction for real!

With a frustrated sigh, Salome pulled at the scarves, then pulled again. Marc had decided to twirl the box around on its caster wheels, desperately bidding for extra time. The theater whirled about her eyes once, then twice. But still she couldn't untie the scarves.

"Ladies and gentlemen," he announced.

She heard defeat in his voice. There was no way she was going to be responsible for spoiling another trick tonight.

With one last mighty tug, Salome pulled the scarf free. To her horror, her hand slammed against the front of the middle section, causing the panel to come unhinged. As she reached over to close it, Marc knocked it shut with his fist. Startled, Salome instinctively fell back. With a sick sensation, she felt the cabinet wobble.

To prevent the entire contraption from toppling, she leaned forward as far as she could, but the movement was too much. A second later, she and the three sections of the Zigzag Mystery Box crashed to the stage. As she lay sprawled face down—still contorted and wrapped in knotted scarves—the audience broke out in laughter and cheers. In a split-second, the act had gone from magic to burlesque.

Above her, she heard Marc fling one of the steel blades against something. Luckily he hadn't thrown it at her.

"Ladies and gentlemen, this now concludes the Zigzag Mystery Box trick." His voice sounded as sharp as broken glass. "As you can see, the real mystery lies in whether our Salome of the Seven Hundred Veils will ever figure out how this illusion works."

A chorus of cheers greeted this; someone even shot off a pistol in a lunatic display of Old West zeal. Suddenly she felt the box lifted off her. As Marc kicked away the remaining sections of the cabinet, she finally got to her feet, ripping two scarves in the process.

She shot a nervous glance in his direction.

Beneath the smeared greasepaint, his eyes blazed

with anger. "You'd better start praying I never find that saber, Miss Hall."

Amazing what a glass of whiskey could do for a fellow's disposition. An hour ago, he wanted to lock Salome Hall into his Tip Over Trunk and ship her back to that Missouri schoolhouse. But after washing up and relaxing with a tumbler of Cutty Sark, Marc felt his anger at Salome fade.

It was all his fault. He had no business hiring Miss Hall to be his assistant. A lady like her should be teaching farm children how to find Mexico on a map or how to write their names on a blackboard. She shouldn't be parading around in front of half-drunk cattlemen, hiding in secret cabinets or carting around magic fish bowls. That's what he got for being softhearted back in St. Louis.

If Jenson hadn't threatened her, he would have felt no qualms about heading off to Kansas City without her. But he couldn't leave a naive young lady like Miss Hall alone to deal with a trumped-up vagrancy charge and jail. He'd spent a night or two in jail in his life, and it was no place for a lady.

Well, tonight had taught him that being onstage with a magician was no place for a lady either. As much as he wanted to help her out, Marc couldn't afford to have her wreck his act. He was too new on the Orpheum Circuit; if he didn't polish his act soon, there would be plenty of dime museum magicians eager to take his place.

Salome Hall had to go.

The bells above the entrance jingled. Marc looked up in time to see Miss Hall walk through the door of Garwood's Sandwich Shoppe and Soda Fountain. He'd briefly considered taking her out for a nice dinner, but the soda fountain was right across from the theater. Marc wanted to get this over as quickly as possible. Dinners in Kansas City were apt to be leisurely affairs involving endless courses of beefsteak and potatoes. But Garwood's would only allow him enough time to buy her a sandwich and sundae, then finish by telling her ever so gently that she was fired.

He stood up, waving her over.

"I'm sorry to be late, but some of the scarves were knotted so tightly I could barely untie them." She sat down in the chair he'd pulled out for her. "As a matter of fact, I still have one scarf wrapped around my knee. I may have to cut it off, and it doesn't even belong to me. I borrowed most of them from Flora the Dancing Girl. She has quite a few."

Marc glanced down at her brown tweed skirt as though expecting to see scarves trailing beneath the hem. "I was wondering where you got all those fool scarves. For a moment, I thought you'd robbed a dressmaker's shop."

Her cheeks colored. "I might have put a few too many on." She tried to busy herself by examining the printed menu card on the table.

"A few?"

This time she met his gaze. The rouge had been washed off her cheeks, and her face looked paler than usual. But her large dark eyes seemed luminous. If only she'd put the proper paint on tonight, all of Kansas City could have seen how enchanting those eyes were.

"Mr. Cooper, I'm sorry if I got carried away with the scarves, but I just couldn't wear that costume. I tried. I honestly did. I put it on before tonight's performance, but even alone in my dressing room, I felt brazen and shameless. And it was much too large for me. Every time I moved, the straps slipped off my shoulders. You can't expect me to walk out there in

75

front of all those people with my legs showing and my top falling down."

He shook his head. "No, I don't expect you to do that."

A look of relief stole over her face. "I'm so glad, Mr. Cooper. I didn't know what I was going to do for the next performance."

He cleared his throat. This was going to be unpleasant; firing people always was. But this young woman didn't have the street sense to realize she was as good as gone. He was hoping she would simply quit on her own, mortified by tonight's fiasco. But he'd forgotten how stubborn she was.

"That's what I wanted to talk to you about. The next performance."

She sat back in her chair, waiting for him to continue.

"You see, Miss Hall, there are just some people who will never get the hang of performing. And you can tell it right off. Theater life is not for them. So rather than let the show suffer, it's always better to—"

"Are you ready to order, folks?" A gangly young man stood beside their table, a long white apron tied about his waist.

Marc looked over at her. "Miss Hall?"

She reached for the menu card. This time he noticed that the card and its metal holder trembled in her hand. So she did have an inkling of what was going to happen. Marc wished now he'd drunk more than one glass of whiskey before coming here.

"Chicken salad sandwich, please. And a cup of tea. Orange Pekoe, if you have it." She pushed the menu card towards him, but he ignored it.

"Bring me a sardine and lettuce sandwich," he said. "And coffee."

76

"No sardine and lettuce sandwiches." The waiter pointed to the menu card. "We only got what's on the card."

Miss Hall pushed it closer to him, but he refused to pick it up.

"You must have ham sandwiches, don't you?"

The waiter nodded.

"Well, bring me a ham sandwich."

Salome leaned over the marble-topped table. "That man and woman by the soda fountain are staring at us. Do you think they recognize us from the show?"

He glanced over. A well-fed couple stood sipping malts beneath the fountain pavilion's glass canopy. Two children sat eating ice cream on either side of them. Marc waved, and all four waved back, wide grins on their faces.

He faced forward again. "I'm sure they were in the audience. They still can't stop laughing."

Her face fell. "I was awful, wasn't I?"

Marc just looked at her.

"I'm so sorry about the performance. You were kind enough to hire me, and then I go ahead and spoil our first night in Kansas City. Don't try to make me feel better. I know I ruined everything tonight." She looked up at him as though hoping he would politely deny it.

"Yeah, you wrecked it all right. If the act had gone on a bit longer, I'm sure you would have gotten around to burning down the theater."

"I wasn't that bad, surely." She sat upright, her dignity obviously affronted.

"You were worse." Marc ran a hand over his hair. "Look, Miss Hall, I wanted to do you a favor. You were in a bind back in St. Louis and I thought bringing you here would help you out. But it's just not

77

going to work. You must see that. You're too respect-able."

She glowered at him. He didn't understand her at all. Since when did a lady resent being called respectable? Looking at her as she sat there in her dark tweeds and sensible shoes—and with that silly straw hat on her head—he marveled again that he'd ever been fool enough to put this little spinster on the stage.

"Prim and proper is just what's needed for a schoolteacher, but it won't help me or my magic act. Sorry."

"I am not prim and proper!"

"Calm down, Miss Hall. I'm not insulting you. I'm just trying to tell you that I can't use you."

"You're firing me?"

Patrons at the nearby tables glanced in their direction.

Marc gestured for her to lower her voice. "Yes, I'm firing you. As much as I'd like to help you, I have my own career to worry about."

She looked as though he'd just slapped her. He felt like the worst sort of heel, but this should teach him a lesson. Stay far away from lady schoolteachers with a liking for scarves and straw hats.

"Won't you give me another chance? Let me work another performance. You'll see. I'll try my best to get at least one of the tricks right."

"I can't do it. You don't understand how hard I've worked just to get on the Orpheum Circuit. I've been kicking around the theater since I was fifteen. Carnival sideshows, dime museums, even small-town circuses." He frowned at the memory of those long frustrating years. "I've finally earned a place on the best variety and vaudeville circuit in the country. This will take me into big cities, New York eventually. And I'm playing legitimate theaters now, not canvas tents or the stages in some backwater saloon. I've caught the eye of big-time promoters, and I can't allow you or anyone else to ruin this for me. I'm sorry."

He sat back, hoping she wouldn't cry. "I'm sorry," he repeated. "But I have to let you go."

She remained silent. "I understand," she said finally. "You've already done far too much. And you have every right to be angry with me. Not only did I ruin the performance, but then I lost your lovely sword."

"Yes, you did. And for the life of me, I don't understand how anyone can lose a saber that big."

"I just misplaced it somehow. I was so nervous." She thought a moment. "I might have accidentally put it in Boblo the Juggler's trunk."

Marc shook his head. "Don't worry. It will turn up somewhere. Besides, it's no longer your concern. I'll do the show solo tomorrow, then ask the stage manager to place another ad in the papers. I'll be in Kansas City for ten days. Time enough to audition a few women for the job."

"You must reconsider, Mr. Cooper. I need this job."

They both grew quiet as the waiter brought their food and drinks to the table.

"Now don't worry about being out of work," Marc said as soon as they were alone again. "I'll speak to the manager about finding you a position with the theater. Preferably something backstage."

She looked down at her sandwich before pushing the plate aside. "Mr. Cooper, I need this job. Oh, not because I long to be a magician's assistant, fine as that might seem to some people."

Sharon Pisacreta

He raised his eyebrows. What was this school-marm going to come up with next?

"If I don't find a job in the theater—and very soon, too—then I'll lose the man I love."

Instead of continuing, she sat back and sipped her tea.

"That's all you're going to tell me?"

"Well, it's very personal. Not to mention humili-ating." She stared down into her teacup. "But you probably should know the whole story, so you'll un-derstand why I need to work with you."

"On second thought, Miss Hall, don't bother. No matter what you say, I'm not keeping you in the act. So save yourself the humiliation and keep any sad love stories under that infernal straw hat of yours."

She touched the small brimmed hat atop her head. "You don't care for the way I dress, do you?"

"Doesn't matter what I think." He bit into his ham sandwich.

"But it does matter. It matters that you know I was engaged to be married last month."

"Was?" Despite himself, she had aroused his cu-riosity.

"Lyndon Joseph Whittier proposed to me on the first Sunday in May," she said softly, almost as if she were uttering a prayer. "It was a beautiful Sunday, with the magnolias and dogwood in full bloom. In full bloom at long last, just like me. I'd waited ten years for that moment to happen, and when it did, I nearly died from happiness."

"It took that man ten years to propose?" Marc shook his head. "I'm not sure a man that leisurely in his courting is worth so much happiness."

She shot him a reproachful look. "Lyndon Whittier is worth a great deal. And it only took him *four* years

80

to propose. We weren't courting when he first came
to Black Horse."

"I don't see what this has to do with any—"

"He jilted me, Mr. Cooper," she broke in. "Two
weeks after asking me to be his wife, he ran off with
another woman. A beautiful, famous singer, a glamorous woman who makes her living on the stage."
She paused. "Jane Dupree."

Marc choked on his sandwich. "He ran off with
Julia's sister?"

"Yes, he did. He told me that he'd always been in
love with Jane, that she was exciting and irresistible,
the sort of woman every man dreams of having.
While I was merely kind and honest." She said this
last with great bitterness. "He recited poetry to her
on bended knee, and claimed his love for her was as
glorious as 'music and moonlight.' And after he said
all that, he ran off with her." She paused. "He ran off
and left me alone once more."

Marc liked it better when he could assume his little
schoolteacher possessed emotions no stronger than
anger and indignation. But now he could discern the
pain in her voice, and see the sadness in those velvety
brown eyes. What was he supposed to say to such an
admission?

"I vowed to myself that I would win him back," she
went on. "I would become the sort of alluring, exciting woman he so obviously wants. And what better
way to make him sit up and take notice than if I, too,
go on the stage."

Finished with his sandwich, Marc pushed his plate
away. "Jane Dupree is pretty famous, Miss Hall, and
it's taken her a long time to get to the top. You're
fooling yourself if you think you can compete with
her onstage." He didn't add that, as far as he could

tell, Salome Hall didn't possess a drop of theatrical talent.

"I don't need to become famous. I don't expect to. All I want is a chance to perform onstage this October at the Columbian Exposition in Chicago."

"Let me guess. Jane is going to be performing at the Chicago World's Fair."

She nodded. "Lyndon and she plan to marry during her engagement in Chicago. And I plan to surprise both of them by appearing onstage there, too."

"How were you going to get there as my assistant? I'm not going to Chicago."

A sheepish expression crossed her face. "I had hoped to persuade you. After all, think of the publicity you would garner from appearing at the Exposition, the crowds of people who would be introduced to your act for the very first time."

Marc drained his coffee before replying. "You know, I owe you an apology. I took you for a sensible woman, but you're actually as crazy as Boblo the Juggler. Miss Hall, there's no way I'm going to keep you in the act. And I venture to guess that no one else in the theater is going to put you onstage. You're wasting your time dreaming about being in Chicago this fall."

"I am going to be in Chicago, and onstage, too."

"Even if you are, why would you try to compete with someone as famous and talented as Jane Dupree?" And as beautiful, he thought. He'd seen Jane perform several times; once in New Orleans, Julia had taken him backstage and introduced him to her older and much more successful sister. Salome Hall was a sweet-looking young woman, but not even those dark brown eyes and long lashes could outshine Jane's golden curls and angelic voice.

"Forget about this Lyndon fellow," he added. "You don't want a man who would run off like that anyway. He sounds like an idiot."

"Lyndon is not an idiot!"

"Of course he is. He ran off with Jane Dupree. Only an idiot would want to marry one of the Dupree sisters."

"I admit that I'm very upset over how Lyndon has behaved. But just because he's made a mistake, that doesn't mean I still don't love him. Or that I don't want him back. And I am going to get him back, Mr. Cooper. In October, I will be onstage in Chicago. Just watch."

"Not with me, you aren't."

"How can I convince you that—" Salome broke off, staring up in surprise at the large gentleman standing next to their table.

Cooper's face grew sullen. "Chauncey, what in blazes are you doing here?"

"Seein' as how the two of you are talking so hot and heavy, I hate to interrupt you, but I got business to discuss." He pulled out a chair and sat down. "Go on, keep eatin'."

"If you or Baer think you can keep hounding me every minute, you're mistaken. I don't need a chaperone, and I won't put up with spies."

"I'm just makin' sure that my boss gets his money. You got your job to do—sawin' ladies in half—and I got my job. Which is to make sure a certain magician don't get any funny ideas about cheatin' the agency you done signed with." He fingered Salome's untouched chicken salad sandwich. "You gonna eat this?"

She shook her head.

He slid the plate over and bit into the sandwich. Half of it disappeared instantly. She thought he had the bushiest yellow eyebrows she'd ever seen. And in

83

his rumpled brown suit and shaggy beard, he looked just like an Ozark bear. Although he smelled—not unpleasantly—of orange peel.

"What you lookin' at, lady?" After devouring the sandwich in less than five seconds, he turned his attention upon her.

"Leave the young woman alone, Chauncey. And now that you've stuffed your face, get your carcass away from our table."

Chauncey wiped his mouth with Salome's napkin. "After I get my money."

"You get your money when the engagement is finished. As always. In case you've lost what little is left of your brains, I'll remind you that tonight was only the first night of our engagement in Kansas City."

"Yeah? Well, now Baer wants his money every day."

"He's not going to get it."

Chauncey leaned over. "Oh, yes, he is. Accordin' to your contract, Baer can demand his percentage every day, every week or every month. Look the contract over again and see for yourself."

Marc's face seemed to purple with barely suppressed rage.

"Excuse me, but could I see a copy of this contract?" Salome thought maybe she could help defuse the situation. Both men looked tense enough to come to blows.

Chauncey glared once more at Marc before turning to her. "Yeah, sure. Seein' as how you're part of the act now, you may as well know where the money is goin.' " He pulled out a long piece of paper from inside his suit jacket.

She took it from him, and unfolded it on the table.

"Keep it, lady. We got plenty of copies. Sometimes we need those copies when Marco here takes it into his head to try and stiff us. But just remember that Baer has the original, and it's as signed and legal as the Declaration of Independence."

Salome ran her finger down the first page. "I don't know how legal this is."

"What do you know anyway?" Chauncey stood up, straightening the lapels of his jacket. "You can't even get a stupid magic trick right. I was in the audience tonight and I ain't never seen Marco come off lookin' so bad. You get better before tomorrow's performance, lady, or you can start huntin' for work at the church mission." His gaze traveled over her body. "And fix yourself up, will ya? Let your hair down from all those pins, put a little rouge on those cheeks. And get rid of them scarves. No use having a woman in the act if we can't see her legs."

"Miss Hall is leaving the act," Marc said curtly.

"Yeah, well, I'm not surprised. You need a chorus girl up there, not someone who looks like a school-marm."

Salome and Marc exchanged amused glances.

"Now where's my money?" Chauncey rapped on the table with his knuckles. "Or do you want to be hauled in again for breach of contract?"

"Look, I don't get paid until the end of the engagement. So I can't give you something I don't have."

"That's your problem, not mine. Talk to the boys who run the circuit and tell 'em you need to be paid daily. Baer don't care what you do as long as he gets his fifty percent." He held out a beefy hand. "Now fork it over."

Salome watched with wide eyes as Marc pulled out his wallet.

"Mr. Cooper, are you certain you want to do this?" she asked.

Her heart sank as he handed Chauncey a fistful of

bills. "You shouldn't give it to him, Marc." She was so upset that she found herself calling him by his Christian name. "This is extortion."

"No, lady." Chauncey stuffed the money into his pocket. "This is business."

"Marc?" She tried to get his attention, but he avoided her eyes. Instead he occupied himself with slowly putting his emptied wallet back into his jacket.

"I don't like this one at all, Marco." Chauncey cocked a finger at Salome. "I'm glad you're gettin' rid of her."

Salome watched as the man sauntered off towards the soda fountain, his large figure reflected in the beveled glass of the pavilion's canopy roof.

She turned back to Marc. He looked at her with an embarrassed expression.

"I'm sorry about Chauncey," he said. "He's nothing but a gorilla in a shirt and tie. But as long he and Baer get their money, there won't be any trouble." Marc shot her a rueful grin. "See, I told you a nice lady like you was crazy to want to work in the theater."

Salome held up the contract. "Did you actually sign this?"

He nodded.

"Then you're crazier than either me or Boblo the Juggler."

"Excuse me, but I'm a grown man and whatever legal arrangements I make for my career is none of your—"

"Oh, be quiet, you great fool!" She felt like a schoolteacher again, having to explain simple addition to a student who should have learned it long ago.

Marc sat back, his mouth open.

"And keep quiet until I figure a way to get you out of this."

She bent over the contract, examining it closely. Up until now she thought she needed him.

But it looked as though he needed her far more.

Chapter Five

After reading the contract, Salome put her head in her hands.

"I think the Devil made Daniel Webster sign something similar to this."

Marc looked offended. "It may not be the smartest thing I ever did."

"I'd like to think so. Otherwise I've allowed a complete fool to aim steel blades at me tonight." She spread her hands out. "Look at these clauses. Indentured servants worked under less punishing terms. What in the world were you thinking of?"

He tried to take the paper from her, but she snatched it up. " 'The party of the first part agrees to forfeit all expected earnings from the contracted period even if illness or incapacitation prevents said party from gainful employment; failure to do so will result in legal proceedings being instituted.' Which means that if you were struck down with typhoid *and* run over by a train, you still have to pay them. Or find yourself hauled into court."

"I know all that, so just hand over my contract. This is none of your business, Miss Hall."

"Oh, I fear that it is. I have never been able to sit quietly by and watch other people being taken advantage of. It is simply not in my nature. That's one of the reasons I became a teacher, so as to give my pupils the tools to prevent the villains of this world from exploiting them."

"Well, I'm not your pupil and I am not being exploited."

Salome held up the contract. "Marc Cooper, if you *were* my pupil, I'd have you write on the board one hundred times 'I will not sign a contract that makes me a slave.' "

"Blast you, Salome!" He slammed his fist on the table, his face red with anger.

She jumped, the contract falling from her hands.

"I knew I should never have hooked up with a schoolteacher. Nothing but trouble with their fancy words, looking down their noses at anyone who hasn't wasted their youth sitting at a desk, writing letters on a blasted board. Well, I've done pretty well so far without schoolteachers. And I don't need one now to tell me that I'm a fool."

"Marc, I'm sorry for calling you a fool. That was uncalled for and insensitive. But it doesn't alter the fact that you were crazy to sign such a terrible document. These conditions amount to little more than extortion. Is there actually an original of this which you signed?"

"I signed it." He sat back, arms crossed resolutely in front of his chest. "That's as good as giving my word. And Marc Cooper doesn't go back on his word, even if it does cost me half of everything I earn."

89

She sighed. He was so stubborn she could shake him. Sitting across from her, he suddenly looked like a young boy who refused to admit he was wrong. He was completely exasperating—yet somehow endearing.

"Well, I'm a lawyer's daughter and I know something of the law. Before I became a teacher, I helped Father write his briefs. I can assure you that this contract is illegal; no reputable court would force you to abide by it. It's riddled with dubious clauses."

He smirked. "Tell that to the judge in Copper Valley, Georgia. I spent three days in jail there last March because I refused to pay Baer and Chauncey."

She shook her head. "One dishonest judge merely proves that this Mr. Baer and Mr. Chauncey—"

"His name's Chauncey Farrell," he broke in.

"All that proves is that Mr. Baer and Mr. Farrell can occasionally buy off a small-town judge. But Kansas City is not Copper Valley, Georgia. In fact, I know a fine attorney in the city. Mr. Frank Kesselbaum is an old friend of my father. I can bring this to his office tomorrow and he'll show you exactly how to invalidate the contract. All legal and aboveboard, by the way, so don't imagine that you've broken your word. You've been cheated, Marc, and shamefully cheated at that. I admire your sense of ethics but not even Spinoza would expect you to abide by these terms."

"I don't need your help. And I don't need to go begging to fast-talking lawyers, so you can forget about visiting these Kesselbaum or Spinoza fellows."

Salome rubbed at her temples, trying to stave off a headache.

"Now hand over that contract," he continued. "It has nothing to do with you."

"Only if you can explain to me how you could sign

your name to a document that includes this final clause."

She turned the contract around so he could see it. "Read that last line. It's abominable."

He stared back at her. "I don't want to read it."

Salome pushed the sheaf of papers aside. They brushed against the menu card and set it jangling on the marble-topped table. She steadied the card, holding it in her hands for a long moment. In the three days since they left St. Louis, he'd never ordered from a menu, she thought. Never even once glanced at a menu card or looked over a blackboard bearing the specials of the day.

She sat back, feeling ashamed for railing at him so.

"You can't read," she said softly.

He flinched as if she had prodded him with a dagger. "You'd like to think that, wouldn't you? This way you can feel even more superior than you do. Educated people like to feel superior."

"That's why you signed the contract." She ignored his bitter statement. "You didn't know how dreadful these clauses were, you had no idea what you were signing away."

Marc took a deep breath. "If you're done eating, I think it's best we leave." He looked around for the waiter. "After all, you have to start looking for work tomorrow."

She leaned over and put her hand on his arm. He tried to pull away, but she refused to let him go. "Marc, I don't feel superior to you. Don't insult me by ever saying such a thing again."

He gave her a sardonic look. "We won't be seeing each other after tonight, so there's no chance of that happening."

"That may be true. But I'm still taking this contract

91

to Frank Kesselbaum tomorrow and getting you released from it."

"You are not!"

"Look, in another minute I'll be losing my temper too, and we'll spend the next hour shouting at each other." She squeezed his arm. "And I don't want to argue with you. Good heavens, I'm trying to help you. Can't you see that?"

"I don't need your help." He paused. "Or your charity."

"Then look on it as my way of making up for spoiling the performance tonight. Or as a gesture of thanks for saving me from vagrancy charges back in St. Louis." She raised an eyebrow. "After all, I have my pride, too. It isn't only stubborn magicians who balk at charity."

"You've some brass calling *me* stubborn," he muttered. "Once you've got your mind made up, you're as immovable as New Bedford rock."

She let her gaze rest on that proud profile. The cadence of his speech occasionally hinted at a New England background; now she could finally connect him to a specific place. "Is that where you're from? New Bedford, Massachusetts?"

"Not New Bedford." He sighed. What was the use in arguing with this woman? "Marblehead. And no jokes about my own head being as hard."

She smiled. "I wouldn't dare stoop to such dreadful humor."

"Well, plenty of others have, including my parents and my cousins." He grew silent, refusing to blather on about his childhood. He hadn't talked about Marblehead in fifteen years, not since his mother died. In fact, Marc couldn't understand why he was still sitting at the table with this nosy schoolteacher, let alone telling her about his people.

"Does your family still live in Marblehead?"

"Not much family left." If only she didn't have such a gentle voice, and large brown eyes that seemed to hold nothing but sympathy. He hadn't met many gentle, sympathetic women since he'd left home. "An uncle and aunt, two cousins. The rest of the Cupertinos either died or never left Portugal. That's my real name—Marco Cupertino."

Now why had he told her that? Not even Julia knew his real name.

"Your parents?"

"My mother's gone. She died of pneumonia when I was fifteen." He clenched his fists, as if somehow he could beat back the awful truth of that statement. New England winters were always too cold for her, and the winter of '78 had been colder than the devil's heart. It was the winter that really killed her. He hated the blasted season.

He reached for his coffee cup and drained it. Even after all these years, he couldn't speak of his mother's death without choking up. The next thing he knew, this little schoolteacher would have him blubbering like a drunken sailor.

Perhaps sensing that she had churned up unwanted emotions, Salome waited before speaking again. "And your father?"

"My father was a fisherman. Signed on a mackerel schooner in '72 and the whole crew went down fishing off the Georges Bank." Marc suddenly felt weary and desolate, as if he also had been on that schooner when the February storm hit. That was always his problem—he had too much imagination and not enough common sense.

"So I never went to school, Miss Hall." He forced himself to speak up, to stop the weight of memories from dragging him into melancholy and despair.

"My father could barely speak English. All he knew how to do was work hard and fish. That's what he believed his son needed to make his way in the world: hard work and fishing. So instead of going to school, I did scut work on the docks." If he let himself, he could still smell the tang of the salt air and feel the bitter wind on his reddened hands.

He looked over at her. There was something serene about her, something steady and strong. He suddenly envied her students—all those apple-cheeked country children—who looked up from their desks every morning into such a calm, intelligent face. His mother would have liked Miss Hall; she would have liked her modesty, her determination, her honesty. Even if she was a book-loving, ruler-wielding schoolteacher, she was nice. Genuinely nice. He would never dare reveal so much of his past otherwise.

"You've never had any formal schooling then?"

He shook his head. "Working on the docks helped put food on the table. Book learning didn't matter, just survival."

The admission—and all that it implied—brought on the old bitterness. No matter how often he told himself he didn't care that he'd never gone to school, it still rankled. He had never liked being kept in the dark, never liked anyone keeping secrets from him. As soon as he saw a magic trick performed, he wouldn't rest until he knew the truth behind the illusion. He had an excellent memory that usually stood him in good stead. Few people ever realized he could neither read nor write, and he'd do nearly anything to keep it that way. But each time he spied a young man reading a newspaper or a woman writing a letter, the shame flared up again. Even street signs seemed to mock him, forcing him to admit anew that no matter how magnificent he might appear onstage, in the real world he would always be viewed as unschooled and ignorant.

"That's a shame. You're an intelligent man. And you must have been a very bright boy."

Marc shrugged. "I was bright enough to know that when my father died, I couldn't earn enough on the docks to keep my mother and me in shoe leather. So I apprenticed out to a locksmith, then a watchmaker. Even spent a summer picking pockets in Boston."

Surprisingly she didn't change expression.

"Lightest fingers this side of Back Bay," he continued, "but I didn't have the stomach for robbing people. Lucky thing I ran across a street magician one day, doing rope tricks and making coins disappear. After he made those coins disappear, I noticed that people were also throwing coins into his hat. Not a bad way to earn your keep, I thought. So I asked him to teach me some tricks in exchange for picking a few more pockets and handing over the haul." He looked over at her. "Am I shocking you?"

She sat back, a knowing expression on her face. "You'd like to think that, wouldn't you?"

"Yes, I would," he said with a grin. "I've always had a desire to set schoolmarms back on their heels."

"Even schoolmarms admire initiative."

"Well, I had plenty of that. I was playing carnivals by the time I was fourteen. And working six shows a day at a dime museum in Boston. My mother was proud of me, even if I couldn't read and write." He was silent. "I wasn't so proud though. I'll admit it. I didn't like not knowing how to read and write. I still don't."

"But that's easily remedied, Marc. You're smart and ambitious. There's no reason you can't learn to read now."

"You think I want people laughing at me? I'm

thirty years old! That's too late to sit in a little red schoolhouse and trace my letters on a slate."

"You don't need a schoolhouse. A dressing room would work just as well. And no one need know but me." She clasped her hands neatly on the table before her. "I'll be your teacher."

"You?"

"Of course. It will work out perfectly for both of us."

"Please don't fool yourself into thinking that I need you. You won't be the only assistant I've had who guessed that I couldn't read. Your old friend figured it out and when she did, she used that knowledge to cut me down every chance she got. I'm not going to let you do the same."

"Julia taunted you about not being able to read?" She seemed genuinely shocked.

He nodded. Marc couldn't believe she could claim to be a childhood friend and still remain so unaware of Julia's true character. Despite her book learning and manners, Salome Hall was remarkably innocent. She needed someone to watch out for her, see that no one tried to take advantage of her natural goodness. Damn, but he hadn't felt this protective about anyone since his mother.

She sat back, her delicate features screwed up in a frown. "Did Julia read this contract before you signed it?"

He snorted. "Of course, she read it. When she discovered I couldn't read, she took over the business side of the act. Read all the contracts. Read this one aloud to me, in fact. But from the sound of it, she didn't read it exactly as written."

"I don't understand how Julia could let you sign this. Maybe she isn't as clever as I took her for."

This time he laughed with genuine amusement.

"My only regret is that I took her for anything for too long. Well, she's out of my hair, and if the price is paying extortion money to Baer, then it's worth it."

"I told you. Mr. Kesselbaum will extricate you from this contract."

He started to object, then stopped. What was he protesting about? After all, this contract had been hanging around his neck like a block of granite. Every time he laid eyes on Chauncey, his disgust with himself grew greater. He should never have listened to Julia, trusting that sly hussy to read over his contracts. No doubt, she could barely read and write herself and had made half of everything up. Landing a spot on the Orpheum Circuit just at the moment when Baer and Chauncey had a way to squeeze him dry had spoiled his success so far. He wanted an end to this robbery, so why not simply admit it? And if the schoolteacher had a way to legally release him from the contract, why was he digging in his heels?

"No doubt the price for Mr. Kesselbaum's services will be to keep you in the act."

"Certainly not. As I said, look on it as a gesture of thanks for helping me get out of St. Louis." Those refined features suddenly took on an impish expression. "Teaching you how to read and write is the price for keeping me in the act."

He fought to keep a straight face. "And Chicago?"

"Of course you'll take me to Chicago. The stage manager informed me that the circuit has a theater there. This way, I get the chance to impress Lyndon and you learn enough to prevent you from ever signing another contract like this again." She held up the offending document.

He sat back. "Can't say as I wouldn't mind knowing how to read a little. And trace my name proper. The way things stand now, it's all I can do to scribble my initials, and that's little better than signing with an X."

"I'll teach you a far sight more than that. First we'll practice the alphabet; I'll have you signing a proper signature before the week is out. And then we'll work on reading street signs." She smiled at him, obviously elated at the prospect of teaching again. "You just wait and see. I may be a terrible magician's assistant, but I'm a fine teacher."

"That reminds me. About those scarves . . ."

She crossed her arms, her lower lip pouting slightly. "You're not going to let me wear so many of them, are you?"

"Try none." He settled back in his seat, amazed at how comfortable he felt with this woman. And judging by her amused expression, she felt at ease with him as well. Maybe magicians and schoolmarms were a better fit than he realized.

"Fair enough. I did look a bit dramatic tonight."

"You looked ridiculous."

"I do have another idea that should work much better." She leaned over. "Flora the Dancer has the loveliest shawl, perfect for draping about my legs. And I'll practice diligently to make certain the fringe doesn't interfere with any of the tricks."

He groaned loudly.

"Luckily the shawl is sapphire blue, which will match the costume," she went blithely on. "And it's lined in black silk, so it should complement your own black outfit. I think it will work perfectly, Marc. The fringe will even allow for a few indiscreet glimpses of my legs that, although it will mortify me, will undoubtedly please you and the other male gawkers in the theater."

"You and I will probably be responsible for the death of vaudeville—and it's only a few years old!"

Even though he wasn't entirely joking, she burst into a peal of delighted laughter.

"You truly are the worst assistant I've ever had, Salome," he said, trying to be serious.

"I know." She was laughing so hard she could barely get the words out. "You should have seen your face when my scarves got caught during the Indian Rope Trick."

How could he forget that fiasco? Instead of seeing Salome disappearing up the rope as planned, the long-suffering audience had to be content with watching him try to untangle a half-dozen blasted scarves from the rope. Then when he finally yanked them free, the whole rope fell on his head.

Tears were running down her face. "You looked like you wanted to throttle me."

"I did!" As embarrassing as the memory of that botched trick was, he couldn't help but join in her laughter.

"Oh, you poor man," she said. "I did everything but turn you into a rabbit tonight."

For a lady, she laughed with great abandon. Head thrown back, her pleasure loud and unrestrained. He liked her laughter.

And he liked her.

Out of the corner of his eye, he saw Chauncey Farrell moving toward the sandwich shop's door. Before exiting, he threw Marc a warning look, and mouthed the words "See you tomorrow."

Marc sobered instantly. How stupid of him to think that just because Salome's friend could find a way to release him from the contract, his troubles were over. Baer had already thrown him in jail for not paying. He had no doubt that Baer and his cronies would resort to violence if they didn't get their share of his salary. Well, damn them and that crooked Dupree female who had helped get him into this mess.

For four months they had been bleeding him of both cash and self-respect. It took a little school-teacher from Missouri to remind him that caving in to bullies only made them greedier. Well, he wasn't going to play their game any longer. They had cheated him once. He wouldn't allow them to get the better of him again.

They might hurt Salome, though. No doubt they would threaten to harm her. But if he sent her away, he would only be giving in to their threats once more.

Salome pulled a lace handkerchief from her sleeve and dabbed at her eyes, an occasional chuckle escaping her. She glanced over at him, her large eyes still bright with laughter. With that absurd straw hat perched on her head, she looked like a cheerful little bird. A bird that could so easily be crushed.

Well, Marc wouldn't let that happen. No matter what he had to do, he'd see to it that no one hurt Salome Hall.

And that included Lyndon Whittier, the fool she thought she was in love with.

Chapter Six

Salome bit back a scream. Two huge rats smeared with yellow greasepaint stared down at her from the shelf on the wall.

"The rats are into the makeup again," she whispered.

Marc looked up from his writing tablet. With a bored expression, he took off his shoe and threw it at them. The jar toppled over, sending the rodents scurrying for cover.

He shrugged at the shards of broken glass. "Never used that color greasepaint anyway."

"Maybe we should set a few traps."

"Nah, I told you. Rats are good luck in vaudeville. You find a nest of rats in your dressing room, chances are there's nothing but good press notices heading your way."

"That's a ridiculous superstition."

He had already turned his attention back to pencil

Sharon Pisacreta

and paper. "Superstition or not, I've never known an act to flop once a rat's paid a visit."

"Then everyone in vaudeville is destined to be a headliner," she muttered to herself.

But Marc was too engrossed in writing to pay attention to either her or the rats. She'd never worked with such a conscientious or devoted student. Between shows, he waited impatiently for her to come to his dressing room, armed with her writing tablets and books. And once the lessons began, his attention never wavered; his efforts to sound out words and laboriously write his name were almost exhausting to watch. Yet his fierce determination to succeed filled her with awe—and a sharp sense of humility. Not many grown men would expose their lack of skill as openly as he did, especially to a woman. But he was so hungry to learn. It was as if he sensed that a wide, glorious world was about to open before him, and he couldn't bear to wait one second longer than he had to.

Although she missed teaching in her little schoolhouse back home in Black Horse, Marc had helped to fill the void. He was more challenging—and brighter—than many of the children she'd labored over and loved these past few years. Of course, he also was a strikingly attractive man, which made the task that much more intriguing.

She fidgeted in her chair. Stuff and nonsense. She liked teaching Marc Cooper because she was a born teacher; a dozen people had told her that ever since she was out of gingham pinafores. Teaching gave her purpose and strengthened her character. Leaving her position at the school to run off after Lyndon had not been done without trepidation. More than likely Black Horse had already hired someone else to replace her.

Teaching Marc Cooper to read and write was an unexpected compensation, and a sweetly satisfying one. She had only been teaching him for a week, but already she looked forward to those afternoon hours between shows; she watching intently as he wrote the alphabet over and over, he listening closely while she sounded out the letters. Outside the dressing room door, performers and stagehands shouted, chattered or snored the time away, while she and Marc sat close together, she with her lesson plan, he with his notebook. Had they spent the time caressing each other, it couldn't have felt more intimate.

Amazingly she had even begun to look forward to being onstage. She was still nervous, her stomach fluttering like a field of butterflies just before she stepped in front of the footlights, but surely she could not do worse than that first disastrous performance. Although she crinkled her nose at the noxious gas fumes, she welcomed the heat emitted by those hundreds of lights, the hush that automatically greeted Marc's entrance onstage, the delighted cheers when the tricks went off well. She only regretted not having any real talent to offer the audience.

Getting rid of the scarves had helped both the act and Marc's humor. She'd even agreed to add a tiny amount of rouge to her cheeks; that, combined with her carmine-painted lips, made her feel quite disreputable, yet somehow pleased. Maybe by the time they got to Chicago, she'd work up the nerve to smear kohl around her eyes and let a tendril or two of hair loose from its pins. But she didn't fool herself that a little rouge and lip paint would win Lyndon back. It had only been five weeks since he'd run off with Jane, not enough time for him to tire of that affected voice and soft powdered bosom. But in a few months, surely he would have wearied of Jane and instead think warmly—and longingly—of what they had shared.

Salome peeked over at Marc. He muttered under his breath, then crossed out what he had just written. A wave of affection swept over her. He was trying so hard, concentrating on the letters of the alphabet as though they were a wondrous yet tricky illusion he had vowed to master.

She leaned towards the dressing table, searching for her teacup in the clutter of face paint, theater programs and playbills. She gave up looking for it and instead picked up a schedule for the Orpheum Circuit.

"You said we'll be playing in Indiana next?"

"Iowa. There won't be a jump to Indiana until August. Now be quiet for a minute so I can finish this."

With luck, she'd understand theater lingo soon. He had explained to her that traveling from one town to another for a performance was called a "jump." "Breaking the jump," involved playing one-night stands until reaching the next longer engagement. Or something like that. Marc Cooper wasn't the only person in this act who had a lot to learn.

Settling back in her chair, she adjusted her wrapper. Since the next show would begin in two hours, they were still in costume. Her scandalous scrap of blue spangles was well-covered by a floor-length cotton wrapper, while Marc's bathrobe was tucked tightly about his barrel chest. Since that first day, he'd taken care to cover up whenever they were offstage. She was grateful for that. Onstage, she concentrated so hard on doing the tricks correctly, she barely noticed that exposed, muscular chest. But in the cramped confines of his dressing room, such a sight would be far too unsettling.

Marc still had on his makeup though, while his long hair hung loose so that it nearly brushed his shoulders. With that gold hoop earring gleaming from one ear, she could easily imagine that she was teaching a pirate. All he lacked was an eye patch and a raucous green parrot.

"Why do you wear the earring onstage?" She wanted to kick herself as soon as she asked. She'd been watching him so intently that she inadvertently blurted out what she was thinking.

"For my mother." He held up the lined paper where he had been practicing his signature. "The 'Cooper' looks fine, but I think 'Marc' still needs work."

Salome nodded. "Let's work on the 'r' a bit more." She tried to control her curiosity, but couldn't. "What does the earring have to do with your mother?"

He chuckled. "Between you and the rats, I'll never get this lesson finished."

"I'm sorry. It's none of my business."

He glanced up at her. "My mother always wanted to be a singer, used to sing all the time when I was a kid. Folk songs from Portugal mostly. And my father taught her some sea chanties." His eyes looked beyond her, as if focusing on a distant memory. "Sang me to sleep till I was near eleven years old. She had a good voice, too. If she'd been born in a different time and place, I think she might have made a name for herself on the stage. That was a secret dream of hers, being able to sing in a real theater."

"Is this hers?" Salome softly touched the hoop hanging from his right ear.

Marc nodded. "She was so happy to watch me performing in front of an audience, even if they were the sort of lowlifes that often wind up at a dime museum. You see, she didn't want me to be a laborer or a fisherman like my father. She didn't want her only child to have as hard a life as she had. So my getting paid good money for doing magic tricks was like a miracle to her, a real step up in the world. When I wear the earring onstage, I feel like she gets to share in the performance. And in the applause, too. Wherever she is, I hope she knows what I'm doing." He paused. "I think she knows, and is happy to be up there with me."

Marc had already turned his attention back to the lesson, but Salome thought for the next few minutes on what he had said. She liked the fact that he'd confided in her, and she liked even more that he didn't apologize for his sentimental gesture. In the past, Lyndon had quoted some melancholy poet to demonstrate his affection for his own deceased mother. Marc's manner of honoring those he had loved and lost somehow touched her far more. Not for the first time, Salome thanked fate and Julia Dupree for guiding her towards the magician. He was not only an attractive and kind man, but a sweet one, as well. No wonder Julia dreaded the thought of losing him.

Marc held out his latest effort at a signature.

She smiled with approval. "I believe you could start signing bank drafts this evening. As long as you don't make any out to Mr. Baer."

He lifted a rakish eyebrow. "Baer never did want bank drafts; it's greenbacks or nothing."

"Do you think he'll send Mr. Farrell again tonight?"

As predicted, her father's friend Frank Kesselbaum had invalidated the contract. But although that freed Marc legally from its harsh terms, Chauncey Farrell had not taken the news well. Two nights ago, Chauncey and Marc had come to blows outside the stage door. It took the stage manager and the Three Hibernian Singing Brothers to finally pull them apart.

"I imagine we'll be seeing Chauncey every night for quite some time. We've put his nose out of joint, you see. Now that we've broken the contract, they can't threaten me with jail anymore." His face screwed up as he slowly wrote out another signature. "I'm sure they'll find something else to threaten me with—broken legs, busted ribs." And hurting you, he thought with a sinking heart, but deliberately left that unsaid.

"Why don't we go to the police? If we let the authorities know this man is making threats, maybe they can detain him, at least until we leave the city."

"And what do we do in Davenport, Milwaukee, St. Paul, Indianapolis or the dozens of small towns in between?" He squinted at the letters he'd just written. "We can't keep running to the police every time Chauncey raises his voice. The cops wouldn't pay us much mind anyway. We're only theater folk, after all. Oh, the law might sit up and take notice if Lillie Langtry had a complaint, but they won't give a tinker's dam about Marco the Magnificent and the beauteous Salome."

He said this in jest, but she blushed anyway. He hadn't meant to embarrass her; perhaps the word 'beauteous' made her uncomfortable. Yet gazing at her just now, it occurred to him that she wasn't that far from beauty, even if he had never met a woman so reluctant to meet that beauty halfway. What he wouldn't give to just once see that rich brown hair unbound from its dozens of pins. And if only she'd put that lavender dress on again, the one she'd worn the day Jenson accosted her in St. Louis. Didn't she own any clothing that wasn't as dreary as New England mud? At least she did appear younger and more daring with that bit of rouge warming her cheeks and lips.

"Don't worry about Chauncey," he said gently. "He's my problem; I'll handle him. And I'll make certain no harm comes to you, you have my word."

"I helped put you in this position, Marc. Not that I regret it. That terrible contract had to be invalidated. Still, it seems I've placed your well-being in jeopardy and I bear part of the blame. Rest assured I will do my best to see no harm comes to *you* either." His little schoolteacher looked as serious as a fisherman who'd just snagged a marlin. No doubt she was just as determined as well. It was a good thing, however, that she couldn't possibly know how low people like Baer and Chauncey could stoop.

He must have looked worried for she leaned over, covering his hand with her own. "As I always remind my students, the only way to defeat evil is to stand firm and refuse to look the other way." She patted his hand again as though he was the one who needed reassuring. "We'll be fine, Marc."

Marc could only shake his head. For the first time since she told him of her plan to win back her former fiancé, he thought that maybe—just maybe—she might be able to do it. Not that this Lyndon idiot sounded like anyone a sane woman would want, but damn, if Salome Hall wasn't as determined and stubborn as ten Missouri mules. For a delicate-looking female, she really was quite fearless. And as good-hearted as his mother had been.

If Lyndon Whittier didn't come crawling on his knees to her, he was the biggest fool east of the Rockies. Either way, Lyndon didn't deserve a woman like Salome.

And to his surprising regret, Marc knew that he didn't deserve her either.

She stood before the footlights, the gas fumes making her cough. The chandelier above the audience revealed a sea of expectant faces, dozens of fans fluttering in the sweltering heat. Things were going well tonight. Marc seemed to finally trust her not to ruin every trick, and he was energetic and commanding. Just now, he was gesturing towards a long box on wheels that stood center stage. A snap of his fingers brought her quickly to his side.

As the music from the orchestra pit swelled, Marc opened the box, then held out his hand to her. She took a deep breath. His eyes were so black and lustrous. For a moment he seemed like a dark, forbidding stranger, then he gave her a quick wink. Before she could relax too much however, he lifted her into his arms so effortlessly that it must seem to the audience as though she weighed no more than one of her scarves.

As he held her in his arms, Salome couldn't help but feel a tremor of nerves, perhaps even desire. After all, Marc Cooper was a striking man and in his guise as Marco the Magnificent, he was outrageously male. That bare, muscular chest of his was pressed against her now, and she marveled again at how strong and hard his body felt. A man of stone might be holding her, except for the steady reassuring beat of his heart, which sounded slow indeed next to the fevered beating of her own.

He held her aloft for only a second. Any longer and she feared they might seem like lovers, rather than magician and assistant. When he set her down gently within the box, she breathed a sigh of relief. She had work to do now and could concentrate on something other than his strong arms.

Like a child being tucked into a trundle bed, she snuggled within the box's narrow confines, her head and feet sticking out from either end. The construction of the box prevented the audience from realizing that her legs never went into the lower half of the box at all. Instead, the moment she lay down, she pulled a lever which released a pair of painted false feet which wore her identical booted heels. Then, while stretching her head straight out so it looked as if she was lying flat, she made certain to turn her body slightly to the side, drawing her knees up nearly to her chest.

When she nodded that she was ready, Marc closed the box's lid over her with a heavy thud. The music rose once more. She couldn't help but feel pleased with herself. Only a week onstage and already she'd mastered the tricks and conquered most of her stage fright.

So far the performance had gone exceedingly well; she hadn't stumbled or made a false move. She was certain it was because of the shawl. Freed of that mountain of scarves, she no longer fretted about exposing her legs and thighs. The blue silk shawl that replaced them now lay wrapped about her waist and hips, covering everything but her calves. Even though her arms and shoulders were still left exposed, she could pretend to herself that she was wearing a formal evening gown, one that permitted only an occasional indiscreet glimpse.

Marc tapped on the box with his saw. She curled her legs up into an even tighter ball, struggling to keep her neck and head ramrod straight. The audience must not guess that she had twisted her body about within the box. As Marc began sawing loudly into the box, the audience murmured among themselves. When he had finished sawing her in half, Salome triggered the mechanism that set the fake feet to wriggling. The drumroll from the orchestra sounded like thunder as he pulled the two halves of the box apart.

She turned her face to the audience—her neck straining from the effort—and smiled graciously.

While the audience cheered, Marc pushed the box together again. She swiftly fumbled for the button that opened the wall between the two halves, and stretched her legs out. As Marc proceeded to spin the box about, she reached down with her hands, pulled on the wires that retracted the fake feet, and pushed her own feet out into the holes. Marc made certain that she was in place before completing the spin.

When he bent over to lift up the lid, the smile he bestowed upon her was dazzling. Working in the theater held definite charms, she decided. To earn such applause and cheers for doing so little seemed almost sinful.

The applause seemed especially enthusiastic tonight. Emboldened by the reception, she decided to sit up with a theatrical flourish, maybe even lift an arm high to court more cheers. As the lid was raised, she took a deep breath and flung herself into a sitting position. In that split second, the shoulder strap of her costume caught on one of the triggering buttons. She heard the material rip loudly, then felt the bodice of her costume fall away. For one excruciating second, her bare breasts were exposed to the world *and* Marc Cooper. She let out a mighty scream that was drowned out by the hoots from the audience.

Salome fell back into the box, banging her head on the way down. She fumbled for her shawl, tugging it until it came loose from her waist.

Marc's face appeared over her. He looked as
though he were fighting not to laugh and losing the
battle. "Are you all right?" he asked, those dark eyes
sparkling.

"Close the blasted lid!" It was the first time in her
life she had ever cursed, but surely even the Lord
would excuse her in these circumstances.

Not only did Marc close the lid of the magic box,
he pushed it gently so that it rolled on its casters
offstage. Trapped inside, she flushed scarlet as the
cheers from the audience grew louder. After all that
worry about displaying her legs, she had gone ahead
and exposed herself worse than any calico queen. As
she spread the shawl over her bare torso, she was
grateful for only one thing: she wouldn't have to
worry about wearing this costume any longer. Even
if it wasn't torn in two, she was going to personally
shred every last scandalous inch of it into a hundred
glittering pieces.

Marc watched as the box rolled smoothly offstage
where it was caught neatly by the performer waiting
to go on next. Luckily it was Flora the Dancing Girl;
she'd see to it that Salome got out of the box mod-
estly covered. Although he dearly wished for just one
more glimpse of his half-naked assistant.

In fact, he'd had to restrain himself from joining
in the cheers ringing from the rafters. Salome might
not have let down her hair tonight, but she had
shown that beneath the shawls, scarves and drab
dresses, a real live woman was waiting to burst free.
As slender as she was, he had been surprised to see
how shapely her breasts were, jutting out from above
her corset. With nipples as rosy as summer berries.
What must the rest of his little schoolteacher look
like, he wondered.

As he bowed to the audience—the men whistling

and on their feet—he reminded himself that Salome Hall was no Julia. His hot, carnal thoughts were best directed at overpainted chorus girls or the bored wives of theater owners. Still, he had to admit that Salome had not only brought down the house tonight, she'd stirred up something in him that would be hard to tamp down.

A good thing he wasn't as dishonorable as Lyndon Whittier. Otherwise he'd be tempted to take advantage of her shaky emotional state—the jilted woman whose pride and heart had been hurt—and seduce her into his own bed and arms. He straightened up as the curtain swung closed. Lucky for her he wasn't a dishonorable man.

But maybe it wasn't so lucky for him.

"I'm telling you, no one backstage saw anything. . . . Salome, wait."

Marc hurried to keep up with her. How could someone with such short legs walk so fast?

She sidestepped the porter who was pushing one of Marc's half-dozen trunks. "Don't tell me that no one saw. Boblo went red as a beet when I bumped into him in the hallway, and all three Hibernian Brothers asked me to marry them!"

He couldn't keep from laughing. "They're just kidding. C'mon. It's no use pretending your costume didn't fall off. Five hundred Kansas City citizens saw it happen." He finally caught up with her, and grabbed her elbow.

The station was bustling with departing passengers, ready to take the night train north. "Half the Orpheum Circuit will be on the train tonight heading toward Iowa, so there's no way you can avoid your fellow performers."

He forced her to turn around. "Salome, as lovely a

sight as you were tonight—" Her brown eyes flashed anger at him beneath the brim of her straw hat. "— these are all show people. We've seen everything from dog-faced boys to naked midgets. One brief glimpse of your hidden charms is not as earth-shattering as you may fear."

"It is to me," she said furiously.

"Then look at it this way. Now that you've exposed yourself onstage like that, maybe you won't feel so funny about wearing the costume."

Her expression mysteriously lightened. "Yes, my costume."

"I hope it can be fixed. I don't have another costume for you."

She stepped back, a tiny smile appearing on her face. "Oh, I fixed the costume, never fear."

"What did you do? Did you rip the rest of it? I'll saw you in half for real if you did."

Turning on her heel, she marched off in the direction of the nearest railcar.

"Salome Hall, that costume better be sewn back together in time for our next performance! Bad enough you lost my saber, I won't sit still for you throwing away the only costume I have."

She waved a hand dismissively in his direction as she stepped onto the train.

"Salome, I mean it. Costumes cost money and I—"

"That's right, Cooper. Costumes cost money, and so do dishonest magicians."

Marc spun around. A flume of steam blew out from the railcar beside him. But even with the swirling smoke, he recognized the lean features of Robert Baer.

"Well maybe we should discuss dishonest contracts first," Marc refused to show his surprise. He'd only seen Baer twice before; usually the man left his dirty work to flunkies like Chauncey. He must be really upset to have left his plush nest in New Orleans.

Baer reached into the pocket of his gray frock suit and pulled out a cheroot. "I don't rightly believe there is such a thing as a dishonest contract. Just dishonest people who sign their names to them." He snipped off the end of his cigar.

"Maybe you didn't get the paperwork that my attorney wired you five days ago. If you had, you'd see that the contract was broken because of its many illegal clauses."

Baer lit the cheroot, his lean, tanned face impassive as always. Marc had never been able to figure out what this man was thinking. He couldn't even rightly guess his age—anywhere between thirty and fifty. All he knew was that despite his elegant dress and clean-shaven cheeks, Baer was a dangerous man. He didn't need to bully and bluster like Chauncey Farrell. His threats were quiet, unemotional— and much more deadly.

"Where I come from, a contract is a contract," he finally said, his hazel eyes barely visible through all the cigar smoke. "A man signs his name to a paper, he's expected to abide by its terms."

"You've been extorting money from me for months, Baer. And extortion is illegal; the law doesn't care if it's done with a pistol or a pen. So stop your moaning." Marc turned up the collar of his suit coat. Despite the hot summer night, he suddenly felt chilled. "Count yourself lucky that you got as much money from me as you did. Hope it bought a few doodads for that house of yours in the French Quarter. Cause that's the last dime you'll ever get from me."

Baer frowned. "I thought you were brighter than this. Maybe I been confusing you with that Marco character you pretend to be onstage. I see now that you're as dim as sunlight in a swamp."

"I admit I've been pretty dim these past four months. But no more."

"It's that mousy assistant you got now, isn't it?" He pointed towards the railcar where Salome had disappeared. "She got you all riled up, made you think twice about our contract. Chauncey told me that she wanted a copy for herself; damn him for being fool enough to give her one. She looks like the sort who makes trouble. Next thing you know she'll be marching in temperance parades. If I were you, I'd hire myself another assistant. One with less brains and more bosom." Baer grinned. "Although I caught the show tonight. The mouse apparently has more hidden up her sleeve than even you do, magician."

"Miss Hall is my business, not yours. And since our contract is now null and void, I'm no longer any of your business either. So shove off, and take that clown Chauncey with you."

Baer took one last puff before flinging the cheroot beneath the train's wheels. "Poor Chauncey. He's back in town, nursing his jaw. For a magician, you have a nice left hook."

"I told him to stay away, but he kept coming around to the stage door every night, threatening me and Miss Hall. Some of those threats were not fit for a lady's ears." Marc shrugged. "If he wants to keep all his teeth, tell him to back off. I'm sure you have other sheep to fleece. Start nosing around for your next victim, Baer. You're not getting another red cent from me."

"So the cheap vaudeville magician now wants to play Sir Galahad. Well, play all you want as long as you keep making money and seeing that I get half." He held up a hand to still Marc's protests. "Damn the contract and damn your Miss Hall. We had a deal and you welshed. You made a fool of me, Cooper, and that don't sit right with a Southern gentleman. If this were fifty years ago, I'd challenge you to a duel. It would give me no end of pleasure to put a bullet right between those black eyes of yours."

"Don't think too long on that." Marc slipped his hand into his suit coat. When he pulled it out again, a derringer lay neatly within his grasp. "I might fancy firing a bullet or two myself."

Baer's expression remained impassive but the slight twitch near his left eye indicated his agitation.

"You owe me half of everything you earn, and I intend to get it." His voice was calm and cold.

"No," Marc said softly, his fingers now curled around the trigger of his gun.

"You've gotten mighty brave since hiring that little mouse. Maybe you'll lose some of that courage if she's taken away from you."

"Don't even think about it, Baer."

Baer glanced once at the gun, then back up at Marc. Something in Marc's expression must have convinced Baer that he was serious.

"We'll talk again. When we do, I assure you, you'll be in a more receptive mood."

The train whistle blew, covering up Marc's curse as Baer walked away, elbowing his way through the crowded station. He knew that Baer wouldn't give up just because the law was now on Marc's side. Since when did someone like Robert Baer give a damn about the law or legal contracts?

And Baer certainly wouldn't give a damn about the welfare of a little Missouri schoolteacher.

He fumbled for his tobacco pouch. With Salome so set on reaching Chicago by October, he knew that he couldn't convince her to leave the act. Especially if she thought that he was in danger as well. He pulled out one of the cigarettes he had rolled earlier.

If anything happened to Salome because of him and that blasted contract, he'd never forgive himself. And the devil only knows what he'd wind up doing to Baer and Chauncey.

He stuck the cigarette between his lips, then lifted the derringer. With one flick of the trigger, a tiny flame ignited at the end of the barrel, and Marc brought it close to light his cigarette. He inhaled deeply. If things kept up like this, he might be forced to buy a real derringer.

With a sigh, he clicked off the novelty lighter. And it also might help if he learned how to shoot a gun.

He feared it was only a matter of time before someone got killed.

Chapter Seven

"Don't tell me that rats in the dressing aren't good luck." Marc walked out onto the veranda of the boardinghouse, beaming as widely as he had after last night's tumultuous applause. "Our names will be second from the bottom of the bill before you know it."

"I refuse to give rats credit for our hard work." Salome looked up from the newspaper. "By the way, *The Gazette* has an article about us. Apparently we're the best thing their reviewer has seen since Lillian Russell and her English ballads."

Marc sat beside her on the porch swing, his weight causing it to creak noisily. "You're kidding? We're being compared to Lillian Russell? Read it to me."

By the time she finished reading aloud the brief but glowing review, Marc's eyes were as dark and glittering as obsidian. He took the paper from her, staring at the words.

"I recognize my name," he said softly. "Yours, too. And a few other words. I wish I could figure out the rest. Who knows how many good things the papers have said about me in the past and I never knew. If you can have me understanding more by the time we hit Chicago, don't worry about Lyndon marrying you. I'll haul you off to the altar myself."

Salome bit back an irritated reply. This past month, there had been too many humorous references about how foolish Lyndon had been to jilt her, and too many lighthearted comments about how much better off she'd be if she trusted her affections to a certain New England magician. Of course, he didn't really mean it. She'd spent enough time around theater folk these past few weeks to realize their lives were far more casual and familiar than the community she'd grown up in. But she did wish Marc wouldn't joke about her plan to win back Lyndon, especially now that he knew how much Lyndon meant to her.

She reached for her palmetto fan and began waving it in front of her damp face. "I can't promise you'll be reading every word of the newspaper by then, but you will understand enough to make you grin." She tapped him on the shoulder with her fan. "Assuming it's complimentary. I seem to recall the Des Moines reviewer describing us as 'shameless and vulgar.' "

"Hayseed," Marc muttered. "That's the type that thinks a vaudeville act is one step from original sin."

"Imagine what he'd have said if I was still wearing that terrible blue costume."

"Well, even I'll admit you look a lot better in the new dress." He folded up the newspaper. "Although you should have told me before you destroyed the first one. I might have been able to sell it to another performer."

"I wasn't going to take a chance on that bit of spangles turning up again in my life. I'm just grateful Flora had the red dress to give me. Even if it only does cover me to the knees."

Indeed the velvet dress she now wore onstage would have scandalized her just two months ago, but compared to the scanty blue costume, it seemed positively demure. The new costume was cherry red, and the rich color warmed her pale complexion. The skirt was short enough so that it didn't interfere with getting in and out of the trick cabinets, but the material didn't cling disgracefully to her curves. And she'd traded her flesh-colored tights for a pair of Flora's black mesh. This way she didn't give the illusion that the audience was seeing an inch of bare flesh on her legs. She only wished she'd gotten better acquainted with Flora Hatcher when she first joined Marc's act.

At that moment, the screen door banged open and Flora herself appeared. She held a cup of steaming coffee in her hand and from the look on her face, it still hadn't woken her up.

"Mornin', you two." Flora gave a mighty yawn, before settling down on the top step of the porch. As usual, the attractive dancer wasn't dressed yet. Instead she wore her flowered cotton wrapper, wavy yellow hair spilling messily about her shoulders. Luckily this was a boardinghouse that catered to theater people and no one raised an eyebrow at such informality.

Marc stood up, then straightened his suspenders. "I'd best be off. Haroldson wants to nail down our fall tour over breakfast. I'd like to get to the cafe before he starts without me. Once Charlie begins to eat,

121

his mind will be on nothing but country biscuits and sausages."

Charlie Haroldson was one of the Orpheum Circuit's Midwest bookers and was notorious for his love of food. He ate like a military regiment on maneuvers, yet had the frame of a stripling.

"Sure you don't want to join us? This way you can put in your Chicago request personally."

She shook her head. "I'm sure you'll overcome your natural shyness and demand it quite nicely."

He grinned down at her. Even under the awning, his dark hair gleamed like a raven's wing. "Wish me luck then. If I buy him a big enough breakfast, he won't book us on the swamp circuit through Florida."

"Wait a moment." Salome stood up and adjusted his collar. Her hands briefly brushed against the nape of his neck, his long hair swept back in that ever-present queue. Who would ever have imagined that she'd find long hair on a man so appealing? A pity it was no longer the fashion. If Lyndon ever let his thick chestnut hair grow to shoulder length, she was certain he'd turn more heads than Gentleman Jim Corbett.

"There, that's better."

In his white duck trousers and wheat-colored blazer, Marc Cooper looked as dapper as any city banker on holiday. Although the pearl silk fedora would look foppish on any other man, it was impossible for Marc to appear anything other than all male.

He gave her a wink before setting off down the porch, whistling. She stood watching him as his figure disappeared down the dirt road. He wouldn't be able to pick up a hired carriage for at least half a mile, but his jaunty walk showed he was in high spirits. In the distance, the bells of Trinity Cathedral sounded, its cheery peal soon drowned out by the clucking of chickens. Their boardinghouse sat on the outskirts of Omaha, smack in the middle of vacant lots and ramshackle chicken farms.

Even if the boardinghouse was shabby and buzzing with far too many flies, the country-like setting reminded her of Black Horse. A wave of homesickness swept over her. Taking a deep breath, she inhaled the mingled scent of field grass and marigold leaves as if it were French perfume.

"That man sure does like you."

Salome glanced down at Flora. "Of course, he likes me. We've been working together for over a month. We're friends."

Flora tapped her polished nails on the blue enameled cup. "The way Marc's always looking at you, I expect any day now you two will be doing a double bill offstage as well as on."

"Nonsense." The July heat seemed to shimmer in waves above the sunburnt grass. "He's just grateful that I've finally stopped ruining the act."

"Marc's had other women who didn't mess up the act. He didn't go around treating them like they were special."

Salome fanned herself a moment, thinking. Honey bees hovered about the black-eyed Susans bordering the veranda; occasionally one would dare to inspect her fluttering fan.

"I'm sure he thought Julia Dupree was special once," she finally said. One of these days, Julia would turn up, expecting Marc to take her back. It was best to remind people occasionally that Marc had had an assistant he was once far more attached to than he ever would be to her. "They were quite close, I hear. Or didn't you know her?"

Flora swept her hair back with one hand, her neck glistening with perspiration. "Julia? Sure, I knew her. We toured through Georgia together this past spring. And two years ago in Ohio. Pretty girl, if you like bleached hair and corsets pulled too tight." She sipped her coffee. "But she was never happy, even when her and Marc were seeing each other regular. Always jealous, believing people were talking against her. Thinking females were panting to get their hands on ol' Marc. Lucky thing for me I'm a married lady, otherwise Julia would have been hissing at me every time I said 'good mornin' to Marc. If you ask me, it was her jealous nagging that drove him away. A regular Southern harpie, that Julia. Cunning, too."

Flora looked up at Salome. "Good thing she's not around now. She'd tear a little thing like you apart with her bare hands."

Salome sat down beside her on the porch step. The long sleeves of her cotton blouse stuck to her arms, while her dark green skirt felt as warm and cumbersome as ten layers of flannel. No doubt it was the summer sun that made her head suddenly swim.

"Julia knows me too well to ever imagine I'd be a threat to her. I grew up with her. We've been friends since we were children. Why, we've never exchanged a cross word."

Flora laughed. "You two ever make eyes at the same boy? I thought not. Julia is a man's woman, which means she don't give a pile of dirt for any female and her feelings. I think we've seen the last of her; leastways I hope so. She's a troublemaker and you can't have someone always stirring the pot when you're on tour. But if you ever see her in the audience, just get your bustle in gear and start packing your trunk. Not even lovestruck magicians will be able to save you then."

"Lovestruck?" Salome's mouth fell open.

Flora leaned close. "Marc fancies you. I'm not sure he even knows it yet, but it's as clear as heat lightning to the rest of us. Why do you think the other men on tour haven't tried to cozy up to you? They don't want to cut in on whatever Marc has up his sleeve." She giggled. "And you know magicians. There's no telling what he's got planned."

"But—but men don't cozy up to me," Salome stammered. "I mean, I'm engaged. Well, I was engaged, and I will be again. Besides, I'm Julia's friend. I would never even consider a man that she had designs on. Julia trusts me."

Flora put an arm about her shoulders and hugged her tight. "Now you don't have to pretend with me. Why, the whole company has seen how much time you two spend locked away together in his dressing room. You don't rightly believe we think the pair of you are just rehearsing card tricks."

Salome bit her lip. She hadn't considered how odd it must look to everyone. Marc and she did spend an inordinate amount of time behind the closed door of his dressing room between shows. Of course, no one guessed she was teaching him to read—nor would they ever, if she had anything to say about it. Still, it must appear as though something licentious was going on.

"Actually, we are rehearsing the tricks."

Flora shot her an incredulous look.

"No, really. You forget that until last month, I was a schoolteacher. I didn't know a limelight from a fire curtain. It isn't just tricks I have to practice over and over, it's the terminology, the stage mechanics. This whole month I've felt like I've been in school, and Marc has been my teacher."

Flora laughed. "I just bet he has."

"Flora!" Salome's exasperation gave way to anger. The last thing she needed was for gossip to start about her and Marc Cooper. News traveled fast among show people, and no doubt both Jane and Lyndon would stumble onto some nasty lie concocted about her if she allowed this silly talk to continue. It could spell doom to any hope of winning Lyndon back.

"Marc and I are friends. *Just* friends. I don't know how life is lived in the theater, but even you must understand that it's an insult to whisper falsely about a lady and a gentleman."

"Damn, if you don't sound like a schoolteacher sometimes." Flora shook her head. "I shouldn't have gotten your skirts fluttering about something that's none of my business. Hey, if you claim to be practicing magic in that dressing room, I won't say otherwise. But don't expect the rest of the world to be as gullible as I am. Especially in this company."

The screen door swung open, cutting short Salome's response. She stood up quickly, hoping no one had overheard their absurd conversation. A half-dozen performers filed out in various stages of undress. Chattering, laughing, bearing cups of coffee or glasses of iced tea, they settled themselves about the veranda like brightly colored birds.

"Anyone here want to read *Variety News?*" Michaela the Acrobat waved a dog-eared newspaper.

"Me." Flora thrust her hand out.

Michaela, otherwise known as Mickey, tossed the paper over to Flora and smiled at Salome, her freckled cheeks creasing in amusement. With her auburn curls and round blue eyes, Mickey Switalski looked like nothing more than an adorable rag doll. Salome had grown extremely fond of the petite acrobat this past month; actually she'd become friendly with all the performers, even Flora's husband, Lorenzo the Tenor, and the wisecracking comedians Bill and Phil.

"Salome, I don't know how you can stand to wear that heavy skirt." Mickey flopped down on the swing, her bare feet showing beneath the ruffles of a striped blue gingham that seemed as thin and airy as a sugar wafer. "I thought you Southern women knew how to dress for the summer heat. Look at Flora here, nearly bare naked beneath that wrapper."

Flora swatted her with the paper. "Now, you just hush. How can I read about a real Southern lady like Jane Dupree if you keep yammering?"

Salome leaned over her shoulder. "Jane Dupree?"

"Yeah, Julia's sister, speak of the devil. Look's like she's made a big splash in San Francisco. Here, take a look. They even printed a picture of her." Flora handed the paper to Salome. "If that woman ain't prettier than Lillie Langtry herself. No wonder her little sister grew up to be so sour and jealous."

Salome stared in dismay at the large photo of Jane, the caption below reading "Songbird of the South." How could she have forgotten how beautiful Jane was, how feminine and elegant and perfect? She felt her head swim again, and stepped back. With a violent gesture, she tore open the screen door and fled inside. In another moment, she feared she'd be ill or start wailing at the bitter injustice of it all.

Why did Jane have to come home just as Lyndon and Salome had pledged themselves to each other? For what man could resist such a glorious visage: eyes shaped like almonds, hair golden and lustrous, a profile that would rivet a painter? And a womanly shape that epitomized the hourglass figure sought by every female under eighty. Then, to add to her allure, she had to possess a voice that was angelic and pure.

Sharon Pisacreta

She was talented, rich, famous, beautiful. And she had Lyndon Whittier on his knees before her. What in the world was she thinking of? Lyndon would never tire of Jane. Never. Salome took one last anguished look at the photo, before flinging the paper to the floor. Taking the steps two at a time, she barely made it to her room before collapsing in tears.

Foolish old maid. The phrase repeated through her mind as she bathed her face once again in the basin of cold water. She had known Jane her whole life; why should a grainy photograph of her now send her into hysterics? Yes, Jane Dupree was beautiful, and yes, Lyndon thought he was in love with her. But she knew Lyndon better than Jane ever could. They shared years of friendship between them, and four years of tender courting. They had memories of soft embraces on the back porch and wet kisses that lingered for a sweet eternity, long walks beside the river, laughter at picnics and Christmas dinners, and carriage rides at dusk when the fireflies turned the surrounding hills to flame. Salome and Lyndon had more than foolish infatuation between them, more than silly notions like "music and moonlight."

And they had passion, too. Her heart wrenched to remember how Lyndon dismissed that passion so easily, but she never would. Nor would she forget the endearments he had whispered in her ear, or the way he made her feel like a woman at last. And she was the first woman he had ever asked to be his wife. She, Salome Ruth Hall, was first, and no "Songbird of the South" would ever take her place. By God, she wouldn't.

She patted her face with a towel, then bent closer to the mirror above her washstand. But men weren't constant, nor did their emotions run as deep as those of women. Lyndon appreciated her intelligence, her honesty, her devotion, but he clearly wanted all those noble attributes contained in a pretty little package. And here she was, still going about like a Missouri schoolteacher, wearing the same dull clothes, hair pinned back, face unpowdered and unadorned. Just because she was strutting about a stage wearing a cherry red dress did not mean she was a temptress yet.

Well, if she could play at being a magician's assistant, then she could very well play at being a siren. And who better to teach her than women who spent their lives in bright feathers and spangles, women who painted their faces and transformed themselves each night into exotic and daring creatures.

She marched to the door. If it was carmine-painted lips and bare shoulders Lyndon wanted, then she'd give him such frippery in spades. She hadn't spent a month in vaudeville without learning how to be vulgar and shameless.

Marc couldn't figure out what they were up to. He'd returned hours ago from his breakfast with Haroldson, and still Salome wouldn't come out of her room. Even more suspicious, Mickey, Flora and Dagmar the Knife Thrower were closeted with her. He paced about the front parlor, sidestepping the basset hound who lay on the hooked rug, panting in the mid-afternoon heat.

And he very much wanted to talk with her, too. Of course, he would break the good news that Charlie had agreed to book them—and the other members of the show—at the Exposition; a stroke of remarkable luck due in large part to the glowing notices this past month. Even better, he wanted to tell her that he had ordered breakfast from the menu for the first time. Maybe he couldn't read everything, but he recognized enough to order fried eggs, toast and juice. If he'd just escaped from prison, he couldn't have felt prouder or more relieved.

So what was she doing squirreled away in her hotel room with three of the brashest females on the circuit? How much could they find to chatter about? After all, the women saw each other every day, seven days a week. He was glad Salome had made friends on tour, but he didn't want them to monopolize her when he had such wonderful news.

He sat down on the prickly horsehair sofa, startling a tiny mouse who scurried beneath the china cabinet in the corner. A pity they couldn't stay in nicer lodgings, but such was life on the Orpheum Circuit. Not that Salome had ever complained, except for the rats in the dressing rooms. Even the bedbugs at the boardinghouse last week in Lincoln hadn't unsettled her, and she hadn't uttered an unkind word about the mattresses here—every last one of them filled with scratchy corn husks.

Well, he'd see to it that they had a decent place to stay in Chicago. A fancy hotel with velvet settees, Oriental rugs and feather bed mattresses covered in fine linen. He'd book it himself as soon as he found a telegraph office.

And what if that's the last time you see her? Once again he calculated the chances of this lawyer fellow leaving Jane Dupree for a schoolteacher named Salome. A month ago, he might have said impossible, but Salome possessed a quiet charm all her own. And, knowing the Dupree females, it was more than likely that Lyndon Whittier had already tired of Jane. If Lyndon returned to Salome, it would make her happy, and he wanted to see her happy. Or did he?

That cheating scoundrel's not good enough for

her, he thought darkly. No doubt if Lyndon ends up marrying Salome, he'll desert her a few years down the road for another pretty face. Poor Salome will be left alone once more—and with a passel of brats to raise besides. He felt himself grow red with rage. How dare that bastard do something so low to his Salome?

"She's not yours, you fool," he muttered aloud. "Leave her to her fancy lawyer, if that's what she wants." The idea set his teeth on edge, however, and he kicked at a nearby ottoman.

Slumped over in the oak rocker across from him, Boblo the Juggler let out a strangled snore. "What did you say?"

"Go back to sleep. You've only gotten in a three-hour nap, so I'm sure you're still tired."

Boblo scratched his head, making his prematurely gray hair even messier. On Sunday, the performers normally spent their one day of rest either asleep, engaged in card games, or sipping a light liquid refreshment. The Three Hibernian Brothers were playing cards on the veranda, while Phil the Comedian weaved past them, a brandy flask peeking from his breast pocket.

"Don't know why you have to wake a fellow up," Boblo grumbled. "I told you that jugglers need more rest than other people. All that physical dexterity and those heavy Indian clubs. If I don't get my ten hours, I'll be dropping clubs on my head faster than you can say Giacomo the Clown, who's a terrible juggler by the way. I don't care how much Tony Pastor pays him. Why, he's not worth a single dollar of—" He stopped. "Well, would you look at that! If that's who I think it is, we've a regular swan in our midst."

Marc swiveled about. Coming down the stairway was a slender young woman, her dark hair arranged

131

a la pompadour so that it appeared to be a cloud about her face. In her claret red skirt and white ruffled blouse, she seemed the very picture of a fashionable Gibson girl. While one hand rested lightly on the bannister, the other carried a closed red parasol, lace peeping out from its folds. And on top of that curled dark hair perched an elaborate leghorn hat, draped in white chiffon and decorated with dozens of tiny red and pink flowers.

Beneath the striking bonnet, familiar brown eyes stared back.

"Salome?" Marc asked in a strangled voice.

She nodded, then hurried down the remaining steps. "Well, what do you think?" she asked breathlessly.

He looked closer. She was wearing face powder over her smooth porcelain-like skin, while an expert hand had applied rouge to those once pale cheeks. Her long lashes now seemed even longer beneath ebony mascara, and someone had drawn a perfect rose colored bow over her lips.

"You're wearing makeup!"

"Yes, I am. The ladies spent all day experimenting on me with their paint pots." She pointed her parasol at the three women who stood at the top of the stairs; the feminine trio seemed beside themselves with glee, like girls who had just dressed up their favorite doll.

"Does not she look vonderful?" Dagmar asked in her German accent. "Like fancy New York showgirl, no?"

"And I did her hair," Flora added. "I copied it from a magazine. It's the latest style, according to *Harper's Bazaar*. And with all that hair puffed out, it makes her neck look even longer."

"Like a swan," Boblo said appreciatively.

Marc shot him an irritated look. "Where did you get the clothes?"

Mickey skipped down the steps, her gingham dress swirling about her bare ankles. "The outfit is mine. I gave it to Salome. I mean, I must have been half-witted to buy a red skirt; red doesn't go at all with my hair." She straightened the sateen ribbon on Salome's hat. "And we're taking her shopping tomorrow. She has to do something with the piddling salary you pay her, so why not buy herself a nice new wardrobe? Plus I have loads of clothes she can borrow." She looked approvingly at Salome's petite figure. "After all, we are the smallest women in the show; might as well take advantage of it."

Salome cleared her throat, forcing him to look at her again.

"What do you think?" she repeated softly.

It was as though he had been gazing at a half-finished work of art for weeks, only to be confronted now by the completed portrait, colorful and dazzling. That beauty Salome Hall seemed to always be running from had caught up with her at last. She looked fashionable, feminine, alluring. She looked like anything but a spinsterish schoolteacher.

Yet somehow he missed his little schoolmarm. He had grown accustomed to those pale smooth cheeks, the long brown lashes that seemed soft as a painter's brush. Lord, he'd even grown fond of that ridiculous little straw hat and the dated, prim dresses. Even seeing that dark nut-brown hair pinned up and hidden away left him room to imagine how glorious it would be to loosen such tresses himself.

Now she looked like any other lovely fashionable woman. His stomach turned over. Now she looked like a female who would give even Jane Dupree pause. Lyndon Whittier had once loved the prim, de-

mure Salome enough to propose. What would he do
if he caught a glimpse of his former betrothed looking this enticing?

"You don't like it," Salome whispered. She
sounded crushed.

"No, no, that's not true at all," he said quickly. "You
look ravishing." Marc stepped back and let his gaze
travel slowly up and down her figure. "No one will
ever take you for a little schoolmarm again."

At the top of the stairs, Flora and Dagmar broke
into applause.

Salome smiled with obvious relief. "I'm glad you
like it, Marc. I need to appear attractive." From beneath her hat brim, she mouthed the words, "For
Lyndon."

"Don't worry about that, my dear." Boblo stood
next to Marc, his hands busily adjusting his cravat.
"You look most appealing. Most appealing."

Too appealing, thought Marc. Too damn appealing, by half.

With a pang, he thought of how he'd arranged
their Chicago engagement only hours ago. All done
to simply please her and pay back her kindness in
teaching him how to read and write. Now he regretted his honest and far too noble gesture.

Salome stepped out into the center of the parlor,
twirling several times so that the crimson skirt
swirled about her ankles. The other ladies and Boblo
applauded. She looked happier than he'd ever seen
her. And more beautiful than he'd imagined.

He had no doubt that Lyndon would be torn trying
to decide between the artful blond singer and the
sweet schoolteacher—especially now that she had
turned herself into a dark-haired temptress. And if
this fool Lyndon had any brains at all, he'd ask Salome to marry him once again.

The very idea caused Marc to ball up his fists, as if the fellow were here before him and daring him to fight for her.

Well, why not fight for her? Marc watched as Salome paraded about the lobby, lifting up her skirts so that Boblo could glimpse her garnet red shoes. Now that they'd become so successful this past month, why let this woman leave his act without a struggle?

No faithless lawyer could ever do right by his little schoolteacher. Marc was thinking of her own good, after all. Her own future happiness.

And his.

135

Chapter Eight

Salome felt her hands grow clammy with fear. She darted back around the corner, dropping her parasol. Maybe she was mistaken. After a moment, she peeked about the brick wall of the theater. It was him. The same man who had been standing ominously outside the stage door in the last two cities they'd played in.

How naive to imagine that simply because Marc's contract was invalidated, these con men would be satisfied to leave them alone. Both she and Marc had been foolish to think that everything was all right, just because Chauncey Farrell had never turned up to threaten them again. Yet somehow Chauncey's brutish presence had not unnerved her like the elegant figure of the gentleman waiting patiently by the stage door.

And patient he was. Whether standing in the hot summer sun or pouring rain—his eyes boring into her as she hurried past—all he ever uttered were the words, "My dear Miss Hall, how are you this evening?"

Clearly they were afraid to use obvious lowlifes and hoodlums to threaten them; instead they'd recruited a middle-aged man who wore broadcloth frock coats, silk top hats, and sparkling stick pins in his lapel. He may look like a city gentleman, she thought nervously, but she had no doubt he'd been sent to keep an eye on her and Marc. And to remind them that Marc owed this Baer person half of his earnings.

She heard a jaunty whistling behind her, and it was as if the weight of the world lifted from her hunched shoulders.

"Oh Marc, I'm so glad to see you. I thought you'd be longer at the tobacconist." His eyes widened when she grabbed his arm. "Sorry, I didn't mean to clutch at you like that."

He covered her hand with his own. "Not at all. Always makes a man feel good when a lady lunges at him so desperately."

Although he grinned when he said this, his eyes looked far too serious. Salome pulled her hand away. He had been making too many suggestive remarks ever since she'd taken to wearing rouge and bright colors. Lord help her, it was as if the spell she wanted to work on Lyndon was starting to take effect instead on Marc Cooper. And the very idea made her almost as nervous as that elegant man by the stage door.

"He's here again," she whispered.

Immediately Marc grew as somber as a judge. He stepped around the corner, pushing her farther back into the late afternoon shadows to make certain she remained hidden. "Blast it, if this scoundrel hasn't followed us here from Muncie."

"And don't forget Evansville," Salome hissed. Indeed, the first time she had glimpsed the fellow had been outside the stage door in Evansville during a thunderstorm. Marc had been so busy trying to hurry her into a waiting carriage, he'd never glanced at the man. But Salome remembered thinking how odd that a man in formal evening clothes would stand exposed to the elements. And he'd been staring at her so.

She had instantly recognized him again in Muncie; his neatly trimmed auburn beard and glittering stick pin—diamonds, no doubt—set him apart from the stagehands, managers and performers who normally milled about the back of the theater.

"So Baer has recruited a fancy man to keep tabs on us now." Marc nodded, as if he'd been expecting this for weeks. "I was afraid we'd got let off too easy. It's not like Baer to give in without at least drawing blood."

"Blood?" Salome tugged at his sleeve. "Look, Marc, maybe we'd better go to the police. Indianapolis is a big city, I'm sure they'll know how to deal with Baer *and* the men he hires."

"The police won't do anything. Why should they? Can't arrest a man for hanging around a theater. No, this is something that only I can take care of." He straightened his plaid vest, preparing himself for confrontation. "You wait here. It's time I spoke to our well-dressed shadow."

"No, Marc, don't. He might be dangerous. What if he has a weapon? Wait!"

But the stubborn magician was already striding towards the stage door. Sometimes she wondered why she thought a man who had himself lowered upside down into a water tank would ever behave in a cautious or circumspect manner. Well, if he was going to stir up trouble, she couldn't let him do it alone. She had made him break the contract, so she deserved to share in the unpleasant consequences.

By the time she ran up to the stage door, Marc was shouting, "See here, I won't have you skulking around me or Miss Hall. You go tell that ape you work for that I don't care how many fops or thugs he sends out after me, I'm not paying him another nickel. Do you understand me? Or do I have to shake some sense into you?"

"Marc, please," she said breathlessly. "Let's just go inside. Curtain is in less than two hours."

The elegant fellow seemed unperturbed by Marc's outburst; his slight smile more amused than angry. "I don't know to what you are referring, Mr. Cooper."

"Aha, so how do you know my name is Cooper?"

"And why shouldn't I know the name of the finest magician in the Midwest? As well as the name of his exquisite assistant." He doffed his top hat, revealing even more auburn hair, clipped short and slicked back with sweet-smelling pomade. "Miss Hall, how are you? I trust you are well."

"Don't you bother to threaten Miss Hall."

"He didn't threaten me, Marc," she said in a low voice, trying to pull him away.

"Indeed not." The man bowed, stick pin glittering. "Allow me to introduce myself. Theodore Tierney, owner of Tierney Furniture Manufacturing in Evansville."

"You're a businessman?" Salome let go of Marc's arm. This close up, the gentleman seemed as refined as his dress. Would Baer really hire such a nicely turned out person to do his dirty work?

"Yes, funny business, isn't that right?" Marc's stance was belligerent and defensive. Tierney was several inches taller, and clearly Marc was trying to

139

expand his chest like a bantam rooster about to scrap. "Well, you just tell old Baer that all the fancy stories in the world won't convince me to hand over any more money."

"I do not know what you are referring to, sir." Tierney reached inside his frock coat, and Marc flung his arms backward, shielding Salome.

"Get down! He may have a gun."

"No, no, please." The man pulled out a silver card case and extracted a card. Clearly too bemused by Marc's behavior, he handed it instead to Salome.

Salome scanned the embossed lettering. "It's a business card, Marc. 'Thomas Tierney, Tierney Furniture Manufacturing, First Avenue in Evansville, Indiana.' " She handed it to Marc. "What exactly do you want with us, Mr. Tierney?"

"I want nothing at all to do with Mr. Cooper."

Marc grumbled beside her.

"Then I don't understand—"

He held up a gloved hand, interrupting her. "I want nothing more than the opportunity to gaze each night upon your beauty, Miss Hall."

"Have you lost your mind, mister?" Marc asked.

"You what?" Salome couldn't have been more surprised if the stranger had started to dance on his toes.

"I rarely attend the theater, Miss Hall. But I did that night in Evansville because I glimpsed you walking towards the stage door, and realized you were no doubt an actress of some kind. I had to see you again, to prove that the glorious vision who passed me on the rainy streets of the city was no figment of my imagination. And watching you that night onstage proved to me that feminine perfection does exist." He laid his hand over his heart. "And that perfection wore a red velvet dress and had silky brown hair.

That perfection was you, Miss Hall. And I have not been able to rest but that each night I seek it out again."

Salome looked at him closely. "Have you been drinking, sir?"

Only moonshine liquor could make a man talk like that—especially about her! Marc was staring at the man as if he were a two-headed giraffe. Such flowery talk had struck him speechless.

"Your beauty is enough to make me drunk with pleasure. How can I prove my sincerity?" Tierney placed his hat back on his head, then clapped his hands together in an attitude of prayer.

Salome felt nervous laughter rising up. "Please, sir. This is most unseemly. In another moment I fear you'll be on your knees."

Tierney's face lit up. "If that is what you wish, Miss Hall." He dropped to his knees, oblivious to the dried mud and refuse that littered the alleyway.

"What the devil!" Marc flung his arms out in exasperation.

Salome gasped. She didn't know whether she should be flattered or frightened.

"I pledge myself to your devotion, Miss Hall. It is enough for me to simply gaze upon you as you enter and leave the theater each night. But if you ever decide to take pity on a besotted fool, I will consider myself the most fortunate man in the country. The world, even."

"I've had enough of this." Marc grabbed her arm and steered her towards the door. "Bad enough we got criminals on our trail, now we have lunatics following us, too."

Just before he pushed her into the theater, Salome looked back. Theodore Tierney was still on his knees.

"I adore you, Miss Hall," he shouted before Marc slammed the door shut.

She stood stunned. How disturbing to have a total stranger accost her like that. No matter how well-dressed he was, the man had to be deranged. After all, he'd first laid eyes on her a mere week ago, and had never had a proper conversation with her. So how in the world could he profess to adore her? Yes, he clearly was mad.

Still, he had knelt down before her. Knelt down just as Lyndon had before Jane!

"Are you all right?" Marc asked her. "Don't let this crazy man get you upset. He probably talks to pigeons in the park and thinks he's Napoleon."

"He got down on his knees before me." She heard the wonder in her voice.

"Yeah, I know. I told you he was crazy."

Salome shook her head. "You don't understand."

Marc waited, his expression growing more puzzled by the moment.

"I don't understand what?" he said finally.

"Lyndon is going to come back to me. I hoped and wished for it to be true, but I know it now. I know it for certain." She felt a wave of relief, joy and—strangely enough—trepidation.

"Lyndon is coming back to me."

That's all he needed. Lunatic lovestruck men panting at the stage door for Salome. Bad enough half the men in the touring company had been staring goggle-eyed at her ever since she'd acquired pretty gowns and rouged cheeks. And without a doubt, Lyndon would be just as struck at how his former little duckling had transformed herself into an all-too-glamourous swan.

Marc spread his legs apart, then pushed back his

flowing sleeves to reveal his bare forearms. For the first time, he took note of how muscled his arms were and hoped Salome was paying attention, too. That is, assuming she favored men with muscled arms. At the moment, Salome wasn't even looking at him. Instead, she paraded before the footlights, displaying the handcuffs she was about to place on his wrists.

In the glare of the stage lights, the jewels in her hair sparkled like red stars. Gilding on the lily, he thought. Her hair was thick and lustrous enough not to need fake gemstones woven among its strands. Ever since their performances in Omaha, his little schoolteacher had become quite the glamour girl. Now when she performed, she dispensed with hair pins. Instead, her gleaming straight hair flowed down her back, its ends brushing lightly against her buttocks. He couldn't help but stare at those buttocks now as she stood before him, demonstrating to the audience how strong the handcuffs were.

And she'd been right to destroy that blue costume, cheap duds fit only for cheap women. In her knee-length red velvet dress, she looked like a dangerous lady, a vixen even, but one with real class. A lady with delectable calves, he noted, and a waist he ached to span with his hands.

She turned towards him, gesturing for him to move to the side. What a change from the nervous, awkward performer of only a few weeks ago! She had become so comfortable and assured onstage that half the time, she directed him. With an amused sigh, he turned, allowing the audience to watch as Salome clapped the handcuffs on him. Once he was locked in, he raised his hands high in the air, then yanked his wrists apart vigorously, showing everyone he was truly confined.

Sharon Pisacreta

As the music swelled, Salome walked over to the magic trunk. She had a nice little walk—all ladylike and measured in those red heels of hers. She didn't sashay about the stage as Julia had; instead she moved with control and grace. He'd seen ballerinas with less style.

Lifting up the lid, she tipped the trunk forward to show the audience it was empty, but for a voluminous red satin bag. As she did so, she bent over slightly, revealing a soft swell of breasts beneath the cherry-red bodice. Marc felt himself grow excited. He didn't blame that lunatic businessman for following her around like a crazed lapdog. Salome Hall combined elegance and seductive charm, and only he knew that lovely exterior hid a kind heart and keen intelligence.

She gave him a questioning look. Damn, but he'd missed his cue. Hurrying over, he stepped into the trunk. Salome quickly reached down and grabbed the red satin bag. As she swept the bag up over his head and fastened it closed, he caught a whiff of her perfume. She used to smell like Castile soap; now her fragrance reminded him of a rose garden just after a gentle rain. If truth be told, he preferred it when she smelled fresh-scrubbed and girlish; when they became more intimate, he would try to convince her to leave off using the perfume. He liked it best when Salome smelled like—well, like Salome.

A moment later, he felt her wrapping heavy chains about his torso. He wondered what it would be like to feel Salome herself wrapped about him.

As he knelt down in the trunk, he heard the lid slam shut over him. It took only a second to free his hands from the cuffs, and only a second more to slip out of the chains wrapped about him. The third second saw him bursting out of the trunk, unencumbered by chains or satin wrappings. The audience suspected the handcuffs and chains were trickery and easily opened, yet the dazzling speed of the trick set them to cheering each time.

He stepped out of the trunk and grabbed Salome's hand, seeing to it that she also shared in the applause. *As she will share in my life,* he told himself with sudden conviction. He had no intention of letting Lyndon—or any man—take Salome away from him.

Ever since he saw her waft down the shabby stairway in Omaha, he'd been thinking of how best to charm her away from that lying oaf, Lyndon Whittier. He couldn't be obvious or ham-fisted; it wouldn't help his cause if she resented him or thought he was bullying her. No, what he had to do was make her realize that she was as attracted to him as he was to her. He only hoped she was.

Well, he'd been giving this some thought, and he had come up with a plan for slowly drawing her toward him. He looked over and shot her a victorious grin. Somewhat puzzled, she smiled back as they both bowed again.

Until now, he had been the perfect gentleman, the consummate professional. Starting tomorrow, he would begin to work some real magic on Salome Hall.

"But I don't want to shoot you." Salome backed away from the rifle he held out to her.

"It's all part of the trick." Marc forced the gun into her hands. "You won't really shoot me. Look, I'll explain it again."

He sat her down on the magic trunk. "Now, first I hand the rifle to you. You act like it's heavy, show the audience that this is a real gun. Which, of course, it is. Then you give me a brief kiss—

"I what?" she broke in.

"You kiss me."

Salome began tapping her foot. "This doesn't sound like any magic trick I ever saw before. Kissing men, then shooting them."

"It's done simply for dramatic effect. You know, the lovely lady kissing her swain farewell, just in case the trick doesn't work and I end up getting shot."

"But you said I wasn't going to shoot you!"

"You won't. See, I hand you the gun, you kiss me goodbye, and when we kiss, you'll pass the bullet to me."

"Do you mean I'm holding a bullet in my mouth, then opening my mouth to pass it you?" She frowned. "I think I'd rather just shoot you."

"Very funny. Anyway, the audience won't guess I've already got the bullet clenched between my teeth. I'll stand just over there—" he pointed to the mark taped on the stage—"and you'll step to the other side of that glass pane."

Salome got up and inspected the thin pane of glass that Marc had set up on a tall pedestal.

"You aim the rifle at me and fire," he continued. "It will make a terrible blast and shatter the pane."

"But—but I've never shot a gun. I hate to even touch them." She looked at the weapon with distaste before laying it carefully on the stage. "I can't guarantee I'll be able to hit the glass."

"You won't have any bullets. All you have to do is pull the trigger. I'll wire the glass pane to explode as soon as you fire. Everything will seem instantaneous. I'll rear my head back, and then open my mouth wide to show the bullet clenched in my teeth. The audience will go wild. I've seen this done before. Believe me, I wouldn't have paid a hundred dollars for this trick if I wasn't dead certain it would make us famous."

Salome ran her fingers lightly along the edge of the glass pane. She despised guns, and had always been grateful her father had never hunted. Even the sight of a rifle or revolver made her nervous. Now she would have to fire a gun as part of the act.

Even more unnerving, she would be required to kiss Marc.

She glanced up at him. He seemed too eager to win her approval for this trick, as though he had suggested something sexual and dangerous. He *wants* to kiss me, she thought. *He's wanted to kiss me for weeks.*

It wasn't vanity that told her so. The way he looked at her, the possessive way he hovered about whenever Boblo or one of the Hibernian Brothers was trying to make innocent conversation, all pointed to one fact. He was jealous, jealous of men she didn't give a careless thought for. And if he's suddenly jealous of them, what would he do when they met Lyndon in Chicago? She sighed. At one time, all this masculine attention might have flattered her; now, it simply made her uneasy.

She liked Marc, she liked him more than almost any man she'd ever met. They had a nice easy friendship, without pretense or guile. And they were both willing to help each other and keep their secrets. Why had everything changed? Why was Marc trying to seduce her? He had to know it was useless. She only loved one man. And she could never love another.

"Won't you at least try, Salome?" he asked quietly. He suddenly looked uncertain and shy. "Or is it that you just don't want to kiss me?"

147

She doubted if anyone had ever seen the Magnificent Marco this vulnerable. She was being silly and spinsterish. After all, Marc had been kind enough to take her on as his assistant. Because of him, they would appear onstage in Chicago, trailing rapturous reviews in their wake. A thought suddenly occurred to her. If she and Marc did kiss during the act, wouldn't that make Lyndon really sit up and take notice? She knew all too well how potent and male Marc appeared onstage. She couldn't resist grinning. Wait until Lyndon took a gander at the muscular magician in black kissing his former love.

"You'll do it then?" Marc took her smile for assent.

Salome looked down at the rifle, lying lifeless and ominous at her feet. "Where's this famous bullet?" she asked.

He dug it out of his shirt pocket. "Here, place it in your mouth. Mind you don't swallow it."

She looked at the gold-tipped bullet in her hand. "I don't see why we have to rehearse the kiss. Let's practice when I shoot you and the glass breaks. Just warn everyone backstage first that we're about to shoot a gun. I don't want people screaming that I'm trying to kill you out here."

"Everyone's at lunch. Besides, they know we're rehearsing." Indeed, he had chosen just the moment when the theater would be most empty—hours before tonight's performance with no one to interrupt their first kiss.

"Then let's rehearse the gunshot," she insisted. "That's the difficult part."

"On the contrary, the key to the trick is the transfer of the bullet. The transfer must be seamless and natural." He stepped closer to her. "It must appear that you are kissing me farewell. That you are fearful of losing me and never having me stand warm and alive before you again. That you will never feel me embrace you or lower my lips to yours." He moved closer, and his breath ruffled the tendrils of hair that fell about her face.

She put her hand on his chest, keeping him from getting any closer. His heart pounded beneath her fingers, and she wondered at the strength and fury of it. If he kept talking and looking at her like this, she feared he'd mesmerize her—just as he mesmerized audiences in his guise as Marco.

"Fine, Marc. We'll practice the kiss. But only once. I *have* kissed before, and don't believe it requires much rehearsal."

Trying to still her own heart, which had suddenly started racing, Salome slid the bullet into her mouth. It felt cold on her tongue. Best to get this over with.

Leaning forward, she closed her eyes. Marc gently grasped her by the shoulders and pulled her close. His strong full lips pressed against hers. This soft kiss was a lovely sensation—even thrilling—but then she remembered she'd have to open her mouth. How else to pass the bullet to him?

His lips pressed harder, and she fought to open her mouth beneath such insistent pressure. Yet once she had opened to him, the kiss grew even stronger, more demanding. His hold on her shoulders tightened, drawing her so close she feared he'd crush her to his chest. Yet, she made no move to back away, not a single gesture to show she wanted him to stop.

Her mouth opened wider, as his tongue slid in, warm and velvety. She felt him push the bullet to the side of her mouth as his tongue danced about hers. She moaned in protest—at least she thought it was protest—but still she didn't break away. Instead, she opened her mouth wide, molding her mouth to fit his, soft, tender, exquisite.

149

Sharon Pisacreta

It had been so long since she'd been kissed like this. Not since Lyndon held her that misty morning in the cabin, not since Lyndon—

Salome stiffened. What was she doing? She was in love with Lyndon Whittier, had pledged herself to him. How could she claim to love Lyndon while she was opening her mouth wide for another man? Had she become as shameless as the Dupree sisters?

As Marc's kiss grew even more passionate—she could feel his arousal—she broke off the kiss and pushed away. A second later, she was choking for breath.

"What is it?" Marc grabbed her by the shoulders once more.

"I—I swallowed the bullet!" she gasped.

After several moments of pounding on the back, a red-faced, tearful Salome finally admitted that the bullet was now wending its way to her stomach. Marc appeared guilt-stricken.

"I'm so sorry." He sat her back down on the trunk, crouching before her. "We should have rehearsed *passing* the bullet, rather than just the kissing part."

Salome shook her head. "I'm fine now, really. I guess I just got carried away." She stopped, hearing what she'd just said. "I mean, I guess *we* got carried away."

"Yes, we most certainly did." Marc smiled at her. His voice was low and musical, a man who was bent on seduction and charm. He suddenly looked all too smug. Then again, why shouldn't he? She'd darn near choked to death on a bullet and all because she didn't want to stop kissing him.

She straightened up. "It won't happen again, Marc. When we do this onstage, we have to remember to keep the kiss exceedingly brief."

"Of course." He looked like the sleek cat who swallowed the innocent canary.

Only she wasn't all that innocent, was she?

She reached out and grabbed Marc. Before he knew what she was about, she leaned over and kissed him once more. This kiss was fierce, strong and almost violent. She ended the kiss as abruptly as she'd begun it.

Marc looked thunderstruck.

"If you want to kiss me, Marc, then don't invent elaborate subterfuges. Simply kiss me and have done with it." She stood up so suddenly, he fell over backward.

"However, I'm in love with another man. A man I fully intend to marry. It would be best if you didn't forget that again."

Without another word, Salome picked up her skirts and walked offstage. But as she closed the dressing room door behind her, she found she was trembling.

She didn't mind that Marc had forgotten about Lyndon. He was a man, after all, and his growing desire for her was unsettling, but understandable. No, the terrible thing was that *she* had forgotten about Lyndon.

And if she had to exchange kisses with Marc Cooper every night, she was afraid she'd forget herself in earnest.

She sank down in the nearest rickety chair. After working so hard these past two months, she'd finally reached a position of strength. A month or two more, and she'd be Lyndon's bride. She could not let it all fall apart simply because Marc kissed like a seductive devil.

But only she knew how weak she could be. And if she fell again, it would be better indeed if she shot

Sharon Pisacreta

herself with a gold-tipped bullet rather than merely swallowing one.

She had no doubt the pain—and the humiliation—would be less.

Chapter Nine

Thanks to Salome, Marc could now read well enough to understand when he was being threatened.

Although the letter was stained and crumpled, the envelope was on expensive vellum and spotless. He looked at the postmark, which he thought read "Columbus, Ohio," but he couldn't be sure. Of course, he needed only to show it to Salome, and she could verify his suspicions. Yet why bother her with this? After all, she couldn't prevent Baer from threatening them, and it would only upset her.

He tore up the letter and tossed the pieces onto his dressing table. These past two weeks, she'd been skittish enough at every performance; she didn't need anything that would make her more uncomfortable. All his fault, too. At times, he wondered if he'd done the right thing by adding the gun trick to the act. Although the audience loved it, the illusion was a blatant attempt to win her over. And she never again

kissed him as she had that first rehearsal afternoon.
Never since had she let him explore her mouth, or
returned his pressure with her own. When they exchanged the bullet now, she slipped it to him expertly with little more than a sisterly peck on the lips.
He told himself each day that he should end her uneasiness with the trick and replace it with the Bed of
Nails or some other showy illusion. Such action
would be the mark of a gentleman, and a patient one
at that. But he'd gone past being patient or gentle-
manly.

For weeks now, he'd been forced into close quar-
ters with a woman who had grown more and more
appealing to him. Blast, but she was all he thought
about. He dreamed of her at night; heard her soft,
low voice reading to him; felt her moist, full mouth
open to him again and again; imagined he ran his
hands over those small rounded breasts and bent his
head to kiss her naked body, from the hollow of her
neck to below her white, smooth belly.

But it was more than just physical desire. Not
since his mother had he felt so comfortable and safe
with another person. She knew everything important about him, and still she liked and respected him.
Never had she shown the slightest contempt or distaste for his rude background or his ignorance. She
was an angel, he decided, and the only thing that
marred her perfection was her obstinate attachment
to another man.

If only he had real magical powers. He'd mesmerize her in a minute, make her forget a lawyer named
Lyndon had ever drawn breath. He'd bewitch her
into loving him as desperately as she claimed to love
Lyndon.

Marc ran his hands through his hair. Staring at
himself in the mirror, he could only shake his head.

The last thing he had ever expected was to stumble upon a little schoolmarm who would upset his life like this. It was discouraging, prancing about with his chest bared, flexing his muscles like a half-witted circus strong man, and all to make this one female sit up and take notice. Sometimes he felt as idiotic as that fool Tierney, who was still dogging their footsteps from city to city, merely for the chance to glimpse Salome. Wasn't he twice as pathetic as the foppish businessman, trying to win her love and attention with everything from bare flesh to cunning magic tricks?

A soft knock on the door interrupted this latest bout of self-pity.

"Come in," he said. He doubted it was Salome; they'd already had their lesson for the day. In fact, the first show was well underway; he could hear the orchestra playing the music to which Boblo juggled his knives and Indian clubs.

That was another thing that was growing increasingly difficult. As much as he hungered to learn how to read, their afternoon lessons had become a quiet torment. Sitting beside Salome—their knees pressed together—it was all he could do to concentrate on the alphabet and not her elegant little nose or long silky hair.

The fragrance of roses wafted into the room, and Marc stopped smearing greasepaint over his cheeks. "We'll be on soon enough. What are you doing here?"

Salome shut the door behind her. "I'm already dressed."

He shot her a quick look as he put the finishing touches on his own makeup. As she sat beside him on a scarred wooden chair, he could see she was in full costume, even to the red jewels in her hair and the elaborate makeup she now wore on her face.

155

He'd grown to hate all that paint covering her up onstage; it made her look foreign and artificial, like a glamorous stranger.

"I just spoke to Epstein."

Epstein was the owner of the theater here in Columbus, Ohio.

"And?"

"He changed the bill tonight. We go on second from last."

Marc swung around, thinking she was joking. But those large kohl-rimmed eyes looked entirely serious. "He's headlining us?"

She nodded, handing over a theater playbill. There in big black letters proclaimed the words: HEADLINING MARCO THE MAGNIFICENT AND SALOME THE FAIR. "And he says he talked to the Orpheum bookers here in the Midwest. From now until Chicago, we're headliners."

Marc grabbed the playbill, his eyes scanning the letters he could finally decipher. He'd waited fifteen years for this moment, fifteen years filled with carnivals, dime museums and greedy managers and agents, but now at last, he had moved up. And he had no doubt that Salome's clever and beautiful presence onstage had been instrumental. These past two months, she'd added class to their act, real style and polish.

"And look what Epstein showed me." She held up a newspaper, pointing to an article on the front page. "The Chicago papers must have picked up some of those reviews we got in Nebraska and Iowa, and ran this. They're calling your water tank trick the greatest illusion ever seen onstage. It even describes our gun trick and the Zigzag Mystery Box." She colored slightly. "According to the reporter, we're a 'dazzling and romantic duo.'"

He laughed. "Let me see." Of course, he could only pick out a word or two, but it was enough to understand that both he and Salome were on the cusp of real fame.

"You know what this means, don't you?" she asked softly.

"Darn right I do. It means our salary will double as soon as I talk to Epstein and the others." He ran his fingers over the printed text, as though it were sumptuous velvet. "It means we now have a real chance at New York, Tony Pastor's even."

"That too, but it also means that Lyndon and Jane can't help but hear about us now."

He looked up at her. Beneath the rouge and face powder, he glimpsed excitement. Damn, but Lyndon Whittier *would* catch wind of this, especially since he now was moving in theatrical circles as Jane's manager. "Yeah, I suppose they will."

She pointed to the paper. "And they call us 'romantic.' Even though it's not true, it will make Lyndon jealous. Especially since they actually call me beautiful, although of course, that's absurd. Here, let me read the whole article to you."

As she read the words in a low-pitched, excited voice, he felt his own excitement dim. Yes, the article was enthusiastic and flattering. But damn, if it didn't also paint a seductive picture of his assistant Salome Hall.

"It's wonderful, isn't it?" she asked when she was done. "If we'd written the article ourselves, it couldn't be more complimentary. Lyndon will be dying to see me again. I know it."

He nodded, turning back to the mirror. Sometimes he thought he'd grow mad hearing about her stupid devotion to Lyndon Whittier. He could barely stop himself from taking her by the shoulders and shaking some sense into her.

"I'm sure he's read glowing notices before." He went back to smearing on his greasepaint. "You forget that he's traveling with one of the most popular female singers in the country. Jane gets reviews like that with her morning coffee." He was being cruel now, but he couldn't help himself.

"That's probably true." Her voice grew quieter. "But he would expect such things for Jane, not me. Why, he doesn't even know that I'm in the theater. Although after he reads this, he will. And he'll be struck dumb, wondering how I ever found the nerve. He'll be eager to see what I look like; the papers call me 'beautiful and exotic.' I wouldn't be surprised if one night he even shows up at a performance, and when he does, he'll be—"

"He's in love with another woman!" Marc met her gaze reflected in the mirror. She looked stunned, hurt. Well, hadn't Lyndon already hurt her a hundredfold, and here she was, preparing to have that bastard hurt her again.

"He's in love with another woman," he repeated. "A woman who's already exotic and beautiful. Why do you think one glimpse of you will send him running to your side?"

She bowed her head. He didn't want to say these hard things, but he was trying to save her. Save her from Lyndon's lies and more heartbreak. He was trying to save her from a lifetime of unhappiness. He was trying to save her for him.

"I realize I can't compare myself to Jane in that way." Her voice was muffled. "She's probably the most beautiful woman I've ever seen."

He swiveled around. "You're a thousand times more beautiful to me. Can't you see that?" He grabbed her by the arms, forcing her to look up at him.

"Salome, I'm not trying to compare you to a woman like Jane Dupree. You're worth a thousand of her. Let Lyndon keep her; she's spoiled and selfish and will make his life a living hell. He deserves her."

She shook her head. "Lyndon deserves to be happy. I know him; you don't. He's a kind, loving, gentle man and he needs a woman who will appreciate those qualities. He needs to be loved, Marc."

"Damn it, he needs to be horsewhipped, not loved!" He couldn't stop himself from cursing in front of her. "He's a bastard! He asked you to marry him, then runs off with another woman. He humiliated you in front of the whole town. Any man who does that can never be trusted again. Never!"

"I don't blame you for thinking so poorly of Lyndon. After all, you know only that he deserted me. What you don't know is how wonderful he was during our years of courtship, and all those years of friendship before."

Marc released her, and sat back. When a woman was this fool in love, nothing could make her see reason. "If he does come back to you, he'll ruin your life. He can never make you happy."

Salome took a deep breath. Obviously, Marc's emotions ran too deep where she was concerned.

"But he's the only man who's ever made me happy. Except for my father." She paused. "I was the youngest of six children, Marc. All girls. There would be no son to pass on the family name or take over Father's law practice. Some men would have resented his daughters and his wife for this, but not Father. I've never known a gentler soul, a more loving man. And I so wanted him to be proud of me. Mother only cared about how pretty we were and how many curls she could tease into our hair. For her, a woman only had value if she married and had a man to admire and protect her. But not Papa. Papa didn't care about such things." She sighed. "I miss him so."

She heard herself revert to her childlike "Papa," but Marc was not the sort of person to think less of her for mourning a parent.

"My sisters all had the pretty curls and the practiced smiles. They were each married before their twentieth birthday. But not me. I wanted to be a lawyer like Papa. I sat beside him in the parlor from the time I was six, reading my books as he went over his papers. He took me to his law office when I was older, and showed me how to prepare briefs and look up legal precedents in his library. We even discussed which law school I should apply to, but Mother put her foot down. No daughter of hers would ever be a lawyer. It was mortification enough that I wasn't pretty and had no gentlemen callers."

He sighed. "But you are pretty, Salome."

She shook her head. "You didn't know me as a girl of sixteen. I was quite the roly-poly."

He stared unbelieving at her now petite frame.

"It's true. I was so unhappy at not being allowed to go to law school—for Papa couldn't bring himself to upset Mother that much—that I simply ate and ate. By the time Lyndon joined Father's practice, I was as round as a bowling ball."

She could still wince at the memory of the fat, unhappy girl she'd been then. Hiding her body in dark colors, baggy blouses. Winding her hair up and hiding it under a multitude of pins, trying to make herself as unobtrusive as possible. But Lyndon had noticed her. Lyndon had seen past her dowdy clothes and shy demeanor and been warm and friendly from the first.

"Lyndon treated me just as Papa had. With respect. He listened to what I had to say, regardless if it was about contract law or the weather. He was interested in my opinions, and he was interested in *me*. What I looked like didn't seem to matter to him, only what I thought and felt."

She had bloomed under Lyndon's affectionate regard. As the years went on, she found herself eating less and strolling by the river more. Gradually, like maple trees shedding their leaves in autumn, she grew more slender with each passing year. And with each passing year, she found herself depending more and more on Lyndon's company and friendship.

"I still regretted not being able to go to law school, but once I became a teacher, I found I had a real gift for it. It helped, too, that most evenings, Lyndon came calling. We'd sit at the kitchen table while I prepared my next day's lessons and he went over his cases. And after Papa died, Lyndon became even more important to me. He was my last link to the world of law. Even if Papa was gone and my own dreams of being a lawyer were dashed, with Lyndon, I still had a place in that world." She sat still a moment, remembering the laughter and conversations of those evenings. "And when Lyndon began courting me, I was happier than I'd ever dreamed."

Marc was watching her with a hooded expression. Now in his full makeup, he looked forbidding, mysterious. And angry.

"We were already such good friends, Marc. The best of friends. Of course, I had loved him from the first moment he walked into Papa's office. It took years before Lyndon began to feel the same way about me. But when he did, it was like stumbling

161

into Paradise. The first time he kissed my hand, I thought my heart would stop dead. And when he kissed me properly one night by the river—" Her voice trailed off. Was it possible she had ever been so young? So willing to think that life would always be that joyous and sweet?

"I love him. Marc. I always have. And he swore that he loved me. He meant it, too. I know him far too well not to realize when he was dissembling."

"Apparently you didn't know him well enough," Marc said in a dangerous voice. "Otherwise you would never have trusted him anywhere near Jane."

She shook her head. "Jane is not the woman for him. I grew up with her. She knows nothing about the law or poetry or painting. And those are the great passions of Lyndon's life. Especially poetry. We read all of Shakespeare aloud to each other in my mother's kitchen, and all of Sir Walter Scott. And Keats."

Marc lifted his eyebrows.

"Oh, I know it must sound boring and silly to you. But to share such beautiful words with someone you love is glorious. I believe he was the only man in Black Horse who had ever read a poem, let alone recited entire volumes of them." She felt a sharp pang as she remembered Lyndon's voice reciting poetry to Jane on that moonlit night in May.

"I don't think I could love a man who didn't also love poetry," she said simply. "It shows he has a tender heart."

Three knocks sounded on the door, making them both jump. The stage manager stuck his head in. "The fellows need help with your water tank."

"I'll be right there." Marc got up, then looked back toward the table as if forgetting something. A moment later, he fastened the gold hoop earring in his right ear.

"Spouting poetry is all very nice, and I'm sure it charms the ladies. But I'd think you'd want a constant heart instead."

She nodded. "I do. Lyndon has just made a terrible mistake. He shouldn't have to pay for it the rest of his life. Neither should I. All I know is that he's the only man to confess he was in love with me. And at the end of a long day teaching, he was the only man who tried to ease the tedium by reciting poetry to me. Both count for a lot."

Marc yanked open the door. The sound of applause and laughter drifted in. "More than loyalty?"

She swallowed hard. Why did the truth often have to be so painful, so humiliating? "I fear so."

Muttering under his breath, Marc stormed out.

Salome sat back, as exhausted as if she'd danced a dozen waltzes. Maybe she shouldn't have told him all that; Marc resented Lyndon, thought only the worst of him. She didn't blame him. Unless he'd known Lyndon for ten years as she had, why should he take into account his otherwise sterling character?

It was just as well she hadn't mentioned the letter. Since Marc hadn't spoken of it, she must have been the only one to receive the threatening note. Maybe Baer figured that Marc still couldn't read. Not that the letter had been signed, but who else could it be but Baer? She reached into her bodice, pulling out the folded slip of paper.

"Accidents happen," it read in big bold letters. "Magic won't save you. Pay up or die."

No matter what Marc said, she was going to the police with this. At least they now had concrete proof that Baer was trying to extort money from them.

She read the note again. "Magic won't save you." That was wrong. So far, magic had saved her from wallowing in lonely self-pity in Black Horse. Magic had saved her from being helpless to lure Lyndon back to her. Magic had given her Marc Cooper's friendship and support, and forced her to look the world head on—while wearing black mesh tights.

If she had anything to say about it, magic would save her love and her life.

Salome hated this trick. No matter how impressed the audience invariably was, just the sight of the seven-foot-tall water tank made her heart leap in her throat. She hated everything: the thick tempered glass; the mahogany and steel frame; the pulleys, clamps and rope. Most of all she hated the gallons of water that were poured into the tank from fire hoses and showy brass tubs.

Whenever the curtain rose to reveal the glass cell, she silently cursed Marc's friendship with a young fellow magician called Erich Weiss. The two men had met last winter in Wisconsin. Late one night, one or both of them had dreamed up this stunt. As far as she knew, Erich—who went by the stage name Houdini—had not yet introduced the water tank trick in his act. Leave it to Marco the Magnificent to jump headfirst into an illusion that was obviously too dangerous.

Salome faced forward. The less time she spent looking at the water tank, the happier she'd be. As expected, the faces turned towards the stage were rapt and excited. One of those faces belonged to Thomas Tierney, who sat in the first row.

In the past three weeks, she'd grown rather fond of the Evansville businessman. He was unfailingly polite, deferential, and had recently taken to sending her gardenias before every performance. A pity he hadn't taken a fancy to some willing woman back home; traipsing around after her was useless. And she hated having to rebuff him every night. If Mickey hadn't just started up with Boblo, she might have tried her hand at matchmaking Tierney with the vivacious acrobat.

Tierney was the only member of the audience staring at Salome, rather than at Marc and the sinister water tank. Not wanting to encourage him, she threw her gaze to the other side of the theater, and felt her uneasiness grow. Somewhere in the back row, she could have sworn she'd caught a glimpse of bushy yellow eyebrows and a familiar black derby. But the lights were shining in her eyes so, she couldn't be sure the man was Chauncey Farrell.

Walking toward the wings, she dared to appear unprofessional and shaded her eyes with one hand. This time, she saw him. The gaslights lining the walls of the theater shone down upon his bulbous nose and thick butter-yellow eyebrows. For one second, their gazes locked. She felt her hands grow cold, even with the footlights blazing with their noxious heat.

If only she could warn Marc, but he was already standing on the tarpaulin spread out on the stage, kicking off his black boots. With one graceful movement, he whipped off his black satin shirt. There were always gasps from the female members of the audience at their first glimpse of that muscled bare torso. As many times as she had seen it, she always felt her eyes widen in appreciation. Except tonight. Tonight, he suddenly looked vulnerable, standing there barefoot, half-naked. Alone.

As rehearsed, three stagehands walked onstage, dressed in oilskin raincoats and Wellington boots.

Salome had to bite her lip to keep from crying out to Marc not to perform the trick tonight. Not with Farrell in the audience, and a threatening note still folded in her boned corset. But she knew Marc wouldn't listen. This had become his favorite illusion, a real showstopper, just as the gun trick was. In fact, Marc alternated closing the show with the Water Tank and the Gun Trick. Their act was becoming so popular that many people were staying for both daily performances, and Marc wanted to give the crowd something different each time.

Although Salome felt uncomfortable kissing Marc when it was time to pass the bullet, at least she had some control over that, and kept her kisses brief and sisterly. But the water tank always bothered her. It seemed cold, monstrous, and deadly. Even when it was drained of its water, she never looked at the tank without feeling chilled and anxious. Tonight, her anxiety had turned into full-blown fear.

She walked over to Marc and took his shirt from him. She leaned over. "Are you certain you want to do this tonight?" she asked as she clapped a pair of handcuffs on his wrists.

While he demonstrated to the crowd that his wrists were truly confined, he shot her a puzzled look. Instead of replying, he lay down on the tarpaulin and raised his legs in the air.

"Be careful," she murmured as she fit his bare feet into a heavy wooden stock that clamped over his ankles like the jaws of a grizzly.

He looked at her as if she were mad. "What's the matter?"

One of the oilskin-clad stagehands attached a steel frame to the wooden stock holding Marc's ankles.

"Chauncey Farrell's in the audience," she whispered.

Ropes dropped down from the flies, and Salome busied herself with hooking them to the rings protruding from the steel frame.

"So what? He can't cause much trouble if he's sitting there in plain view. Now move away. The windlass is ready."

From the wings, a windlass started to crank, slowly lifting Marc upside down into the air. She held her breath during this part of the trick. If the winching ever jerked, the sudden movement would snap Marc's ankles in two.

Five minutes, she kept telling herself as Marc was raised higher and higher. In less than five minutes, the illusion would be completed and Marc would be taking his bows. The show would be over, no harm done, nothing to worry about. As Marc swayed above the open water tank, Salome found herself nervously twisting her velvet skirt in her hands. For the first time, she wished she were the one about to be immersed into the water. Baer and Farrell didn't want money from her; it was Marc who had angered them. It was Marc who was in danger—tonight more than ever.

As Marc was lowered into the water tank, he folded his arms tightly to his body, his long dark hair flowing about him. His body dislodged several gallons, sending water gushing over the sides of the tank and onto the tarpaulin-covered stage. Salome was so anxious, she forgot to move out of the way and got a good soaking. A little water didn't matter. Nothing mattered but that Marc free himself from the tank and stand beside her again.

The three stagehands hurriedly climbed stepladders, making certain to lock the frame into place. Now Marc was totally submerged from head to toe.

167

The burliest stagehand fastened an enormous pad-lock over the lid.

"Hurry," she murmured. "Let's get this over with."

She allowed the audience only a brief second to see Marc submerged upside down, his hands and feet locked into place. Then she wheeled a dark curtain onstage, positioning it before the tank. The curtain covered only the dimensions of the water tank and not an inch more. As she moved away from the curtain, she released the escape latch hidden on the side of the tank. The entire trick took three minutes. Marc could hold his breath three minutes. He'd done it dozens of times, she told herself. Even now, if she pulled away the curtain, she would see that by tripping the escape latch, Marc had already released his feet from the lid. At this moment, he was probably taking the handcuffs off. The remaining time was spent simply to keep the audience in suspense.

Meanwhile, she mustn't forget the audience. Marc would never forgive her if she ruined their closing number.

She began counting down with the audience. Pacing before the tank, her hair dripping from being splashed with water, she counted, "One hundred and fifty, one hundred and forty-nine, one hundred and forty-eight . . ."

This was taking forever. Why couldn't she calm down? She began counting quicker, the audience following her lead. "Five, four, three, two, one!"

Salome grabbed the satin curtain before the tank and yanked. She heard the screams before the curtain hit the ground. One of them was hers.

Marc was still underwater. His hands and feet were free, but he seemed to be struggling with the lid of the tank. Had it jammed? But that was impossible.

168

Magic & Moonlight

The stagehands raced up the stepladders.

"Hurry, he's already been in there three minutes!" she shouted.

Her stomach twisted in knots as they grunted and pulled, cursing, but the lid would not budge.

"He's going to drown! Get him out of there!" She could feel hysteria start to take over, but was helpless to prevent it.

The stage suddenly swarmed with performers, some trying to clamber up the ladders, others trying to break the glass.

"He's turning blue!" someone shouted.

Salome ran to the front of the tank, having to push through a morass of people. Lord in heaven, but Marc *was* turning blue. He saw her, and pointed at the closed lid,

"We can't get it open!" she shouted. "Hold on!"

But he could be unconscious in another minute. Or dead.

She banged her fists against the tank.

Flora grabbed her by the shoulders. "Don't worry, hon. Bill's gone to get the fire axe. That will crack this thing open."

For one second she felt a lessening of the terror that was threatening to paralyze her. Of course, the axe would break him free of the tank. A second more and he would be out, breathing and alive.

"Where's the axe?" a male voice yelled.

Flora turned white.

"What's going on?" Salome cried. "What's he saying?"

"They—they can't find the fire axe."

Salome's knees buckled and she fell to the floor. "He's going to die. He's going to die."

She felt someone lift her to her feet. "Are you all

169

right, Miss Hall?" It was Theodore Tierney, looking pale and stricken.

She clutched at him. "Get Marc out of there, please!"

He nodded. "We just need something heavy to break the glass with. Never fear, Miss Hall. I shall do my best."

He ran off, only to be swallowed up by the mob surrounding the water tank. The audience was yelling and shouting as well.

Marc had stopped struggling with the lid, and was now only floating. It seemed as though he were watching her. Gazing at her among this screaming crowd as though he desired only a last glimpse of her before he died.

She groaned, as the horror of what was happening grew ever more real. Why had she let him go in the tank? Why hadn't she told him how much his friendship meant to her? Why hadn't she given him a proper kiss during that blasted gun trick?

The gun! She screamed again, this time with relief. Fighting her way through the crowd, she ran backstage, yanking open their prop trunk. Fingers trembling, she loaded the gold-tipped bullet into the rifle.

"Get out of the way!" she yelled at the top of her lungs.

People turned to see her waving the rifle. Everyone ran for the sides of the stage.

Marc was pressed to the glass now, his eyes half-closed.

"Don't move, Marc. Please, God in heaven, don't move."

Putting the rifle against her shoulder, she took only a second to aim. She looked for where there was the most clear space of water.

"Don't move!" she cried again, then pulled the trigger.

The gun blast sent everyone yelling once more, as a huge burst of water flooded the stage. The water splashed up to her knees, nearly sending her sprawling.

She flung the rifle down, and waded through the water and broken glass. Marc was lying face down five feet away from her, a rivulet of blood running down one of his bare arms.

Kneeling beside him, she grabbed him by the shoulders and gently turned him over.

"Someone get a doctor!" Flora yelled beside her.

People crowded about them so, Salome feared Marc would lose oxygen a second time. But she couldn't spare breath to warn them off. All that mattered was that she was cradling Marc in her arms, and that he was looking up at her with those dark, beautiful eyes. Nothing mattered. He was alive!

"Marc, are you all right?" She was crying so hard, she could barely get the words out.

He turned and coughed up a mass of water. She held him tightly, afraid to let him go for even a second.

When he was done choking that accursed water out of him, he lay back in her arms, his eyes closed. Someone handed Salome a towel to staunch the cuts made on his arms from the flying glass.

"They've sent for a doctor, Marc," she said soothingly. "Everything is going to be all right."

He opened his eyes, and smiled. That devilish grin finally quieted her own fear. She smiled back at him, her tears falling on his cheek.

He reached up and touched where her teardrop had fallen. "I thought you didn't care for guns," he said in a hoarse voice.

"I don't. But I care about you a lot more."

She brushed back his wet hair. He caught her hand with his own and brought it to his lips.

"I love you, Salome." He kissed her hand again. "I love you."

As though it had cost him a great deal to speak, Marc lay back, closing his eyes once more. Salome continued to press the towel to his many cuts, sobbing with relief—and joy.

Chapter Ten

"So Cooper didn't pay up."

Chauncey cleared his throat before replying. Even beneath the courtyard's potted palm trees, he felt as though his skin would fry off. The air was so moist and warm, the flagstones seemed to glisten in the dappled sunlight. Who in their right mind would live in a swamp during summer? If he weren't so nervous, he'd curse both New Orleans and the infernal heat.

"I'm afraid not, Mr. Baer." He reached for his cup, swigging down the chicory-flavored swill. Only a Southerner would be fool enough to drink hot coffee in the afternoon heat. But then maybe Baer wanted to see him sweat; maybe he had ordered him back to Louisiana to accuse him of failure. And to punish him.

Chauncey set his cup back on the table with a rattle. Maybe there were a couple of lowlifes waiting for him out in the alleyway. Big, violent men on Baer's payroll. Cajuns, probably. Baer was always saying that no one did a job better for him than a Cajun. Like gators, they were. Come up on a man so quiet, the victim wouldn't know he'd been caught until the moment his neck snapped.

Chauncey pulled out his handkerchief and mopped his face, glancing over his shoulder just in case.

Robert Baer leaned back, puffing on a thin cheroot. In his open white shirt and Panama hat, he looked like a prosperous planter or successful entrepreneur. That was how Baer wanted the legitimate world to view him, and no doubt much of New Orleans did. He had his fancy house on Chartres Street decked out in wrought iron balconies, paved courtyards and furniture imported from France. He even boasted a convent-school wife of old Creole lineage to give him some respectability and class. Only Chauncey and Baer knew how fraudulent this French Quarter idyll was. And how precarious.

"I got word from Ohio that the magician nearly died last week." Baer blew a long plume of smoke, watching it waft lazily over the hibiscus flowers. "Seems he couldn't get out of a water tank and almost drowned. That is, until his little assistant put a bullet through the tank and rescued him." He flicked his ashes. "Pity I missed it. Sounds like it was a melodramatic evening."

"Yeah, it was pretty excitin'." Chauncey bunched the wet handkerchief in his hands. "I tell ya, I don't know why Cooper couldn't get that padlock open. I rigged it so he'd only have to take an extra minute to figure out how to trip it. I spent six years in the penitentiary for knowing how to bust open locks, didn't

174

I? I thought that fool woulda figured it out, too. Seems I overestimated him."

Baer continued to stare at him.

"I mean, I know you didn't want him dead, boss. Can't collect any money from a dead guy, right?"

"That's right. The dead won't put money in my pocket. Or yours." Baer's voice sounded as smooth and thick as molasses.

Chauncey rubbed his damp palms together. "Yeah, I know that. Got me worried when I seen how he was just floating in that tank, not knowing how to get out."

Baer fixed his attention on a hummingbird feverishly suspended over a honeysuckle. "What happened to the fire axe?"

Damn, but if this man didn't have people paid to be his eyes and ears in every hellhole in America. "Now, I had nothing to do with that, boss. How was I supposed to know that those lunkheads at the theater up and lost their fire axe? Stupid show people. Don't have the sense of geese."

But Baer only nodded as he watched the hummingbird and smoked his expensive-smelling cheroot. *He knows,* Chauncey thought, *or at least he suspects.* Well, even if Baer brought in a dozen Cajuns, Chauncey wouldn't admit that he had fiddled with the padlock on Cooper's water tank *and* concealed the fire axe. Not that he didn't know what Baer's explicit orders were: scare the magician and his assistant into paying up. Rigging one of his tricks to fail was exactly what Chauncey had done. It wasn't his fault if Cooper wasn't as clever with locks as a good second-story man like himself.

Hiding the fire axe had been Chauncey's own idea. It stuck in his craw to see Cooper thumb his nose at him and Baer. He was out there getting rich and fa-

175

mous with his silly tricks, then he had the gall to refuse to fork over one dime. And he was an arrogant bastard to boot. Making the ladies swoon over his bare chest, strutting about the stage like a bull about to choose his heifer. Scaring him wasn't enough. Just in case Cooper couldn't get the lock open—and Chauncey had ensured it would be devilishly hard for him to do—he wasn't about to see that dumbbell get rescued with one blow of an axe. Who would have imagined his mousy assistant would turn into Annie Oakley and save the day?

Baer finished his cheroot, stubbing it out in a glass saucer. "Seems like an amazing coincidence to me. You fix the lock on his tank the same night that the axe can't be found. Amazing coincidence." His eyes bored into Chauncey with a dark green fire. "I don't believe in coincidence."

"Well, it's the blamed truth, boss, I swear it. Now why would I—"

His air was suddenly cut off. He found himself gasping and choking. When his fingers clawed at his neck, he discovered a thin cord wrapped tightly about it. Kicking out at the table, he knocked it over, cups and French pastries falling to the ground. He could only stare helplessly at Baer as someone strangled him from behind.

Just as the blood threatened to burst out of his bulging eyes, Baer nodded and the pressure ceased. Chauncey fell onto the flagstones, cradling his raw neck and retching.

He lay there a long time, half-conscious, before a strong arm set him back upon his chair. Chauncey dared to glance behind him and saw a tall man standing there. The brown face wore an impassive expression, but beneath the rolled up shirt were muscled arms and massive hands. Damn Cajun thugs, he thought.

Baer stared at him with a cool snakelike gaze, like a diamondback getting ready to strike. "Listen carefully. Keep your excuses and your lies for the suckers of the world. Don't ever try them out on me again. Do you understand?"

His throat burning, Chauncey nodded.

"Marc Cooper is now a headliner," Baer continued. "He's pulling down close to one thousand a week. By the time he gets to Chicago, it could be even more. What good is a dead magician to me? I need him alive and well, I need him to become even more rich and successful. That only adds to my own bank account. Now Marc Cooper stays alive until I know for certain that he can't be made to pay. If that sorry day ever comes, you can slit him open a dozen times over for all I care."

"Yes, boss." His voice sounded as though cut glass had been scraped across his vocal cords.

"I know you don't like Cooper. Neither do I. The whole circuit has heard about how he defied me. I have dozens of pigeons now trying to weasel out of their contracts. Cooper has to be brought into line— quickly. But you're letting your personal feelings get in the way of business. Do that again, and I'll have no further use for you." He flicked a crumb from his spotless white trousers. "It'd be a pity to see you lose it all just because a little tramp chose Cooper over you."

Even with the pain searing his neck, Chauncey had to speak. "Julia has nothing to do with this, boss. I don't care what that hellcat does. She's nothing to me."

Baer held up a warning finger. "No more lies, Mr. Farrell."

Chauncey was all too aware of the Cajun breathing heavily behind him.

"I want my money, and I want the interest owed me, too. You go back up north and get it for me. Convince those two idiots that if Cooper doesn't honor his contract, they'll both disappear for good. And if that doesn't work. . . ." Baer shrugged. "Get rid of the woman first. That should rattle Cooper's welching bones."

Although he nodded meekly, Chauncey Farrell's temper was rising as fast as the August heat. He'd always done what Robert Baer wanted; such blind obedience got him sprung from a Pennsylvania prison, and lined his pockets with cash earned from bribes, blackmail and extortion. He'd worked twelve years for Baer—done everything he'd been asked— but he didn't like being choked and threatened as though he were one of the suckers they were accustomed to shaking down.

He'd go up north and do as he was told. For now. But if Cooper gave him too much grief, then damn Baer and his Cajun thugs. He'd take him down whether Cooper was making more than Rockefeller every week. Money wasn't everything, after all.

Even killers had their pride.

Marc stuck his finger in the center of the cake, swiping a large dollop of frosting. It melted on his tongue, as sweet and heady as pure sugar cane. After codfish baked in seaweed, Marc didn't think anything tasted as fine as birthday cake. Especially his. It meant he'd survived another year, no small feat for a fellow whose father died before he saw thirty years. And whose mother went to her final reward at two and thirty.

He was thirty-one now. If he managed to live two

more years, it would be victory indeed. A week ago, however, he'd almost joined his parents in premature death. Marc looked around the empty dining room, soiled lunch dishes waiting to be cleared away. He grabbed a fork and dug out a huge bite of buttercream cake. Damn, but he'd almost drowned last week. He'd felt his body begin to give up the ghost, floating trapped in that water tank. Everything seemed to slow down—the people yelling and banging on the glass, even his own futile efforts to open the jammed lid of the tank had seemed dreamlike.

He had been dying. And he had felt at peace with it, as though his will has been vanquished before a greater power. He'd been ready to let go. It was less painful to let go, and it gave him some comfort to understand that to drown wasn't the horror he'd always feared. Instead, drowning was a surrender, a shedding, a soft, slow taking away. That night, he had shared something of his father's death, and the knowledge gave him solace.

Yes, he'd been on the brink of surrender, except his gaze kept falling on Salome. Dear girl, running about the stage, eyes wild, hands flailing, apparently yelling for help. Nearly unconscious, he watched helplessly as she grew frantic with fear. She'd acted desperate and grief-stricken. And all for him.

Then there was that spectacular moment when he looked up to see Salome aiming a rifle right at him. Some dim part of his mind realized she was trying to rescue him, not shoot him. And just before the glass shattered, he knew for an absolute certainty that he was in love with her.

"If you eat another piece of that cake, you're going to have trouble fitting into your costume." Salome breezed into the hotel's small dining room. She looked as fresh and happy as he felt. Wearing a crisp yellow shirtwaist and skirt—two golden clips glittering in her hair—she brought all the warmth of summer into the room. "I seem to recall you eating three pieces last night, then two more this morning for breakfast. I guess Mickey was right to order such a large cake."

She sat down across from him, clasping her hands on the table. "I've never seen a man enjoy a birthday party as much as you."

"I love surprises." He shoveled another bite of cake into his mouth. "All magicians do. To be honest, I expected a little celebration today, but not yesterday. Very clever of you and Mickey."

Actually, the circuit's performers had surprised him with a party at midnight. After a late supper, Marc had returned to the hotel, tired from the night's performances and disappointed that he couldn't convince Salome or any of the others to dine with him. He'd been feeling a bit sorry for himself until he walked into the hotel lobby to be greeted by what looked like the entire Orpheum Circuit singing "Happy Birthday," as Salome and Mickey carried in a preposterously large birthday cake.

It had been a wonderful party, filled with laughter, good food, whiskey—even Salome had ventured a sip or two—and gifts. He looked down at the silver pocket watch hanging from his vest.

"So you like the watch?" she asked shyly.

He gazed at her for a long moment. "You know I do."

She looked away, as if embarrassed. "Well, it wasn't doing any good locked away in its case. Father would have wanted you to have it. You've been a good friend to me, Marc. I think it would please him to know that you're wearing his watch now." She gave a nervous laugh. "Maybe it will make up for that saber sword I lost for you."

"Hang my saber swords," he said softly. "You and this watch are worth a dozen trick swords."

She ignored that. "So how does it feel to be thirty-one?"

"Feels wonderful." He finally pushed the cake away. "If it wasn't for you being such a crack shot, I never would have known how wonderful it was to turn thirty-one."

"It was sheer luck that got you here in one piece. For all I know, that bullet barely missed your skull."

"Hardly matters when you're a second away from drowning. It's the thought that counts. Which reminds me." He reached for his linen jacket draped over the chair beside him.

"We should be leaving for the theater soon. Everyone is getting a late start today. Not surprising since the party lasted til near dawn." She looked behind her to make certain no one was in the hallway. "Did the hotel manager really get up on the table and dance the cancan?"

"I think Mr. McCrory doesn't hold his liquor as well as the theater folk he houses." He pulled out a folded piece of paper. "Although I do recall Boblo waltzing past me at some point with a Tiffany lamp shade on his head."

"Poor Boblo. Mickey's upstairs right now nursing him through his hangover." She grinned. "He says his head hurts worse than if he'd dropped an Indian club on it."

"For my next birthday, you make sure to serve him only sarsaparilla."

Salome felt her smile vanish. Not again. Didn't he understand that she wasn't going to be with the circuit—or him—next year? In less than six weeks, they'd be in Chicago. And she had no intention of leaving Chicago except on the arm of Lyndon Whittier. If only Marc wouldn't persist in this mad infatuation. That Evansville businessman Tierney she could dismiss, although she had no idea why he'd fastened on her as an object of desire. But Marc understood that she was only here to win back Lyndon.

She rubbed nervously at the stained tablecloth. Saving his life had only heightened his attachment to her. When Marc proclaimed his love for her right after the rescue, she'd told herself it was gratitude and lack of oxygen that prompted the words. But in the week since, he had repeated his love, confirming it daily with every look, every touch. She sympathized with him. Didn't she know too well what it was like to yearn for someone, to be in love with a person who—however mistakenly—claimed to love another?

"You know I won't be here for your next birthday," she said softly, refusing to look at him. The coffee stain on the cloth suddenly consumed her attention. "But wherever I am, I promise I'll be thinking of you. Of all of you. Boblo, Mickey, Flora. . . ."

Her voice trailed off as he set a piece of paper in front of her.

"What's this?"

"I didn't know how to thank you for saving my life."

She finally met his eyes. He wore an uncertain expression, almost fearful.

"There's no need for thanks, Marc. I care about you. I consider you a great friend."

His eyes darkened.

"I—I wish you didn't believe you were in love with me. It's not true. Really, it isn't. You're just grateful for my getting you out of the water tank. I understand that. And maybe, maybe if I weren't already in love with Lyndon, well, I couldn't say what my feelings might be for you." That wasn't exactly what she wanted to say, but after all this time, Marc was making her tongue-tied. And confused.

"Read it," he said.

With a sigh, she unfolded the heavy vellum. It looked like expensive stationery: ivory-colored and watermarked. She felt her throat close up with tears. The paper trembled in her hand as she ran a finger over the large childlike script.

"You wrote this?" she asked in a whisper.

"Yes, for you. For my teacher." He leaned across the table and gently touched her hand. "For the woman who saved my life—in more ways than one. You said that no man but Lyndon had ever declared his love for you or recited poetry. Well, until now, I've never told a woman I loved her, and I never knew any poetry to recite. I still don't. That's why I wrote my own. I know it's not fancy and it's spelled all wrong, but I mean what it says, Salome. I swear I do. No magic tricks or illusions now."

"Oh, Marc." She could barely get the words out. "This is the most beautiful poem I've ever read."

He clasped her hand. "The poem's a sorry thing. But my inspiration is beauty herself."

The big, childlike letters on the page swam before her eyes. She bit her lip to prevent the tears from spilling over. He was too close. She didn't need to feel his strong hand cover hers, so warm, so protective, so strong and sure. What was she feeling? Grief, perhaps, or regret. For she couldn't love this magician. She'd only known him a couple of months. She had loved Lyndon for ten years, had pledged herself to him, had proven her love in the most serious manner. This wasn't the time to lower her guard just because Marc was sweet and kind and endearing. Lord, she'd never met a man so endearing. All the more surprising given his rakish appearance and scalawag background.

It would be so much easier if he were as piratical and swaggering as he acted onstage. That sort of devilish fellow she might feel a passing attraction for. What female would remain unmoved by that muscular chest, those tightly clad legs? But his sweetness cut her to the quick. His gentleness and honesty sometimes made her doubt herself—and her love for Lyndon.

Her throat burned from the effort of fighting back a sob. Thankfully, footsteps clattered down the stairway behind them.

"What are you two still doing down here?" Flora's voice rang out. "We'd best all get a move on for the theater. Matinee today."

Salome stood up so quickly, she banged the table, spilling the contents of a glass of lemonade. "Let me get my hat," she murmured.

"What's the matter with her?" she heard Flora say as she took the stairs two at a time.

What *is* the matter with me, she asked herself when she reached the landing. Shaken, she sank onto a nearby window seat. So he wrote a poem. Probably the first thing he'd ever written on his own, save for his signature. She felt a teacher's pride in the accomplishment, of course, but she also felt much more.

It's because he almost died. That had to be why her emotions had been raised to a higher level. Seeing him trapped in that tank had nearly paralyzed her with fear. She was just so grateful that he was alive and well that she was confusing it with something deeper, more tender.

184

Outside, the omnibuses and carriages of Cincinnati rumbled by. She let the everyday traffic sounds soothe her, calm her down. After a moment, she dared open the paper again.

> I want too say too you
> I love you moor then gold,
> I want too say its tru
> My hart is yors too holed.
> If evr you com too me
> My joy will be compleet,
> And I will give my lif
> For one werd of love, my sweet."

Salome leaned her head against the window, warm from the afternoon sun. If she lived to be a hundred, she knew she'd always treasure this piece of paper. She'd make sure to lock it away with mementos from her childhood and her first days as a teacher. Her tokens of love from Lyndon. Marc's poem was a gift that was rare and beautiful. And it somehow wiped away all the pain she'd felt when Lyndon knelt before Jane.

Jane may have had a minute or two of public glory with Lyndon declaiming another man's high-flown words. But she wouldn't trade Marc's misspelled verse for a dozen public recitations of Shelley. For this was meant only for her eyes. And her heart.

If she'd only met Marc years ago. Before Lyndon had entered her life and claimed her as no man ever had. She knew that if she could love Marc, she would.

But she couldn't.

The act had grown more cautious since last week's attempt on Marc's life. Salome had no doubt it was

Chauncey's hand that somehow rigged the water tank so it would trap Marc inside. And discovering the fire axe hidden beneath a pile of old backdrops convinced both her and Marc that the act had been sabotaged. At her insistence, the water tank trick had been eliminated from the act, even though the Orpheum front office offered to pay for a new tank.

Walking about the stage, Salome kept a wary eye on the audience and one on Marc. She worried about him, fretted over him during every showy trick. As he had warned, the police weren't much help. Anonymous notes weren't enough to lead to arrest warrants. Besides, the police sergeant said, how did they know the tank hadn't simply gotten stuck on its own?

Beneath all the excuses, however, Salome sensed the law's indifference to the plight of show folk. Just a step up from the circus was how the authorities viewed them. Their problems were unimportant and slightly ridiculous. How many times had a police detective been called in because a man had been nearly murdered in a seven-foot-tall water tank? No, she would simply have to keep her wits about her onstage. Both she and Marc checked and rechecked their props endlessly before each performance.

But every time she glimpsed the cuts still evident on his arms and chest, her throat tightened with fear—and rage. If Chauncey and Baer tried to hurt Marc again, she'd go after them with that rifle herself.

The spotlight played on that weapon now. As Marc explained to the audience what was about to occur, he held up the rifle. She walked over to him as he pulled out the gold-tipped bullet from his pocket. She took the bullet from him, also showing it to the audience. As she brushed back her long hair, she

186

smoothly slipped the bullet into her mouth, with no one in the audience the wiser.

The orchestra softly played the sinuous theme from "Scheherazade." Salome turned to him, her heart beating faster as he came ever closer. She hadn't properly thanked him for writing the poem, although he must have seen it did not leave her unmoved.

The desire and the need on his face as he drew her to him were all too apparent. *I wish I could love you,* she thought. Marc deserved the love and loyalty of a woman, someone who could see past the theatrical makeup, the gold earring, the long hair, the bulging muscles. Marc needed someone who knew his heart, who kept his secrets, who stood by him no matter the danger.

She put her hands on his shoulders. He smelled of tobacco and soap, bay rum and greasepaint. His scent was familiar and intoxicating. As was Marc. Could she let herself forget for one moment that she was on her way to another man? Could she give Marc and herself one unrestrained moment of love and passion?

She wound her arms tightly about his neck. He seemed to feel the urgency of her embrace and bent his head closer. "My little schoolteacher," he whispered.

When his mouth closed over hers, she pressed herself against him until she could feel every muscle of his pressing back. His tongue dipped into her mouth, caressing her, teasing her. She molded her mouth to his, as though his touch was giving her life.

Her own tongue explored his mouth, as he let out a groan. She dimly heard the rifle clatter to the stage. Marc must have dropped the weapon, for now he had both arms tightly wrapped around her. She was

Sharon Pisacreta

barely aware of the orchestra still playing, the mur-
mur of the audience. She could feel only Marc, was
aware of only him. Their embrace grew tighter, and
that one kiss had turned into several, as they sur-
faced briefly to come up for air, then back to kissing
each other again and again.

Only this one time, she promised herself. They
would never kiss like this again. She wouldn't dare.
Her head was bent back as his kiss grew fiercer, more
passionate. His kisses tasted as sweet as warm
honey, and she clutched at his shoulders, bringing
him even closer, as though they could somehow
merge and become one simply through a searing
kiss.

The applause was like a bucket of icy water. Both
of them jumped at the raucous yells and cheers, each
taking a step back.

She peeked over at the commotion, surprised to
see the first few rows on their feet whistling. Several
ladies looked disapproving in the flickering gaslight,
but most of the crowd seemed vastly entertained by
this unexpected display of affection.

Marc grabbed her hand and squeezed it. With a
wink, he gestured to the audience. He bowed low,
and she followed suit. She knew she should feel embarrassed. As they bowed again, laughing, she had
to admit that what she felt instead was exhilaration.

Maybe she had become shameless and vulgar at
last. But looking at Marc's blissful face, she didn't
really care.

Not all of the audience was on its feet cheering. From
the back row, a young woman got up from her seat,
pushing her way into the aisle.

Once there, she turned back for one last angry look
at the smiling pair onstage. Disgraceful exhibition,

disgusting. If she'd been closer to the stage, she would have thrown something. Her shoe perhaps, or her purse. Heaven knows, she wasn't carrying anything valuable anymore, not after all these months of being out of work.

And now this. Betrayed by both Marc and that deceitful little mouse. Only Salome didn't look like a mouse anymore. Not in such a low-cut red dress, with a tight bodice, and showing off her legs in black mesh. Not to mention all that gaudy makeup, and long hair flowing about her shoulders like a riverboat whore.

So this is what she got for trusting a woman. Well, those smiling liars were in for a nasty surprise after the performance.

They'd both be sorry either of them had underestimated Julia Dupree.

Chapter Eleven

Marc felt as though he'd been set on fire. Salome had kissed him tonight. Kissed him with passion before a thousand people, lights blazing for all the world to see; she had done everything but shout her love for him from the stage. No woman had ever given herself to him so openly, so publicly. Even the women he'd taken to his bed had not surrendered to him as she had tonight. He had never felt this excited before, this hopeful. But he had never been in love before. He knew that for a fact. No woman had ever made him so happy—or so vulnerable.

He poured a glass of ice water. Maybe it would quench his thirst and cool him down. He was feverish inside. If the audience hadn't been there hooting and hollering, he would have taken her there on the stage. He knew he would have. No doubt, part of the reaction from the crowd had been from his obvious arousal. Well, he didn't care. What man wouldn't get excited by a brown-haired beauty pressing herself against him, kissing him with so much hunger, so much abandon?

He drained the glass in one gulp. Let her try to deny it now. Maybe they were good friends, but they were far more as well.

"She's mine," he said to his gleeful reflection in the mirror. "She's all mine, and Lyndon Whittier can go to the devil."

Someone knocked on his dressing room door. It was probably Salome come for their reading lessons between shows, although usually it took her longer after a performance to get ready. She must be as eager to be alone with him as he was to be with her.

"One minute," he called out. Marc whipped off his shirt, toweling his sweaty arms and chest. He reached for his robe, then stopped. Why cover himself up now? Maybe this was the time to keep as few clothes on as possible. After all, the door had a lock on it, and they had two hours before the next show. This time he could play teacher. This time, he would show her just what magic he was capable of producing.

"Come in, sweetheart." He opened the door wide. His smile froze as Julia Dupree pushed past him.

"Hey!" He spun around. "What the hell are you doing here?"

Julia gestured to the open door. "I suggest you close the door," she said calmly. "Unless you want half of Cincinnati—and your little 'sweetheart'—to watch us get reacquainted."

Shutting the door, he prayed that by the time Salome came in for his reading lesson, Julia would be long gone. He intended to make sure she was.

"All right, Julia. I don't have much time. Make it quick."

Julia shook her head. "Still the same ol' rude fellow, aren't you, darlin'?" Sitting down on the chair in front of his dressing table, she pulled off her gloves in a leisurely manner, as if he'd asked her to stay for tea and biscuits.

"Don't bother taking off the hat and gloves. We've said all we're ever going to say to each other."

"Oh, I doubt that. After all, we've been apart for months. I'm sure you have a lot to tell me." Her dark blue eyes looked up at him. "Or are you ashamed to let me know you've been playing footsie with your new assistant?"

"It's none of your business what I do, now or in the future. I thought I made it clear back in April, but I see I have to repeat myself. Listen carefully this time. We're finished, Julia. It's over. There's nothing left to be said or done between us."

Instead of replying, Julia leaned back in the chair. Her gaze traveled slowly over his bare arms and chest; her expression was both curious and lewd. "Looking good, Marco honey. Right good. I always did love them muscles of yours. Seems like you been in a fight or something." Her eyes narrowed. "Or are all those cuts on your body from rough love play with that tramp you got working for you?"

Marc yanked her to her feet. The white feathers on her hat brushed against his forehead. "That's enough polite conversation. I want you out of here. Out of this theater and this city. I want you out of my life. You have no call to be coming around acting like you have some claim on me. I'm not your husband, your swain or your bed partner. Not anymore."

She pressed against him. As always, she had drenched herself in honeysuckle fragrance. At one time he'd found it delightful, but now the cloying scent threatened to choke him.

192

"Well, we can fix that soon enough." Her voice became throaty and seductive. "All you got to do is lock that door, and you can show me how much you've missed me."

Her eyes were rimmed in kohl, and this close up he could see the mascara caked on her lashes. Julia had smeared so much powder and rouge on her cheeks, she looked as though she were ready to face the limelights this minute. He knew she was only twenty-three, but the heavy makeup made her look much older, and hard as a waterfront whore.

Before those red-painted lips could claim his, he pushed her away. "Get out, Julia. This is pointless."

"So, we're gonna play hard to get, are we?" She shook her head. "Well, maybe a beanpole schoolmarm has been sneaking into your bed at night, but take a gander at a real woman for a change. Then tell me that you don't miss what Julia knows how to give you."

She lifted her arms as though she had just stepped onstage into the spotlight. As she slowly turned around, Marc sighed. Did she really imagine he was panting for a sight of that corseted waist? Too tight, as usual, which exaggerated the swell of her hips and breasts. Her turquoise blue blouse was decorated with a great bow in front, yet another obvious device to draw attention to her full bosom. The turquoise ruffles lining the hem of her white skirt looked as gaudy as her shiny patent leather pumps, large satin bows flopping over the sides.

She obviously thought she was a great beauty, irresistible to men. And at one time, Marc had been excited by those lush curves, the flashy clothes, the bleached blond hair that looked nearly white in sunlight. Even her crude manners had once amused him. But he'd tired of her garish charm within weeks, and then paid for his weakness for nearly two years. Well, he'd broken with her. It had been unpleasant and upsetting, but by heaven, he wouldn't spend another minute in her presence if he could help it.

As she faced him once more, her smile knowing and sly, his anger faded. Poor girl. Posing there in her cheap bows and ruffles, that painted, hard face suddenly looked pitiful beneath the feathers and plumes of her braided straw hat.

"You're looking well," he said quietly. "And I wish you the best. I hope you've found honest work elsewhere. I'd hate to think you're struggling for money. But coming here after all these months is foolish. Please don't start following around after me, thinking we're getting back together. It won't happen. We've both hurt each other enough. So let's just call it quits. Now if you need a few bucks to get started elsewhere, I'm sure I can—"

"You believe I came here to beg for a few measly dollars?" Julia put her hands on her hips. "Well, ain't we the hoity-toity gent. Do you think 'cause you're headlining now that I don't remember how things used to be? Think again, honey. Don't forget I was with you near two years. Most of that time I was warming your bed, or helping you with your act. You wouldn't be headlining now if I hadn't been here first, telling you how to polish your tricks, giving the men in the audience a real show just so they kept their eyes on me and not on your fool illusions!"

"Okay, lower your voice." Marc glanced over at the pocket watch lying on his dressing table. Any minute, Salome would be knocking on his door. The last thing he wanted was for Julia to have a go at her.

Julia noticed he was looking at the time. "What's the matter? Afraid prissy Miss Hall is gonna come traipsing in here and catch the two of us? Although from what I seen tonight, she ain't so prissy anymore. Why, you got her gussied up like a hansom cab pony. Even has that skinny bosom of hers pushed up for the peanut gallery to ogle."

"Let's leave Salome out of this." Marc didn't want to get angry again. If he did, the two of them would be screeching at each other for all the theater to hear, just like the old days.

" 'Salome,' is it? I'm not surprised you two are on a first-name basis. Especially after that slobbering kissing you both entertained the crowd with tonight. Almost made me puke, Marc, seeing how the two of you done stabbed me in the back!"

"Blast it, Julia, I broke it off clean with you months ago. I'm free to care for any woman I please."

She glared at him, her chest heaving with emotion beneath that voluminous bow. "And Salome is the woman you care for?"

Oh, the hell with it. Might as well give her the whole truth. "I'm in love with her." He no longer cared what effect it had on Julia or anyone else. "I'm in love with her and I want to marry her."

Julia went nearly as white as her hair. "Marry? You want to marry her?" She turned to the dressing table, frantically searching among the clutter. With a cry, she dug out a jar of greasepaint and flung it at his head.

He ducked and it shattered against the door.

"Are you insane, woman?"

"Insane? That's a hoot. You lying bastard! I begged you to marry me—begged you!—and you turned me down flat. Said you weren't the marrying kind. That you'd never met a woman you ever cared to marry."

"And I hadn't." He stared hard at her, meeting her bitter gaze head-on. "Until I met Salome. Blast, I don't mean to hurt you, Julia, but what do you expect me to say? I've never lied to you, and I won't start now."

"Hah! You've done nothing but lie to me from the moment I joined your act. Pretending that you cared, seducing an innocent girl like me—"

"Innocent? You gave me a laundry list of the men you bestowed your charms on long before you met me. Not to mention the fellows you entertained yourself with whenever my back was turned."

Her face took on a sulky expression. "Well, maybe I'm not a dried-up, prissy schoolmarm, but I'm no whore either. Even though that's how you treated me. Leading me on, using me up and then throwing me away. Throwing me away after I pleaded with you to make me an honest woman. And now you tell me you want to marry that deceitful old maid. That schoolmarm tramp!"

"I said to leave Salome out of this." His voice was now cold as ice. A bad sign. The angrier he got, the colder he grew. If she went on like this, he'd start saying things to her that he would rather not have on his conscience.

"Oh, we can't say a bad thing about the little schoolteacher who lied and cheated her way into my job—and my man!" Julia grabbed her gloves, yanking them on so violently, one of her fingers ripped through the worn seam. "I'm sure you think you got yourself a real lady now, don't you? An aging maiden! Well think again, Marco. That one is slyer than even my sister Jane, and she'd double-deal the devil himself. You know, she's only hanging on to you cause she wants to get that lawyer fella back."

"I know all about Lyndon Whittier."

"Oh, I doubt that you do. You know, they were keeping company for almost ten years. That's a long time, Marco boy. Not even a plaster saint remains untouched after ten years of spooning. Course, you already know she ain't as pure as she pretends."

"Shut up. You don't know what you're talking about. Not every woman is like you or your sister."

She pushed past him, but turned to face him once she reached the door. "You idiot! She's only using you to get to Lyndon. You think an educated woman like her—a lawyer's daughter—would marry *you*? She reads books. Thick books, I seen 'em. And she has her sights set on a lawyer just like her old man. Lyndon went to Harvard. Harvard! My daddy tells me that Lyndon plans to go into politics, leastways he did before my sister got her hooks into him. If Salome gets him back, he'll probably be in Washington one day. A senator, my daddy says. Or, at the least, governor of Missouri. You think Salome wants to marry a dumb show performer like you? A man who lives out of a suitcase, who plays with scarves and knives onstage?"

She shot him a vindictive glance. "A man who don't even know how to write his own name. Salome Hall ain't gonna dirty her hands marrying an ignorant fellow like you. You're even dumber than I thought you were if you believe that. Or maybe she don't know you can't read or write. Maybe she don't know you can't even find your way around a city 'cause you can't read the street signs. Can't even order a ham sandwich from a menu, can you? Or read your own contracts. Well, maybe I'll tell her. She's a teacher, after all. She's used to dealing with stupid people."

"Say one more word and I'm going to pick you up and throw you bodily out of the theater."

"Do that, and I'll have the police haul you away before the next show begins. I don't know why I bother with you, Marco. I really don't." She paused. "I guess it's because I love you."

Following on the heels of her bitter outburst, the declaration of love only made him laugh. "Love?"

"Yeah, I love you. And I ain't gonna let you go. I staked my claim on you a long time ago. Don't matter to me what kind of wild oats you been sowing since you sent me away. I'm back now, and I'm staying."

"Good-bye, Julia," The words came out as hard and unfeeling as stone. "I don't want to see you around me or Salome again. Or I'll take matters into my own hands."

"Why, I'm trembling in my li'l ol' shoes now." Julia yanked open the door. "You get rid of that woman tonight, or I will."

Marc cursed aloud as he caught sight of Salome leaving her dressing room across the hallway. She met his gaze and smiled. But her expression turned to one of shock as Julia stormed in her direction.

"Julia, what are you doing here?" Salome asked in a stunned voice.

"Protecting what belongs to me, you whore!" Before Marc could reach the two women, Julia punched Salome smack on the jaw, sending her flying backward.

As Marc hurried over to where Salome lay dazed on the floor, he heard Julia cursing her way out of the theater.

He cradled Salome in his arms, gently caressing her jaw.

She winced. "What did Julia want?" she whispered, obviously in pain.

"She wants to make trouble." He bent down and brushed her forehead with his lips. "That's all the Dupree girls ever want."

*   *   *

She could barely get through the next performance. Her jaw ached where Julia had struck it. Beneath the greasepaint, she knew a bruise was forming. The back of her head hurt where she'd hit the floor. She felt sick inside from guilt or dread—she wasn't sure which. Or maybe her jaw pained her so much that it was making her ill.

Whatever the reason, she walked through their last performance as if hypnotized. Indifferent to the applause or to Marc's gentle looks, she merely went through the motions, praying for the curtain to fall. When it came time to pass the bullet during the gun trick, she gave Marc no more than the briefest kiss. He looked at her with a worried expression, but she didn't bother to reassure him.

She was feeling too low even to reassure herself. What humiliation this day had brought! First, she had totally forgotten herself and kissed Marc as though he were her lover. And she'd done it in front of a theater full of people. That was all her fault. Marc had taken his lead from her; she couldn't blame him for that kiss. She'd played the wanton and kissed him like a shameless hussy.

No, like a whore, she thought, remembering Julia's last words to her. Of all nights for Julia to be out front. How could she blame Julia for thinking she was trying to steal Marc away? She'd behaved badly tonight, worse than she ever had. Punishing herself, she refused to let Flora bathe her face in tincture of arnica, and turned down Marc's invitation to dinner. She wanted to be alone with her throbbing jaw and her guilt. She deserved it.

Marc helped her down from the carriage. "Salome, why won't you come with me?" he asked for the tenth time since leaving the theater. "Albert Stevens wants to discuss our engagement at the Exposition. He's an important promoter here in the Midwest. Don't you want to hear his plans?"

She shook her head. "After everything that's happened tonight, all I want to do is put a cold rag on my face and go to bed."

He cursed under his breath. "I could strangle that woman for hitting you. Are you sure you're all right? Why don't you let me call for a doctor? Your jaw looks awfully bruised."

"No, it's fine. Just a little sore." She pulled her hand away from his almost desperate grip. "I need sleep. And time alone to think."

"Think about what? About us?"

She closed her eyes. The throbbing in her jaw had spread to her temples. By the time she got to her room, she'd be nursing a whale of a headache. "I just need to think. Good night, Marc."

Before he could stop her, she hurried up the steps of the hotel. Once inside, she waited until she heard him climb back in the carriage and drive away. She breathed a sigh of relief. Her nerves were so on edge, and Marc's questions and pleas were only making things worse.

"Room Three Forty-Seven, please," she told the man at the front desk.

When he handed her the key, he leaned over the mahogany counter. "There's a young woman waiting to see you, miss."

Her heart leaped in her throat. She simply was not up for another confrontation with Julia. "Where is she?" She scanned the empty lobby.

The desk clerk gestured to the right. "She's in the smoking room, miss. I tried to tell her that ladies aren't allowed in there, but she didn't pay me any mind. If Mr. McCory was here, I'd have him deal with her. Especially as she looks like the excitable type, if you don't mind my saying. At this hour, the room is empty, so I thought it wouldn't do any harm." He lowered his voice. "She's not the sort of woman the night manager wants hanging around the hotel. If you could manage to keep your conversation as brief as possible, I'd be much obliged."

So would I, she thought nervously as she walked into the smoking room. Two oil lamps were lit on either side of the fireplace, throwing most of the room in shadow. She could barely make out the sporting prints on the wall or the morris chairs by the window. The room seemed as empty as the lobby. Since it was after midnight, she wouldn't be surprised if that were the case. For the first time, she was grateful that they were staying in a decent hotel rather than another rundown boardinghouse. In a boardinghouse, she'd have no privacy, and Julia would be forced to create a scene in front of all and sundry.

"Is anyone here?" she asked softly, as though a loud voice would somehow disturb the aspidistra in the corner or the knickknacks lining the marble mantel.

She took a deep breath, inhaling the aroma of pipe tobacco and cigarettes that permeated the room like a woman drenched in fragrance. "Thank heaven, she's gone," she whispered to herself.

" 'Fraid not," a voice chimed out behind her.

Salome jumped. She peered into the shadows. "Julia?"

Someone was sitting on a settee in the corner.

"I'm here to stay, Sal. Sorry to spoil your fun."

Heart pounding, Salome walked over to an oil lamp. "If we're going to talk, I refuse to do it in the dark." She carried the lamp over to where Julia lay sprawled on the velvet settee.

Sitting on a straight-backed chair across from Julia, Salome placed the lamp on a side table. She turned up the flame as much as possible. "There, that's better."

But when she sat back to face Julia, it wasn't better at all. Or maybe in this light and at this late hour, Julia simply looked unsavory. She had taken her hat and shoes off, and propped up her stockinged feet on the settee. Her stockings were bright turquoise blue and matched her skirt ruffles and blouse. The bow on her blouse had come undone, and her breasts strained against the thin material. Looking even harsher than usual, her hair was coming down from its pins, and her thick makeup had dried and caked over her skin, giving her a brittle appearance. Salome thought she looked just like a confection that had been left in the bakery window too long.

"I warn you, Julia. If you attempt to strike me again, I shall hit you over the head with this lamp." Salome sat ramrod straight, hands clasped, prepared to jump up to defend herself at the slightest movement.

"I see I gave you a nice bruise." Julia took a long drag of her cigarette. "Actually, I'm sorry about that. Marc made me lose my temper. Not that you don't deserve to be hit for your shenanigans, but you're such a little thing. I didn't need to hit you so hard. One tiny shove would have knocked you over."

Salome reached up a hand and stroked her own jaw, as though trying to shield it from another blow. "Well, little or not, I'm not usually so easy to knock over. It's just that I had no warning."

"Well, neither did I." Julia took another long drag of her cigarette, then stubbed it out in the ashtray lying beside her on the settee. "How do you think I felt out there tonight? I come all this way to see you and Marc, only to find the two of you going at it like a pair of dogs in heat."

Salome bit her lip. "I know it must look awful. I mean, the way I kissed him tonight was hardly proper."

"Don't you take all the blame. Marc was doing his share of the kissing as well. Course, I expected Marc to slip up now and then. He's just a man, ain't he, and men are weak-minded fools. Can be talked into anything, as long as it's a willing female who's doing the talking. The one I'm really disappointed in is you."

Salome groaned aloud. "I feel terrible about all this."

" 'Course, I shoulda known better than to trust any woman around Marc." Julia yanked off one of her earrings, then proceeded to rub vigorously at her earlobe. "But seeing as how you were so in love with that Lyndon fellow, I thought Marc would be safe with you. Or maybe you forgot that I begged you to watch over him for me? You were supposed to keep away any sashaying females aching to get their hooks into my man. Instead you sank your claws in yourself."

"Nothing has happened between Marc and me. Well, except for that kiss. And it will never happen again. Never. I must have lost my head. You see, Marc wrote a poem for me, and I was so moved by its sentiments that I—"

"Hold on there. Marc *wrote* you a poem?" Julia shook her head. "Girl, you must be sampling his Cutty Sark. Marc did not write you or anyone else a poem. It just ain't possible."

Sharon Pisacreta

"Well, it is. A beautiful poem, the loveliest thing I've ever read."

A pitying smile appeared on her face. "Marc's pulling one of his tricks on you. Getting somebody to write for him and passing it off as his own. That man's too ignorant to write a poem. Or anything else for that matter. So don't use some phony poem as an excuse to steal him away from me."

Salome silently counted to ten. She refused to start a quarrel with Julia tonight. She was too tired, too downhearted. All she wanted was to crawl into bed and shut out the world. "I'm not trying to steal him away. You know that I'm in love with Lyndon. That's why I'm here."

"Marc may believe that story, but don't try to pawn it off on me. Why, look at you. Look at the fancy clothes you're wearing, the girlie way you're fixing your hair. You're not even onstage right now, and you got rouge and powder on. Lip paint, too. What's all this primping for then? Not Lyndon. He's off with Jane right now, he can't appreciate the show you're putting on. No, it's all for Marc Cooper. And don't try to tell me otherwise."

"I'm not going to try to tell you anything. I'm too exhausted to continue this conversation." With a sigh, she got to her feet.

"Well, ain't that a pity then, seeing as how your mama gave me a letter for you."

"Mother wrote me a letter?" Salome sat down again.

"Didn't say that. I said she gave me a letter to give you. Told her I was coming north to visit you and Marc. Asked her if she had any messages she'd like me to pass on."

Salome waited eagerly, fists clenched in her lap. If only her mother had sent one word that showed she

204

understood why Salome was doing all this. Just one kind or understanding word.

Julia dashed her hopes immediately. "But your mama claimed she had nothing to say to you. However she did ask me to pass on a letter. Seems your former beau has gotten round to writing you."

"Lyndon?" Emotion flooded through her. "Lyndon wrote me a letter?"

She nodded. "He sent a note to your mama saying he didn't know the tour schedule and could she pass this letter on to you. And here I am nice enough to play Cupid, not that you appreciate it. You or Marc."

"Well, where is the letter? Give it to me."

"I left the fool thing by mistake back at my hotel. But if you agree to pack your bags and leave, I'll send it right off to the train station after you."

Salome shook her head, cursing herself for being a fool. "Did you really think you'd get me to believe such a foolish lie?"

"It isn't a lie, damn it." Julia sat up. Her sudden movement upset the ashtray, spilling out its butts and ashes onto the carpet. "I forgot the stupid letter. It's sitting big as life on the night table in my hotel room."

Once more Salome got wearily to her feet. "We can argue about this tomorrow. I'm tired."

Julia jumped up as well, eyes flashing. "You won't be here tomorrow."

For the first time, Salome felt a frisson of real fear. Julia was a good four inches taller than her, and far more robust. If Julia chose to attack her now, who would be able to stop her? Salome certainly had no faith in the timorous desk clerk.

"What do you mean?"

"I mean that I want you to pack up and leave. Your adventure in the theater is over, Salome. I been seeing the great notices in the newspapers these past few months. That's why I finally decided to come up here. Marc and me belong together. This is our act, not yours. Now that he's a headliner, it should be me sharing all this applause and money, not you. Or maybe I have to remind you that you wouldn't even be getting all this attention if it wasn't for me. I'm the one who told you to ask Marc for a job. Or maybe your memory is as shaky as what's left of your virtue."

"I *am* grateful for your advice. I don't know what I'd be doing now if I wasn't part of Marc's magic act. But I can't leave yet. We're booked into Chicago in six weeks. I have to stay until then, otherwise all of this has been for nothing."

Julia shook her head. "That won't wash. You wanted to make Lyndon sit up and take notice. Well, these stories about you and Marc have been in all the papers. Lyndon can read just fine. He already knows what you been up to. And if he's interested, he'll come find you. You got no reason to be hanging around here."

"I'm sorry. But I've come too far to give up now. All I need is six more weeks. In six weeks, Marc and I will be performing in the same theater as your sister. Lyndon can't help but be in the audience. I have to stay until then."

Julia walked over to her; in the silent room her taffeta petticoats sounded like thunder.

"I want you gone. Whether you meant to or not, you've come between me and Marc. He'll never give us a chance as long as you're hanging around."

"Six more weeks. That's all I ask."

"No way." This close, Julia stank of honeysuckle, tobacco and sweat. Salome felt a wave of dizziness.

She feared the blow to the jaw was starting to make her seriously ill.

"It's not up to you, Julia. This is Marc's act, after all. And if you ask him, I'm sure he'll insist that I remain with the act until Chicago."

She turned to go, but Julia caught her by the arm. Her long fingernails pinched Salome's flesh through the shirtwaist. "I guess you've forgotten how it feels to love a man and have him stolen away. Or maybe you think I don't feel love the same as you?"

Salome stared into Julia's eyes. She wanted to feel pity for her. After all, she did know what it was like to have the man she loved desert her for another. But she didn't see any love in Julia's eyes, or any tenderness or longing when she spoke of Marc. No matter how Julia protested, Salome didn't believe she really loved him. At least, she didn't love him the way he deserved to be loved.

"Take your hands off me, please," Salome said softly.

Julia let out a long breath. "I see how it is then. You're in love with him yourself, ain't you? Of course you are. Well, don't that beat all."

"You're wrong." But her voice sounded weak and unconvincing. If only she wasn't so tired, she'd protest more.

"Don't do this to me, Sally. I thought we were friends." To Salome's dismay and shock, tears welled up in Julia's eyes. "I love him just the same as you love Lyndon." She choked back a sob.

Salome didn't think she could feel worse, but she did. "I'll be gone in six weeks. I swear it."

She tried to leave, but Julia caught onto her bustle, holding her back. "Please, I'm begging you. Leave him. Give me a chance to win him back." She sobbed aloud. "Damn you, he's mine!"

Salome turned towards her. Her head pounded so, she could barely see the blond woman clutching at her.

Tears streaming down her face, Julia looked down at her. "Promise me you'll go. You're a good woman at heart. I know you won't refuse me. Promise me you'll leave tomorrow."

For one shaky moment, Salome was ready to do just that. She felt a wave of sympathy for her—and pity. Wasn't she being selfish to deny Julia her chance at happiness just so she herself could try to be happy once again with Lyndon?

"I wish you wouldn't carry on so." She fumbled for her handkerchief and gave it to the sobbing woman. "This is most upsetting."

Sniffing loudly, Julia wiped her eyes, leaving large black smudges beneath her lashes. "So you'll go then?" She looked up from the handkerchief, waiting.

The lamp beside them shone brightly, and for a disquieting moment, Julia resembled nothing more than a vixen about to pounce on her prey. Salome suddenly had the unreasonable fear that if she pulled away the handkerchief, Julia might bare her teeth, revealing razor sharp incisors.

The sobbing and tears had ceased completely as Julia now watched her with a knowing expression. "So you'll go?" she repeated.

Salome shook her head, feeling like someone who was fighting to awake from a trance. "I can't leave now. It's too late for that. I'll be gone in six weeks. That should be enough to make you happy."

She put a protective hand over her bustle, forestalling any more attempts to keep her here.

As she walked out of the smoking room, Julia

shouted after her, "I was right about you. You are a whore!"

Cradling her throbbing jaw, Salome kept on walking. Maybe Julia was right.

After all, Julia was right about Salome's tender feelings for Marc. She might not be in love with him, but she couldn't bring herself to leave him at the mercy of such a she-cat. He deserved the love of a better person than Julia, she decided.

And Salome intended to take the next six weeks to ensure that Julia was one woman who would *not* sink her claws into him.

Chapter Twelve

Marc could hear Salome grumbling even before he unlocked the door to her hotel room. "One more day, Salome," he said, setting the vase of flowers atop a walnut dresser. "The doctors said that was quite a nasty blow you took to the head. Three or four days bed rest is the wisest remedy for a concussion."

"It's already been three days."

"And tomorrow makes four, just to be on on the safe side."

"And when has Marco the Magnificent ever played it safe?"

"Since he had an assistant named Salome to worry about."

Marc turned to her. Sitting up beneath a faded quilt, hair flowing loose, her white nightgown demurely tied with a neat bow, she looked like a schoolgirl sent to bed with a cold.

"But think of all the performances I'm missing.

210

You must be trimming the act considerably in my absence."

He shrugged. "I've taken a few things out. Not even Flora can fit into the Zigzag Mystery box. And I don't trust the children anywhere around the sabers." A tightrope-walking family known as The Nardinis had recently joined the show; their arrival had been a godsend for Marc. The five Nardini children had served as able assistants in Salome's absence, and he'd started imagining how delightful it could be if one day he and Salome had children of their own who would be part of the act.

"I'm feeling fine now. There's no reason I can't work tonight. In fact, I don't even have a headache any longer. I'm touched by your solicitude, but there's no reason for me to stay in bed any longer."

"That jaw doesn't look fine to me." Without makeup, the large purple bruise was painfully evident to him. He felt a wave of anger every time he saw it. "And I'm sure that bump on your head still hurts like the dickens."

She made a small face. "Maybe it hurts a little, but not enough to keep me in bed like this."

"One more day." He sat on the edge of the bed, pulling out a pair of handcuffs.

"Not the handcuffs again. Why can't we have a reading lesson instead?"

"Nope. Doctor says to rest those eyes. The reading lessons can wait till next week." He grinned as he locked the silver handcuffs around her slender wrists. "But it doesn't demand any eye strain to slip out of one of these."

For the past three days, Marc had been demonstrating how to escape from a pair of locked handcuffs. But no matter how often he showed her how the feat was accomplished, she couldn't loosen even one link, let alone the entire pair of cuffs.

"You're the magician and escape artist. Not me. I don't understand why I have to learn this trick."

"Because I might want to lock you in a trunk one day and have you spring out in the blink of an eye. I can't be the one doing all the work onstage." He pulled out his pocket watch. "Go."

Frowning, Salome tried to move her fingers enough to trip the release mechanism.

"One minute," Marc announced.

She tried twisting her wrists at a certain angle as Marc had taught her.

"Two minutes."

By the time he announced that three minutes had passed, she was ready to call for a hacksaw and beg to be released.

"Patience, patience," Marc clucked as he snapped them off her. In one smooth motion, he locked his own wrists in the cuffs. His hands turned a certain way and, an instant later, he was free.

"*You* have been practicing with them for half your life," Salome said wryly. "So try not to look quite so smug."

"The secret is remembering not to panic. Even if you have thirty seconds to free yourself, your hands must remain steady, your mind clear and cool. There's no situation a true artist can't escape from."

She raised a skeptical eyebrow. "Even romantic situations?"

Marc gave her a sour look. "All right. That's enough handcuff lessons for today." He slipped them back into the pocket of his sack coat. "For a school-teacher, you make a rotten pupil."

Salome crossed her arms, pouting. "Who are the flowers from? If they're from you, I insist you take them back to the florist. You've already bought me enough to fill a greenhouse."

She gestured to the rest of her room. Every side table, wardrobe and stool had a flower arrangement decorating it. The room smelled like the Cincinnati Botanical Gardens.

"Sorry, but this one is from another admirer." Marc lifted a small card from the spray of yellow roses and white gardenias he had carried in. "I daresay you can guess who."

She took the card from him with a resigned smile. "Poor Mr. Tierney. I would love to know who's running his furniture business back in Evansville while he's chasing around after me."

"What does it say?" Marc kept his tone light, but the elegant gent's presence and gifts always made him jealous.

Salome cleared her throat. " 'My dear Miss Hall, I pray this humble offering will brighten at least one minute of your day. I wait anxiously for your return to the stage where you will brighten the days and nights of your many fans. Your faithful and concerned Teddy.' " She put the small card back into its envelope. "Dear man. I wish he could stumble on a willing chorus girl or two. His steadfast devotion makes me rather nervous."

Marc frowned. "He signs himself 'Teddy'?"

She settled back on the enormous pile of pillows stacked behind her. "At least *my* admirers don't go around punching people in the face."

"That infernal woman. If she ever turns up again, I swear you'll see me cut someone in two for real."

She laughed, the sound soft and sweet. He hadn't heard her laugh in days. He found he'd missed it terribly, as he missed having her beside him onstage. He missed their lessons in his dressing room, the easy conversations over breakfast and their midnight suppers when both of them were still exhilarated from the night's performance.

"I don't think anything about Julia is funny."

Her laughter subsided, but her eyes still looked bright with amusement. "A few days ago, I would have agreed with you. But I've been thinking about the whole matter. We really can't blame Julia for being upset."

"Oh yes we can. I broke off with her months ago, What right does she have to come here now, demanding I take her back?"

"She says she loves you."

"Julia doesn't love anyone but Julia. The only reason she's here is that she's heard the act is so successful. I'm sure it's killing her that I'm a headliner now."

"She was with the act for two years. If you hadn't broken off with her, she'd be sharing all these lovely notices with you, garnering all this attention. Not me. She must feel it's unfair."

"No, what's unfair is the two years I was saddled with her. I tried a dozen times to end things between us. I even offered to buy her off if she would just leave me and the act alone. You're wrong, Salome. It's because of you that I'm headlining now. Half the tricks we do now, I couldn't attempt with Julia. That large bosom of hers gets in the way of too many trick cabinets, for one. And all she was interested in was parading in front of the audience. Got so that there was less magic in the act every night, and more of Julia sashaying in the spotlight." He walked over to the window and pushed it open. Even talking about Julia made his head ache.

"I've done a lot of foolish things in my time." He took a deep breath of morning air. "The worst was starting things up with Julia. I'd have been better off taking a sea monster to my bed."

"She's not that bad, Marc."

He turned towards her. "Are you sure you've known her since childhood?"

"Julia just doesn't think before acting. She's impulsive and thoughtless and it gets her into all sorts of trouble. Back home, she started playing truant when she was just seven years old. By the time she was nine, not even the minister could get her to go back to school. She ran wild after that. No one could control her, and when her sister Jane left to be a singer, she followed after her."

Salome looked at him in a slightly reproving manner. At such times, he could just see her sitting behind a desk, talking to a stubborn pupil. "She's hardly more schooled than you are, Marc. Neither of us should blame her for not warning you about that contract. For all we know, she can barely read and write herself."

He sighed. "You're the dearest woman alive, Salome, but also the worst judge of character. Unless we count Boblo. Last year, he gave a hundred dollars to a man who promised he was going to invest it in a gold mine."

"So?"

"The gold mine was in Michigan; Kalamazoo, to be exact."

She giggled. "At least you can't accuse Boblo of being a pessimist."

"Maybe. But I can certainly accuse Julia of a lot of things—all of them bad."

She was silent for a time. "I need to know this, Marc. Do you have any regrets about breaking things off with her? Does she mean anything at all to you?"

He shot her a sardonic look. "The whole time she

was hanging all over me, she was jumping into the beds of half the men in the Orpheum Circuit. One afternoon, I even caught her with Chauncey Farrell."

Her mouth fell open. "Chauncey?"

He nodded. "She had her skirt hitched up to her waist, grinding against him in the alleyway behind the theater. Just like two gutter rats."

"Then she must have known what sort of contract you were signing. Maybe she's in league with Chauncey and Baer."

"Who knows and who cares anymore? She was nothing but bad news. Cheating on me, stealing any spare cash I had lying around. Treating me like I was a stupid lout with nothing to offer a woman but my muscles." He cursed under his breath. "No, I do not have any tender feelings towards Julia Dupree. Does that satisfy you?"

She seemed to be relieved. "Then it's all for the best that no one has seen or heard from her since the night she hit me."

"Never fear. She's holed up somewhere plotting what to do next. Look, let's not talk any more about Julia. I came in here to amuse you before I have to leave for the theater."

Marc paced about the small room, enjoying the way it smelled of Salome, liking to look at her books stacked neatly on the table, her straw hat lying on the window seat, the skirts peeking out from the half-closed wardrobe. Even more, he liked having her as a captive audience. Knowing that beneath the chaste white nightgown, she worn no corset or stays, no stockings. That if she were willing, all he need do was lift the thin cotton material up, pull it over her arms and head, then stretch out along her slender naked body.

He banged into a little table by the wardrobe, send-

216

ing a perfume atomizer and picture frame toppling. When he righted the picture, he found himself staring into the eyes of a handsome young man.

He turned to Salome. "Is this Lyndon?"

She nodded. "I usually take it out of my suitcase only at night. I'm afraid if I left it out during the day, one of the maids might knock it over and shatter the glass." Her voice faded away. "Or somehow tear the photo."

"I see. And we wouldn't want to harm even a hair of his pretty head, now would we?" Marc couldn't keep the sarcasm out of his voice.

"No, we wouldn't," she said softly.

Before putting the picture back on the table, he held it near the window, letting the sunlight reveal a mass of wavy hair, smooth clean-shaven cheeks, eyes that looked too confident, almost arrogant. He was a good-looking devil, even Marc would give him that. But it was a polished charm, well-oiled like the prosperous men who waited outside stage doors for dancing girls.

This was the sort who thought highly of himself and hardly at all of the woman who had the dubious privilege of hanging on his arm. Marc couldn't let Salome go back to such a popinjay. It would be as wrong as him taking up with Julia once more.

"Maybe when you see him again in Chicago, he won't seem the same to you. Mooning about a photo is one thing, but the real man might be disappointing."

"I doubt it."

He shrugged. "He could have grown a beard or one of those handlebar mustaches. Maybe taken up chewing tobacco or wearing shiny derbies."

"And maybe he's as handsome and impressive as

ever." Her eyes were serious now, a hint of pity evident in their brown depths.

Marc dropped the bantering tone. It hurt too much to continue. "I do wish you'd find someone else to moon over."

"I wish you'd find someone yourself."

"I have." He looked at her so intently, he felt he could burn her with his gaze. God, he wanted her so.

"You need a woman who is unattached, Marc," she said solemnly. "A woman who can give you all her love, all her devotion. A woman who knows her own mind and her own heart."

"Exactly." With each word, he moved closer to the bed. "I need a woman who has a straight little nose and big brown eyes that turn amber in the spotlight. A woman who has hair that's as soft and sweet-smelling as a spring morning. A woman who's generous and kind, honest and loyal. A woman who pokes that elegant nose into a book every chance she gets, but never looks down on those who don't fancy reading books—or can't."

"Marc, please."

He sat on the edge of the bed. She was so close, he need only lean over and take her in his arms. But her sad expression held him off.

"I need a woman with a tiny mole on her left wrist, a woman who loves lemonade and frankfurters, who can't pronounce French words, and laughs at all of my terrible jokes." He took her hand in his and squeezed it. She didn't return the pressure. "I need a woman who loves deeply and is honorable. I need a woman who makes my blood hot just by sitting beside me in a dingy dressing room. A woman who keeps me up at night because I want her so much that I think I'll die if she—"

Salome put her hand over his mouth. "You need a

woman who is not in love with another man."

Frustrated, he tore himself away and stalked back over to the window. "You just think you're in love with him! No woman who kissed me the way you did the other night can be in love with someone else."

"I lost my head that night. You'd given me the poem. I was moved by it." She hesitated. "And you're a very attractive man, Marc. I'd have to be made of marble not to respond. Surely you realize that women can be physically attracted to more than one man in their lives."

"Yes, women like Julia and Jane. Not someone like you."

"I'm more like Julia that you imagine."

"Never! You're nothing like her. You're sweet and honest. And innocent."

"Not as innocent as you believe."

He looked over at her, ready to let his temper fly loose if she were playing games with him. Damn, but he was trying to open his heart to her. "Are you going to tell me that you've a scarlet past like Julia? I won't believe it, little schoolteacher."

She gazed down at the quilt, her fingers plucking at the edge. "I don't know how scarlet my past is," she said quietly. "But I do know it would be enough to scandalize my family." She looked up at him, her eyes even sadder than before. "And maybe you."

He felt sick to his stomach. She wasn't lying now, or pretending for argument's sake. Something had happened in the past, and he suddenly didn't want to know about it.

"I don't understand what you're talking about," he mumbled.

"I told you before that Lyndon was the first man who ever recited poetry to me. And the first man who said he loved me."

"Yes?" His fists clenched at his side.

She took a deep breath. "He was also the first man who—who knew me in that way. Oh, why can't I say it straight out? Lyndon was my lover. He was the first man—the only man—I've ever known intimately. So you see, I'm not so innocent as you believe."

"You were his *mistress?*" He said the word with shock. He'd known countless woman who played loose with their virtue, but he didn't want to think that his angelic Salome was one of them.

"I suppose, although that makes me sound far too sophisticated." Her expression turned soft and dreamy. "It was a misty April morning. Lyndon had taken me to visit one of his former clients: an old bachelor who lived in a cabin by the river. But when we got there, we found a note saying his sister had died, and he'd gone to Joplin for the funeral. We should have left as soon as we saw we were alone together. But then it started raining, and the air smelled so fresh. We stood looking out the window, as the rain fell softly. We were really alone. No one would stumble upon us unawares." Her voice dropped to a whisper. "And I loved him so."

"I see." Marc felt as though he'd been cuckolded. "So you gave yourself to him."

"You needn't say it with so much distaste." Her dreamy demeanor was gone. "After all, I haven't said a harsh word about your carnal activities. And I'm sure Julia wasn't your first conquest."

"That's different."

"Of course it is. You're a man and allowed to roam like a tomcat in season and out. But pity the poor female who dares to act human!"

He squirmed under her accusing gaze. "Okay, okay. So Lyndon and you were lovers. Well, in my book, that only makes him more of a cad."

"He's not a cad. He was always mindful of my reputation. We only lay together once. A week later, Lyndon proposed and we both thought it would be better to wait until after the wedding. If I had conceived before then, my mother would have died of shame."

"I see. He behaved like quite the gent, right up until the moment he ran off with your friend." He had composed his face, hoping none of the disappointment showed in his expression.

"It bothers you that I'm not a virgin, doesn't it?" Salome sighed as she threw back the coverlet. "Men! They swear it doesn't matter, they swear up and down that they'll feel just the same whether a girl gives in or not, but it's not true." She reached for her robe, wrapping it around her. "Look at you. You've lived like a gypsy these past fifteen years. Probably bedded dozens of women and I'd be shocked if you remembered even half their names."

She held up a hand. "Oh, don't bother to protest. And here you are looking positively stricken because I gave myself to the man I love. As though I even knew you then." Salome pushed past him, picking up brush, comb, hairpins. "As soon as I wash up, I'm getting dressed and I'm going to the theater."

"Now wait a minute."

"No, you wait. I feel fine, and I'm tired of lying in that bed all day like a blasted invalid."

He raised his eyebrows. If she was upset enough to curse, she must be very upset with him indeed. "I'm sorry if I made you angry. It's just that I didn't expect that—that you—I mean, that you actually—"

She whirled around on him. "That what? That I'm flesh and blood like everyone else? That I loved a man so desperately, wanted him so badly that I dared give myself to him? Well, here's something else

221

to shock you. I liked it. I enjoyed every scandalous minute lying in his arms. And if he walked through the door this minute, I'd do it again." She tossed her head defiantly, sending that long hair streaming behind her. "I wouldn't even mind if you wanted to watch. So there!"

Marc's mouth was still hanging open when she stormed out of the room.

After a stunned moment, he started chuckling. So Salome was a temptress, after all. Damn, but it bothered him that Lyndon had been the man to take her innocence. He had wanted to be the first; he had wanted to be the only man to undress her, stroke her flesh, sink himself into her. See her find ecstasy and pleasure for the first time.

"You're an arrogant bastard, Cooper," he said aloud.

He could hardly expect innocence of her when he had been around the block more than a few times. Next thing he knew, he'd turn into one of those Bible-thumping hypocrites who wanted their females as pure as spring water, while they experienced more sins of the flesh than the prodigal son. At least now he knew that she wasn't afraid of desire, of physical love. Of men.

He wanted her more than ever.

Her anger had finally cooled. Perhaps it had been fear. She hated to disappoint Marc. She knew he had put her on a very high pedestal. That was a precarious place to perch any woman, especially a woman in love.

Well, even if he was shocked and disappointed— and he had no reason to care this much anyway— she wouldn't apologize for either her admission or her love affair with Lyndon.

Blue jays and sparrows fluttered in the trees overhead. They were walking to the music hall through Fountain Square. The splashing of the great marble fountain was soothing over the horns and traffic of Elm Street.

"I'm sorry if I upset you." Marc leaned closer to her, his straw boater clutched in his hands. "It's none of my business what you did before you met me. The way I see it, before they're pledged to each other, a man and woman can be as wicked as they like."

Salome peeked at him from under her parasol. "But Marc, I don't feel that I did anything wicked."

She paused beneath the rustling leaves of a giant elm. Thirty feet away, an elderly woman sat on a bench feeding the pigeons, while children rolled hoops around and around the fountain. They would not be overheard.

"I felt many things the morning I gave myself to him. A little fear, I'll admit that. But what I mostly felt was joy and wonder. Gratitude, too."

"Gratitude?" Marc frowned. "If Lyndon made you feel grateful for bestowing himself on you, I swear I'm going to punch *him* in the face when I see him in Chicago."

Salome tried not to smile. Trying to reason with men was only a step above dealing with schoolboys fighting in the schoolyard. "No, Lyndon was wonderful to me. But we'd known each other so long. There were times when I was positive that he loved me the way a man should love a woman. He'd say something, smile at me a certain way." She paused, remembering. "Or brush my hair back from my face, his hands so gentle and tender. When he did those things I was convinced that he was in love with me."

With a sigh, she began walking again, her heels making scraping sounds on the pathway. "But then

223

months would go by, and there would be no such touches, no meaningful smiles. Just lovely conversations, rides in the carriage. Evenings spent reading and talking like good friends. At those times, I feared he would never ask me to be his wife. I saw my whole life ahead of me, a woman alone, no house of my own, no children."

"I can't believe Lyndon was the only man to court you. What sort of dolts live in Black Horse anyway? Must be a town filled with deaf, dumb and blind men."

She shook her head. "No, just your regular sort of men: farmers, storekeepers. Good decent men for the most part. One or two even came calling, but I didn't want them to hold my hand, let alone court me seriously. Not one of them made my heart do little flips when I saw them; none of them kept me up at night, dreaming of their touch. And when I was sixteen, Lyndon moved to Black Horse. I knew as soon as I walked into Papa's office and saw him sitting at his desk that I'd met the man who *would* keep me up nights." She kicked at a pebble on the ground. "I didn't give a fig for any man but Lyndon after that. If it meant I'd stay unmarried my whole life, so be it. I'm afraid that once you've seen what you really want, nothing else will satisfy."

Marc took a deep breath beside her. "I know."

The emotion in his voice tugged at her. She curled her hand about his arm, pulling him close. "I value your friendship, Marc. Please believe that. And I admit there are times when I find you overwhelmingly attractive."

He stopped and faced her. His hair was coming loose from the string he had tied it back with. Black strands fell into those dark, dark eyes. Above the collar of his shirt, she could see the scar of one of the many cuts he had sustained the night he almost drowned. His expression looked hurt, vulnerable.

"I know. You find me attractive when I'm striding about onstage, all in black, chest bared like a circus strong man."

She tucked a strand of his hair behind his ear. "No. I did once. I thought you were the most gorgeous man I'd ever seen up there. Just like a pirate."

He gave her the hint of a smile.

"Now I find you most attractive when you're standing beneath the trees, looking like a little boy who's just lost his puppy."

She stroked his head again and he kissed her palm. She didn't know how it happened. Or even who made the first move. But a moment later, his arms were crushing her to him, her arms were laced tightly about his strong neck. And they were kissing.

God help her, she loved his mouth, loved the way it molded itself to hers—strong yet gentle—refusing to let her go until she surrendered something of herself. Lyndon had kissed like an angel; she would never be able to deny that. But Marc kissed her so that it shook her and upset all her previously held notions, her conviction that the path she was on was the right one. When Marc kissed her, she dared to think that she could give herself to another, that another man might make her happier, or set her aflame even more hotly and fiercely than Lyndon had.

When Marc kissed her, she became afraid. Maybe she had pledged herself to the wrong person, had made the most serious commitment a woman could make, giving up her virtue and her honor to a man she was convinced would make her his wife. A man whom she told herself each day would make her happy.

Sharon Pisacreta

The kiss finally ended, but they remained locked in each other's arms.

"Why won't you admit it to me and yourself?" Marc asked in a hoarse voice. "Why won't you admit that it's me you love. Me, not Lyndon."

She was so confused. Maybe the concussion was making her behave like Boblo, flying off every which way. Even worse. Maybe she was in love with two men.

"Marc, I do care about you. And if Lyndon weren't still part of my life, I might even allow myself to love you."

Marc grabbed her by the shoulders, shaking her slightly. His eyes were darker than night. "But he's *not* part of your life. What do I have to do to make you see? He left you for another woman. He hasn't tried to contact you in the four months since. Why do you persist in clinging to this hopeless fantasy? He doesn't love you, Salome. I don't care how many poems he recited in that kitchen back home. I love you. *I* do!"

Her heart ached now, as it had in the weeks after Lyndon had deserted her. So now two men were capable of breaking her heart.

"I can't dismiss ten years that easily. I wish I could. Do you think I would have given myself to him if I hadn't been convinced he was the only man for me? That I hadn't been so sure that he would love me forever, and never leave me?" She heard the tears in her voice, but refused to cry any more. "Don't you understand how much he hurt me when he ran off? How much I hurt still! I can't stop loving him simply because he betrayed me. Lord, I wish that I could. It would be so much easier."

She broke away, stepping over to the tree, and leaning heavily against its gnarled trunk. "I dream about him every night." She gave a sad little laugh. "Of course, I dream about you, too. So where does that leave me?"

He gently touched her shoulder.

"I have unfinished business with Lyndon. That's all I know for certain. Not until I see him once more, hear his voice, feel the touch of his hand—" She closed her eyes. "Until I do all that, I would never know if I was coming to you for the right reasons. Maybe I would be with you only because Lyndon had rejected me and I didn't want to be alone. I'm so hurt and angry, Marc. Maybe part of me would use you to bolster my confidence, use you to make me feel like a desirable woman again. Maybe I would use your love—and your loneliness, too—to reap revenge on the man who jilted me. And you're too fine a person to treat that way. You don't deserve that." She took a deep shaky breath. "Neither of us do."

Marc took her hand. "Come on," he said, tugging her back along the path.

He gave her a few moments to compose herself. "I do love you, Salome. I'll love you whether you stay with me or go back to Lyndon. I'll love you for the rest of my life."

Salome felt something inside her give way. As if her broken heart had made the first tentative steps to being whole again.

She couldn't bring herself to look at him. If she did, she'd be lost. "I think I love you, too."

Thankfully, he only squeezed her hand. And when he began whistling a minute later, she felt light-headed and shaky once more. She was afraid she loved this man very much indeed.

They were too intent on each other to notice him. Chauncey tipped back his bowler hat, squinting in

227

Sharon Pisacreta

the sun after their retreating figures. All wrapped up in each other, kissing like lovers right in the city square.

He rattled the bag of peanuts in his hand, wishing he had a beer to wash them down with. Well, at least his patience had paid off. Salome Hall was now back on her feet and out of her sick bed. She certainly looked hale and hearty, mincing about in her fancy lilac dress and her dainty parasol. Yeah, she looked just fine. No wonder that fool magician couldn't keep his hands off her.

Although for his money, he'd take Cooper's former assistant any day over the skinny schoolteacher. Now Julia Dupree looked like a woman ought to. His contempt for Cooper grew ever greater for having sent her away.

Any man who chose little schoolmarms over a buxom doll like Julia deserved to suffer plenty. And Chauncey was just the fellow to oblige.

He took a last look at Salome and Marc before they disappeared through the doors of the Music Hall across the street. Now all he had to do was wait for the chance to lay his hands on the schoolteacher. Cooper or one of the other performers couldn't always be hanging around her. Sooner or later, he'd catch her alone.

Then Cooper—and Salome Hall—would be in desperate need of some real magic.

228

Chapter Thirteen

Backstage, Salome and Marc were greeted by very worried faces. Even Lorenzo the Tenor looked frightened.

"What's wrong?" Marc asked. "Has someone shot President Cleveland?"

Dagmar rubbed her arms as though she were chilled. Salome looked at her with consternation. As usual, the backstage area was as sweltering as a delta riverbank.

"Has the theater been closed down?"

Even though she had only been on the Circuit a short time, she'd already had the unpleasant experience of arriving in a town only to learn that bankruptcy or a narrow-minded civic group had shut the local theater down. But neither seemed a possibility with Cincinnati's new, impressive music hall.

"You probably should not be walking about, Salome," Dagmar said. "Dat bump on head must still be there."

"Yes, I think Salome should turn right around and get back to the hotel." Boblo stepped forward and grabbed her elbow.

The other performers chimed in with their various reasons for Salome to continue her bedrest. Marc finally had to stick two fingers in his mouth and give a piercing whistle.

"Okay, what's up? C'mon. Salome is not going back to the hotel and I'm not moving until someone tells us what this is all about."

They looked at each other

"We might as well show him," Flora said with a gloomy expression.

Salome felt her stomach turn over. Just how bad could this be?

"Show me what?" Marc asked.

Phil the Comedian stepped forward, his lined face looking crestfallen and slightly embarrassed. "It made the front page," he said, holding out one of Cincinnati's daily newspapers.

Marc grabbed the paper. Dead center was a photo of him and Salome, a publicity still taken of the two of them looking dark and mysterious in full makeup and costumes. He read aloud the caption beneath the photo. "Marco the Magnificent and the . . . Salome."

"What does s-c-a-r-l-e-t mean?" he whispered to her, not recognizing the word directly in front of her name.

"Trouble," she replied, snatching the paper from him.

"The Orpheum managers ain't gonna like this one bit," Mickey muttered.

Salome cleared her throat and began reading,

" 'Famous magician Marco the Magnificent has more tricks up his sleeve than even this reporter imagined. During a stellar engagement here in our fair city, it has come to light that the theatrical Mr. Cooper takes particular delight in demonstrating his sleight of hand with the ladies.' "

"What the devil does that mean?" Marc asked.

"Let me finish. 'Although Mr. Cooper is ably assisted by a young woman known by the stage name Salome the Fair, it seems that Miss Hall is not his first assistant. That dubious honor was bestowed on a lady, who until this past April was not only Mr. Cooper's partner onstage, but offstage as well. It has been verified that this long-suffering lady was married to the magician earlier this year, then abandoned by him.' "

"What!"

Salome could barely continue reading. "Left alone in Missouri with no funds, Mrs. Cooper, nee Miss Julia Dupree, has finally learned of the whereabouts of her husband. She has come penniless and alone to our city, and asks that the law compel Mr. Cooper to honor his responsibilities. Failing that, perhaps the good citizens of this bastion of Midwestern values will make their disapproval known. 'I don't want to be a burden to anyone,' Mrs. Julia Cooper tearfully told this reporter. 'Marc took a fancy to this Salome woman, and left me high and dry. If it was only my broken heart, I'd let him be. But I'm ashamed to say that he left me in the family way and I've nowhere to turn.' "

Salome let the paper fall to the floor. "Julia is going to have a baby?"

Marc looked angrier than she'd ever seen him. "How would I know? And if she is, it sure as hell ain't mine!"

Sharon Pisacreta

"I think I'm going to be sick." Salome pressed a hand against her stomach.

Mickey patted her shoulder. "Julia has that effect on all of us."

"Marc, you aren't really married to her?"

He began pacing in the narrow corridor, kicking at props and ladders. "Are you mad? Of course I never married her, nor got her with child either. I'd as soon marry a toothless prospector panning for gold!"

"But why does the reporter say it's been verified?" She felt unsteady on her feet. Whether the charges were true or not, the article painted a very sordid picture. And she was smack in the middle of it.

Phil capped his brandy flask, neatly shoving it inside his coat pocket. "My dear, this is not one of Cincinnati's finer newspapers. In fact, it's little more than a penny sheet that's handed out to the denizens of the Basin's slums. Look closer and you'll see all four of its pages are devoted to murder, wife beating and sexual peccadilloes. I wouldn't take any of this seriously."

"That's easy for you to say. You're not being portrayed as a husband stealer and scarlet woman." She turned to Marc. "We can't let her get away with this. We must contact the paper and give the true version of this story immediately."

"I wouldn't." Flora picked up the paper from the floor, scanning the front page. "You'll only add fuel to the fire, and that's just what Julia wants. You didn't think she was going to let you get away with just a sore jaw, did you? She wants to get back in the act, and back with Marc, too. Spreading lies about you two is one way to do it."

"I can't let this go unanswered." The very idea chilled her. If one paper ran this story, what was to prevent another, or ten others? "We have to do something. What if this gets back to my family in Black Horse? And what if Lyndon hears of this? Marc!"

He finally stopped pacing. He looked preoccupied, worried, angry. But something in her expression must have alarmed him, because he instantly tried to give her a reassuring smile. "I'll have the theater manager ring up the paper. Tell them to send this fool reporter down here so we can set the record straight. After all, there's no way she could have verified a marriage that never took place. We'll catch her in that lie without even trying very hard, and they'll have to print the truth." He put a finger under her chin, trying to make her smile. He couldn't. "It will be all right. I promise. Only drunken sailors read this trash anyway."

"Are you sure?" She wanted desperately to believe him. Otherwise her reputation and her entire future were in jeopardy.

Before he could answer, Douglas James, the manager of the music hall, came out of his office.

"I want to see you, Marc, and you too, Miss Hall." He chomped on his lit stogie. "Looks like we got a mess of trouble brewing. Paper's only been out a few hours and I've already had some idiot throwing tomatoes at your names on the marquee."

"Oh, no. What a dreadful thing to do."

Marc put his arm around her.

"That's nothing. If I were you two, I'd get ready to face an ugly crowd today. I'm sure there's a mess of lamebrains who are already packing tomatoes to throw at the real thing."

"We can't go on, Marc. We mustn't. It might be dangerous." She swallowed. "And so humiliating."

"Now, don't let Doug here get you upset. One tomato gets tossed on the sidewalk, and he wants to make a federal case out of it." He hugged her to him. "If we don't go out there tonight, it will just confirm the gossip. They'll say we were too ashamed to show our faces, and if that sort of talk gets going, we won't be able to ever go onstage again."

She took a deep breath. "You're right, I'm sorry. It's just that I didn't expect any of this. I've never been the target of vicious gossip. But we have to go on, otherwise Julia and her lies will have won."

"That's my brave little schoolteacher." He kissed her on the cheek.

But she didn't feel brave at all. In fact, she would have preferred being submerged upside down in a seven-foot water tank to going out tonight in front of a disapproving mob.

"It won't be that bad," Marc whispered. "I promise."

She attempted a smile for his benefit. There was no point in protesting. They had to perform onstage tonight; it was inevitable. As inevitable as the fact that the performance would turn into a complete disaster.

Things were worse than she'd feared—and her fears had been considerable. As soon as the curtain rose to reveal her and Marc standing in the spotlight, a muttering swept through the hall.

By the time they had completed the Zigzag Mystery Box trick, a woman yelled "Hussy!" When Salome paraded before the footlights, holding up the handcuffs she was about to place on Marc's wrists, the first few rows erupted in hissing. She wished that theaters made a practice of turning down the house lights. At least she wouldn't be able to see the glowering faces near the stage, nor the people standing up in the aisle, whistling or shaking their fists.

For months now, she had grown accustomed to being onstage. She no longer felt exposed or awkward; surprisingly she now found she enjoyed the experience, enjoyed the applause that swept over the stage like a wave of approval. She enjoyed the rapt attention paid to the climax of each trick—the anticipation palpable, almost sexual. Yes, that was it. She found performing physically thrilling, with its endless risks, the ever-present possibility that a trick would go wrong, or that the audience's attention and interest would wander. And she dearly enjoyed being onstage with Marc. They worked as a team now, each anticipating the other's moods and movements. She was always aware of him watching her. Those dark eyes shone with affection and approval, and she basked in his attention like a bird welcoming the warmth and lengthening days of spring.

But tonight, his affectionate regard was not a comfort.

"You should be ashamed of yourself, girlie!" another female voice rang out.

Salome felt particularly vulnerable. Marc was diligently sawing away at her body, while she lay trapped and contorted in the trick box. She made far too easy a target if any of these hissing fools chose to start slinging tomatoes.

"Don't let them get to you, sweet," Marc whispered as he sawed through the box. "I wouldn't be surprised if Julia was the one out there doing all the yelling."

Salome nodded. If he worried too much about her, he might make a mistake and that could be costly in some of his more risky illusions. Marc finished sawing and, with a bold gesture, pulled the two parts of the box apart.

She turned her face to the audience to give her

customary smile when she saw a large object heading right for her. Letting out a small yell, she tried to
move her head out of the way, but the box had her
in a vise-like grip. Luckily the object only grazed the
top of her head, but a chorus of approving cheers
erupted from the crowd. Marc quickly moved the
two pieces of the box together and released her.

"What was that?" she asked as he helped her out
of the box.

"Cabbage, I think."

She looked behind her to see a head of cabbage
lying by the stack of saber swords, green leaves scattered about the stage.

"You should be ashamed of yourself, young
woman!" someone shouted. "Husband stealer!"

"I'll have no more of these interruptions!" Marc
bellowed, silencing the muttering that was racing
through the crowd like brush fire.

She was grateful that Marc knew how to intimi-
date an audience. As the silence continued, Salome
felt like they were facing a pack of jackals, eager for
the kill.

"If none of you can behave decently, then I'll ring
the curtain down now!" he continued.

For a moment, she thought it was going to work,
that the dark magician had cowed the mob. But then
a woman piped up, "You're a fine one to talk about
decency. Leaving a wife and babe to take up with the
likes of her!"

Salome tried to spot the person who had just
shouted. Marc was right. It did sound like Julia. And
if she was in the audience, she wouldn't let Marc or
anyone else stop her from inciting the crowd.

"She's right!" A male voice chimed in. "Who do
these two think they are?"

Another cabbage went whistling past Marc. It

struck the top cabinet of the Zigzag Mystery box and sent it crashing to the floor.

All Salome had time to say was "Uh oh" before two more cabbages and several tomatoes were flung on-stage. This seemed to release a wellspring of ill will, because suddenly a chorus of shouts and whistles rang out. People hooted insults, while the few rascals who had actually brought bags of vegetables to the hall now began flinging them in earnest.

"Cowards!" Marc shouted just as a tomato hit him smack in the face. Spluttering with rage, he wiped off the dripping fruit, his expression murderous.

Salome ducked and bobbed about the stage, praying that the stage manager would ring the curtain down. But the only people she glimpsed in the wings were Flora, Mickey, and five very excited Nardini children. She was sorely tempted to run offstage, but she couldn't leave Marc out here alone.

"You pigs don't deserve to see my magic tricks!" Marc shouted, shaking his fist. A moment later, a tomato splattered against his trousers.

Salome winced. If she had to, she'd carry him bodily off the stage. The audience had turned into a self-righteous mob, and nothing would stem its stupidity. But as she grabbed his arm, an egg came flying out of the first row and cracked open on her forehead. Wiping away the runny yolk, she heard mocking laughter greet this latest indignity.

"How dare you!" Salome glared in the direction of the laughter. She stooped down to pick up a cabbage, and flung it with all her might.

Her aim was good. The man who had thrown the egg never expected retaliation, so the cabbage hit him soundly on the nose. The next thing she knew, the air was filled with tomatoes, eggs, and lettuce. Some dolt actually flung up a plucked chicken. Her fear was long gone. Now she scrambled about the stage, grabbing anything that hadn't smashed to bits and hurling it right back at the crowd.

At some point, she found herself standing next to Marc, shoulder to shoulder, ducking and weaving, both of them throwing insults and vegetables at the audience.

Despite the anger she felt, she began giggling at the absurdity of it all.

Marc looked over at her as he heaved two tomatoes at the third row. "You find this funny?"

She yelped as a cabbage bounced off her knee. "Yes, I do." With that, she burst into laughter, which made her miss the woman she was aiming a cabbage at.

Marc shook his head. "I think you're better suited to vaudeville than I am."

As her giggling grew even louder, Marc began to chuckle. By the time the curtain was mercifully rung down, they were covered in cabbage leaves, egg yolk and tomato seeds. What the stage manager couldn't understand, however, was why both of them were hysterical with laughter.

As they walked offstage, Flora and Mickey handed them towels.

"You poor things," Mickey said. "It's been years since I seen a crowd turn wild like that."

Flora dabbed at the egg yolk dripping off Salome's bare arms. "My Lorenzo once had tomatoes thrown at him, and all because he cracked his high C singing a Puccini aria. Took him months to get over it. He refuses to sing in Texas now. The place is filled with nothing but tone-deaf cowboys and drunken ranchers."

Salome patted her face dry. "Well, we're not in Texas. So what is Cincinnati's excuse?"

Flora thought for a moment. "Could be a lot of Texans visiting the city right now."

"Okay, okay, we still got a show going on and one more act left." The stage manager tapped Mickey's shoulder. "You all right with closing the show, or do you want me to get Phil and Bill to do another set?"

Mickey flung off her wrapper. Her green costume glittered in the gaslight. "The night I can't close a show by myself is the night I hang up my tights."

"All right, everyone back to their dressing rooms," the manager whispered. "Let's get this show over with and those bunch of animals back on the street again."

Salome breathed a sigh of relief when she heard the scattered applause that greeted Mickey's first somersault.

"I only hope that she doesn't slip on all the vegetation lying about the stage," she said.

Marc walked her to her dressing room. "Mickey's a pro. She started out in the circus when she was just ten. It would take a lot more than a couple of cabbages to rattle that redhead." He reached over and lifted a cabbage leaf from Salome's skirt. "And it looks like you're just as tough to rattle. Where did you get such a fine throwing arm? Every time I looked, you were nailing people right and left with tomatoes."

She grinned. "To my mother's everlasting shame, I spent early childhood with a slingshot in my back pocket, hitting anything that moved. It was the only way I could protect myself from the villainous little boy who lived next door."

"Well, remind me to get you a slingshot. I have a

239

feeling we're going to need it. At least for the rest of our stay in Cincinnati."

Her smile faded. "You don't think this is going to continue? It can't."

He shrugged. "I think it will take a while to burn itself out. But I doubt things will get worse than tonight."

"Wishful thinking there, Marco, boy. Pure wishful thinking." Chauncey Farrell stuck his head around the corner.

"How did you get in here?" Marc looked about the corridor.

"A sawbuck in the right place will get me into the White House, let alone a cheap music hall." He turned his attention on Salome, who stood rigidly in the doorway of her dressing room.

"Enjoyed the show tonight, Miss Hall. Indeed I did. Always did like a good comedy act."

"At least tomatoes and cabbages won't kill a person, Mr. Farrell," she said in a cold voice. "But trapping a man in a water tank will."

Those thick yellow eyebrows furrowed over his watery eyes. "Don't know what you're referring to. Has there been some sort of accident lately?"

"Cut out the performance, Chauncey. We've had enough play-acting for one night. You know you sent us both a note ten days ago warning us to pay up or else." Marc stepped in front of Salome, putting his arm across the open door. "And that night, someone mysteriously jammed the lock on the tank."

Salome pulled his arm down. She wasn't afraid to face Farrell or Baer. Her rage over Marc's near demise was still as hot as ever. "And you hid the fire axe as well, didn't you?"

Chauncey's mocking grin vanished.. "I gave you both your chance. You had your warning. Ain't my fault if you're stupid enough to ignore what any person with half a brain would listen to."

"It's you that's stupid, Chauncey. And Baer. too. I'm not paying. You got that? You've robbed me long enough. And if you think you're going to sabotage my tricks again, you'd better be a lot more clever than you've proven yourself so far."

"We've gone to the police as well," Salome added. "They have the notes in their possession."

"Yeah? Well, the police can't protect you. And neither can this fellow's bragging lies." He wagged his finger at Salome. "At least you got some brains. Too much brains, since it was you that got him out of the contract. But I'll let that go if you talk some sense into him. Me and Baer ain't going away. And you're going to pay the money you owe, or I'm going to take both of you down."

"If I see you again, Chauncey, get ready to fight." Marc pushed the bigger man back so hard that he nearly fell.

Chauncey straightened his plaid jacket. "If I see *you* again," he said hoarsely, "get ready to die." He glared at both of them, then nodded as though he'd come to a decision.

When he finally left however, Salome felt no relief.

"He means it, Marc. What are we going to do?"

To her surprise, he bowed his head, obviously dejected. "To tell you the truth, I don't know."

She fell back against the doorjamb, feeling exhausted and very afraid.

The next four days were the longest Salome could remember since that first desolate week after Lyndon had abandoned her. Unfortunately, they had a two-week run in Cincinnati and, even though the crowds had quieted, there were still catcalls and an

241

occasional rotten apple. The hostility alone was so strong, it sometimes threatened to choke her onstage.

Their last day in Cincinnati found Salome eagerly packing her trunk. The Cleveland-bound train was due to leave at eleven o'clock the next morning, and the departure couldn't come soon enough. She ached to leave not only Cincinnati, but the entire state of Ohio. They'd had nothing but bad fortune since they'd arrived.

Before snapping shut her leather cabinet bag, she ran her fingers over Lyndon's photograph. Despite her blithe assurance to Marc, she wasn't sure what she would do when she was face to face with Lyndon at last. Maybe he would seem changed, callow perhaps, or coldly indifferent. Or maybe he would be contrite, loving, and as sweet and gentle as she remembered. With a sigh, she rewrapped the photograph in the satin damask towel she always carried so as not to scratch the glass frame.

Dagmar breezed into the room, twirling an enormous brown silk umbrella. "Is time to leave for theater, *ja?*"

Salome nodded. "It's a bit early, but I'm all packed, so we may as well go. Besides, Marc wanted me to remind the conductor not to rush the intro to the Flying Scarf trick."

"Marc vill be back for show?" Dagmar asked as they walked down into the hotel lobby.

"He'd better be. I can't very well saw myself in half."

Although both women laughed at the thought, Salome did wish Marc wasn't spending the afternoon buying a new steamer trunk. He traveled with a multitude of trunks, all crammed with expensive props. The lock on one of them had rusted, so he was out trying to secure another. He'd left strict orders, however, that she was not to go wandering about Cincinnati alone. Not with Chauncey Farrell and a vindictive Julia also in the vicinity.

Salome suppressed a grin as she looked up at the statuesque knife thrower. Dagmar was taller than Marc, and probably as strong. If anyone dared threaten her in Dagmar's presence, they would be in for quite a surprise. Few people knew that the sweet-natured performer made a habit of carrying a knife concealed on her person at all times. With her jaw still sore from Julia's blow, Salome wondered if perhaps she herself shouldn't start carrying a weapon as well.

"*Ach,* is not good."

They were strolling across Fountain Square, the music hall in sight. Salome didn't see anything to cause them concern.

"What's wrong?"

Dagmar pointed to a woman sitting on a park bench near the fountain, her back turned to them. "Is Julia, *ja?* Hair like tail of horse."

As they neared the bench, she could indeed recognize the pale yellow hair piled beneath a fancy hat adorned with aigrettes.

"Ve go other vay," Dagmar pointed to a more circuitous route to the nearby music hall.

Salome shook her head. "No, Julia must be here for a reason. She probably wants to talk with me again." The very idea made her irritated, and a bit nervous. "Running away won't stop her. Besides, I'd like to talk with her about that newspaper story."

Dagmar tried to dissuade her, but Salome refused to budge. She was tired of looking over her shoulder for Baer, Chauncey, and now Julia. They were the ones who were cheating, spreading lies, issuing

243

threats. So why was *she* acting like the furtive criminal, bent on escape?

"Go on." She gave Dagmar a gentle shove. "I'll only be a few moments. Besides, the park is a mere fifty yards from the music hall. And in clear view, too. I'll be fine."

Only after a reluctant Dagmar had disappeared among the carriages, carts and omnibuses of Elm Street did Salome walk over to the park bench. She had no doubt that Julia knew she was there.

"See you finally ditched your chaperone," Julia said, without turning around.

Salome dusted the bench lightly with her handkerchief, then sat down, careful to keep her skirt from brushing against Julia's.

"So you've been watching me?"

"I been waiting for you to act like the smart girl I always thought you were and leave. But I guess being around Marc has rubbed off on you. The man ain't exactly got the brains of an educated fellow like Lyndon, does he?"

She swiveled around to face Salome. Julia had not layered so much paint on today, which made her look younger. And the blue serge dress she wore would have seemed demure, if not for the snugness of her Eton jacket that clung to her curves. The delicate material strained perilously at her slightest movement.

"Look, I do not take orders from you, Chauncey Farrell or Robert Baer."

Julia gave her a sour smile. "Bet you jump when Marc gives the orders, though, don't ya? Especially when it's time for bed."

Salome stifled a rude response. What was the use of trying to convince her that she and Marc weren't lovers? Besides, she suspected that Julia would like nothing better than for them to engage in a screaming brawl right in the middle of Cincinnati.

"That was a very entertaining interview you gave the paper the other day."

Julia chuckled.

"I especially liked the part where you claimed to be Marc's wife. And that you were carrying his child."

"Can't prove that I'm not." Her blue eyes sparkled in amusement. "Leastways, you can't prove it for a while. By that time, the ugly stories will have ruined Marc's career. Yours, too."

"I thought you wanted to return to the act. If you destroy Marc's career, then what was all this for?"

Julia's smile faded. "I'm no fool. So I got one of these slimy reporters to print my lies. Had to entertain him privately before he'd do it, if you know what I mean. But it's a waste of my time in the long run. Marc and the Orpheum people get riled up, force the other papers to print their own stories, and that tidies up the mess in one little town. But since you and Marc treat me like dirt, that means I gotta keep doing this every stop on the tour. Might take me three, four months to smear Marc enough to end his ride to the top. Luckily, I don't think you have the stomach to stay around that long and watch it happen. Not if you care for him like I know you do." She poked her in the arm. "Not when you know that the moment you leave, my lies stop and Marc can get back to being a success."

"But I told you that I have no interest in staying with the act once we reach Chicago. That's less than five weeks away."

"I don't believe you."

"I'm a schoolteacher, Julia, not a vaudevillean performer. Do you imagine I'm going to be Marc's assistant for the next twenty years?"

Julia stared at her. That hard gaze was not only bitter and accusing, but shrewd. "I don't think you're going to leave his side willingly until one of you is stone cold dead. Even if your sufferin' mama came up here and begged you to come home, you'd turn up your little nose at her. And all five of your sisters, too. Poor ladies are wondering what you're up to, by the way. They're afraid you're dragging your daddy's name in the mud."

"Please don't start concocting more lies. My mother and sisters know exactly what I'm doing since I write them faithfully every week."

"And how often do they write you back?" Julia looked like a jungle cat about to close in on her prey.

Salome bit her lip. Her family had not responded once to her dozens of letters home.

"My family and my letters are no concern of yours," she said stiffly.

'Well, ain't that a pity then, seeing as how I still got that letter your mama gave me for you."

Salome's heart skipped a beat. "Is this the mythical letter that Lyndon was supposed to have written me? No doubt, you don't have it on your person once again, so I'm simply supposed to take your word for it."

"Not at all." She reached into her drawstring bag and pulled out a letter. "Maybe this will change your mind about chasing after some fool magician."

Salome snatched the letter from her. Thankfully, it was still sealed. Her hands trembled. She needed only a second to verify that the handwriting on the envelope was indeed Lyndon's. Merciful heaven, but he *had* written her. Thoughts in a jumble, she wondered what he had at last sent to her. What did the letter contain? A confession that he was desperately unhappy and wanted her back? Or perhaps he'd finally left off reciting poems in the moonlight to Jane and found the time to pen an apology, complete with explanations, good wishes and polite farewell.

Just the sight of his forceful, elegant handwriting on the envelope sent a wave of memories through her. Ignoring Julia's gloating presence, she lifted the letter closer and sniffed. Beneath Julia's cloying scent, she could still discern the clean, aftershave Lyndon always used. It smelled as welcome as the first lilacs after a dry, cold winter.

"I know my sister," Julia said in a soft voice. "She may be pretty, but she strains a man's nerves something awful. I bet that letter is from a man crying out to be forgiven by his lady love."

Salome stared at the envelope. She felt shaky and disoriented, like a person jolted awake from a deep sleep.

"So maybe you lost your head about Marc," Julia continued in that gentle tone. "I know how them muscles of his can get to a woman. But a man like Lyndon Whittier don't come along every day. That man's special. A gentleman, a smart fellow that's going places." She paused. "And I think now he wants to go to those places with you."

Salome took a deep breath, reminding herself that Lyndon had told her to her face that he loved another woman. Perhaps this letter simply bore a longer explanation.

Julia pushed herself to her feet. "Well, looks like rain."

Salome gazed uncomprehending at the overcast sky.

"Best leave Marc to me," Julia said with a grave expression.

247

Letter or no, Julia was not to be trusted.

"I refuse to leave a friend of mine at the mercy of someone who delights in spreading ugly lies." Salome stuffed Lyndon's letter deep into her skirt pocket. She would not read it in front of Julia. Or anyone else for that matter.

"I'll keep on spreading those lies till you don't have a reputation left. Then see how many letters Lyndon writes to you."

"Good day, Julia," Salome said primly, instinctively knowing that her refusal to argue would only infuriate the young woman more.

"I'll go to every paper between here and Chicago. And mind you look for me in the mezzanine, too. I'll be the woman throwing the rotten tomatoes."

"Yes, Marc and I heard your sweet voice during the vegetable free-for-all the other night. What did you do? Hire a couple of dolts to buy out a greengrocer and join you in your childish games?"

Julia's spiteful expression told her that she'd guessed right. "Maybe next time, we'll be throwing something harder than tomatoes."

"Maybe we'll have you arrested for disrupting the peace."

"And maybe once you read what Lyndon has to say, you'll stop playing the whore with my man and go after your own."

Salome had her mouth open to speak, but Julia had already turned on her heel, marching off toward Elm Street. The wind had picked up, and fat raindrops spattered Salome's face. A gentleman held on tight to his hat as he hurried beneath the trees. After the humid heat, the prospect of a summer thunderstorm seemed welcome.

She lifted her face to the rain, now starting to come down in earnest. So Lyndon had written to her.

She felt a kaleidoscope of things, some sweet and joyous, some troubling and unhappy. She had nearly three hours before the performance. How much better she'd feel if she returned to the hotel, retired to her room, and read the letter in privacy.

Yes, that sounded wise. Especially since a roll of thunder crashed overhead, reminding her that she sat here alone and exposed beneath far too many trees. Lightning flashed in the sky, bringing her to her feet instantly.

"Let me help you out of the storm, miss."

At the sound of that familiar voice, she gasped and turned around. Three men crowded around her, their large frames dwarfing hers.

"We know a place where a woman like yourself can be kept nice, dry and protected." Chauncey wore a smug and chilling smile.

She started to protest, then stopped. The expressions of the men blocking her way told her it was futile.

So did the gun pressed against her back.

Chapter Fourteen

Marc hadn't felt so trapped since he'd found himself drowning in the water tank. For the fifth time, he made the rounds of the theater, running through the lobby, the dressing rooms, the storage closets, even knocking aside music stands in the orchestra pit, but his efforts were in vain. She was gone. Salome had vanished as quickly as he did in his Tip Over Trunk, but this time there was no trap door to explain her disappearance. No hidden lever or sleight of hand.

He raced backstage once more, banging open Dagmar's dressing room door. "Are you sure you didn't see anything suspicious? Think, Dagmar! You say you left her sitting on the park bench with Julia. Did Julia strike her, or try to drag her away?"

Dagmar looked up from pinning on her feathered headdress. Her eyes were as sad and mournful as the sigh she uttered. "*Nein, nein*, I see nothing. Salome and Julia just sit there talking. So I think I go to dressing room for one minute. Ven I come back to look, it is raining like *Katze und hund*. And I see no one. No one is in park now. Just rain and trees." She shook her head. "Just rain and trees."

Marc hurled himself down the corridor once more. Julia was behind this. No one else would have the brass to somehow kidnap Salome in broad daylight. And she was mean enough to do a lot more than just kidnap her.

As he pushed open the backstage door, Doug James, the theater manager, came running after him. "Marc, where do you think you're going? The show's already started."

Oblivious to the rain pelting him in the face, Marc yelled back, "I'm going back to the hotel to see if she's turned up there."

"But you've already been back to the hotel twice, and all over the park, too. Now look, you have to go on. The crowd will set this theater on fire if the headlining act doesn't show. Bad enough that your assistant has hightailed it off, but I can't have you letting me down, too."

"Hang you and the theater! Salome has been kidnapped."

"You don't know that. She just hasn't bothered to show up yet. If you'll get into costume, I'd bet ten poker hands that she's backstage five minutes before you're ready to go on, and with a perfectly good explanation, too."

Marc shook his head in disgust. "Go back to counting your pennies, Doug. I'm not coming back until I find her."

As he ran down the wet alleyway, Doug shouted after him, "If you're not back in time, I'll sue you *and* that assistant!"

Marc uttered a curse that was lost in the fury of

the storm. Even though it was not yet sunset, the sky was dark and roiling. The howling wind and pounding rain reminded him of a New England squall. All that was lacking was the crash of cold surf and scattered lobster pots.

He was drenched before he got halfway through Fountain Square. It reminded him too much of a brutal nor'easter, the same kind of storm that took his father's life at sea. He couldn't bear to think of Salome in danger in such a storm. She must be frightened. Maybe she's already dead, he thought wildly, then pounded his fist into his hand to drive away such a lunatic thought. No, she was alive, she was alive and well and waiting for him to find her. But where was she?

With the storm howling at his back, he struggled to open the doors to the hotel. When he finally did, the wind that whipped through the lobby knocked over two potted palms and sent an elderly woman shrieking as her switch flew off her head.

He left it to the porter to shut the doors behind him. He had no time for apologies or manners. Instead, he sloshed over to the desk clerk. Disapproving guests took care to avoid the water he splashed with each furious step.

"I need to find Miss Hall," he demanded, his fear making him angry at everyone now. "Has she come back to the hotel yet?"

The desk clerk shook his head nervously. "No, sir. She hasn't. But—but there is a young woman in your room."

"What?"

The clerk took several backwards steps, his eyes looking for escape. "She claimed she was your wife, sir, and insisted we let her in your room."

Marc pounded his fist on the counter. "Julia!"

"Were we in error, Mr. Cooper?" the porter asked in alarm.

But Marc was already taking the steps two at a time. He cursed to find his room unlocked, and threw open the door with so much force that it came off one of its hinges.

The blonde lying on his bed sat up with a jolt. "Lord have mercy, what a way to be woken out of a sound sleep. You near scared me to death!"

"You're right about one thing," he said. "If you don't tell me where Salome is, I'll strangle the very life out of you."

Julia had more nerve than any tightrope walker or sword swallower. Instead of being cowed by his obvious rage, she simply propped the pillows behind her back, then neatly straightened her skirt, which had gotten rumpled during her nap.

"I see the storm hasn't let up yet. Why, honey, you're wetter than a toad in Judson's Swamp. You better get out of those dripping clothes or you'll—"

"Where in the hell is Salome?" he shouted at the top of his voice. Out in the hallway, several pairs of footsteps hurried past the open door and down the stairs.

Even Julia paled as he took a step closer to the bed. "How should I know where she is?"

"Dagmar last saw the two of you sitting on a park bench in Fountain Square about three hours ago." He grabbed a towel from the nearby washstand. "And Salome told her she wouldn't be more than a couple minutes. I repeat: where is she?"

He dried off his face, then flung the towel to the floor. "Julia, if you don't tell me where she is in the next two minutes, I'm going to hurt you. I've never raised a hand to any female—and damn few men, too. But you've gone too far this time."

Julia sat up, drawing her knees to her chest protectively. "Now calm down, hon."

"I am calm." It was true. His rage had turned ice cold. His hands were steady and his intention clear. If Julia didn't tell him what he wanted to know, he was prepared to strangle the truth out of her. This she-wolf had plagued his life for two years of lies, misery and humiliation. All that he could forgive her, put behind him, but now she had done something terrible to Salome. Salome was alone and terrified somewhere, maybe hurt. Or worse. And that he would never forgive, or allow to go unpunished.

Her eyes round with fear—the first time he had ever seen her afraid—Julia grabbed one of the pillows and held it in front of her like a shield. "Marc, I don't know where she is. I swear it on my daddy's life."

"You were the last person seen with her."

"Damn that Dagmar! She don't know nothing. I was the last person *she* saw with Salome. But I only sat talking with her five minutes, no more. Soon as I gave her the letter—"

"What letter?"

"A letter from Lyndon. He sent it to Salome's mother, and asked her to see that her daughter got it." Julia said this very quickly, clearly hoping something would stem his anger. "And then she gave it to me seeing as how I was coming up north to call on the two of you."

Marc stood beside the bed, motionless except for the heaving of his chest. "What did the letter say?"

"How do I know? You don't think I'd be fool enough to open it? Miss Prissy woulda thought I'd fooled with the letter otherwise and she would never have believed anything in it." She lifted her chin defiantly. "And I want her to believe what's in it, Marc, cause I bet he wants her back. You don't think I want to spoil a sweet little letter like that."

He didn't want to believe her, but the unblinking gaze told him she was telling the truth about this, if nothing else.

"So you just handed over Lyndon's letter and walked away?"

"Sure did. I knew she wasn't going to read it in front of me, not the letter she's been waiting for, the letter from her best and favorite sweetheart. Cause that's what he is, Marc, no matter how much the two of you slobber over each other. I figured the sooner she read the letter, the sooner she'd realize that she had to hustle off to wherever Lyndon is, not stick around with the likes of you."

Julia tossed aside the pillow and crouched towards him. Her full breasts strained against her ivory blouse, and her red lips parted in anticipation. "Not that I have any problem with the likes of you. I like you right fine. Right fine indeed."

She tried to caress his thigh, but he grabbed her wrist.

She winced. "You're hurting me."

He only increased the pressure on her wrist, forcing her to kneel on the bed before him. "I have no reason to believe a word you say. This is the first I've heard about any letter from Lyndon. But I do know that you hate Salome, that you'd do anything to get her away from me and the act."

"Why shouldn't I? She doesn't belong here." Julia tried in vain to free her wrist. "She stole my job, then she stole you."

"So you went to the papers with all those lies. That's the only way you know how to get anything—lie and cheat."

She cursed, then gave up trying to struggle out of

his grip. "What's wrong with that? A woman's got to fight for what belongs to her. And I'll keep on lying and cheating till that tramp wises up and clears out."

"Exactly. You'll keep on lying." While he kept hold of her with one hand, he placed his other about her neck. "Just like you're doing now."

She turned white as chalk. "I'm telling the truth!"

"Where is she, Julia?" he said quietly.

"I don't know, I tell you." Her voice came out high-pitched and nervous.

"Where is she?" he repeated. For a terrible moment, he felt the world go silent, except for Julia's heart thudding frantically against his chest. It was as though he were watching himself from a distance: emotionless, determined, implacable.

Tears welled up in Julia's eyes as he slowly tightened his grip on her throat. "One last time, Julia." He paused. "Where is she?"

Before the frightened woman could answer, Marc heard a man call his name out in the hallway. Reluctant to release his grip on Julia, Marc had to shake his head before he realized the man standing in the doorway was Thomas Tierney.

Tierney appeared not only wet and bedraggled, he looked positively fearful. Realizing he still had Julia by the throat, Marc at last released her. She flung her hands about her neck and sank gasping onto the bed.

"What do you want?" Marc asked, feeling like a man slowly coming out of a drunken stupor.

"It's Miss Hall." Tierney glanced over at Julia, before daring to step inside. "I think she's in trouble, Mr. Cooper." The businessman gave an anxious cough. "I've been worried about Miss Hall ever since her convalescence in the hotel these past few days. Every morning I wait outside to see if she will finally appear, and today I was at last rewarded. I followed her through the park at a discreet distance, for I didn't wish to burden her with my presence. But I did want to make certain that she was well enough to be walking about. I saw the two ladies talk for a few moments by the fountain, then this woman here left." He pointed to Julia.

Julia glared at Marc. "I told you," she said with quiet venom.

Now Marc felt an even colder fear. If Julia didn't kidnap Salome, that left only Chauncey and Baer. "So what happened?"

"Several very large men surrounded her, I'm afraid, and shortly afterwards, Miss Hall and these gentlemen walked out of the park together."

"Was she struggling? Did they have a weapon?"

Tierney shook his head. "She seemed to go willingly and, as for a weapon, I did not see one, but then they were all crowded so close about her, I could barely discern Miss Hall's diminutive figure. One of the gentleman did appear in high spirits however, a husky fellow with bushy yellow eyebrows. Wearing a brown derby."

"Chauncey," Marc said hoarsely.

"I followed them at a distance. Imagine my chagrin when I saw that their destination was a disreputable establishment in a very disreputable part of the city."

"Where did they go?" Marc was trying to keep his frustration in check, but if Tierney didn't hurry this tale along, he feared he'd be strangling him next.

"A place called the Sapphire Queen, which is located right in the middle of a slum known as the Basin."

"Sapphire Queen," Marc repeated to himself.

"I fear it is occupied by the frail sisterhood," Tierney said in a stage whisper.

Julia piped up, "He means it's a whorehouse."

Marc ignored both her and Tierney's embarrassed blush. "How do you know she's still there?"

"I stood across the street for two hours—nearly caught my death of cold—but Miss Hall did not reappear. Finally, one of the gentlemen who had brought her there did leave about thirty minutes ago. I followed him, and he went straight to the music hall. He left a moment later quite angry, and I went in right after to talk to you, but they told me you had left. I didn't know where else to go, so I came to your hotel, hoping someone here would know your whereabouts."

"They're holding her for ransom," Marc guessed with a calmness he did not feel. "For the money they claim I owe Baer. That bastard probably brought a ransom note to the music hall for me. They'll be mad as hell to learn I've given them the slip. If they've hurt her. . . ." He couldn't bring himself to finish the thought.

"Chauncey's a mean one," Julia lay back on the pillows once more, one hand still rubbing her neck. "She could be dead by now."

Tierney went pale, but Marc had no time to spare for Julia nor her spite and hatred. "Come on, we've got to move fast." He pushed past Tierney. "I want you to go to the police and tell them a woman has been abducted and is being held against her will at the Sapphire Queen."

"But—but we don't know that for sure," Tierney stammered. "Maybe there is a legitimate reason for her being there. I'd hate to involve the police if we don't have to. Then the papers get wind of this, and my name could somehow be bandied about. In Evansville it doesn't look right for a businessman to have his name linked with disreputable establishments."

"You're married, aren't you?" Julia asked with a sly smile.

"Why, yes, yes I am. And you see, although I do want to help Miss Hall, I believe I'm through chasing after her. I would prefer not to—"

He never had a chance to finish. Marc snapped his fingers, then pointed his hand at the gentleman. His stance was as dramatic and commanding as any displayed by his stage persona. "You run to the police station as fast as you can and make damn certain they get to the Sapphire Queen immediately. I'm going there now to try to rescue Salome. If I find out you turned coward on me, Tierney, I'll hunt you down."

Tierney looked at him with sheer terror.

"Now go!"

Tierney ran out of the hotel room without a backward glance.

Marc started to hurry after him, but Julia called out, "You were ready to kill me, weren't you?"

He paused in the doorway. "Yes."

She looked grim beneath all that bright blond hair, now falling in disarray about her shoulders.

"Stay far away from me, Julia," he said solemnly. "If you interfere in my life or Salome's life again, I'll finish what I started tonight. I swear it."

As he ran down the stairs and out into the storm, however, some part of him felt sick. He had come close—perilously close—to killing Julia. He had never been a violent man, but tonight he'd felt a monstrous rage, a rage so overwhelming that he'd been prepared to choke the life out of a helpless woman. It was as though his normal character had been ripped away by the force of his emotions, and a primitive, dangerous man had fought his way to the surface. And God help him, if Salome's life hung in the balance, he'd let that primitive part of him take over once more.

Julia had almost lost her life tonight at his hands. Luckily, for her, she had played no part in Salome's kidnapping.

The men holding Salome captive at the Sapphire Queen might not be so lucky.

She should have paid more attention. For three days, Marc had instructed her on the art of escaping from handcuffs and she still couldn't slip even one of her wrists free.

Salome sat back, exhausted. She was locked in an upper room in what was clearly a brothel. From what she had seen walking through the streets, they were in a fearsome slum district where few people would give a hang for the welfare of a young woman.

The storm outside was still rattling the window panes with thunder and gale force winds. Even if she could scream, no one would hear her over the storm's fury and the laughter and piano music downstairs. In addition, one of her captors had tied her ankles to a spindle-back chair, so tight in fact that her legs tingled from the poor circulation. Chauncey had gagged her with his large cotton handkerchief; she knew it belonged to him since it reeked of orange water. If she ever got out of this alive, she'd never be able to peel an orange again or tolerate the scent of a bride's orange blossoms.

When one of the women of the household came in, dangling a pair of handcuffs from her bejeweled hands, Salome's eyes widened in disbelief. Where would a prostitute acquire such a thing? But as

Chauncey clapped the handcuffs on her, he joked that the customers tonight would have to engage in fornicating without being chained to the bed.

Whenever she left off trying to free herself, Salome pondered the mystery of men's sexual practices. Why would anyone want to be bound during the act of love? One of the deepest pleasures in her tryst with Lyndon had been the glorious opportunity to caress and hold him, to explore with her own hands the body of her lover. Then again, the denizens of this establishment were probably engaging in all sorts of sexual acts right this moment that might turn her brown hair snow white.

"Won't do any good giving me those looks, missy." Chauncey sat across the room, his feet propped up on a vanity table, and his weight causing the chair to lean back on two legs. "Ain't no one going to set you free until your lover boy coughs up the money he owes us."

Salome could only lift her chin defiantly. How frustrating not to be able to answer this brute. Not that he would listen to a word of sense anyway. Her sole consolation was that if she managed to get out of this sorry predicament, she could at last bring charges of kidnapping against Chauncey Farrell. Let the police try and explain away her abduction and being held hostage in a house of ill repute. They'd have to arrest not only Chauncey, but the other two men.

Chauncey reached into his jacket, pulling out a slim nail file. As he did so, she glimpsed the revolver nestled in a dark shoulder strap. The sight of his weapon reminded her that she might not live to accuse Chauncey of anything. Lightning illuminated the room, the gaslit fixtures dim in comparison to that blinding flash. She might end up dying before

261

the storm was over, unable to fight back, ignorant of what would befall Marc when he at last discovered where she was being held.

Chauncey turned his attention to wielding the nail file. "Course, it looks as though Marco has flown the coop. Seems he left the theater right before he was to go on, and ain't no one seen him since. Bad luck for you if he decided to save his own skin and hopped the first train out of here."

Salome sighed. She knew Marc was right here in Cincinnati, desperately searching for her. When she didn't show up for the performance, the poor man would have gone mad with worry. And the last person anyone had seen her with was Julia. That alone would convince him that she was in considerable trouble. The only question was how long it would take him to learn that it wasn't Julia who was behind her disappearance.

She peeked over at Chauncey again. The man was paid to extort, threaten and—she had no doubt—kill. Such men were not likely to be patient. And he'd already proven that he was itching to destroy Marc. Her murder would simply be the tragic prelude to Chauncey's aim at the real target of this mad scheme: the all-too-successful Marco the Magnificent.

No, she had to find a way out of this. Once again she turned her attention to the handcuffs. A calm mind and dexterous fingers were what was needed, Marc told her repeatedly. That or a lockpick, he had joked. Well, she had no lockpick. Just pearl buttons closing the sleeves of her blouses, a jet brooch on her collar that she couldn't get to, and the pins in her hair. And how could she get the pins out when her hands were chained behind the chair?

Chauncey had left off filing his nails, and was now

looking over a penny newspaper. What if she somehow knocked her chair over? The violent movement would loosen the hairpins. Of course, it could also knock her clean unconscious.

Luckily, he seemed engrossed in the paper. Holding her breath, she dared to give a violent shake to her head. Nothing. But at least, the movement hadn't drawn his attention. She tried again, and then again. This time she was rewarded as a pin slipped out of her coiffure and fell onto her skirt. She couldn't reach that one either, but there were dozens more nestled in her hair. Ten minutes later, she was dizzy from shaking her head, but several more pins had fallen out, one of which grazed her bound fingers.

The door to the room burst open. One of the fellows who had abducted her rushed in. "It's him."

Chauncey sat up, his chair finally coming to rest on four legs. "The magician is here?"

Salome froze.

The man nodded, a wolfish grin on his face. "The lunkhead rushes in big as life, demanding to know where his lady friend is. He didn't get two steps inside the front parlor before me and Ethan brained him. We got him in Lola's room on the second floor, trussed up like a turkey and still out cold."

Behind her gag, she let out a small scream. Poor Marc, risking his own life to rescue her. Now he was as helpless and vulnerable as she was. And in even more peril. She tried to yank the cuffs off her wrist and wanted to howl in frustration.

Slapping his knees, Chauncey laughed until tears showed in the corners of his eyes. The sound plunged her into icy despair.

"Seems like we got not only the little chicken, we got the sly fox as well." Chauncey stood up. Her eyes widened in horror as he pulled out his revolver and checked it for bullets.

"Let's go down and see if Marco boy has been as clever as his audiences think he is and brought our money." Chauncey was almost out the door when he turned back to her. "If you happen to hear a gunshot, missy, you'll know that your boyfriend came up a little short." Laughing again, both men walked out, Chauncey making sure to kick the door shut behind them.

Heart pounding, Salome began shaking her head furiously, like a woman who has just discovered hornets nesting in her hair. One pin fell out, then two, then two more—all eluding her fingers.

Theoretically, this was possible. She knew it was. The odds, however, were against it happening in time. But with Marco the Magnificent—and Salome the Fair—the impossible had to become possible.

Or she'd die trying.

He'd done a lot of stupid things in his life, but barging into a whorehouse like a jealous husband was right at the top of the list. It was a wonder they hadn't just shot him dead as he stood there bellowing for Salome to be brought out to him. He hadn't even brought a weapon. Sometimes he forgot that the real world wasn't as easy to control as the world of magic. And sometimes he forgot that his tricks only worked onstage, not in a slum brothel where armed men were holding Salome for ransom.

His rage would do him in one of these days. As he tried to clear his senses, he realized he was tied to a chair. In the dim light, he could see a four-poster bed, a pile of towels on the floor next to it, and a changing screen that was partially hidden by a scarlet corset.

Salome had to be in one of the other bedrooms somewhere. He prayed she wasn't hurt. He doubted they would dare harm her before he had a chance to pay up. Not even Chauncey was that foolish. Well, he couldn't sit around here waiting for the goons to show up. He felt the knots securing his wrists. Child's play.

Taking a deep breath, he nearly choked on the thick perfume permeating the air. He sniffed again and discerned sweat, cheap tobacco and the unmistakable smell of sex. No doubt about it, he was in a whorehouse. And he was damned if he was going to let either Salome or himself die in one.

Closing his eyes, he let his body relax while his fingers expertly untied the knot. It wasn't even a decent fisherman's knot that would have occupied him for at least a minute. By the time he heard the footsteps outside the door, his hands were free and the ropes that had been wound about his body were looped and clutched in his fists.

Just as the door swung open, he let his head drop down, then put his hands behind the chair and pretended to be still bound. He hoped that in the dim gaslight, they wouldn't immediately notice that the ropes about his body were gone.

The door creaked open. Between claps of thunder he could hear music downstairs. Pretty dramatic setting, he thought wryly. One of these days he'd have to use the sound of thunder and flashes of lightning in his act; he now could attest to how eerie and chilling were their effects. But then Chauncey chuckled and spoiled the sinister mood. He had known this crude fellow for too many months, and understood that although Chauncey was not unintelligent, he was unimaginative. And that might be enough to save Salome's skin . . . and his own.

"Hey, Marco boy." Chauncey kicked at his foot. "You fall asleep on me? Or did Roy here rattle what little brains you got?"

Marc shook his head, as if slowly coming back to consciousness. He pretended to be dazed, but beneath his eyelashes he saw that the wiry man called Roy had closed the door and stood leaning against it. Chauncey sat down heavily on the bed, leaning forward, a shiny revolver cradled in his hands.

"Open those dumb eyes of yours and take a look at what I have here for you." He gestured with his revolver. "You've cost Mr. Baer and me a lot of time and money. If it had been up to me, I'da made an example of you long ago. But, no, I gotta go chasing around after you and that assistant of yours."

Marc straightened in the chair. "Where is Salome?" He tried to keep his voice lethargic and dazed. "Is she all right?"

"Don't worry about that skinny little thing. She's doing just fine, and she'll do even better if you pay up." He snorted and then added confidentially, "But if you ask me, I don't know how you could trade a gal like Julia for someone like her."

"Yeah, I seem to recall you and Julia being friendly one night in an alley."

Chauncey grinned, yet his expression seemed pained. "I miss that filly, don't mind telling you. But then you went and spoiled everything by firing her. What was she supposed to do, except run back home? Baer wouldn't keep paying her, and she didn't have no salary from you anymore. But the day she left for Black Horse, I wanted to bust you in the mouth something fierce."

"Whoa, what are you talking about?" Marc was so jarred by his statement that he abandoned his helpless pose. "What do you mean, Baer was paying her?

266

Are you telling me she worked for him all along?"

Chauncey shook his head. "We didn't hook up with Julia until this past winter. I caught your act in West Virginia, and told Baer that audiences were just gullible enough to make your magic tricks a success. And that your blond assistant was a tempting sight for the gents buying tickets. We managed to have a few words with ol' Julia and told her that if she got you to sign a contract with us, we'd hand over ten percent of our share."

"Damn, but I should have known." Marc remembered now that Julia had started talking about how much he needed a manager several weeks before Baer showed up with his infamous contract. And she had been the one to read aloud the contract to him before he signed it. Of course, now he knew that every word she'd uttered had been a lie.

Chauncey only sneered. "We didn't think you'd ever figure anything out. After all, if you'd been really smart, why would you waste your time being a magician? Then you proved just how dumb you were by tossing out Julia and hiring that Salome." He pointed the revolver towards the ceiling where Marc assumed she was being held. "I told Baer that she was the one causin' all the trouble. Get rid of her and you'd fall back into line."

Marc glanced over at the man guarding the door, who likely had a weapon concealed on him. Otherwise Marc could risk rushing Chauncey and slipping his gun away from him. Salome was expendable to them, he realized; the sooner he got Chauncey out of the way, the better.

Before he could move, however, a loud thud sounded from overhead.

"Damn, what is that woman doing up there?" Chauncey gestured towards the ceiling. "Roy, go see what kind of trouble our guest is getting into. But first make sure that idiot I hired hasn't drunk every keg of Lola's beer. I don't think I'm going to need any help with our fancy magician here, but I still don't want Ethan drunk as a skunk if there's trouble."

Stifling a yawn, Roy nodded, then slipped out of the room. Marc frowned. Obviously Salome was securely tied up since no one was showing any undue haste about checking up on her.

Chauncey turned his attention back to Marc. "I'm trying to be nice to you and that little brunette, giving you a chance to pay up and walk away still breathing." He laughed. "Not that I'd hesitate to put you both away, but I'd rather not do it in Ohio. Got a couple of old warrants out on me in this stinking state, so I'd just as soon not draw attention to myself with a pair of corpses."

"I'm touched." Marc said.

"Can the sarcasm, Cooper. You and Miss Hall have run out of choices. We're down to two: make your peace with the Almighty before I kill you both, or open your wallet and start emptying it of those greenbacks you've been raking in all summer."

"I see. And you think I've come here with my pockets stuffed with cash. But as you can see, my hands are empty." With a swift movement, he raised his hands out to the side.

As Chauncey cried out in surprise, Marc flung the coiled rope he'd been grasping behind him straight at the gun. Startled, Chauncey shot off his revolver, its bullet smashing the mirror on the wall.

As agile as a cat after fifteen years of escape artistry and magic tricks, Marc dove to the floor to avoid the next bullet. When he appeared on the other side of the bed, he was holding his little derringer. A quick stride, and the silver snub was at Chauncey's head.

"Now, you just hand the gun over to me and I won't have to bloody this pretty green jacket of yours." Marc fingered the stiff collar. "Although a little blood might improve its looks. This is damn cheap material, Farrell."

"You dumb son of a bitch," Chauncey muttered.

"Give it to me." Marc pressed the derringer to the man's temple, nearly burying the small gun beneath a large yellow eyebrow.

Chauncey handed over his gun, swearing all the while. Marc took it gratefully, switching the derringer to his left hand, and cocking the trigger of the Colt revolver.

"Of all the dumb luck. When Baer gets wind of this—"

"You'll be in jail," Marc finished. "In fact, the police should be here any minute. Now just sit nice on the bed. No funny business. I got two guns pointed at you, remember."

The footsteps racing up the stairs belonged to Roy. The younger fellow had his own gun ready, but lowered it when he saw that Marc was armed with two guns.

"Empty the bullets, then toss the gun over in that corner."

Marc waited impatiently while Roy did this. Damn, but where were the police? If Tierney had turned coward on him, he'd go after him next with this new arsenal he was acquiring.

"Now pick up that rope and tie up our friend here. And make sure those knots are tight."

Chauncey shot him a murderous look as Roy wound the heavy rope around his body. Marc didn't know what he was going to do with Roy. If only he was still carrying around those handcuffs in his pocket—but this past week, he'd stopped giving Salome her lessons in escaping from them. He glanced at the ceiling. What kind of shape was Salome in, he wondered anxiously.

Roy stood in front of Chauncey, his task done. "Now what?"

Behind him, Marc glimpsed a quick movement. Then he heard the unmistakable sound of a rifle being cocked.

"Magic show is over," a nasal voice announced from the doorway.

Standing there was a tall, ruddy man holding a rifle pointed at Marc. He heard Chauncey snicker. Marc again pressed the revolver to Chauncey's head. This had to be the other fellow who had helped kidnap Salome.

"Lower your weapon, or Mr. Farrell will be in a sorry way."

The other man shrugged. "Don't matter to me what you do with him. I was paid to kidnap the lady and get some money from you. If this pig here ends up dying, it's no skin off my nose."

Chauncey uttered a string of violent oaths.

Marc stood with one gun trained on Chauncey, the little derringer aimed at Roy. A regular standoff, and one that was likely to get him killed. Sleight of hand and tricks weren't going to help him now. I've failed you, Salome, he thought with a stab of remorse. *I've failed both of us.*

The man with the rifle gave a little laugh. "If you're going to shoot those fellows, then have done with it, because I got you dead in my sights."

Roy started to tremble, his shaking shoulders partially blocking the gunman from view. "Ethan, you don't have no call to let me die. I'm the one who got you hired on for this job."

"Thanks, Roy. I owe you one. But if it's between

me taking a bullet or you, I'm afraid it's gonna be you."

Marc quickly shifted the revolver from Chauncey's temple, and pointed it straight at the gunman. "This is a no-win situation, sir. And if you want to prove your stupidity, then on a count of three, we'll all just fire and see who's left standing."

"No, I tell you, I ain't gonna die!" Roy yelled.

"Shut up, all of you!" The gunman steadied the rifle, but suddenly a large object came crashing down on his head. As the man collapsed, the rifle went off and shot Roy in the foot.

Roy fell to the floor, screaming in pain. Marc looked in astonishment at the unconscious gunman, blood running down his face. Most astonishing of all was the welcome sight of Salome standing there, the remains of a wooden chair clutched in her hands.

"Do you think I killed him?" she asked anxiously.

"Thank God, you're all right," he cried in relief. She looked exhausted. Her hair was hanging down in an awful tangle, and a pair of handcuffs dangled from one wrist.

Stepping over the wailing Roy, Marc picked up the rifle and emptied those bullets as well. He felt the gunman's pulse.

"He's alive." Marc stood up and drank in the sight of her. "We're both alive, thanks to you."

She dropped the remains of the chair and fell into his arms. "I was so worried about you."

"Me?" Marc hugged her close. He reached down and lifted up the wrist still clasped in handcuffs. "Did you get free of these like I taught you? Good lord, woman, you're a better magician than I am."

She shook her head, a tired smile on her face. "I tried shaking pins out of my hair, but I couldn't catch any to use as a lockpick. I finally tipped over the chair

271

I was tied in and fell to the floor. I thought that would make it easier to grab the hairpins I'd already spilled. But then I realized that crashing to the floor had broken the lock on one of the cuffs." She displayed the smashed links. "So I can't take credit for escaping."

"Sweetheart, I've never seen an escape so neatly done." He kissed the tip of her elegant little nose, then remembered she'd been recently injured. "I forgot about your concussion, Salome. Did you fall on your head upstairs? Do you think you're hurt?"

"I'm fine, especially since I see that you're alive and well." She pointed to the derringer in his left hand. "Is that what you were holding these men at bay with? Your trick lighter?" She laughed.

"What? Trick lighter!" Chauncey tried to break free of the ropes knotted about him, his face red with anger.

Marc lifted up the derringer and pulled the trigger. A flame appeared by the hammer. "No magician should be without one. Especially a magician who has a taste for tobacco."

"If I ever get my hands on you, Cooper—"

Marc gestured toward the shouting coming from downstairs. "Don't think you will. Sounds to me like the police have finally arrived."

Salome stepped past him. She knelt beside Roy, staunching the wound on his foot with a towel. He moaned with every gentle touch. "If you don't want to find yourself in this sort of painful predicament," she scolded, "then you shouldn't go around kidnapping people at gunpoint."

Chauncey rolled his eyes in disgust. "Bad enough she can get out of handcuffs, now she's Florence Nightingale as well. A woman like that would drive me crazy in one afternoon." He looked over at Marc

272

who had his revolver trained on the unconscious gunman, just in case.

"I think you finally met someone as stubborn and impossible as you are, Cooper. Hell, but if you two don't deserve each other."

Chauncey was wrong about that. Marc didn't deserve a woman as fine and brave and sweet as Salome. He didn't deserve the sort of love and happiness he was sure she would bring to him.

But he swore he was going to spend the rest of his life *trying* to deserve it.

Chapter Fifteen

The city was calm again. And so, finally, was Marc.
The thunderstorms had ceased, leaving the streets
damp and littered with broken branches. Getting up
carefully from the rocking chair, he crept over to the
window and opened it wide. A church bell tolled the
third hour of the morning, its lonely chimes the only
sound aside from the rattling of the milk wagons.

He leaned his elbows on the sill, breathing deeply
and uttering a silent prayer of thanks. Salome was
safe. That was all that mattered. He didn't want to
reflect on his murderous rage, didn't want to admit
that he wasn't always in control of his emotions and
his actions. But Salome Hall had swept him away as
surely as the summer storm had swept away the
branches of a hundred city trees.

A sigh escaped Salome's lips, and he spun about.
In the moonlight pouring through the window, he
could clearly make out her sleeping form, restless

now beneath the sheet, her dark hair spilling about the white pillow like skeins of black silk. He didn't want to wake her; she needed to sleep, to try to forget tonight's madness.

They hadn't been able to return to the hotel until after midnight. Exhausted from an endless round of police questions, they at least found relief in the knowledge that Chauncey and his henchmen were behind bars. And with Chauncey's record and arrest warrants, it was a certainty that not even Robert Baer could pull enough strings to keep him from another decade or two in the penitentiary.

But even knowing that Salome was safe and sound in the room next to his wasn't enough. Once he was sure she'd fallen asleep, he picked the lock on her door and kept a watchful vigil in the chair beside her bed. No one would harm her again, he vowed. Not jealous, cruel women like Julia or greedy, clever men like Baer. He sat down once more, his eyes fixed on her sweet profile. Nor would handsome, deceitful ex-lovers like Lyndon Whittier.

Surely after all they'd been through this past summer, Salome would realize that they were as fated to be together as his own mother and father, whose love had never wavered even during years of hardship in a land where they had few friends or family, only each other. Yes, Salome and he shared a love as deep and sure as Jorge and Rosa Cupertino. He leaned over, gently brushing back a strand of hair from her cheek. And they would have a couple of little Cupertinos, too, he thought happily. Before Salome, he had never given fatherhood even a passing consideration. But with Salome—and Marco the Magnificent—all things were possible.

Although he touched her face with the lightest gesture, she stirred.

"What? Marc, what are you doing here?" Still half-asleep, she turned toward him, oblivious that her shift left one shoulder bare. "Is something wrong?"

"Shhhh." He reached for the sheet and tucked it up around her neck. Even though the night air was still and humid, the sight of her smooth bare skin was too distracting, and he was only here to watch over her, protect her, even if it meant he must protect her from himself.

"Nothing's wrong, darling," he whispered. "I just wanted to make sure you were sleeping soundly."

She smiled. The moonlight turned her skin to alabaster. "Did you pick the lock again? I think you did it every night I had the concussion." A soft laugh escaped her. "You've probably broken into more locked rooms than a cat burglar."

"Go to sleep. I didn't want to wake you."

Yawning, she turned onto her back. "It's so hot. I thought the storm would cool things off." She flung the sheet down, leaving the top half of her body exposed.

Marc couldn't resist a yearning gaze at the small rounded breasts jutting against the thin linen of her nightgown.

She reached out and touched his arm. "Marc, please go back to your room and get some sleep. I'm fine, really."

His eyes fastened on her wrist, which even in this light showed the marks left by the handcuffs. Although he was here with the best intentions in the world—the dark knight protecting his lady fair—he couldn't stop himself from bending down and pressing his lips against her bruised wrist.

He heard her gasp, then felt her other hand cradle his head.

"If something had happened to you, I would have

gone mad," he murmured, kissing her wrist again, and then again. "I don't think I can bear life without you. Knowing those men held you tonight chilled my blood."

"I've never met a man as brave as you, Marc. When I heard your voice downstairs in the Sapphire Queen, I knew that everything was going to be all right." She lifted his face with her hand. "I knew that you would make the magic happen."

Then she leaned over and kissed him. Not like the sisterly pecks she'd bestowed onstage, or those few passionate kisses the night Julia had witnessed the Gun Trick. This was a kiss of promise, anticipation, a kiss of quiet desire. He knew with thrilling certainty that she was inviting him into her bed.

He slowly left his chair, and eased himself beside her. Her hand still curled about his neck, her fingers teasing the cord that tied his hair back. To his surprise, she pulled it off, letting his thick hair fall loose.

"My dark pirate," she whispered.

He felt himself grow hard at the husky quality of her voice. Lying there before him, bathed in the summer moonlight, Salome was the realization of every erotic, sensual dream he'd had of her. No perfume of roses masked her own musky scent now, no glittering costume or corset or black mesh stockings covered her smooth, pale body. There was only a warm, willing woman, naked beneath a thin nightgown, and her hands on his shoulders were pulling him toward her.

She had given him permission, he realized with aching excitement. He caressed her bare arms, feeling her breasts pressed against him. With a groan, he sat up quickly and tore off his shirt. He needed to feel Salome's bare flesh against his own, needed to feel every ridge, pore, every naked inch of her

277

melded to him, damp with his sweat, and his desire.

Salome wiped her own brow, obviously as hot and impatient as he was. In the aftermath of the storm, the room was airless, silent, and drenched in moonlight.

He kicked off his shoes, but hesitated before unbuttoning his pants. He didn't want to hurry her or make her nervous. It was she who sat up in bed, dark eyes luminous but unreadable. With her chin raised defiantly, she pulled her nightgown over her head, then tossed it aside. For a moment, he was riveted by the spectacle of a half-naked Salome sitting before him, a true Venus rising, but this one rose from moonglow and a sea of white linen. Her long straight hair hung down her back and about her shoulders but couldn't hide those small firm breasts, their dark aureoles tempting and delectable.

In a fever, he stripped off his pants, his arousal so hard, he feared he'd lose control before he even laid a hand on her.

But summoning the strength of will that had made him a master escape artist, he finally sat naked before her. With one swift motion he pulled the sheet away, and Salome at last seemed to grow shy. She lay on her side as soon as the sheet was gone and curled her legs slightly, hiding her inner thighs and the triangle of soft hair he could barely discern now.

Laying stretched out beside her, Marc didn't bother to hide his excitement. He couldn't even if he'd wanted to.

Salome looked at him. The silence was charged with heat and desire and love. She lay back on the pillow and slowly uncurled her legs. Although her thighs remained pressed together, she was stretching herself out beside him like a lioness, letting him look his fill at her, drink in her nakedness, her vulnerability.

Marc moved closer, leaning down to kiss her. But as he did, he wrapped his arm about her, scooping her up and pressing her to him. He moaned as her soft breasts were crushed against him. Kissing her eager mouth wasn't enough, he had to feel his mouth on her neck, her collarbone, and then claiming those lovely erect nipples. Hooking one of his legs over hers, he drew her ever nearer. This time there would be no trick levers, no way possible to escape this breathless illusion save through climax, fulfillment, surrender.

"Marc, I want you so," she said breathlessly. She wrapped her own arms about him so that they lay entwined, limbs entangled. And still this wasn't close enough.

The only response he could make was to explore her glorious body, that slender waist, the smooth belly, the rounded buttocks he'd dreamed of caressing a hundred nights. His hands couldn't get enough of her. She was like a magic trick that had somehow turned real, an escape that at the last moment erupted into a miracle of wonder and spectacle.

He was hard and aching. His wet tip grazed against her thighs and slowly she opened to him. His hand cupped that soft, damp center of hers, the center that she now offered. As they kissed feverishly, desperate yet lingering, he at last eased himself into her. At the snug feel of her around him, he broke off their kiss, and let out a cry. Then he plunged slowly into a wet heat that proved to him there was one thing more thrilling than magic.

Salome clutched at him, wrapping her legs about his back instinctively, knowing only that she had to draw him closer. He was crying out, moaning a sound that made her own need even greater. The man who seemed so masterful, so controlled on-stage, was like a wild animal now. And she loved it, she loved the fury of it, the hunger, yet beneath it, the tenderness.

Oh, she'd wanted him for so long, she admitted to herself, from the moment she'd seen him flashing those sabers onstage, the moment she'd laid eyes on those black eyes and blacker hair, and that muscled chest covered in hair. She ran her fingers over his chest now, playing with the stiff black curls, rubbing his own hard nipples. Then she lowered her head and rained wet kisses over his chest, her hands fondling his straining buttocks. How she enjoyed the masculine feel of his body, the smell of sex, the groans, the hard pounding that she heard herself begging to be even harder.

She was no longer Salome Hall, but Salome the Fair, the wanton who dressed in cherry red and fired guns at men in water tanks. This was a Salome who flung off her clothes eagerly, and who cried out with as much abandon as the fevered man now deep in-side her. This was a Salome who believed in magic, the magic between a man and a woman, the magic that could erupt on a hot summer night between two people who had denied their feelings for far too long. The tense waiting—the denials—were vanquished before such magic. *She* was vanquished. And when her utmost pleasure shuddered through her, she pressed herself even closer to the man who had given it to her.

Lost in a haze of emotion and desire, she heard Marc give a great moan as he himself reached ful-fillment. It was all magic with him, she decided, as they lay spent and exhausted, still wrapped about each other. Their tender feelings for each other were magic, so was their friendship. The fevered desire that still coursed through her was a rare and dangerous sorcery. She tried to understand why it was so dangerous, but sated and happy, she instead drifted off into sleep.

"Magic," she murmured, and closed her eyes to the blinding beauty of the moonlight.

Fastening the long row of pearl buttons on her dress, Salome kept looking over at Marc's sleeping form. She really should wake him. Their train was due to leave in little over an hour, and he probably hadn't packed yet. Still, she liked watching him sleep, liked having a strong naked man sprawled across her bed, rumpled sheets flung to the floor, allowing her to gaze shamelessly at her magnificent magician.

Sitting on the rocking chair, she cupped her chin in her hands and simply watched him for a long while. Scars and cuts covered his arms and chest, terrible reminders of his near drowning in the water tank. Thinking about how close she'd come to losing him made tears well up. And remembering how brave he was to storm the Sapphire Queen made her heart swell with pride.

He was a beautiful man. How could the whole world not realize how extravagantly handsome and imposing he was? To think that only a few months ago all she could appreciate was his manly chest and raven black eyes. Marc Cooper was far more splendid than that, with a spirit and mind as impressive as his physique.

And such a man had possessed her last night, and she him. She had seen Marc at his most primal—his most vulnerable—and the mere memory quickened her breathing, and set her to summoning up a dozen images of him inside her, moaning, plunging, holding her so close they might as well have been one person. She shut her eyes, the better to remember that electrifying moment when they were indeed one.

Yet there was no shame, no regrets. She had wanted him so, cared about him so deeply, and after the emotion of last night's kidnapping and rescue, mere words were inadequate to release all the built-up tension. Mere words could not express what had to be expressed finally between them. Never had she needed a man's touch as desperately as she had needed Marc's last night. Not even on that misty morning when Lyndon—

Salome sat bolt upright. Lord in heaven, Lyndon! Had last night's moonlight blinded her to everything but her body's own hunger and need? To keep from crying out, she clapped her hand over her mouth. What was the matter with her? Lyndon. She had completely forgotten about the man she was determined to win back. Wildly glancing about the room, her eyes widened when she spied the skirt she had worn yesterday hanging over her packed trunk.

The lilac dimity was stained and torn. She'd been going to leave the skirt here for the maids to throw away, or use as cleaning rags. Except in all the excitement and terror of yesterday, she had totally forgotten that Lyndon's letter still lay nestled within its pocket.

Marc let out a loud snore. She froze, praying he wouldn't awaken. When he quieted once more, she got up softly from the chair. Just pulling the letter from the skirt pocket made her feel dishonest and callow. She had forgotten—forgotten!—that Lyndon had at last written to her. Had she gone mad? Or was she really as whorish as Julia claimed she was?

With trembling fingers, she unsealed the envelope.

Taking a deep breath, she unfolded the paper and dared to look down. "My dearest Sal," she read silently. "Words cannot adequately express how much I have missed your sweet face and angelic spirit these past months. Nor can words convey how bitterly I regret my unforgivable actions. For I love you, dear heart, more than I ever knew. . . ."

Her legs gave out from beneath her and she crumpled to the floor.

He stretched, feeling sore and sweaty, but otherwise glorious. Last night had been magic indeed, he thought, as he grinned from ear to ear. Eyes still closed, he reached out to the other side of the bed but found only a pillow. Finally opening his eyes, he called out sleepily, "Salome, where are you?"

He saw her trunk next to the door, a straw boater sitting atop it. Maybe she was already dressed and downstairs having breakfast. He sat up with a grunt. If he could only find his pocket watch, he could figure out how long he had to pack up his own things. The blasted train was due to leave at eleven this morning, but after such a night, he could have slept hours more. Especially with Salome stretched out naked beside him. Damn, but he'd wanted to wake up with her next to him. He wanted to cover her body once more with his own, and start off their day the same thrilling way they had ended their night. Where could she be?

As he turned around, he jumped to see Salome sitting on the floor by the dresser, her eyes red and swollen.

"Good God, what's the matter?" He rushed over to her, kneeling down and taking her gently by the shoulders. She looked pale and drawn. And very, very unhappy. "Are you ill? Salome!"

With what seemed like a great effort of will, she pushed him away. She got hurriedly to her feet, but stumbled twice on her way to the rocking chair. Only when she sank down in the cane rocker did he see she had a paper clutched in her hand.

"Blast it, Salome, tell me what's wrong?"

"Lyndon's letter," she said in a dull voice.

For a moment, he was completely confused. When did that idiot write her a letter? Then he remembered Julia's smug smile yesterday as she'd told him how Salome's mother had asked her to carry this letter to her daughter. A cursed letter from Lyndon Whittier, of all misbegotten people!

A sickening dread swept over him, but he beat it down. After all, she had given herself to him last night as only a woman in love could. He had no need to worry about a bloody letter. But Marc felt suddenly naked and exposed.

Grabbing his trousers from the floor, he hurriedly stepped into them. "So what does this letter say?"

"He says he made an unforgivable mistake, but he begs me to forgive him." She took a deep breath. "He says he loves me more than he ever realized. More than he could ever love any woman, including Jane." The letter trembled in her hands.

Marc had a violent urge to knock over furniture, but instead busied himself with buttoning up his shirt. "How sad for him, then. Maybe this will teach him a lesson about women. A man shouldn't go around proposing to one lady just before running off with another. At this rate, he'll have more wives than Bluebeard by the time he's forty."

"I've done him a terrible wrong, Marc," She looked up at him with guilt-stricken eyes.

His mouth fell open. "Wait a minute. You've done *him* a terrible wrong? This is the lying dog who jilted you back in Black Horse. He ran off with your pretty childhood friend. And to crown it all, he took you to bed first." He shook his head. "You're an intelligent woman, Salome, but I've known two-bit whores who showed more sense."

"Well, that's exactly how I feel! Like a whore!" She wrapped her arms about herself and shivered. "I left my home and my teaching post because I was set on winning back the man I loved, the man I'd given myself to, the man I promised to marry. And just a few weeks before I'm to see him again, I take *you* to my bed!"

He clenched his fists at his side. "Don't make it sound so awful. You seemed to enjoy it as much as I did."

"Oh, I did. You know I did." She wiped a tear from her cheek. "That's what makes this all so dreadful and terrible. Lyndon says he's prepared to grovel at my feet when he sees me in Chicago. How can I let him do such a thing when I've behaved just as dishonestly?"

"Dishonestly!" Marc felt as though his world had just spun wildly out of control. He could shake her senseless, the stubborn, misguided fool of a woman that she was. How could she not see the truth standing right in front of her? How could she not know that he loved her more truly and deeply than a hundred Lyndons ever could?

She looked up at him with a sad and fearful expression. "I don't want to hurt you, Marc. That's why I didn't want anything to get started between us. I told you it wasn't fair. I told you that I couldn't sort out my feelings until I saw Lyndon again, heard from

285

him. And now that I have—" She held up the letter as if it were sword of vengeance.

"Now that you have, you're going to scurry back to him like a grateful little mouse. Yes, I understand perfectly well."

Marc had to get out of this room. He couldn't breathe in here, couldn't bear another second watching the woman he loved sobbing over another man, especially a man like Lyndon. He especially couldn't remain in a room where they'd shared so much passion and love just a few short hours ago.

"I care for you so much, Marc," she whispered.

"Sure, sure. Just like Lyndon cared for Jane, no doubt. Well, now that you two hayseeds have had your little flings with the lowborn show folk, you can both go skipping back to Missouri. Now you've got something shameful and exciting to put in your scrapbook. Along with all those nice press clippings."

"Don't say such things. You know you don't mean them."

He shook his head. "You're wrong. I always know what I mean. I've known for months that I love you, Salome."

Tears welled up once more in her eyes.

"I knew that I loved you and wanted to share the rest of my life with you. Onstage and off. And I knew that a liar like Lyndon was worthless to any woman, especially a woman like you. Well, now I know you're so convinced you're destined to be Mrs. Whittier that nothing I say or do will make a drop of difference." He took a deep, shaky breath. "Not even what we shared last night."

Salome leaned forward, clasping her hands before her like a woman in prayer. "If only you knew how confused I am, Marc. And how wretchedly miserable."

286

He walked over to the door. "The confusion I'll leave to you. But the misery I'm afraid you'll have to share with me."

"Don't hate me, please." she said in a ragged voice.

He had to wait a moment before replying, trying hard to control the emotion welling up in him. "I'd give up the secrets to a thousand magic tricks if only I did hate you."

Refusing to look back, he forced himself to leave the room. But once the door was shut behind him, he bent his head and shuddered. Even through the thick oak door, he could hear Salome crying.

He hadn't known such desolation since the day his mother died. It certainly felt as though a life had ended.

And he feared that something very precious just had.

Chapter Sixteen

Salome stared at the fearsome spikes overhead. She was once again locked in handcuffs, but this time the cuffs were chained to the bedpost. With her arms stretched above her, she could barely move her neck enough to see her bound feet.

As magic tricks went, she found this one a little too real. Perhaps she wouldn't have minded being chained if the memory of being held hostage in the Sapphire Queen weren't still so fresh.

"As you can see, ladies and gentlemen, Salome the Fair is trapped on this bed of nails, unable to move her hands or feet." Marc paused dramatically. "Unable to do anything but wait for the deadly canopy to impale her with its steel spikes."

The woodwind section of the orchestra broke into an eerie melody, as Salome tugged hard at the chains that held her. Turning her head, she gave a desperate glance towards the people in the front row, as if beseeching them for help. They stared back at her with wide, excited eyes.

Marc snapped his fingers at the two audience members he had brought onstage. Tonight it was a portly gentleman decked out in a white summer suit, even though autumn had at last set in, and a pretty girl young enough to still be wearing her hair down. They had already ascertained that Salome was indeed locked tight to the bed.

They would be the ones to draw the curtains about the canopied bed of nails, after which Marc would direct them to stand on either side so that they could see that Salome had no avenue of escape. Even the mattress was no thicker than a pillow; no one would be able to assume she had fallen through a trap door.

As the portly fellow and the young girl began to draw the red silk curtains, Salome caught a glimpse of Marc's solemn face. No longer were there any whispered endearments or tender smiles when the audience couldn't see. Onstage, they were merely a highly accomplished magician and his very able assistant. Professional, unemotional, and cordial. Her heart ached with how things had changed between them.

The curtains closed around her, cutting off the stares of the audience and Marc's indifferent scrutiny. She stared up at the deadly sharp spikes that studded the canopy above her. Since omitting the Water Tank Trick, Marc had been searching for another showstopper, and decided to reinstate an illusion he hadn't performed in over a year: the Bed of Nails. How fitting that he had added this trick to their act these past few weeks. For she indeed felt trapped, trapped by her feelings for two men, trapped by guilt, fear, confusion. And love.

The music grew louder. Salome reached her fingers to the side, pushing a button which released her from the handcuffs. Sitting up quickly, she tripped open the cuffs that bound her feet. Marc was circling the bed outside the curtains. Two more bars of music and he would send the canopy crashing down. Scurrying to the lower right-hand corner of the bed, she knelt, arms to her side. Luckily none of the spectators took the time to wonder at the size of the bed, much larger than normal. The proportions were exaggerated in order to allow space at all four corners for a slender assistant to huddle unharmed when the spikes came down.

The music stopped on a high note. She covered her face with her hands. A second later, the spiked canopy slammed down on the empty mattress. She heard the usual gasps and screams from the audience. To the sound of a drumroll, the canopy slowly began to rise. By the time it was back in place, she was once again handcuffed to the bed in the same position as before, but miraculously unharmed.

When the two volunteers from the audience drew back the curtains, they both let out astonished cries of delight and surprise to see her lying there, alive and well.

Taking her curtain calls with Marc, Salome no longer felt the pleasure or thrill of just a few weeks ago. Performing had become stale, routine and joyless. Marc turned to her and bowed. She smiled at him with what she hoped was her old warmth, but his expression remained stony.

Her spirits sank even further. She had done this to him, made him melancholy and cold. She had broken his heart, just as Lyndon had broken hers. Such bitter knowledge only increased her guilt and pain—which was already sharper than any of the spikes that threatened her each night.

*   *   *

They wouldn't arrive in Chicago for another week, but he had lost her. He'd lost her as surely as if she had hidden in his Tip Over Trunk, then disappeared in a puff of smoke. For five weeks, they had been cordial, but distant to each other. Watching them, no one would guess that they'd lain naked and shameless together little over a month ago. No one would guess that he loved her more than anything in the world, and that she had confessed that her own feelings ran deep. Too deep. She wasn't a brave woman after all, he thought. Physically, she seemed willing to take more risks than any fire-eater or escape artist—she'd demanded to perform the Bed of Nails trick, to add spice to the show—but emotionally, she was a coward. And he was helpless to change it.

What more could he do? He'd tried seduction, poetry, magic tricks, honesty. And, most heartbreaking of all, a night filled with passion and moonlight. None of it had been enough. She still wouldn't admit that what she felt for him was stronger and more real than anything she could pretend for Lyndon Whittier. Even worse, that damn letter had drowned her in a sea of guilt and self-recrimination. This past month, he'd even begun grasping at pathetic straws, hoping perhaps that he'd gotten her with child.

Surely if he had, she wouldn't still insist on returning to Lyndon. She would have to come to him, and he would be able to possess her at last—as his wife, and the mother of his child.

But as the weeks passed, there was no sign from Salome that such a thing had occurred. His patience at an end, at last he'd asked her outright.

He winced to recall how indignant she had been,

as if the very idea of being pregnant with his child was repugnant.

"Don't even think on such a dreadful possibility," she had said, even paling a little at the suggestion. "I have enough guilt to live with as it is. The last thing this situation needs is an innocent child to complicate matters more. Which, thank the lord, is not the case."

It was the one personal conversation they had allowed themselves since the morning after their lovemaking. Both of them seemed to silently agree that the only decent way to get through the weeks before their arrival in Chicago was to remain professional and unemotional. The other performers had commented on the sudden coolness between them, but he let them assume they'd had a lover's spat. Everyone in the circuit believed they had been lovers anyway, so there was no point in trying to insist otherwise. This way, there were fewer questions, less curiosity. Passionate trysts among performers were common, as were stormy and sudden breakups. Whatever had passed between Salome and himself had therefore been explained away as the usual theatrical funny business.

No one would guess that his feelings for Salome were so strong that he could barely face another day without her, let alone the rest of his life. If she did indeed leave him in Chicago, he would be destroyed.

He had no idea how things had come to such a melodramatic and sorry pass, but they had. Marc Cooper—the invincible Marco the Magnificent—had been laid low by a slip of a woman. A schoolmarm, no less. For the first time in his life, he felt an affinity for those tales of star-crossed lovers: heartsick fools who flung themselves on daggers or sipped poison rather than continue on without their love.

Not that he would resort to suicide if and when Salome left him. He was besotted but not insane. Yet the first morning he awoke knowing that Salome would not be there to smile at him, share confidences, listen to him read from the newspaper, brush against him with her smooth body that held all the delight and promise of paradise . . . on that first morning, he was certain his own heart would stop within him.

To Salome's relief, the Nardini children had never had a proper education. Boasting a brood ranging in age from seven to thirteen, the Nardinis were one of the many family acts on the circuit. When Signor and Signora Nardini discovered Salome was a schoolteacher, they prevailed upon her to tutor their rambunctious offspring. Although it was a shame they had never had time for school, their abysmal classroom skills gave Salome an excuse to spend less time with Marc.

She no longer tutored Marc every afternoon. How could she justify devoting that much time to one student when there were others, younger and just as needy, who also needed her attention? Her lessons with Marc had been reduced to three days a week. The rest of her free time—even on weekends—was now spent teaching the Nardini children backstage.

She stood before them now, a linen wrapper covering her costume, and a chalk slate in her hands. "Now think, children. If c-a-k-e spells 'cake,' then l-a-k-e spells what? And remember the 'e' is silent so that makes the first vowel—"

"Long!" Although seven-year-old Lucia Nardini was the youngest of the family, she was the most intelligent.

Sharon Pisacreta

"That's right, Lucia. And what does that sound like?"

As the child piped up with the right answer, Salome saw Marc leave his dressing room down the corridor. Actually, she sometimes imagined she felt his movements before seeing them. After sharing so much with him this summer, it was as if his very thoughts communicated themselves to her. How often had she glanced up, feeling that he was near, only to see him gazing at her with those haunting, dark eyes.

As he was doing just now. He stood just outside his dressing room, his black hair loose, his robe tightly belted. For a moment, she could do nothing but stare back at him, while dear little Lucia asked her a question about long vowels. What would things be like between them if Lyndon had not sent her that letter? Would they have continued to share a bed as they had that searing night after the storm?

She flushed to remember how she had clung to him, begging him to do things to her that she hadn't even dreamt of. Without Lyndon's heartfelt letter, she might have shared Marc's bed every night, and maybe found the courage to tell him just how important he had become to her. Now her future—and his—seemed as daunting as the Bed of Nails illusion.

Marc broke their tense gaze, walking past the children perched on crates without even a polite nod.

Suddenly her throat felt thick with tears. The romantic pairings and mismatches of these last few months seemed as confusing as anything in Mr. Shakespeare's *A Midsummer Night's Dream*. She remembered that dreadful Mr. Jenson back in St. Louis who had tried to seduce her with promises to appear in a touring company's rendition of that very play. Little did he know she was engaged in a scenario every bit as fantastical and bewildering.

"Why is the 'e' silent? I do not understand this, Miss Hall. Such things make my head ache," Paolo asked.

Salome forced herself to answer the eldest Nardini's question; he was a diligent boy, but clearly reading and writing were not going to be the mainstays of his life. Just like Marc.

After two more examples of long vowels, Salome dismissed her makeshift class early. It seemed that neither the teacher nor the children were in the mood for school. As the Nardinis ran shouting down the corridor, Salome picked up the chalk and slates, then slowly stacked the crates against the wall. She wondered where she would teach next, or even if Lyndon would want her to continue teaching once they married.

"Mrs. Lyndon Whittier," she said aloud.

The words no longer entranced her, nor did they conjure up images of domestic bliss. After all, until a few weeks ago, Lyndon had every intention of bestowing that name on the golden-haired Jane Dupree. The honor of being his wife could be a dubious one. Such a man might not be suited for marriage, for constancy and trust. Maybe—just maybe—she had been wrong about the importance of the ten years they had shared. Maybe he didn't love her as deeply as he should. And maybe her love for him wasn't enough to last them through the inevitable travails of a lifetime.

"Saying your daily prayers?"

She turned around. Marc leaned against the wall, arms crossed in front of him.

"What are you talking about?"

"I heard you say 'Mrs. Lyndon Whittier.' I assumed

you were praying." Despite his sarcastic tone, his eyes wore a pained expression.

"I didn't realize I'd spoken aloud. I'm sorry."

She didn't know what she was apologizing for. But these past few weeks, nothing came easily to her when Marc was around. She still hadn't gotten over his asking if she was pregnant. After their cool politeness towards each other, such a question shocked her with its bluntness—and the realization that he'd wanted the answer very much to be yes. Even worse, for a brief wicked moment, *she* had wanted to be carrying his child. But too many lives were already in upheaval. To bring a baby into this morass would be unforgivable.

"Well, you'll be his wife soon enough." He shrugged. "I'm only surprised you're not writing it on the blackboard every morning for practice."

She wasn't in the mood for his sarcasm today, even if genuine pain was behind it. "I'm not sure I want to be anyone's wife. These past few months have taught me that men and love rarely lead to happiness. The joys of spinsterhood have much to recommend it."

He lifted a skeptical eyebrow. "Once you lay eyes on the glorious Mr. Whittier in Chicago, I'm sure your enthusiasm for spinsterhood will vanish." He paused. "As well as your enthusiasm for vaudeville and flashy theater folk."

"And magicians?" she snapped back.

Marc took a deep breath. "Oh, that's long gone. Or hadn't you noticed?"

Before she could answer, he walked into his dressing room, slamming the door behind him. Close on his heels, she flung it back open.

"For weeks, we have maintained a chilly, but polite distance," she said in a low, angry voice. "If you want such civility to cease, fine. But I do wish you would give me advance warning before you start discussing my marriage plans or any possible state of impending motherhood."

Although startled by her assault, Marc quickly recovered. The pain in his eyes was now replaced by anger. "Well, maybe if you didn't stand in the hallway reciting the words 'Mrs. Lyndon Whittier' like they were the Lord's Prayer, no one would feel moved to comment on it."

"Don't exaggerate!"

"And as for imagining whether you're pregnant or not—" Marc reached behind her and shut the door. He was inches away, his arm brushing her shoulder. As always, his presence affected her senses like fiery brandy. "I find it hard to understand why you're insulted. I'm a man who honors his responsibilities. If I had gotten you with child that night, would you have preferred it if I had abandoned you and the baby?"

"I didn't say that. Don't twist things around, Marc."

"No, I'll tell you what's twisted: your idea of what makes a proper man. You gave up your friends and family back home, you gave up your teaching position, just to run after a weak fool who deserted you. And now you're giving me up."

Salome grabbed the doorknob. "I'm not listening to this again."

But she was no match for the strong arm he flung against the door, pressing it closed. Nor was she a match for the emotion she felt emanating from him like the rays of a blinding sun.

"I've tried to keep my distance this past month. Damn it, but I have tried. I let my guard down once only because I needed to know if our night together had resulted in a child. Do you think I'd let you go

297

to that bastard Lyndon with *my* child in your belly?" His dark expression told her she'd be mad even to consider such a thing. "I'd run him through with my sabers to prevent that from happening. Or do you think my emotions run as shallow as his?" He took a ragged breath. "Or yours."

She swallowed hard, wishing she could escape from this man who flooded her senses so entirely with emotion. "I never lied to you, Marc. You knew from the beginning what my feelings were for Lyndon. I should have prevented anything from happening between us, but I didn't. I couldn't." She touched his face gently, but he jerked away as if her touch burned. "I wanted so much not to care for you, but you're—you're magic to me. The way you speak, the way you look, the way you move like a panther."

Although he held himself apart from her, at her words his expression grew less forbidding.

"But this isn't real, Marc. The excitement, the costumes, the audacious illusions: *all* of it is illusion for a person like me. I'm a small-town girl, a schoolteacher who prepares her lessons, quilts on Monday evenings, and oversees church rummage sales. I have no place in this world or with a man like you."

He tried to protest, but she put her hand over his mouth. "For a brief moment, I lost my head and dared to act as though this were real. What we shared that night was wondrous and thrilling, but Lyndon's letter jarred me awake. It did, Marc, and I can't pretend otherwise. We've only known each other for a summer. Just one sweet summer, but Lyndon and I have a decade between us. And those ten years demand that I give him another chance."

She lowered her hand, grateful that he hadn't tried to kiss it. A single kiss now would undo her.

Marc looked away. For a moment, she thought he

was saying something under his breath, but she couldn't be sure.

"You'd better go." He yanked open the door. From down the corridor came the sounds of the orchestra rehearsing, and the younger Nardinis screaming with laughter. "I'm probably keeping you from your lessons."

Suddenly awkward, she stepped out into the hallway. "Actually, I've finished teaching the children for today."

His face remained averted, as though he couldn't bring himself to look at her.

She hated hurting him so, but didn't know how to make amends. "We have time for at least one reading lesson ourselves." Now he did look at her, his eyes glowing like black embers.

He shook his head. "No, Salome. I require no more lessons. We've already learned far too much from each other."

Even after the door shut in her face with a soft click, she couldn't move. If she did, she feared she'd shatter in a thousand fragile pieces.

Chapter Seventeen

The extravagant beauty of the Chicago World's Fair had turned even the voluble vaudeville performers momentarily speechless. Flora and Lorenzo gazed wide-eyed at the endless white buildings of what was called The White City—flags, peristyles, porticoes, and statuary festooning every imposing inch. Like children seeing snowflakes for the first time, Marc, Salome and Boblo spent thirty minutes transfixed by Mr. Edison's Kinetoscope, a marvelous machine that showed moving pictures on celluloid film.

The Nardini children's excitement was so great at their first glimpse of the sweeping lagoon and gondolas that little Lucia nearly fell headfirst into the canal. Only Mickey's speed and dexterity prevented the mishap, even though the petite acrobat was gaping the entire time at *The Republic*, a 65-foot-high gilt statue that gleamed like gold in the October sun.

Surely there had never been a World's Fair as spec-

tacular as this. Christopher Columbus could not
have felt more gratified or awestruck at discovering
America. How fitting that all this beauty was the result of an Exposition honoring the Italian explorer's
momentous discovery four hundred years earlier.

Salome had never seen anything to rival the two
hundred white buildings housing everything from
technological wonders to art treasures to her personal favorite: the artificial mountain and Crystal
Cave beneath the Dome of the Horticulture Treasure
House.

Out of suffering comes enlightenment, she
thought while strolling among the throngs eager for
a glimpse of the Viking ship bobbing on Lake Michigan. Had Lyndon not broken her heart and set her
on this course, she would never have seen such a
kaleidoscope of wonders. She would have continued,
placid and content, among the people and things she
had known since birth. She'd never realized how terrifying and thrilling the world could be for a woman
who dared set out on her own.

As the crowd grew ever greater, Marc took her
hand. He whistled toward the others in their party.
Laughing, they all converged near the water's edge.
Salome hadn't felt this happy in weeks. Marc's broad
grin and joking patter showed that the festive atmo-
sphere had lifted his own melancholy spirits. She
squeezed his hand impulsively and was rewarded
with a dazzling smile. Had she not left Black Horse
she would never have met Marc nor any of these
warm, gifted people.

As Dagmar babbled excitedly about the beauty of
The Golden Doorway, a wave of love for her new
friends suffused Salome. She'd only known them a
brief summer, yet she felt closer to Flora, Dagmar
and the others than to her own mother and sisters.

To her family, she was merely an aging spinster who read too much and dreamed of impossible things, like law school and Lyndon Whittier.

But to these engaging and colorful show folk, she was a daring young woman, bold as brass, one of them. Her family would never understand how life in the theater could be so rich and filled with fun. Her family would disapprove of such fun anyway. Salome didn't know how she would feel when she went back to her old existence of schoolhouses and church socials. Of course, if she married Lyndon, life would change. He was going into politics, and her world would expand again, wouldn't it?

But as she giggled at Bill and Phil's imitations of the Hussar guards, she wondered. Lyndon was a decorous, conservative gentleman, and the wife of a governor or senator would be expected to be decorous and conservative as well.

Marc bent over double at Bill's jokes, tears of laughter running down his face. Marc had demanded nothing from her but that she be herself. Even when she was losing his props and knocking over trick cabinets, he had been exasperated, but never disapproving. Had Lyndon not abandoned her, she would never have met Marc Cooper, and never known that magic could exist both on- and offstage. Her throat constricted as she watched him. Head thrown back, his infectious laughter rising above the babble of the crowds, he stood in the fading October light, as robust and impressive as the marble statues lining the lagoon. He was as filled with life and color as this glorious World's Fair, and to think such a ferocious individual claimed to love her. Euphoria and fear swept over her at the thought.

"Look at the lights!" Boblo cried out.

As the sun set, the statues and paintings decorating the white buildings faded from view. In their place a million electric lights twinkled on. As though the crowd spoke with one voice, a great "Ahhh!" could be heard. Salome squeezed Marc's hand, while Mickey grabbed her other hand excitedly. The dome of the Administration Building gleamed with a fiery light, as flames illuminated its facade.

She had seen electric lights before; Black Horse's own auditorium had a string of them out front, and at least two theaters on the circuit had boasted electricity. But compared to those meager incandescent bulbs, gaslight shone brighter and fiercer. Not here. Entranced, her gaze traveled over the endless lights lining every cornice and peristyle. It was if the night had been set afire by strings of glittering diamonds.

The new century was seven years away, but Salome suddenly felt as if she stood on the brink of the future. The world was changing all around her, and it was daunting, fearsome and glorious.

Suddenly colored lights illuminated the awesome jets and sprays of the fountains, turning them violet, gold, silver, emerald green and scarlet. A searchlight swept over the mesmerized thousands, and lit the angelic statue atop the Agricultural Building. Her outstretched wings seemed to hover over them all, the one comforting point in a thrilling new landscape of color and light.

She moved closer to Marc, and slipped her arm about his waist. He embraced her, and she felt his lips brush the top of her head. She'd lost her hat long ago to the lake breezes and bustle, but didn't care. She was so exhilarated, she wouldn't have minded if the winds had stripped her of all but her corset and petticoats.

Suddenly the lights playing on the fountain ceased, but before the crowd could voice disappointment, a rocket soared into the night sky, followed by another, then another. As fireworks exploded above them, Salome knew she could never desire anything more than to relive this night, to experience once again the aching beauty and spectacle, made all the more magnificent by being held in Marc's arms.

She might never know such happiness again. But she had no time to grieve. The sky was exploding with fury and color, and she was helpless to do anything but cry out in wonder.

If he died this minute, Marc knew he would die happy. Surrounded by his friends, with Salome's hand firmly tucked around his, he wandered through the fair like a desert boy come upon his first bazaar. He had always dreamed of fantastic things, believed in the impossible. Since he was a child in that hard fishing village, he had hungered for a world that dazzled with promise, a landscape peopled with daredevils and artists. And he was proud of his ability to make others forget their disappointments, their limitations. Proud that, if only for a moment, he could make the impossible seem possible. Women floated in midair, men burst free from chains, and a magician and his beloved assistant cheated death again and again.

Taking in the chaotic delights of the Midway Plaisance, Marc knew that he had indeed come home. His roots weren't with the sea air and codfish of Marblehead. Instead, he belonged among the Midway's camels and conjurers, the Moorish palace, the Bedouin encampment, the dancing girls with their castanets, and the Temple of Luxor.

"Watch out, Marc!" Laughing, Salome pulled him out of the path of a camel wending its way imperviously through the crowd.

He looked at the beast swaying down the narrow, brick-paved street. Atop its cushioned back sat two familiar figures. "Is that Mickey and Boblo?"

"Who else has hair that color?" Salome tried to shout a greeting at the couple, but it was futile in the surrounding din.

He looked around. Bill and Phil were busy flirting with the Egyptian flower girls, Flora and Lorenzo had set off for the Chinese Theatre, and Dagmar had just disappeared into the Labyrinth of Mirrors. He wouldn't even attempt to figure out where all the Nardinis had scattered, although he did spy Mama Nardini haggling over a brass lamp.

Looking down into Salome's happy face, he was relieved that they finally had a moment alone. Even if they were surrounded by Bedouins and Nubian tribal chiefs.

He cocked a thumb towards the camel stand. "Care for a ride yourself?"

"The ride looks a bit bumpy. But if you can find a reasonable-size elephant anywhere, I'll give that a try."

"Hmmmm." He pretended to scan the lights and movement of the enormous Midway. "Could be there's an elephant or two by the Hawaiian volcano."

"Let's go."

Pressed close together, they pushed and jostled their way through the excited throng.

"Been quite a day, hasn't it?"

She sighed like a woman after a night of pleasure. "I would never have imagined such wonders were only a nickel streetcar ride from downtown Chicago."

"After all this, I'm not sure Chicagoans will be all that impressed by my magic tricks. I might have to

305

throw myself into Lake Michigan, bound in chains and trapped in a trunk."

"If you even think about such a stunt, I'll lock you in the Zigzag Mystery Box and keep you there until the Fair is over."

"Worried about me?" He said it in a teasing tone, but was entirely serious.

"Always." She glanced over at him, and he saw that she was serious, too. "We've been very lucky. Julia has finally left us alone. And according to that last telegram from Cincinnati, Chauncey and the others should be sentenced to at least ten years."

Both of them left unspoken the still real threat of Robert Baer. Marc knew all too well that Baer was a man who didn't live well with failure. But the day had been too glorious to spoil with the grim face of reality. And the night promised to hold its own riches.

Salome had stuck close by him since they entered the fairgrounds hours ago. Every wonder, every new delight, had been immediately shared with him. It was as if the extravagance and greatness of the Fair had made their problems pale into insignificance. Maybe the endless possibility presented here in Jackson Park had convinced her that a life with him was far more possible—and marvelous—than any dull existence Lyndon Whittier could offer.

"Marc Cooper? Is that you? I'd heard you were going to be performing downtown during the Fair!"

A stocky young man stood behind him.

"Erik!"

The two men embraced.

"Salome Hall, this is Erich Weiss," Marc clapped his friend on the shoulder. "The second best magician in the country."

Erich gave him a scornful smile. "Don't listen to him, Miss Hall."

"Hah!" Marc gave him a playful shove.

"—in a showdown of illusion, the audience will always choose Houdini over Marco the Magnificent."

"So *you're* Houdini. I should be angry at you for helping to dream up that dreadful Water Tank Trick." Salome shook the young man's hand. Still in his teens, she guessed. But like Marc, he had piercing eyes and thick black hair. Perhaps such dramatic coloring was a requirement for magicians, she thought in amusement.

Erich's expression grew sober. "I heard about the accident. I told you it wasn't nearly ready, Marc. Why, it might be years before I'll risk such an illusion."

Marc grinned. "That's why you're not billed as 'magnificent.' "

"The last act billed as 'magnificent' showcased a trained mule called Millie."

"A second cousin," Marc shot back. "But she doesn't rehearse enough."

Erich laughed. "Well, I'm working tonight. Come to the corner of Cairo Street by the minaret in fifteen minutes. My brother and I will be mystifying the crowd for a few shekels."

Salome nodded her farewells.

"Nice to meet you, Miss Hall. And remember to take care of this daredevil here. He risks everything for a little applause or a smile from a pretty woman."

After the young man had disappeared in the crowd, Marc turned to her. "He's right, you know. I do risk everything." He took both her hands. "Risk everything with me, Salome."

She stared back at him, the lights and noise of the Midway fading to a dull distant roar. His eyes were

307

as bright and compelling as the electric lights decorating the White City. What woman could resist such a yearning gaze, or a man who revealed his heart so eagerly? Increasingly, she'd found herself staring at that gilt-framed photo of Lyndon. His handsome face was becoming more difficult to conjure up. Especially when Marc stood so close, his hands holding firmly onto hers, his body near enough to stir her windswept hair with his breath.

"If I risk everything," she finally said, "I may lose it all."

He pulled her closer, trapping both her hands against his strong chest. "Never me, Salome. Never me."

Standing amid this fantastic spectacle of camels and dancing girls, she could well believe that her life was destined for vaudeville, dark-eyed magicians, and nights filled with fireworks and electric lights. She wanted to believe she had no commitments elsewhere, no sense of duty to her family back in Black Horse, or to that weak, elegant man who now begged for another chance.

"I want to believe," she murmured.

With so much noise in the air, Marc couldn't possibly have heard her, but his eyes brightened as though he had. He bent his head over hers, blocking out the minarets and the lights of the great Ferris Wheel. All she could see for a moment was Marc's haunting and beautiful eyes. Then she wound her arms about his neck, meeting his lips hungrily.

She pressed herself hard against him, wanting to feel every ridge, every muscle of a body she now knew intimately. She had dreamed of being melded to this body for weeks now, dreamed of seeing those dark eyes look at her with tenderness once more. She had dreamed of feeling his furious heartbeat drumming beneath her own.

And he felt better than all of her dreams, richer, more overpowering, sweeter. Lyndon had not branded himself upon her as this man had. She broke apart for a second, but Marc didn't let her come up for air long. He possessed her mouth as completely as he had possessed her body on that moonlit night. She could do nothing else but cling to him, fingers digging into his broad shoulders like a person clinging onto her last chance at life.

Finally, he backed away, but only to rain hot kisses upon her face, her brow, the hollow of her throat. Surely passersby must be staring in disapproval, but she was oblivious, oblivious to everything but Marc's mouth on hers, and his hands running urgently along her waist, her hips. The exotic music from the Turkish tent broke upon the night air. Salome had never heard a melody so sensual, so filled with desire and longing.

"I love you, Salome," Marc whispered in her ear, then planted another kiss along her neck. "Say you love me. Say it."

She ached with the desire to forget everything but Marc. And everyone.

Trying to catch her breath, she cradled Marc's face in her hands. "You know the truth. You've always known." She kissed him. "I do. I do lo—"

"Salome! Salome and Marc!"

She looked up in alarm. Several people were shouting their names.

"Blast, what is it now?" Marc's expression was positively stormy.

Spying Flora's flowered yellow bonnet in the crowd, Salome broke away from Marc's embrace. A second later, the dancer and Lorenzo emerged from the crowd.

"There you are," Flora said breathlessly. "Mickey and Boblo told us they saw you walking towards the volcano."

"What is it?" Marc asked in an obviously irritated voice.

Flora ignored him, and instead grabbed Salome by the elbow. "You'll never believe who we ran into at the Chinese Theatre. An old friend of yours from Missouri."

Salome felt the joy of this day vanish. Obviously, Julia Dupree was not done with them, but of all the wretched times for her to upset their lives again. Looking about wildly, she thought she saw a blond woman walking through the crowd, but the honey-gold tresses looked far too natural and elegant to belong to Julia.

Just as she lost sight of the woman, she heard a mellifluous voice ring out.

"My dear Sally, what a delightful surprise."

She gasped.

A tall, brown-haired man was making his way towards her. He was handsome, smiling and confident. And even in this shouting, raucous throng, he was elegant as only a gentleman could be.

Especially a gentleman like Lyndon Whittier.

Chapter Eighteen

Stunned, Salome could only watch helplessly as Lyndon took her hand and bowed low. Pulling her hand back, she stared at it a moment as if wondering how an apparition was able to plant a kiss upon it.

"You are looking exceedingly well, Sal." Lyndon's gaze swept over her with obvious approval. "What a fortuitous occurrence. If Jane hadn't recognized Miss Flora from their time together on the circuit, I would never have known you were at the Fair tonight. Although, of course, I was aware you were performing here in Chicago this week."

When Salome still didn't respond, he looked over at Marc. "I assume you are Marc Cooper. Or should I call you Marco the Magnificent? We've read the most laudatory reviews regarding your magic act these past few months. In fact, Jane and I have tickets for your first show tomorrow night."

Marc took a deep breath, which ended ominously

in a low rumble. Salome broke out of her amazed stupor in time to see him glare at Lyndon, like a jungle cat whose dinner has just been snatched away.

"Where is Miss Dupree, by the way?" Marc asked in a cool voice that betrayed none of the agitation she knew he was feeling.

"Where is she indeed?" Lyndon scanned the shoving crowd. "There she is. Jane, over here!"

He didn't sound like a solicitous man in love, Salome thought. In fact, he'd obviously forgotten about Jane in his haste to come see her. And now he was leaving the young woman to fight her way through the mob alone. A most unchivalrous gesture for a man as well-mannered as Lyndon Whittier.

Yet, when Jane did at last appear, Salome's heart sank. She was as beautiful as ever. Her memory hadn't been playing tricks on her all these months. Even the pushing throngs couldn't dishevel the upswept blonde curls or the green crescent-shaped hat that perched daintily atop them. Dressed stylishly, Jane's shapely figure was enhanced further by her apple-green serpentine skirt and double-breasted jacket trimmed in lace. She belonged on the marble steps of one of the Fair's more impressive pavilions, not being jostled here among the camels and Turkish dancing girls of the Midway. Jane's expression showed that she would have gladly preferred to be elsewhere as well.

"How are you, Jane?" Salome was surprised that she could actually manage a polite smile for the woman who stole Lyndon away from her.

Jane nodded, her lovely face grave and pale. "A bit tired, actually. I've certainly had my fill of all this." She gestured towards the Midway barkers, Nubians and babbling tourists.

Lyndon brushed off a speck of dirt from her jacket.

312

"It's my fault she's so exhausted. I really should not have insisted we leave the pavilions, but everyone told us that the amusements of the Midway were spectacular."

"Instead, we find nothing but buffoons and camels." Jane sighed, bestowing a hint of a smile in Marc's brooding direction.

"Oh, but then you must not have ridden the Ice Railway," Flora said, her bonnet bobbing with enthusiasm. "Or seen the lions at Hagenbeck's Animal Show."

"This Hagenbeck fellow has got trained lions climbing over horses, and tigers riding velocipedes!" Lorenzo's eyes opened wide with wonder, still moved by the memory.

"How charming it all sounds," Jane said in a flat voice. "A pity we must take our leave."

Lyndon cleared his throat. "I think perhaps we could stay another hour. After all, you haven't seen Flora in years. And certainly we have much to discuss with Salome. Our old friend from Black Horse is now trodding the boards. Think of the anecdotes she must have to tell us about her sojourn in the world of magic."

Marc muttered something about "fools" under his breath.

"We're all going to be in Chicago for the rest of the week," Salome said quickly. "I'm sure we'll have time to reminisce."

Jane pulled at her gloves. "Exactly. It was a pleasure bumping into everyone, but I do have a rehearsal tomorrow afternoon. Singing isn't like magic, you know. Our art requires long hours of devotion and work."

"I beg your pardon," Marc said. "But I doubt you

313

practice your pretty songs more than we do our illusions."

"Now, Jane didn't mean to offend." Lyndon shot the blonde a warning look. "But it has been a frightfully long day."

Salome held out her hand. "Till later in the week then." Although she had been looking forward to seeing Lyndon ever since that dreadful night in May, now that he was standing before her, she was shocked at how uneasy she felt in his presence.

And Jane wasn't looking her usual serene self. Beneath the fashionable hat, her face wore a petulant, strained expression. She looked like a woman who hadn't been happy in a long time. But she was with Lyndon. So how could she not be happy?

Lyndon took Salome's outstretched hand, but instead of shaking it, he merely clasped it. His luminous brown eyes held the old affection and regard. For a moment, they might have been back in her mother's kitchen in Black Horse, reciting Shakespeare and gazing at each other across the wooden table. But now she was all too aware of Marc breathing heavily beside her, while Jane's blue gaze held anything but friendship for her old girlhood friend.

"Good-bye then." She had to pull her hand from his firm grasp.

"Let's go, Lyndon." Jane tapped the ground with her parasol.

Lyndon refused to take his eyes from Salome. "I have an idea. Why don't we all take a ride on the Ferris Wheel? First of its kind in the world. Who knows if we'll ever see its like again?"

"Are you mad?" Jane tugged at his arm. "I told you that I was tired. And I'm beginning to have heart palpitations again." She turned towards the others. "I fear that the strain of touring has upset my nerves. When I tire, my heart begins racing most grievously. Doctors have warned me that I might die one day from overexertion." She pulled at Lyndon again. "I don't want to risk an attack here in this forsaken Midway."

Startled by Jane's admission of nerves, Salome was even more surprised by Lyndon's apparent indifference.

"You'll be fine, my dear. Why don't you remain behind with the others while Sal and I take a ride on the Wheel?"

Before she could answer, Lyndon grabbed Salome's elbow and was steering her away through the crowd.

"Lyndon!"

Salome looked back to see Jane staring after them in complete disbelief. Marc had his fists clenched at his side, his expression dark, furious and resigned. Poor Marc. He must think Lyndon was running off with her for good, that they'd disappear in Mr. Ferris' great wheel, never to be seen again.

"I'll meet you in front of the Old Vienna exhibit in one hour, my dear!" His hand tightened on Salome's arm. Wordlessly, he pulled her into the throngs until Jane's outraged cries and Marc's desperate gaze were lost.

Only when they were at last in front of the gigantic Ferris Wheel did Lyndon stop and look down at her. "You're all mine, now," he whispered. "Mine."

Not for the first time, Marc wished he wielded real magic powers. If only he were a dark sorcerer, robed in violet and ebony, able to wave a wand and enchant a woman. Or command the destruction of his enemy. As Lyndon carried Salome off into the crowd,

Marc had no doubt that the well-dressed lawyer was his enemy, a more deadly one than even Robert Baer and Chauncey. They only wanted to destroy his career, while Lyndon was intent on destroying his only real chance at happiness.

For a blazing second, Marc wanted to run after them, but he couldn't do it. As much as he wanted to, he couldn't force Salome to stay with him. She had to make that decision herself; she had to understand, as he did, that they were meant to be together as surely as the stars blanketed the night sky. Not all of his seductive pleas or angry looks could weigh in the balance. She must know it in her heart. And maybe time alone with that fool Lyndon would open up her eyes.

Beside him, Jane fumed like a woman scorned. He didn't blame her. But he couldn't summon up much sympathy. Even if she was lovelier and more polished than her sister, there was a steeliness in her expression that reminded him of Julia. He was certain that Lyndon had had his fill of the golden-haired singer, who obviously needed a lot of cosseting and care.

And he'd noticed how Lyndon's eyes lit up at his first sight of Salome. He didn't blame him. She did look ravishing tonight. She'd lost her hat to the winds off the lake this afternoon, and her gleaming dark brown hair lay soft about her face, tendrils hanging about the nape of her neck, amber clips keeping her smooth tresses from spilling down her back completely. Her cheeks were flushed from both excitement and the cool breezes of early autumn. The short plum-colored jacket she wore set off her tiny waist, and he was certain Lyndon had noticed how provocatively that pale lavender skirt swirled about her hips. No, that popinjay would have missed nothing about Salome.

He would have seen that the demure little woman he'd deserted in May had become as stylish and assured as Jane Dupree, but far lovelier, far sweeter, and infinitely more full of life and energy. Lyndon would know in an instant that he'd run off with the wrong woman.

If only he could make Lyndon Whittier and both tiresome Dupree sisters vanish in a blaze of light. If only he could convince Salome that she need only look into his eyes to see her own future happiness. But without the powers of a sorcerer, Marc could do nothing but watch the swirling activity of the Midway.

And pray.

"You're mine," Lyndon repeated, and pulled her close.

Just before his mouth claimed hers, she pulled back. "I hardly belong to you." She straightened her velvet jacket. "You or any man."

"I understand how you must feel."

"I doubt that."

He looked at the line of people moving onto the cars of the Ferris Wheel. "Let's get on. At least that way, I won't have to worry about you leaving before I've said what I must."

She looked at him for a long moment. "*I* wasn't the one who ran away."

He held out his arm, which she took after a brief hesitation. "Then allow me to abase myself before you." He pointed to the great spokes of the wheel looming above them. "And what better place to seek forgiveness than among the stars."

"Should I expect poetry next? Shelley, perhaps?"

317

"For you, only Shakespeare. Or have you forgotten how we read the sonnets together?"

"I've forgotten nothing."

As they stepped into the glass-enclosed car, he leaned over her shoulder. "You will forgive me, won't you? The gentle woman I've known all these years would never be so cruel as to turn me away."

She settled herself near the end of a row, the glass on all sides allowing her a spectacular view. Lyndon sat swiftly on the plush-covered seat beside her. He seemed oblivious to the fifty other people sitting in the car with them. "You did get my letter, didn't you? Good lord, maybe that's why you're acting like this. I wrote you a letter, and sent it to your mother. I begged her to forward it to you, but since she didn't—"

She turned to him, just as the door of their wood-veneered car slammed shut. "Never fear. She gave it to Julia, who then passed it on to me."

"Is Julia here in Chicago, too?"

"No. The last time I saw her was weeks ago in Cincinnati."

He breathed an audible sigh of relief. "Well, then you know how deeply sorry I am. I regret every day I've spent apart from your sweet presence. Every lost hour."

The wheel slowly began to move, and she felt the car lift up into space. The people in the car moved excitedly on their swivel seats, chattering like birds.

"I remember warning that you would regret marrying Jane," she said softly, trying to keep her attention on the slow movement of the car. Lyndon was undoubtedly looking at her with pleading eyes, and she didn't think she could deal with yet another heartsick man.

"Thank heaven I haven't married her. Although

she expects us to wed next week. She's even had banns posted. I told her not to do such a thing, but she wouldn't listen. Now I fear she'll be most upset when I refuse to go through with it."

Salome did turn to him now. Even in the dim light of the car, Lyndon still had the power to make her catch her breath. That mane of brown pomaded hair was achingly familiar, as was his expensive gray serge suit. His hat of nutria fur was new, as was the pearl stick pin in his cravat, but his old, accustomed elegance permeated the very air he breathed.

Sitting beside him now, she understood why he had entranced her for so long. Who would have imagined that a handsome, worldly fellow such as this would bother to pay attention to a chubby, little bookworm? A goose girl being courted by a prince could not have felt so grateful, or giddy. No wonder she'd fallen helplessly in love with him: she'd been in love with everything about him, from his gentle smile to his soothing voice, his tall, graceful figure and his impressive intellect. And, above all, in love with his kindness and rapt attention.

When had he turned unkind? He had, she could see that clearly now. It was in the way his eyes turned hard whenever he mentioned Jane. Certainly he had been most unkind that night in May, when he stepped out from under the willows with another woman clinging to him.

"So you haven't told Jane you won't marry her?"

He shook his head. "Not yet. Jane is a bit of a handful, emotionally speaking. One must take great care when broaching unpleasant topics to her."

"She suffers from heart palpitations often?"

"Palpitations, headaches, vapors, crying jags that would fill Lake Michigan. I never suspected that the artistic temperament was so fragile." He paused, gazing out at the vista below them. "And exhausting."

They remained silent. The Ferris Wheel moved very slowly; one revolution would take twenty minutes. No matter the outcome of this conversation, Salome would be forced to stay beside Lyndon for a good while more.

"She's not what she seems." Lyndon wore a sad expression, but his voice was tinged with self-pity. "She's high-strung, and requires a great deal of attention. Without it, she becomes overwrought. We actually canceled two performances in California. I confess I've grown quite impatient with her this past summer. We've had some nasty quarrels on tour, which certainly don't help her nerves."

"Jane never seemed like the nervous type in Black Horse."

"When you knew her she was just a country girl, not a famous singer. I've learned that fame isn't as appealing as it seems, at least not theatrical fame. It carries all sorts of responsibilities and expectations. And some shoulders are too weak to bear them well."

"Poor Jane." Amazingly, Salome felt genuine pity for her. "To think that nerves could wreak such havoc on a person's life."

"Well, to be fair, it isn't only nerves. While performing out West, we consulted a specialist about her palpitations. He confirmed that she does suffer from a faulty heart valve. Surgery will not adequately correct it, so . . ." His voice trailed off.

"Is Jane dying?" Even if she had stolen away her fiancé, Salome would never have wished such calamity on Jane Dupree—or any woman.

"Now, now, I've upset you. You do have a gentle heart, my dear Sal. Let me put your mind at rest. Jane is not in immediate danger, but the doctors say she is highly unlikely to see her dotage. If she can manage to control the stress in her life, she might live another eight or ten years."

Salome sat back. All this time, she had been jealous of Jane, envying her beauty, her talent, her success. And, above all, envying her possession of Lyndon Whittier. Instead, the lovely young woman was to be pitied, not only for her deteriorating health, but for her poor choice in men. A wave of disapproval swept over her at Lyndon's eagerness to desert Jane, like a child exasperated with a broken toy.

She shook her head. "Then you must not leave her, Lyndon. The pain and stress might kill her."

"Nonsense. She's not on her deathbed yet. I told you, she has ten more years. And you wouldn't want me to stay with her out of pity." His voice became as smooth as honey. "Not after I've realized how wrong I was to leave you. I lost my head back in May. I don't know what came over me. Perhaps I was as bowled over by her celebrity as any stage-door Johnny. But I've regretted it every day since. Regretted giving up my life and my future plans. Above all, I regretted giving you up."

Suddenly she wished he weren't leaning so close. The pomade on his hair sickened her, and he seemed as if he would overpower her objections with sheer elegant will alone. "You claimed to love *her* only a few months ago. If a man loves a woman, he should do all he can to help her."

"Exactly. A man who loved Jane would do just that. He'd have all the patience in the world and would do all in his power to ease her stress and strain. But I feel none of those things. Not any more."

She stared at the lights of the White City below, glittering like a thousand stars. So he was running away again. But this time, he planned to run back into her sensible, safe arms.

He reached over and took her gloved hand in his own. "Do you remember the plans we made back home? Moving to Jefferson City after we married, starting my own practice. Then in a year or two, running for office. We can still do all that. You'd be the finest politician's wife ever. Intelligent, poised, loyal—"

"And slightly scandalous now. I fear I'm no longer a candidate for the position of governor's wife. Not after a season as Salome the Fair."

He lifted her chin, forcing her to look at him. "The right politician can conceal that easily enough. After all, you only spent a brief summer working with that ridiculous magician."

"He's not ridiculous."

"Oh, hang the magician. He's not important to us or our future. We can put this ludicrous past behind us and get on with our lives together."

She felt numb. For ten years she had loved this man, been slavishly devoted to him, even when he deserted her. Her heart had ached for months at his absence. So why, when he was hers for the taking once again, did she feel nothing?

"Why did you ask me to marry you this past spring?"

Lyndon looked genuinely startled. "What an absurd question."

"You knew me for ten years, we courted for four. What finally prompted you to propose?"

"I loved you, of course. How could you ever doubt that?" He leaned forward and whispered, "Didn't I prove my love that morning in Old Man Schiller's cabin?"

She remembered all too well the misty rain that

fell outside the cabin that day, the way Lyndon held her and undressed her slowly, the feel of a man moving within her for the first time. The sharp, unexpected pleasure, the relief that Lyndon did indeed desire her. All that she remembered very well. But it faded beside her memory of the night she'd spent with Marc, rocking with him in passion: hungry, shameless, ecstatic. Both of them lost to each other, bathed in sweat and moonlight, vulnerable and willing, out of control but safe in the other's arms.

"I've sometimes wondered if guilt didn't play a role in your proposal. Stealing a young lady's virtue and all that."

"Silly girl. I would have proposed eventually, but there were times when I felt we were friends more than lovers." He squeezed her arm. "I always knew you'd make an impeccable wife for a lawyer or politician, but that morning convinced me that marriage to you would hold other advantages."

"How romantic." She didn't want to look at him any longer, nor hear his confident voice. If only the Ferris Wheel would move faster.

"I love you, Sal." Despite the other people in the car, Lyndon laid his cheek against hers. "Forgive me, my dearest. Forgive my weakness, my foolishness. What I feel for you is stronger than—"

"Music and moonlight?" she finished.

He laughed. "You'll never let me forget that bit of poetic nonsense, will you? Never mind. Yes, what I feel for you is stronger than music and moonlight."

She pulled away from him. Clasping her hands in her lap, Salome looked out the glass panes.

"You're still angry. I know that, darling. But I won't go away again. I'll be by your side for the next fifty years. I swear it."

Below her the entire Fair spread out like a cornucopia of wonders and delights. But confined in this glass-enclosed box, she could hear nothing of the music and shouts below. She couldn't feel the crisp October breeze or smell the candied apples and Turkish sweetmeats. Trapped up here, the throngs of humanity couldn't press themselves against her, so that she felt their warmth and vitality. The electric lights seemed farther away and their fire cooler. It was safe in here, she decided, safe and predictable. The wheel would slowly go round, moving as methodically as a mill grinding wheat, and then the ride would cease just when expected.

She preferred the chaos below. She wanted to walk through the Midway once more, feeling Marc's arm tightly about her. She wanted to hear him laugh at the marvels, and talk extravagantly of the even more extravagant illusions he was planning. She wanted his unrestrained emotion and honesty, his unmasked pain and longing. She wanted Marc's love, which now seemed as majestic and wondrous as the illuminated white buildings below. Not until she sat beside Lyndon, listening to his sorry excuses, not until this moment had she known she wanted all of that so much.

She didn't want the ordered, acceptable life Lyndon was laying out for them. Decorous, useful, and admired. She didn't want to be a politician's wife, nor any man's wife—unless the man was a dark-eyed magician who floated upside down in water tanks and sawed women in half each night.

She wanted Marc. She wanted him more than anything she had ever known in her twenty-six years. And the overwhelming need to see him and hold him made her break out in an eager smile.

Lyndon mistakenly thought the happiness was for his sake.

"I'm glad you're pleased that we're together again, Sal. Exceedingly glad. I feared I'd have to grovel for weeks before you finally forgave my stupidity." His voice grew husky. "I would be loath to waste more weeks apart from you. This past summer has been torture. And seeing you now, my need for you is even greater than I'd imagined. You're different somehow. More vibrant, more desirable. I don't know what it is. The way you're wearing your hair perhaps, these smart new clothes, the manner in which you carry yourself. I don't know what it is, but you seem suddenly full of beauty and life. By God, you're different, and I like it."

She turned to him, her smile now touched with a hint of regret for what she must do. "It's because I'm in love. Desperately in love."

His eyes shone. "My dearest girl, I knew you would not be—"

"With Marc Cooper."

Lyndon froze. "What?"

"I'm in love with Marc Cooper." She felt joy at finally declaring it aloud.

"The magician?" Lyndon sat back, his hands spread out on his knees. "You're joking. This is some way of getting back at me for running off with Jane."

"No, I love him. Not as I loved you. My feelings for you were that of a grateful young girl, hero worship I suppose. But my love for Marc is that of a grown woman for a wonderful man." She took a deep, contented breath. "And I'm going to marry him."

For a moment, Lyndon could barely get a coherent word out. "Have you been drinking beer in the Irish Village? You can't marry someone like Marc Cooper. He's a cheap vaudeville performer."

"Oh, hardly cheap. The Orpheum Circuit pays him eight hundred a week."

He turned towards her, his body rigid with anger. "See here, Sal, I've had enough of this. I understand that you want to hurt me as I hurt you—"

"But I don't. All these months, I only wanted one thing: to see you again. I'd hoped everything would be the same, as it was before Jane upset our lives. But they're not. You're not the dependable, kind gentleman I always believed you to be. And I'm not the shy little schoolteacher trying to please everyone but myself."

"I don't believe this! This man can't mean anything to you. Think of all we have shared. All those years. Not to mention that morning in the cabin."

Salome was suddenly aware that the car was completely quiet. She wondered how long everyone had been paying rapt attention to their urgent conversation. Lyndon would probably be mortified, and the Salome of only a few months ago would have been, too. But now she didn't care if the whole world wanted to listen in.

"I've shared far more with Marc," she said gently, finding no pleasure in rejecting Lyndon now. "Friendship, laughter, working together as equals. And so much love. More love than I thought existed in this world." She paused. "And desire."

He grew very still. "Sal, I hope you are not implying that anything immoral has occurred between you and Mr. Cooper this summer."

Her steady gaze was her only response.

"This is unconscionable! Are you telling me that you've taken that fool magician to your bed?"

As the car erupted in tittering and gasps, even Lyndon became aware of their audience. He glanced around quickly at the faces turned towards them.

"I have," she said proudly.

"We have nothing more to say then." He pulled off

his hat and crushed it in his hands, as though needing to exert physical violence somehow. "You've already chosen your path. I'm sure you'll regret it. At least I cloaked my folly in poetry and silly notions of music and moonlight, but you've done nothing more than wallow in the mud."

"Now, Lyndon, surely you're not saying you've been a monk these past few months. Aren't you and Jane lovers?"

"No gentleman would answer such an impertinent question." He shot her a bitter look. "And no lady would dare ask it."

She sat back in her seat, the wheel moving so that the moon finally appeared in her field of vision. "I suppose I'm not a proper lady any longer."

"I should say not!"

Salome began laughing. "I'm so relieved."

"Have you taken complete leave of your senses?"

She was trying to take Lyndon's chagrin seriously. But she felt too jubilant—too free—to do anything else but laugh with joy. "I'm sorry, Lyndon, but if only you knew how lovely it feels *not* to be a proper lady."

Lyndon stared in disbelief as Salome dissolved in laughter. "What in heaven's name is responsible for this shameless display?"

"Blame it on magic," she said, then pointed to the moon shining outside their windows. "Magic and moonlight."

Chapter Nineteen

Trying to find one lone magician among the throngs of gawkers at the World's Fair was as frustrating as searching for a coin dropped into the sea. Salome pushed and squirmed her way into every Midway exhibit, stopping only once to gape at the startling gyrations of a dancer known as Little Egypt. But Marc was nowhere to be found.

The Fair would close soon for the night. Common sense told her to simply turn around and take the streetcar back to their hotel. Surely he would turn up eventually. But the longer she stayed away, the more certain he would be that she had gone back to Lyndon. She had already caused Marc enough pain with her vacillating and pigheaded devotion to her former love. She dreaded being responsible for bringing even one more anxious hour to her magnificent magician. The word 'magician' brought to mind Marc's young friend Erich Weiss. Of course, where else would Marc be but standing before another master of illusion and escape?

For ten minutes, the possibility gave her hope, but not a single familiar face greeted her in the small crowd watching an act billed as "The Brothers Houdini." Two men stood on a makeshift stage in a small corner of the Midway. Although he was in the midst of performing a card trick with a fellow she assumed was his brother, young Erich glanced over and gave a brief smile of recognition.

Her heart sank. Marc wasn't here. With each moment that passed without him, she felt more a failure. How could she have been so foolish all these months? She'd turned away from a man offering her love, friendship and a future filled with promise, holding back like a kitten trembling near the edge of a precipice. If she'd only had the courage, she would have peeked over the edge and seen what lay beyond: a breathtaking vista filled with wonders, an exciting landscape waiting to be explored by her and the daredevil she had come to adore.

Instead, she'd refused to tell him how much she loved him, him and no other. That cold omission on her part had caused him a misery not even the master of illusion could conceal.

And for what had she done all this? For a chance to win back a man who had deserted her for a pretty face, a man who callously wanted to now abandon that woman, and was using Salome as a convenient excuse. If the whole scenario weren't so pathetic, she might work up a righteous indignation. Yet she had no one but herself to blame. It was her blind stupidity that had refused to relegate Lyndon to the past, her inability to believe that the soft-spoken gentleman who had singled her out for conversations about law and poetry might not have a character as noble as his profile. Indeed, he had shown himself to have no character at all. And the man who had cared for her, the man who had always been honest and kind, passionate and gentle, that man was now alone somewhere in the Fair, thinking that she had abandoned him.

Dispirited, she turned down the alleyway towards Cairo Street. The exotic music from the Turkish tents wafted over her. To think that just an hour ago, she and Marc had kissed to the strains of such lush melodies. And now she was wandering about like a lost camel in the desert.

She stopped. A camel. If she were riding one of the camels that were forever bearing tourists through the Midway, she would have a much better chance of being seen by Marc. Jumping over a puddle of spilled beer, Salome hurried towards the camel stand. Why hadn't she thought of this before? For a schoolteacher, she could be remarkably stupid. It was a wonder she had been able to teach Marc anything.

She stopped in her tracks again. That gave her another idea. Maybe the late hour and the smell of cotton candy and incense were causing her to think in appropriately dramatic fashion. The tents and walls of the Midway attractions were decorated with playbills announcing the treasures within. She snatched one off the walls of the Moorish Palace. As expected, the reverse side of the bill boasted nothing but plain white paper. A few yards away, a street artist was making charcoal sketches of tourists. Surely he didn't need all those bits of charcoal and chalk scattered about him. And even if he did, Salome hoped a few dollars would convince him to part with at least one stick of charcoal.

If Marc were anywhere near the Midway, he would

not be able to miss her messages. She might know little about love and men, but she did have a talent for teaching. And Marc had been a very apt pupil.

Little did he know, but tonight was his first big test. For both their sakes, she prayed that he would pass.

Each minute weighed heavily on him until he felt like a man slowly being buried alive. Yet even with the knowledge that Salome had chosen Lyndon, Marc could still dredge up amazement and wonder as he stood before the entrance to the Hagenbeck Animal Show.

Just above the doorway to the arena, a huge iron cage hung suspended in midair. The cage dazzled onlookers with its myriad electric lights, the bold brightness revealing five lions circling their trainer. With each snap of his whip, the trainer directed the great beasts to move about the confines of the cage like jungle dancers. Despite Marc's heartache, for a brief moment, even he forgot about his doomed romance as he watched the marvelous sight of man and beast performing in midair. And when the trainer shot a revolver into the air, he found himself gasping with the crowd when, as if by magic, lions and trainer vanished from sight.

Staring intently at the empty cage, its lights extinguished, Marc tried to find the trap door that permitted such an impressive illusion. Before he left Chicago, he must talk with Hagenbeck and discover how he pulled off this stunning feat. As far as he knew, no other magician had yet used wild animals in his act. Such a thing could make him world-famous, although he couldn't resist grinning at imagining Salome's reaction at working with a lion or two.

Sharon Pisacreta

He sobered instantly. What a blasted idiot he was. Did he really imagine that she was going to stay with him and the act? After all, she had left with Lyndon over an hour ago. To ride the Ferris Wheel only took twenty minutes, so where was she? With Lyndon, of course. When that fool lawyer dragged her away, she hadn't uttered a word of protest or tried to shake off his grip.

No, she had what she'd longed for this whole summer. Time alone with Lyndon Whittier, time enough to convince both of them that they'd made a terrible mistake in getting involved with show folk. Time enough for them to pledge their love to one another, and maybe express relief at being spared even one more day in the sordid world of the theater or its sorry denizens.

Shoving his hands in his coat pockets, Marc started off towards the exit. Salome wasn't going to show up. She was gone. Maybe she was already back at the hotel, packing her bags. He had a hard time breathing, his chest tight with bitter tears he refused to shed. He had done all he could, everything in his power to convince her of his love, but it wasn't enough. Blast Lyndon's deceitful smile and Salome's stubbornness, but it wasn't enough.

Head down, Marc didn't see the man in front of him until he knocked him over. When he pulled the fellow to his feet, Marc was amused to see he had knocked down one of several Egyptian conjurers on Cairo Street.

"Be careful." The wizened man pulled out a hen's egg from behind his ear. "Samir has spells to help and hurt."

Marc brushed the dust off the older fellow's robes. "How about spells to forget?"

The conjurer closed his eyes, his brown face

screwed up in dozens of wrinkles. After a moment, he opened his eyes once more. "Now is not time to forget." He cracked open the hen's egg, allowing a tiny bird to fly out.

Marc couldn't help but grin. Was the whole Fair peopled with magicians?

The conjurer tapped Marc hard on the forehead. "Look about you. Your destiny has been written."

Marc stared after the old man as he disappeared into the Temple of Luxor. A veiled Egyptian flower girl offered him a single perfect lotus, then surprised him by refusing the coin he offered in return.

"For your lady," she murmured.

He was long accustomed to dealing with illusion and trickery. Life was fuller for having secrets that could not be plumbed. Yet even he was caught off-balance by the Midway. It was as if the real world beyond these lights and minarets had vanished and he was now wandering in a land of real magic. He had no control over this, he thought wonderingly, his gaze sweeping over the nearby Bedouin encampment.

His mouth fell open. A piece of paper fluttered on one of the tents. "MARC," it read. "I LOVE ONLY YOU. SALOME."

"What the devil?" He tore the paper away from the nail holding it in place. Running his fingers over the words he could at last read, he felt a wave of relief and joy. He didn't know how such an impossible thing had happened. Obviously he'd just gotten a miraculous sign. Salome had chosen him. Him, not that fancy fool Lyndon.

He stuffed the paper inside his jacket. Maybe the old Egyptian had conjured this up. Maybe it appeared out of thin air. Why not? On such a night, anything might be possible.

Sharon Pisacreta

Marc had to find Salome. He would show her this paper as proof that miracles existed. But as he hurried down Cairo Street, he saw yet another paper on the wall of the Irish Village.

This one read: "MARC. I'M LOOKING FOR YOU. DON'T LEAVE THE MIDWAY. I LOVE YOU. SALOME."

By the time he found the fifth piece of paper declaring her love for him, Marc was laughing out loud. So this wasn't a conjurer's trick or angelic assistance. This was even better. Salome was leaving notes of love for him strewn about the Midway, hoping he would find at least one. Thanks to her, he could finally read their thrilling message.

But where was she? He shouted her name, but was drowned out by the chants of the sweetmeat sellers.

Adding to the cacophony were the drums that heralded the appearance of one of the camels. He stepped to the side, knowing that the camels always swayed in unexpected directions. Now that he'd learned of Salome's love for him, he didn't want to get stepped on by a desert beast.

"Marc!"

He looked around sharply. Beneath the drums and the cries of the street sellers, someone was shouting his name.

"Marc, up here!"

He looked up in time to see Salome waving at him from atop the passing camel. Her petite body swayed dangerously with the motion of the beast, and Marc feared she'd slip off the gaudy saddle.

"Hold on! Wait for me."

He pushed through the crowd until he reached the flanks of the camel. The driver said something angrily to him in Arabic, and tried to shoo him away with a thin stick.

"I'll come down," Salome said through the din.

Before he could prevent her, she swept her legs over the pommel and leaped into the air. As she fell, he grabbed onto her waist, but her weight staggered him and they both toppled to the ground.

Nearly trampled by the other fairgoers, Marc dragged Salome safely out of the path of yet another camel.

Pressed against the walls of the Moorish Palace, Marc hugged her so tightly, he feared he might end up bruising her ribs. He eased up a bit, only to kiss her repeatedly.

When he finally let her come up for air, she laughed softly and said, "I've never jumped off a camel before."

"And they call *me* a daredevil. You're only lucky I was there to catch you." He smoothed back her hair.

She nodded, a tender smile on her face. "For a moment, I was afraid you were going to let me go."

He hugged her tight once more. "Never," he promised fiercely. "I'll never let you go."

To the east, the sun was beginning to lighten the sky over the great sleeping city. Marc and Salome hadn't slept yet, but lying in each other's arms, neither seemed willing to surrender to the dream world yet. Not when reality had suddenly become far more enchanting than even the most blissful dream.

"Can you ever forgive me?" Salome ran her fingers through the luxurious mat of black curls covering his chest.

Marc's strong arm tightened about her, softly caressing her bare breast. "Never," he said with a teasing grin.

"I can't believe I ever thought him a kind man, let alone a gentleman."

Sharon Pisacreta

Marc raised her chin. "Let's bid farewell to Lyndon Whittier. All that matters now is that we're together. Nothing will ever keep us apart again."

They exchanged a lingering kiss. Salome pressed her naked body against him, enjoying the feel of his arousal. He teased her nipple, and she reached down and grabbed him. Marc pulled her even closer.

She loved lying here with him. She would never get enough of sharing Marc's bed—and his heart. They had made love three times since returning from the Fair, but her need for him seemed greater than ever. She flung her leg about his, both of them on their sides, facing each other.

He fondled her breast once more, then left off to explore the curve of her waist, the roundness of her hips and buttocks, and at last the wetness between her legs that was proof of her aching desire.

Large and erect, he slipped smoothly inside her, and she opened to him. They fit together perfectly. As they exchanged a deep kiss, she let out a soft moan. He moved slowly within her at first. No doubt he was as sore as she was. Their lovemaking this evening had sometimes turned wild and out of control. She was amazed the guests staying in the room next door hadn't complained to the hotel management over their occasional shouts and cries.

When had she learned to wrap herself about a man like this? How had she known to take him into her mouth and pleasure him so? And surely a woman wasn't supposed to enjoy the way a man's tongue felt exploring her most intimate place. But she reveled in it all. Luxuriated in every touch of his, every thrust, every kiss and every movement. No doubt this was quite shameless behavior for a Missouri schoolteacher. But if this was shame, she would never be able to get enough of it.

They began moving faster now, his movements becoming harder, more urgent.

"You'll kill me, Salome," he panted. "You'll kill me with pleasure."

Instead of answering, she pushed Marc onto his back, then straddled his body. He groaned, grabbing on to her hips.

He pushed her down hard, and she held onto his wrists as she lifted her body up and then pushed down. Though both tried to go slow, neither could wait, neither wanted to. She rode him, head thrown back in delight, while he tried to control his own excitement, trying to slow down her movements. But she would have her pleasure—and his.

With a wrenching cry, he held her tight about him, and spilled his seed within. She sat very still. Just as his own cries faded, she clutched at his shoulders, overtaken by her own pleasure.

When they lay once again, exhausted in each other's arms, Marc let out a small chuckle.

Smiling, she looked up at him, his expression barely discernible in the early dawn.

"What's so funny?"

"I was thinking that my little schoolteacher was actually a wild jungle cat. You probably wouldn't be at all afraid of lions and tigers."

"Don't know about that." She rested her chin on his damp chest. "All I do know is that I'm a woman in love."

"I'm gratified that love has that effect on you."

Salome tweaked his nose. "You're something of a wild man yourself. Or maybe it's your particular brand of magic."

"After all the lovemaking tonight, I suspect that soon enough we'll have a little piece of magic of our own. Someone who will have their own way of keeping us from getting enough sleep every night."

Tears pricked Salome's eyes, but these were happy ones. "A baby," she whispered.

"Yes, our son or daughter, so we're going to get the marriage license as soon as possible. I may be a daredevil magician, but on matters of family, I am very old-fashioned. Cupertinos are always born in wedlock." Even though he wore a wide grin, Salome sensed his seriousness.

"Is this a marriage proposal?"

In answer, he waved his hands swiftly about her head and the pillow. Mystified, she could only watch. "Will you marry me?" he asked, opening up his hand and revealing a ring inside.

"When did you buy this?" The gold circlet twinkled with a red jewel and what looked like diamonds on either side. She slipped it on her ring finger. It fit perfectly.

"I bought in back in Omaha."

"Omaha? But why would you buy a ring back in Omaha? Nothing had happened between us yet."

"For me it had. That night you saved my life in the water tank, I knew for a fact I was in love with you. Buying the ring was a way of convincing myself that one day you would feel the same way, too."

This time the tears did flow. He pulled her close.

"I'm so sorry for making you wait this long. I was such a blind fool. I think I've loved you from the moment you jumped down from that stage in St. Louis and scared off Mr. Jenson. You must think me the biggest fool who ever lived to even consider choosing someone like Lyndon over you."

"Careful. No one can call the woman I love 'a fool.' Not even you." He looked at the ring on her finger, kissing it once. "We're together now, now and for the rest of our lives. That's all that matters."

Magic & Moonlight

Feeling her soft and warm in his arms, Marc knew that nothing else did matter. Until Salome entered his life, he had never known how lonely he was, how empty he felt inside with only applause and magic tricks to keep away the pain. But having her by his side, being able to go through life graced by her gentleness and laughter made him swell with pride—and deep, deep gratitude.

She snuggled against his chest, and sighed with obvious contentment. "Music and moonlight," she murmured.

"What, darling?"

Salome yawned. "My heart once broke because Lyndon said his love for Jane was as wonderful as 'music and moonlight.'" She laughed sleepily. "How silly."

"The man doesn't know what he's talking about." Marc reached down for the blanket and tucked it around them both. "Any fool knows that magic and moonlight are far more powerful."

"That's what I told him," she whispered.

A moment later, she was fast asleep.

Marc tried to stay awake as long as possible, as if to be sure that he hadn't dreamed up this woman now safe in his arms. Everything was going to be fine now. In the brief summer they'd known each other, so many forces had tried to pull them apart. But not now. They belonged together, and nothing could change that.

So why did he still feel afraid?

Chapter Twenty

The excitement of the White City in Jackson Park had stirred up every neighborhood and district of Chicago. Marc was pleased that their two-week engagement at Loew's Theater was completely sold out. But he wasn't arrogant enough to give the credit to either to his magic tricks or to the charms of the other Orpheum performers. Even Flannagan's Flea Circus on State Street was drawing record-size crowds. Until the Fair closed its doors at the end of the month, the city's thirst for entertainment would be unquenchable.

He knocked on Salome's dressing room door, then peeked in. She had hairpins sticking out of her mouth, and her long hair was in beautiful disarray about her shoulders.

"Show starts in twenty minutes, darling. Do you need anything before I change?"

"Just you," she muttered, as two pins fell from between her lips.

He planted a kiss on her bare shoulder. "Adorable wench," he teased. "See you soon, and break a leg."

She winked at him in the mirror before he shut the door. Neither of them had slept more than a couple of hours last night, yet he felt excited, jumpy even. And with more energy than if he were a rambunctious ten year old. Well, why shouldn't he? His whole life was just beginning, with Salome as his wife and partner. No wonder he felt exhilarated and restless, as though the world were too slow and sedate to contain his newfound happiness.

But when he opened the door to his own dressing room, that happiness dimmed. A man sat before his dressing table, cigar smoke as thick as a cloud about his thin face.

"What in the hell are you doing here?" Marc let the door swing wide open. He wasn't going to give Robert Baer an opportunity to do any harm.

"I came to see the Columbian Exposition, of course," Baer said smoothly. "My wife had a hankering to see what all the fuss was about. We'll probably spend a week here before heading home."

"I really don't care about you or your wife's travel plans."

"But I care about yours." Baer examined the lit end of his cheroot. "Word is that you're going to be playing Tony Pastor's in New York next month. Big money to be made in New York."

"Yeah, and you're not going to see any of it. Now get out. Or haven't you heard that Mr. Farrell and his friends are doing time in Cincinnati? Keep hounding me and Miss Hall, and I'm sure the authorities can

find enough dirt to land you in a nice prison somewhere."

"I didn't come here to threaten, Marco. You do me
a disservice. On the contrary, I'm here to offer you a
contract."

"What!"

"An equitable contract, all legal and aboveboard."
With the cheroot clamped between his teeth, he
slowly withdrew a slip of paper from his vest pocket.
"Here, read it for yourself."

Marc took the paper.

"Or would you like me to read it for you?"

"Not necessary." He unfolded the paper. "Well,
what you lack in imagination, Baer, you make up for
in nerve. This looks just as underhanded as my last
contract, except you're willing to let me keep sixty
per cent of my earnings, instead of fifty."

Baer sat up straight, his face registering surprise.
"I thought you had difficulty reading."

"My only difficulty was with you and the clowns
who work for you." He tore the paper in half. "Play
these dirty games elsewhere. I'm not signing, and I'm
not giving in to any more threats. You're right about
one thing, I'm getting pretty famous. Lot of people
are paying attention to me now. That spotlight on
me is bright enough to expose your double-dealing.
If I see you around again, I'll spend every dime I
make to find a way to publicize your rotten business
deals."

"You couldn't prove anything."

"With enough money and enough time, I can prove
that Columbus didn't discover America. Eventually
you'll get too greedy and trip yourself up, but if you
keep bothering me, I guarantee it will happen much
sooner."

Baer stared coolly back at him, but for once Marc

sensed the nervousness beneath his French silk suit and velour fedora.

"Always knew I should have stayed away from magicians." He stubbed out his cigar in a jar of greasepaint. "Lying tricksters, every last one of you."

"Look, if you don't mind, I'm working and you've wasted enough of my time."

Baer stood up abruptly, then pushed past Marc. But as soon as he was out of the dressing room, he turned to face him. "You can't keep escaping trouble, Cooper. No one is that lucky. Eventually your luck will run out and you'll have nothing but cheap tricks to fall back on."

The image of Salome smiling at him came suddenly to mind. "You're wrong. I have a guardian angel who will take care of me just fine."

"Idiot," Baer spat out. "I only hope I'm around when you and your guardian angel come crashing down."

"Never," Marc said firmly.

Nothing could possibly spoil his happiness with Salome.

It couldn't.

She was dazzling. Who would have imagined that his little Sally, a bookish schoolteacher, for pity's sake, had turned herself into a siren? Lyndon felt crushed all over again.

From the moment the curtain rose on her and that magician fellow, he couldn't take his eyes off her. In all the years he'd known her, he'd never seen Sal with her hair hanging loose about her shoulders. Glorious hair, gleaming and dark brown, framing her petite shapely frame. He'd never seen her in such a revealing dress either, bright red velvet, its neckline scooped, and its skirt skimming her knees. Strutting

up there in her black mesh tights and little heels,
Sally was more woman than he'd seen in a long time.
And that included the lady sitting beside him in the
theater. No wonder Cooper had taken her to his bed.

"How long are you going to ogle her?" Jane asked.

Lyndon forced his gaze away from the stage. "I've
always found magic acts amusing."

"Please. You couldn't care less what was happening onstage, as long as you could drool over Sally
Hall in her red dress."

Under the gaslit chandelier, Jane looked tired, her
smooth cheeks pale beneath the powder and rouge.
She was a fragile person, as fragile as a porcelain
figure already suffering from tiny fractures. It
wouldn't take much to shatter her, he knew. Rejec-
tion, failure, too many nights fretting that he no
longer adored her.

Lyndon glanced back at the stage, wanting to
throttle that vibrant young woman in the red velvet
dress. If only Sal were still in love with him; if only
she hadn't turned herself into the magician's whore.
Then he could have gone to Jane and said he was
returning to his former fiancée. The world would
have approved such a scenario; his career would
have remained intact. And if Jane sickened after his
departure, the censure would fall on the loose
woman who had tried to break up a happy, respectable betrothal, not him.

Now he was trapped.

As though sensing his discomfort, Jane reached
over and laid a slender hand on his arm. A sapphire
bracelet glittered on her thin wrist. She was losing
weight, and growing more out of breath after each
performance. Perhaps the doctors were wrong. Perhaps she had far less than ten years to live.

"I know you're disappointed, Lyndon," she said in

a low voice, the music from the orchestra pit nearly drowning her out. "But she's not right for you. Be glad she turned you down."

"What are you talking about?" He pretended to be engrossed in Marc Cooper's flying scarves. "We merely took a ride on the Ferris Wheel last night." He shot a bitter look at the bare-chested magician. "Besides, I told you. She's in love with that fool up there."

"I'll make you much happier."

Lyndon gritted his teeth. Oh yes, he thought, he'd be happy as a clam hunting for her heart medication, fanning her when she grew dizzy, trying to calm her down when the tears began flowing right before every performance. Years of being at her hysterical beck and call unrolled before him. Even her money and celebrity couldn't make anything of that scenario but a living purgatory.

Applause erupted about them as Marc completed his tedious trick with the scarves. Then, as Salome wheeled a long cabinet onstage, the magician brandished a shiny saw with jagged teeth.

"Oh, good, he's going to saw her in half." Jane settled back in her seat, pleasure evident in her voice for the first time tonight. "Maybe she'll get nicked. Or seriously wounded."

"And to think that I once thought you were the precious jewel of Black Horse." He crossed his arms in front of him.

"There are no jewels in Black Horse. Just cow manure and restless females dying to get out." She laughed. "And restless men, too. I certainly didn't have to try very hard to convince *you* to leave everything behind."

"We all live to regret our baser impulses."

345

"How droll of you, Lyndon dear. I would almost think you possessed a sense of humor."

"Could you just let me watch this tiresome act in peace? It's probably the last time we'll ever see our old friend Sally."

"This had better be the last time. If you're thinking of chasing after little Sal, let me remind you that I am constantly being asked for interviews. What do you think would happen if I began complaining about how my future husband deserted me for a magician's trollop? I'm sure it would have a deleterious effect on your political career. Not to mention my nerves. A lot of people have a soft place in their hearts for the 'Songbird of the South.' They wouldn't want anything to happen to me."

That's only because they don't know you, he thought sourly. Once again, he hoped that the doctors were wrong about how much longer Jane had to live.

They had never performed so well before. Every movement of theirs was perfectly synchronized. Although their act was polished to a fine sheen already, tonight the illusions seemed quicker, more dazzling and completely effortless. It was like their lovemaking, she realized—Both of them totally focused on the other, on trying to please their partner. And by doing that, they ended up creating true magic.

The applause and appreciative gasps flowed across the footlights in delightful waves. As the Bed of Nails was wheeled onstage, Salome felt near euphoric. To be so happy was intoxicating.

Just watching the back of Marc's head as he chose volunteers from the audience gave her intense pleasure. To think that this glorious man was hers. As wonderful as the performance had been, she couldn't wait for it to be over. She needed to be in Marc's arms again, to reassure herself that she was really his.

The music quieted as Marc explained to the audience what was about to occur. For this trick, he normally chose just two audience members to inspect the bed and stand nearby while the trick was performed. But because the Chicago theater was so enormous, they decided it would be more impressive if six volunteers from the audience were selected instead. As the three men and three women were helped onstage, Salome sat down on the expansive bed, then lay back. Stretching out her arms, she waited patiently, letting the music of Rimsky-Korsakov waft over her.

When the audience volunteers were at last gathered at the foot of the bed, Marc took his place opposite them. Just before snapping the handcuffs on her, he gently stroked her hair. She caught his eye, they exchanged tender glances.

As he bent over and locked her in place, he whispered, "I love you."

She smiled, then remembered she was being chained to a bed of nails and assumed a properly somber expression. Marc directed two of the volunteers to secure her ankles in the heavy cuffs. When she was locked in, all the volunteers were invited to inspect the cuffs and chains. As usual, everyone confirmed that Salome the Fair was truly confined. Before drawing the bedcurtains about her, Marc also asked the volunteers to reach up and touch the nails.

Since the nails were made of shiny hard steel, no one could claim that the threat hovering above his assistant wasn't real. At last everyone was satisfied, and Marc motioned the volunteers back. With a majestic wave of his arm, he then grabbed the satin curtain and pulled it closed on all four sides.

As soon as the audience was cut off from view, Salome reached with her fingers to spring the hidden button on her handcuffs. Two minutes more and she would be taking her bows. Five minutes more, and both she and Marc would be backstage, laughing, talking, safe in each other's arms.

"Slow down," she murmured. She was so eager to finish the illusion that she found herself fumbling for the trick button.

Forcing herself to go slower, she ran her fingers along the inside of the cuffs. Nothing. Her heart leapt in her throat. This was impossible. Again, she tried. Then again.

Dear God, where was the trick button? Had Marc somehow used the wrong handcuffs tonight? Or maybe in all the excitement of their first performance in Chicago, an unknowing stagehand had attached the wrong ones to the bed. No, she and Marc checked their equipment right before each performance. In fact, ever since that night when Marc nearly drowned in the water tank, they had checked everything twice.

Panic swept over her. Perhaps this was another attempt by Robert Baer to extort money. Only this time, they had correctly figured out that she was the logical one to kill, not Marc. She pulled hard at the chains that bound her hands and feet.

"See how Salome struggles to break free!" Marc shouted on the other side of the curtain.

Her heart sank. He thought the added noise was her way of increasing the dramatic effect. She did that sometimes if the performance was going extremely well.

"Marc!" she shouted.

But the trick was nearing its climax and the music from the orchestra pit thundered.

"Marc, help me!" Again, she struggled fiercely with the chains. "I can't break free!"

The music continued, its growing volume mirroring her wild panic. Calling for Marc once more, she stared horrified at the canopy of nails overhead. In one minute that canopy would crash down, impaling her. For a terrified instant, she allowed herself to feel the agony of such a death. And just as horrifying would be poor Marc's reaction when he realized she had just been murdered.

Nonsense. She wasn't going to die now. Not when her life finally beckoned with so much love and promise. The music was nearing its dramatic conclusion.

Shutting her eyes to the deadly spikes overhead, she let out a bloodcurdling scream.

Marc shot a disapproving glance at the orchestra pit. Some musician in there had a tin ear. Twice he'd heard a discordant sound, like a woodwind screeching. Usually he would let such mistakes pass, but the sold-out house tonight had been unusually enthusiastic. He hated to have the performance marred because of a lazy oboe player.

He had almost completed his second circle about the bed. In a moment, he would touch the lever on the corner bedpost that would release the canopy of nails. Already he had heard Salome rattling her chains. She did that if she was in a playful mood, and tonight both of them had been understandably jubilant. He'd given her more than enough time to trip open the handcuffs and scurry safely to the side of the bed.

Coming to a halt, Marc lifted his arms high in the

Sharon Pisacreta

air. He could feel the audience's excitement and fear. In fact, their fear was so great that he tasted it himself. Funny, but he had never let an audience's mood affect him. That was good though. It showed he was weaving a powerful spell over the sophisticated Chicagoans. It showed that he was such a master of illusion that he could occasionally spook himself.

Just as he was about to lower his arms and press the lever on the side of the bed, a heartrending scream rang out. He froze.

"Salome?"

The next scream made the hairs on the back of his neck stand on end. For one insane second, he thought he had somehow tripped the lever and sent the spikes crashing down.

Noticing Marc's stricken expression, the orchestra conductor froze as well, and the music died out.

Marc turned and whipped back the bedcurtains. To his horror, he saw Salome struggling to get free of her handcuffs.

"My God, what happened?" He flung himself on the bed and tried to unlock the handcuffs on her wrists.

"They won't open," she gasped, her eyes wide with fear.

She was right. These weren't the handcuffs normally used for this trick. However, he did recognize them. He had bought these cuffs in March, but discarded them because they wouldn't open reliably, not even with his vast array of picks. He could have sworn he'd gotten rid of them, but maybe he had simply told Julia to throw them out. This is what he got for assuming a Dupree would ever act sensibly.

"Blast, how did such a thing happen?" Marc tried to calm himself down. If he couldn't steady his hands, it would take forever to free Salome.

"I don't know. Maybe Robert Baer hired someone to switch the props." Despite her obvious fear, Salome managed a tremulous smile. "I'm so glad you heard me scream."

"*You're* glad?" In fact, he had been only a heartbeat away from lowering the deadly canopy. To think he had almost been responsible for destroying the person he loved most in the world.

Furious at himself, he turned his attention to the cuffs holding her ankles. With a cry of relief, he saw that these were the correct props and snapped open easily. As soon as he set her legs free, he began working once more on the chains clamped over her wrists.

The audience was growing restive. Their murmurs had turned to shouts. They seemed angry that the trick hadn't gone as planned. But for the first time in his life. Marc was oblivious to the audience. He was aware only of the woman lying beneath him on the bed. He had to get her free. For all he knew, Baer had rigged the canopy to fall at the wrong time.

As though she had read his thoughts, she said, "Baer must be the one responsible for this. Unless it's an accident."

"It's no accident," he muttered darkly. He should have called the police as soon as he saw Baer in his dressing room tonight. Instead he'd dismissed him from his life as though he were no more than a pesky salesman. And his arrogance had nearly gotten Salome killed.

Frustrated, he turned to the six audience volunteers who were crowded around the bed. "Will someone go backstage and see if anyone there has an axe or mallet? I need to break these chains."

Two men hurried away.

Salome sighed. "I thought escaping from hand-

Sharon Pisacreta

cuffs required only a calm hand and a cool head."

"Unfortunately, I don't have either at the moment."
He took a deep breath. If he would only calm down,
he'd get her free.

"Maybe you should tell the stage manager to ring
down the curtain?" she suggested.

"The devil with the manager!"

"Marc, it will be all right," she said soothingly, as
though she weren't the one trapped in chains. "You'll
have me out of here in no time."

But she'd no sooner spoken when the canopy
above them shuddered and dropped several inches.
The audience screamed, drowning out her own cry
of terror.

Marc looked up, cursing. He feared this was going
to happen. Damn Robert Baer. Damn any man who
tried to destroy the life he and Salome were planning
so happily.

"Marc, you have to get off this bed! You'll be killed
if you don't move." Salome tried to sit up, but her
arms were chained at an impossible angle.

"I'm not moving until I have you out of these," he
said grimly.

Another shudder sounded from above and the canopy fell two more inches. The theater was in an up-
roar. He was dimly aware of people crowding
around the bed. Some were performers still in costume, others stagehands. A good number were audience members driven by curiosity, or the desire to
help.

He would not let Salome die like this. If the canopy
moved another inch, he'd just throw himself on top
of her, and let the nails drive themselves into him.
But for now, he had to steel his nerves, forget that
Salome was trapped in a truly death-defying illusion.

352

He had to treat this as any other trick. Calmly, coldly, he must keep his wits about him.

"Marc, I'm begging you. Getting yourself killed won't save me! Please move away. Please!" Salome had tears in her eyes. "This is impossible."

"Nothing is impossible for us."

"Escape is impossible," a feminine voice said softly.

Both Salome and Marc looked behind them. People were shoving and pressed as close to the bed as they dared. Their expressions were anxious, fearful, and shamelessly excited.

He cursed under his breath. Now was not the time to be distracted by mysterious whispers.

"Honeysuckle," Salome said in a shaky voice.

"What?"

"I smell honeysuckle."

They exchanged a brief, meaningful glance. Marc could smell it now, too. An overwhelming scent of honeysuckle, cloying and sweet. The last time he'd smelled that much honeysuckle, he'd had his hands about Julia's throat.

"Where are you, Julia?" he shouted.

Salome pulled desperately at her chains. "I have to get out of this. She means to kill me!"

Damn, but these chains wouldn't yield. The taste of defeat was bitter and overwhelming. Billed as the great escape artist, boastful that no chains could bind him, now he was helpless to unlock a ten-dollar pair of defective handcuffs. God in heaven, if Salome died because of his failure . . .

He didn't have time to look for Julia, now hiding among the onlookers clustered around the bed. He didn't have time to do anything but try to force these cuffs open. He didn't have time to think of another solution. He didn't have time!

353

Sharon Pisacreta

The canopy moved another inch. Damn that woman!

"Everyone move away from the bed!" He could feel the veins stand out on his head as he bellowed. "You're likely to hit the lever and kill both of us!"

With fearful looks at the canopy of nails, the entire crowd took a step or two back. Except for one person. Even with her blond hair hidden beneath a dark turban, he'd recognize that bitter face anywhere.

Julia stood a foot away from the bedpost, her gaze holding more hate than he'd ever seen in a human. Hate for him, and for the woman trapped beneath him.

He dared not move. Instead, they stared at each other for a long moment. He heard Salome gasp out, "No, Julia!"

Her gaze flickered toward the bedpost. Julia had performed this trick dozens of times with him. She knew that each bedpost had its own hidden lever that manipulated the canopy. When they did this illusion, he had teased the audience by bringing the canopy down in heartstopping inches. Julia preferred that to having the canopy crash down all at once. She said she enjoyed hearing the cries of terror from the audience.

As she was no doubt enjoying this death by inches now.

"Don't do it," he warned in a low voice. "Killing us is a death sentence for you."

She shrugged. "You told me that you'd kill me if I ever came near you again. Well, I can't stay away." Her skirt rustled as she moved closer. "I can't stay away from you, Marc. How can I? You're everything to me. So either you kill me, or I must kill you."

"Julia, please." Salome reached out a chained hand to her.

She barely spared a glance for her rival. "I didn't think you'd let this tramp die alone. Fine then, die together. Just what both of you deserve for betraying me." Her voice was oddly impassive, almost mechanical.

Marc knelt on the bed. If he shouted for someone to grab her, Julia would still have time to hit the lever. If he could only get one of the handcuffs loose.

"You've made a fool of me, Marc. Laughing behind my back, cheating me out of marriage and all this success, while the two of you become rich and famous. You've left me with nothing. Nothing! Except this."

She put her hand on the corner bedpost, two feet from Salome's head.

Marc got up on one knee. Behind him, he reached his hand down, trying to unlock the chains on Salome's left wrist.

"Listen to me. We can work this out. Talk about it like civilized people." He tried to gauge how far he could lunge towards her. If only this bed wasn't so blasted wide.

Julia shook her hand. "You and me ain't got nothing to do with civilized."

A shriek went up from the crowd near the foot of the bed. "Julia, what in heaven's name are you doing"

Out of the corner of his eye, Marc spied Jane Dupree. Lyndon stood beside her, looking as pale and stricken as Julia's sister.

Startled, Julia's attention shifted for one breathless second. In a fever, Marc bent down, fingers working at the clasp, forcing himself to be calm, cold, controlled. He would break Salome free. He would. By sheer will alone, if need be, but these chains *would* break.

"Marc," Salome whispered. "Hurry."

He had it. Now. She had to get off this bed now. "Move!" he hissed, then shoved her with all his might. Even though one wrist was still shackled to a corner bedpost, the remaining chain would still allow Salome to get off the bed.

"No!" Julia saw too late that her quarry had fled.

She lunged for her, but Salome had already flung herself off the bed, her left wrist straining in the handcuff.

"Damn you!" Julia fell onto the bed, but sprang up instantly. She grabbed Marc's wrist and pulled him towards her.

For a second, everything became a blur of spikes, honeysuckle and mad blue eyes. He heard both Jane and Salome crying out, pleading for someone to help.

Pushing Julia away, Marc threw himself off the bed.

Julia knelt in the center of the bed, tears of fury running down her face.

Jane was weeping, too. "Please, Julia. I don't understand. What are you doing?"

"Get away from me!" Julia shut her eyes, as if repelled by the sight of so many enemies. "None of you care about me. None of you."

"But I care. I'm your sister!" Her face pale and wan, Jane staggered, leaning her weight against the bedpost. Obviously feeling faint, she was struggling to support herself.

Cradling Salome in his arms, Marc looked up in time to see Jane clutching the bedpost. "Jane, no! Keep away!"

Julia turned in time to see her older sister lay a trembling hand on the bedpost. She opened her mouth to cry out, but it was too late.

The canopy of nails came crashing down.

Both Marc and Salome were too shocked to utter a sound. Even if they had, their cries would have been drowned out by Julia's last cries and the screams of her sister.

The stage was chaos and madness. Salome was vaguely aware of Marc holding her. At some point, she realized that Marc had also released her from the remaining handcuff.

She looked at her freed hand as if it belonged to someone else, then flung both arms about Marc's trembling neck.

"How terrible," she whispered. "How terrible for both of them."

She couldn't bring herself to look at the Bed of Nails. Bad enough she could hear the babble of cries and shouts about her, but above it all was the dreadful sound of Jane's anguished weeping.

Salome finally lifted her head. Careful to avoid looking at the horrible bed of nails, she instead sought out Lyndon. He was standing off to the side, holding a distraught Jane in his arms. He was as white as a ghost.

"Lyndon!" she called out.

His head shot up.

"Take care of her, Lyndon," she said. "Stay with her. She needs you."

He nodded, and for the first time in a long time she saw genuine kindness in his eyes. Then the swarming crowd mercifully cut the sad couple off from view.

Late that night, Salome woke from a restless sleep. She had dreamt she was bound to that bed once more, straining to be free. Her heart was racing just as it had earlier onstage.

Taking a deep breath, she reminded herself that

she was safe now. That she was lying in bed next to the man she loved. A bed with no canopy and no spikes. She shuddered, trying to forget Julia's horrible death. She'd never be able to sleep in a canopied bed again.

Marc moved restlessly beside her, but his even breathing told her he was still asleep.

Getting up softly, she walked over to the window and opened it wide. The night air was refreshing and cool. In the distance the White City slept. Occasional traffic sounds rumbled from State Street, and a mournful train whistle was carried on the autumn wind.

Turning her face upward, she gazed gratefully at the moon, a full moon just as it was that first night she gave herself to Marc. In the bracing air, it seemed as white and glowing as a jewel.

"*Our* moon," she said aloud. "And our magic."

"Salome, what's wrong?" Marc asked in a sleepy voice.

She hurried back to bed, chilled from having left the warmth and heat of the blankets and Marc's strong body.

Snuggling under the covers, she sighed with contentment as Marc hugged her close. "I just wanted to let in some fresh air."

He yawned. "No bad dreams?"

"None," she lied. He had already worried far too much about her.

Nestling in his arms, she heard his heart beating steadily against her. She felt her body relax, and sleep begin to overtake her once more.

"That was good of you," Marc said quietly. "Asking Lyndon to take care of Jane."

"She needs him far more than I ever did." She hadn't yet told Marc about Jane's heart condition.

Marc yawned again. "And will you take care of me?"

She stroked his cheek, reveling in the life and warmth beneath her hand. "We'll take care of each other. Only you have to promise me one thing."

His embrace grew tighter. "Anything you want. You know that."

"I never want to be chained again. Not even for the most spectacular illusion."

"I promise." He kissed her forehead. "I'll wear all the chains in this family."

Several moments passed. Salome was nearly asleep when Marc's low voice roused her again. "We've been using the chains too much in the act anyway."

"I agree," she said sleepily.

"Besides, I've come up with a half-dozen illusions that won't require anyone to be chained or tied up." Just before he fell asleep again, he murmured, "Not even the lions."

Snuggled against him, Salome's eyes opened wide. "Lions?" She shook him. "What lions?"

But his snores only got louder. The moonlight pouring in from the window showed that the man she loved was smiling like an angel.

Or a magician who had just come up with another showstopping trick.

She lay back, staring up at the ceiling. "If he thinks I'm working with lions . . ."

The snores rattling beside her ceased.

After a long pause, she heard Marc ask, "Then how do you feel about tigers?"

As soon as she stopped laughing, Salome had every intention of telling him.

AUTHOR'S NOTE

The facts pertaining to the Chicago World's Fair of 1893 were fun to research, and easy to substantiate. Boasting exhibits by Western Electric, American Bell Telephone and Thomas Edison, the Exposition helped to usher in the new century seven years early, as well as introducing the Ferris Wheel and the term "midway" into the popular culture. Fortuitously, the Brothers Houdini performed on that midway, allowing me to include an encounter between my magician hero and the nineteen-year-old Harry Houdini.

In contrast, my research into the history of vaudeville was often conflicting and far from straightforward. Although some books claim that vaudeville officially appeared with the opening of the Keith Theater in Boston in 1894, other theater historians claim that it was the great showman Tony Pastor who began the transformation of variety into vaudeville.

Before Pastor opened his Fourteenth Street Theater in New York City in 1881, inexpensive popular entertainment was mostly to be found in beer halls and dime museums. Instead of catering to rowdy saloon crowds, Pastor was determined to attract a family audience by offering wholesome entertainment. He did so with a variety of acts on a daily bill in a theater that was clean, safe and respectable—what we've come to know as vaudeville.

Despite the attempt by some historians to pinpoint 1894 as vaudeville's official start, variety was increasingly being called—and reviewed as—"vaudeville" years before Keith opened his theater in Boston.

DEBRA DIER
SHADOW of THE STORM

He is her dashing childhood hero, the man to whom she will willingly surrender her innocence in a night of blazing ecstasy. But when Ian Tremayne cruelly abandons her after a bitter misunderstanding, Sabrina O'Neill vows to have revenge on the handsome Yankee. But the virile Tremayne is more than ready for the challenge. Together, they will enter a high-stakes game of deadly illusion and sizzling desire that will shatter Sabrina's well-crafted facade.

___4397-1 $5.99 US/$6.99 CAN

Dorchester Publishing Co., Inc.
P.O. Box 6640
Wayne, PA 19087-8640

Please add $1.75 for shipping and handling for the first book and $.50 for each book thereafter. NY, NYC, and PA residents, please add appropriate sales tax. No cash, stamps, or C.O.D.s. All orders shipped within 6 weeks via postal service book rate. Canadian orders require $2.00 extra postage and must be paid in U.S. dollars through a U.S. banking facility.

Name_____
Address_____
City_____ State_____ Zip_____
I have enclosed $_____ in payment for the checked book(s).
Payment <u>must</u> accompany all orders. ❏ Please send a free catalog.
  CHECK OUT OUR WEBSITE! www.dorchesterpub.com

A FAERIE TALE ROMANCE

VICTORIA ALEXANDER

Ophelia Kendrake has barely finished conning the coat off a cardsharp's back when she stumbles into Dead End, Wyoming. Mistaken for the Countess of Bridgewater, Ophelia sees no reason to reveal herself until she has stripped the hamlet of its fortunes and escaped into the sunset. But the free-spirited beauty almost swallows her script when she meets Tyler, the town's virile young mayor. When Tyler Matthews returns from an Ivy League college, he simply wants to settle down and enjoy the simplicity of ranching. But his aunt and uncle are set on making a silk purse out of Dead End, and Tyler is going to be the new mayor. It's a job he takes with little relish—until he catches a glimpse of the village's newest visitor.

_52159-8 $5.50 US/$6.50 CAN

The Snow Queen
Anne Avery

When Boston-bred Hetty Malone arrives at the Colorado Springs train station, she is full of hope that she will soon marry her childhood sweetheart and live happily ever after. Yet life amid the ice-capped Rockies has changed Michael Ryan. No longer the hot-blooded suitor Hetty remembers, the young doctor has grown as cold and distant as the snowy mountain peaks. Determined to revive Michael's passionate longing, Hetty quickly realizes that no modern medicine can cure what ails him. But in the enchanted splendor of her new home, she dares to administer the only remedy that might melt his frozen heart: a dose of good old-fashioned loving.

_52151-2 $5.99 US/$6.99 CAN

Dorchester Publishing Co., Inc.
P.O. Box 6640
Wayne, PA 19087-8640

Please add $1.75 for shipping and handling for the first book and $.50 for each book thereafter. NY, NYC, and PA residents, please add appropriate sales tax. No cash, stamps, or C.O.D.s. All orders shipped within 6 weeks via postal service book rate. Canadian orders require $2.00 extra postage and must be paid in U.S. dollars through a U.S. banking facility.

Name_____
Address_____
City_____State_____Zip_____
I have enclosed $_____ in payment for the checked book(s).
Payment <u>must</u> accompany all orders. ☐ Please send a free catalog.

Archer's Crossing — Jean Barrett

Crossing Archer Owen seems like the last thing anybody would want to do, or so Margaret Sheridan thinks. Bringing dinner to the convicted murderer is terrifying—for though he is nothing like her affluent fiancé, he stirs a hunger in her she has never known. Then the condemned prisoner uses her to make his getaway. In the clutches of the handsome felon, Margaret races into the untamed West—chasing a man Owen claims could clear his name. Margaret wonders if there is anything Archer won't do. And then he kisses her, and she prays there isn't. For if this bitter steamboat captain is half the man she suspects, she'd ride to Hell itself to clear his name and win his captive heart.

___4502-8 $5.99 US/$6.99 CAN

SONYA BIRMINGHAM

Song of the Lark

When the beautiful wisp of a mountain girl walks through his front door, Stephen Wentworth knows there is some kind of mistake. The flame-haired beauty in trousers is not the nanny he envisions for his mute son Tad. But one glance from Jubilee Jones's emerald eyes, and the widower's icy heart melts and his blood warms. Can her mountain magic soften Stephen's hardened heart, or will their love be lost in the breeze, like the song of the lark?

___4393-9 $5.50 US/$6.50 CAN

Dorchester Publishing Co., Inc.
P.O. Box 6640
Wayne, PA 19087-8640

Please add $1.75 for shipping and handling for the first book and $.50 for each book thereafter. NY, NYC, and PA residents, please add appropriate sales tax. No cash, stamps, or C.O.D.s. All orders shipped within 6 weeks via postal service book rate. Canadian orders require $2.00 extra postage and must be paid in U.S. dollars through a U.S. banking facility.

Name_____
Address_____
City_____State_____Zip_____
I have enclosed $_____ in payment for the checked book(s).
Payment <u>must</u> accompany all orders. ☐ Please send a free catalog.
          CHECK OUT OUR WEBSITE! www.dorchesterpub.com